Black Star

Or The Desecration of Silver Gorge

A Novel by Adam Wynn

www.Adam-Wynn.com

Copyright © 2022 by Adam Wynn

All rights reserved. This book or parts thereof may not be reproduced in any form, stored in any retrieval system, or transmitted in any form by any means—electronic, mechanical, photocopy, recording, or otherwise—without prior written permission of the publisher, except as provided by United States of America copyright law. For permission requests, write to the publisher, at "Attention: Permissions Coordinator," at the address below.

ISBN: 9798619728132
Library of Congress Control Number: 2022900476

Any references to historical events, real people, or real places are used fictitiously. Other names, characters, places and events are products of the author's imagination, and any resemblances to actual events or places or persons, living or dead, is entirely coincidental.

Book Cover and Cover Design by Adam Wynn.
Book Design and Layout by Adam Wynn.
Written Content Edited by Mark Bilbrey.

Printed by Amazon's Kindle Direct Publishing (POD)

First Printed Edition 2022

Published by Adam Wynn
Athens, GA

www.Adam-Wynn.com

For my boys. I haven't had a day of peace since they were born, and I wouldn't want it any other way.

-Adam W.-

-Chapter One-

Shootout at the Rusty Spittoon

A sheriff's duty is to keep the peace. Sheriff Boone protected that duty with everything he had, making it his waking and dying oath to keep the peace in Silver Gorge, Nevada day in and day out, even when it made him a bit uncomfortable with what he had to do. It was especially in those times, when his conscience was called into question, that his creed kept him sound. Keep the peace, he would tell himself. Keep the peace.

Sheriff Boone first heard the gunshots, then he heard the shouting. Cattle drivers and saloon gals filled the dusty streets of the town, pouring out of every door and alleyway in that old watering hole they called home every evening after the workday was done. The miners from the Mason Company mostly conducted their business well outside of town, primarily staying up in Mason City, but a few occasionally ventured into the saloon when their shift was out. Word came to Sheriff Boone that those miners were being held up in the saloon by a masked gunman.

Nobody could see the man's face, on account of the matted red bandana and the long, greasy hair he wore under that flat black hat, but folks said he was tall as a mountain and wide as an ox. Sheriff Boone unholstered his weapons and pushed through the crowd of scattering onlookers under the dust-caked awning that covered the walkway into the Rusty Spittoon Saloon. God-awful name, Sheriff Boone thought. Just God-awful.

Ready for a fight, he near kicked the swinging doors right off, but saw the gunman seated at the bar with three miners cowering in the corner and the barkeep looking horrified as if staring into a mirror with no reflection, pouring drinks while his rattling hand knocked glasses together without a lick of control. The frosted, red-orange windows let in just a little of the fading evening light as Sheriff Boone stared down the back of a supposedly vicious gunman who wasn't even holding his guns. Instead of a pistol, the mystery figure was armed with a bottle of Mule Skinner and a shot glass resting on the bar. The behemoth perched on a wobbly stool that was at least fifteen years old. The reports of the man's size were not exaggerated, nor were the descriptions of the oily black hair that fell out of his hat and over his shoulders, but that's where the truth died. It seemed the threat was overstated. Still, Sheriff Boone felt it wise to keep his guns trained square on the stranger's back. At the man's side, Sheriff Boone noticed that matted red bandana mopping up dust on the floor, sopping wet and soiled with something murky brown. Could be blood, but he wasn't sure.

"I'm gonna have to ask you to let these men go, stranger," Sheriff Boone requested calmly, as if he were asking for a drink.

"I should've known you'd come, Duke. I oughta guessed it'd be you. After all, you are still the sheriff."

Sheriff Boone dropped his hands to his hips. His jaw went slack. He couldn't believe his old friend would go so far as this. After what happened, Sheriff Boone knew the man was dangerous, but this hardly seemed possible.

"Zeke? What happened to your hair? God, man, I haven't seen you in three months. I haven't seen you since…

well, since…"

"Since when, Duke? Since when?" Zeke challenged the sheriff.

"You know when, Zeke. I'm awful sorry about your boy, but you know there was nothing I could do. Boss Mason wasn't at fault for what happened to your boy. Mining is tough work. Things… things go wrong," the sheriff justified, well knowing it was a lie.

"Did they ever even tell you what's in that mine, Sheriff?" Zeke returned, putting a little bite on that last word. "Did they ever tell you what it was they had those boys mining down there?"

"Town's called Silver Gorge, Zeke, what do you think they're mining?"

Zeke laughed. He remembered Duke's quick tongue well. He'd rather talk a man to death than shoot him, Zeke recollected, but being sheriff rarely affords you that option.

"Silver here's been dried up for years, you know that."

"Zeke…" Sheriff Boone whispered, nearing an apology, but not quite managing it.

"I know. You were just keeping the peace. Is that what you called it when you tried to shoot me that night? Keeping the peace?"

"Let these men go, Zeke. You got me here, and that's all you need."

Zeke's head turned a touch and tilted to the side where Sheriff Boone could almost see the corner of his old friend's eye, but the hair still covered it up. "You, Sheriff? What makes you think I want you?"

"Then what are you doing here, Zeke? Why'd you corner these men?" Duke looked at the men in the corner hiding their faces from view. They were Mason's men. He'd run them out of town a few times for harassing folks. Zeke had planned something else.

"Crying out loud, Zeke, you can't kill Boss Mason. You wouldn't live through the night! His boys'd have you strung up from a tree quicker than you could saddle a horse!"

"I can saddle a horse pretty quick, Duke. You know that. We made the trip out here together all those years ago, after all."

The friends kept silent for a minute, but Zeke spoke up, his voice fading and his words catching wind. "Besides, I'm a dead man, anyway. I snuck into the mines last month trying to corner Boss Mason, but he was gone. I saw what it was they're mining down there."

Right then, Zeke stood to turn, facing Duke with a swift step. His hands reached down to his belt, but his eyes fixed on the sheriff clear. The sheriff's eyes weren't on the guns either, as he reeled in horror at the rot that was left of Zeke's face. His eyes were replaced by putrefaction and his bones gave way to decaying sinew. The empty sockets that once held Zeke's glare shot straight into the shocked open eyes of Sheriff Boone. "Did they ever even tell you what was down in that mine, Sheriff?" Zeke whispered as his jaw fell to pieces, and the big man spilled out into the floor, letting loose a stench like death, the foulest black bile splattering all over Sheriff Boone's boots. The threat was no more. The gunman was dead. But the sheriff knew, and he knew it for sure, that he could never keep this peace again.

★ ★ ★

Sheriff Boone woke up night after night with the same dream, seeing Zeke's face as it dissolved into dust and bile on the bar room floor. The big man's body seeped through the saw mill slats that made up the base of the saloon and went who knows where, but the undertaker prepared no coffin for Zeke's body. There was nothing left of the man but his bandana and his hat, both sopping with the blackest ooze that had corrupted the earth.

The vision of his friend falling to pieces haunted Duke Boone from time to time, whether in a drop of water flowing out of a trough only to be swallowed by the red dirt of town or in the way Mason's miners avoided Sheriff Boone's eyes whenever they made their even less frequent visits into town.

It had been three weeks since what was infamously and inaccurately coming to be known as the Shootout at the Rusty Spittoon, and Sheriff Boone still kept Zeke's bandana in a glass jar by the jail. He'd gathered it up with a gloved hand after questioning the three miners as to what it was that caused Zeke to fall away so gruesomely. For all of his work, all Duke knew was that the men were afraid to touch anything that had been on Zeke's person. They didn't want his guns, his hat or, least of all, his bandana, so the dutiful sheriff held on to it as evidence. As proof that Zeke had been there, since no grave would accompany his death.

Sheriff Boone had been present when they dug the grave for Zeke's boy earlier that year, just before the ground froze solid. The whole thing was a bit of a farce since they had no body to bury, but Duke had argued that it would give Zeke some kind of closure to have a burial. Boss Mason told Zeke and Sheriff Boone that Josiah had died in a mining accident of an unspecific nature that left the body unrecoverable. When Zeke asked what killed the boy, whether it was crashing timbers or gas buildup, nobody at the mining company had an answer. They would only say that he'd died in a mining accident.

Duke had been around the Mason company long enough to know that you took them at their word. Not because they were trustworthy people, no, but rather because there was never any profit in questioning the unscrupulous. If they told you something, it was because that's what they wanted you to believe and you'd better believe it. Those who chose to believe other things had ways of disappearing. Like Josiah.

The morning sun was still an hour or so out, but Boone knew that rest was not coming for him, not tonight. He feared going back to sleep. He resisted seeing Zeke's body rot where it stood. No, rest would have to wait until Duke had built up his courage and tolerance for the unspeakable a bit further. The sheriff rolled out of bed and let his bare feet touch the dusty floor of the Silver Gorge jailhouse and constabulary, as the more erudite citizenry referred to it. To Duke, it was just home.

The last embers of the evening fire churned in the office where Duke worked, just steps away from the room where he lived. On bitter winter mornings, Duke was glad to live in the sheriff's station. There were days when he would keep to himself and not venture past the front door unless someone came calling about trouble.

It was one of the last days of cold, Duke remembered well, when someone came clamoring in the middle of the night about a hold-up at the mines. The last snows had melted in the early spring sun, but ice was still forming on the red rock faces outside of town at night. Duke remembered it well, that night. It was cold. Colder than the wind coming off the Devil's wings.

Zeke always had been a fool, the sheriff thought. The two men met on the road headed out west some years back before Josiah was in tow or Zeke's wife had come around. Marybelle. It had been at least three years now since she'd run off with the stage to San Francisco leaving Zeke and Josiah all alone. Zeke was just a small-time cattle farmer trying to tame the open range. He had nothing to offer an eastern woman such as Marybelle, so she ran.

Josiah never forgave his father for that perceived

Ch. 1 | Shootout at the Rusty Spittoon

betrayal. In Josiah's mind, Zeke ran Marybelle off, and Zeke was just fine letting the boy believe it. It wasn't right to vilify a boy's mother to him, Zeke would often tell the sheriff after Duke would come out and break up fights between the father and son outside the saloon.

No matter how many times that boy raised his gun to Zeke's chest, the father in him would not let Duke take the shot. That man loved his son more than life, it seemed, and that's the result you're going to get when you love someone more than life. You'll lose it just to prove a point.

The fire started to kick up with a little prodding, bringing more light into the room. The desert nights were still cold, even when the daylight sun burned the grass and dried the rivers, so Duke kept the windows drawn tight. It would be a little while yet before sun would come up over the valley where Silver Gorge called home, but Duke needed the light now.

Imagine that, Duke thought. A grown man. A sheriff in town afraid of the dark.

Thinking back on Zeke's eyes and his vacant smile gave Duke a shudder not unlike that of a coyote trying to warm itself under the chill of a frigid January wind in the open desert. The lazy fire could not grow fast enough for Duke's liking. Sheriff Boone sat just a hundred yards from the spot where Zeke's body disappeared into the clay. Darkness in this place just would not suit him.

In the morning quiet, as the slowly building fire warmed up Sheriff Boone's coffee, Duke could hear a faint rustling over the cracks and pops of the adobe hearth at his feet. At this hour, there was only one possible thing that could mean.

"You might as well come on in, Mort. I hear you shivering out there like a naked man in an ice house," Duke shouted to the air outside. "It ain't no use you dying just to save your pride."

The door burst open on command as a young man trotted through and melted in front of the fire. Mort was the occasional deputy in town, a youth that some of the elders had convinced Duke to take on in an apprenticeship of sorts. He was a good looking young man with coal black hair and eyes like a mountain pool, and his reputation with the saloon girls took a healthy portion of the deputy's meager wage. Most mornings Duke would hear Mort sneak in from his forbidden forays just before light, but he hadn't counted on the sheriff's restlessness this time around.

"I'm sorry, boss, I went out to check the outskirts of town for cattle thieves I'd heard were crawling through this area and my horse got spooked by a rattler and ran off without me," Mort spit out his words in rapid succession.

"No you weren't," Sheriff Boone responded in a steady flow. "You were at the Cathouse visiting Charlotte and you thought you'd come crawling back in here before I noticed you were gone."

"Well… yeah. I was," Mort finally answered back, facing down his accuser with the courage owed a field mouse before flashing back to his trademark quick-talking style. "I promise you sir, I'll never do it again. I swear off of women. I swear off of booze. I swear off of… of… shoot, I don't know. I swear off of shooting!"

"You'll do no such thing, son," Sheriff Boone asserted before belying his serious demeanor with a grin. "It's alright, Mort. Just make sure you get your rest and you're here for work in the morning if you have to go out. It don't seem right to leave a woman like that lonely when you know how she feels about you."

"With all respect, sir," Mort offered, a bit sheepishly at first, "she left me. Turns out her mamma needed her back home."

Ch. 1 | Shootout at the Rusty Spittoon

The pair shared a laugh at Mort's expense in what was one of the few moments that Sheriff Boone could tolerate with the eager go-getter. It wasn't that Mort was a bad deputy. He did just fine. Boone just wasn't too keen on having company around all the time. Sometimes a man just needs a break from people. After all, what's the use in moving away from the crowds back east if you're just going to invite them all in once you find the quiet?

The coffee finished brewing about the time Mort's tale had ended and Duke poured two cups. He knew Mort wanted to sleep off the last few minutes before daybreak, but Sheriff Boone had to make sure he paid for his indiscretions somehow, even if it was in directly contradicting what he had just ordered the boy to do.

"Did you make up that story about cow thieves, Mort?" Duke asked between sips.

"Not entirely," Mort returned. "I've heard rumors from the men at the saloon that there are some bad fellows coming this way. Cattle thieves and brigands, the whole lot of 'em."

"What do you propose we do about it, boy?"

"I think we need to post up on the edge of town with a posse and deputize some of the miners and get them to teach those fools how we deal with their kind. We take no prisoners, sir."

Mort's fervor for the job was unmatched, that's for sure. Not even Sheriff Boone would have taken such bold action, and for good reason.

"That might work, sure," Boone said thoughtfully, noticing a glint of what looked like pride in the boy's eye, "but you forgot a few things, Mort."

In a flash, his look turned to frustration and disappointment as the sheriff started to lay out just what was wrong with the plan.

"First, we have no way of knowing which crews coming to town are bandits and which crowds are just range ranchers looking for a drink and a warm bed to sleep in. Second, we're liable to start a fight where there need not be one. Once these cattle thieves come into town and start making trouble, we send them on their way however we need to, but until then, we shouldn't antagonize anybody. Finally, and this is the most important part, you know we don't allow the miners in this town to carry guns through the streets."

Mort stared at his cup and slowly took in what was left of the morning's coffee while he thought over the things that Sheriff Boone had said. They made sense, after all. Mort respected Sheriff Boone and knew he was a good man, which is why just once it would have been nice if Duke took notice of his ideas and listened to what he had to say.

"You're right, Sheriff. Sorry. Not sure what I was thinking," the boy obliged.

Mort and Duke each rocked back in their chairs and breathed in the morning air that squeezed its way through the cracks in the walls and the chinking. There was a chill to the mountain valley morning, but both men knew that any semblance of cool air would be gone soon enough. Once the sun came up and cast light over the town, the heat was soon to rise.

"If you don't mind my asking, Sheriff..." Mort trailed off, gauging the sheriff's likely non-verbal response before continuing, "what are you doing up so early? Were you waiting for me to come in?"

Sheriff Boone closed his eyes and leaned back, thinking about his words. "No, son. No, I was not waiting for you to come in. I couldn't sleep much."

Mort cast his eyes down as well and kicked the legs of his own chair with the heel of his boot. "Sir, you can't keep blaming that on yourself. You had no other options with Zeke.

You had to shoot him."

Duke nearly laughed at how absurd it was that people believed that flimsy fish tale. There was no grave. No body. Nobody could really recall how many gunshots there were, if any, and it had only been a few days. Yet, in light of all that, nobody questioned the official line from Sheriff Boone and the Mason Mining Company. Zeke had been shot in a fair draw, and that's all that there was to it. Not that anyone would be surprised at Sheriff Boone outgunning the beef herder.

"The moment he drew on you, Sheriff, that man forfeited his right to life. You've taught me that well, sir. If you draw on a sheriff, then you'd better be prepared to finish it."

"That was a rough day, Mort. It's going to take me some time to get past watching my friend die, and if a few restless nights are all I have to pay for my sins, then so be it."

Mort was the first to see it, and he was glad of a reason to break the silence as Sheriff Boone's gaze descended further and further into a chasm which the deputy did not want to follow him into.

"Look. The sun's coming up."

Sure enough, Sheriff Boone turned and noticed a sliver of pink light breaking up the black horizon, shortly joined by a band of orange and yellow. Within a few minutes, the opposite horizon turned purple about the time the first shades of blue washed over the eastern sky. The sun was coming up and the day was shortly getting started.

"I guess it's time for us to get moving, huh, boss?"

"I guess it is, Mort."

Mort, uncomfortable with prolonged silence, broke into the quiet and forced some conversation out of the sheriff.

"What do you need us to do today, Sheriff?"

"I want you to mind the office and the town, Mort," Sheriff Boone answered, looking at the boy and waiting for the obvious question.

Mort rarely got to mind the town's business by himself, so he was looking forward to it, but it took quite the occasion for Mort to get a day around town without Duke's watchful eye. He couldn't let Sheriff Boone go without an explanation. His curiosity got the best of him.

"Where are you going, Sheriff?"

Sheriff Boone stood up from his chair behind the desk and walked to the window, which Mort had summarily opened without formality as soon as he spotted a little sunlight. Duke wanted to be indignant of the little sedition Mort perpetrated in assuming he could just assume control of the place, but then Duke was glad to see the sun. Morning light was good for his soul. It scared away the demons for one more day.

As Duke grabbed up his rope and his gun belt, he pinned the metal star to his chest and started towards the door. He let Mort think he'd forgotten his question for a moment, but he looked back as he was almost out onto the street and said casually what was on his mind, despite the weighty implications of it.

"I think I'm going to pay Boss Mason a visit," Duke commented with the formality of a breakfast order. "Mort. You clean this place up."

-Chapter Two-

Meeting the Boss

Duke's horse strode along at a steadily held pace towards the mines up in the lower mountains above Silver Gorge. Sheriff's bronze mount blended in with the rocky terrain around it, often making it look as if Boone floated above the horizon towards infinity like a legend long gone by. He'd never bothered to name the horse, though folks often suggested he should. People would suggest names like Bullet and Dusk and Carl, but nothing ever sat well with the sheriff. He just patted her mane and called her "Old Girl," if anything at all.

The road out of town ran east and west, leading travelers towards Carson City one way and San Francisco the other. To hit the mines, though, people usually stole out of town through a back alley around the end of the Rusty Spittoon. It was quicker and it kept miners from being too visible in town. Although the men were officially allowed to go wherever they pleased, neither Boss Mason nor the honest townspeople preferred to see the trademark Mason-yellow bandanas on the streets of Silver Gorge.

Mason had built himself a little village of his own up in the hills, complete with shops and homes and bars, but they paled in comparison to what Silver Gorge could offer in the

way of temptation and distraction. Of course, Mason also paid his men in Mine Bills, good only at the miner township, making it even more difficult for the boys to traverse into the city beneath them unless they first traded goods with the Indians and then sold those goods at the trading post in Silver Gorge for actual cash, but some men found it worth all the trouble for a night at the Cathouse.

Sheriff Boone hated visiting Mason's little empire, called Mason City by most of the locals. He visited only when urgent business brought him out that way. As much as he enjoyed watching the sun rise over Silver Gorge, Duke hated seeing the clock tower appear over the ridge. That accursed clock tower was always the first sight a man would see entering the faux town, and it was always the last shadow that would darken his saddle on the way back down the mountainside. For the men living and working there, that clock tower was gospel. When its bells rang, shift change. When its whistle blew, lunchtime. Though the men down in the mines were far too deep for the sounds to make their ears, they often said you could still see the more seasoned miners flinch when they anticipated their bell.

Boone hated Mason City and he hated Mason, but it was not his place to stir up trouble with the rich and powerful in town. It was his place to manage the calm and keep the peace, and so he dealt with them. He dealt with Mason because he had no choice.

The fastest route to the mines was through the Wilson ranch, but the Wilson family frowned upon riders traipsing through their property like they had the right. As a result, they loved to see Sheriff Boone come through. On more than one occasion he'd been summoned to settle a heated standoff between the Wilson boys and some free-range fool thinking he can drive a couple hundred head of cattle through another man's river. Yes, when Sheriff Boone came through, the Wilsons opened up their home. They offered their table, they offered their wine, and they offered their girl.

Ch. 2 | Meeting the Boss

She was a beautiful young woman, it was true, but not enough to make Sheriff Boone a fool. Mr. Wilson wanted the sheriff on his side in case things ever came to pass between the ranchers and the miners, and those sorts of disputes never went over well for anyone involved. The only reason Mason himself hadn't spent time and money to get the sheriff out of Silver Gorge was because he stayed neutral. Neutrality was a valuable currency in Silver Gorge, and it was one that seemed to disappear at an alarming rate.

As Sheriff Boone got about halfway through the ranch, just before he crossed the broad river that made up the lower boundary of their best grazing fields, he noticed a plume of smoke rising over the trees off to his left. As hesitant as he was to get to Mason City, he was more hesitant to deal with some drifter hiding out on Wilson land just yet, but being a good man Sheriff Boone made a note to double back around and take a look at the situation later. With any luck, whoever it was would have already left or been shot by the time he got back.

Boone soaked in the mountain vista that surrounded the greenest pasture for a hundred miles. As the road started to rise, though, and the grass turned to clay and stone, Sheriff Boone knew that he was headed for what some would consider hostile territory. By all interpretations of the law, Sheriff Boone still had authority in Boss Mason's autonomous society, but he never felt very powerful when in the presence of men as desperate as Boss Mason liked to surround himself with. Of course, as he drew closer to the mine, Zeke's words echoed in Duke's ears.

Did they ever even tell you what's in the mine?

As the sun reached its noontime peak, the forsaken clock tower came into view. At first, all that Duke Boone noticed was the glinting of the weathervane atop the tower. After a few more strides, the ivory face made a fine contrast for the flashing gold hands of the clock, pointing just a shade off of the top of dial. He was right. It was a little past noon, and thankfully the miners would all be eating their lunch. The only man who enjoyed the company of miners less than Sheriff Boone was Boss Mason, so the men being on a lunch break meant that Mason would be tucked away safe and sound in his office.

    The miners who sat along the rails and at tables near the entrance to the mine gave Sheriff Boone a couple of quick glances, but nothing too incendiary. Except, of course, for the three men he rescued from Zeke's imprisonment. Those three men, who had talked extensively with the sheriff after that night, sat apart by themselves and gave the familiar stranger a long stare. It was not an unfriendly stare, but more the stare of someone who is confronted with a haunting truth they'd hoped to put behind them. Sheriff Boone did the men no favors by returning their glance and tipping a hat in their direction. The rest of the miners, already wary of Duke's blonde horse riding into the town atop the mountain, tossed his three amigos a glance that brandished hate for colluding with the enemy.

    Boone smiled at his little trick, further pitting the three buffoons against their coworkers and co-citizens of Mason's town.

    He rode his horse slowly up past the shops and the craftsmen along the mountain face, the wooden offices built into one side of the mountain like the Hopi houses farther out in the desert, though these were built of cedar and pine from back east instead of the mud and adobe of the west. The sunburnt orange mountain face, jutting straight up into the Nevada sky, sheltered Mason City from the harsher winds and storms, and it shaded them from the dark evening sun. Were most of Mason City's work not already under ground, it would be a fine place for day laborers.

    The shelter had drawbacks, though. The airy western breezes flowed right on by Mason City. When the rest of the

Ch. 2 | Meeting the Boss

valley cooled in the afternoon's grace, Mason City broiled in its own fetid air until nightfall finally brought relief.

Mason's secretary, one of the few unmarried, employed women in town who worked somewhere other than the local saloon, walked out of the office and offered to help Sheriff Boone tie up his horse. She'd been standing on the steps of Mason's office under the awning's shade for a while yet and only stepped out to meet the Sheriff when he was close enough to shout. He'd met the lovely brunette before, a tall woman with dark eyes who preferred to leave dresses to the dancing girls, and her punctuality never surprised Sheriff Boone. Even still, she walked out to greet Duke as if she'd been expecting him.

Glorietta. Her name rolled off of a man's tongue like rain off of a flower blossom in a late summer storm. Though she worked hard to hide her beauty in the rusted shades of mining life, an observant man like the sheriff never missed the sight of loveliness hiding behind the thorns on a rose.

Her hands, guarded by shimmering black leather gloves, gripped the reins of the bronze horse and wrapped them around the cross post in front of Mason's office while Duke hopped off of the animal and filled the trough.

"Not too much, Sheriff Boone. We don't have water to spare up here," Glorietta chided with a smile.

"Horses don't drink silver, Miss Glorietta," the sheriff returned. As loathsome as Mason City was, moments stolen with Miss Glorietta made the trip that much more tolerable.

"Let me have your hat and gloves and I'll show you into Boss's office," she said, offering a hand.

Boone obliged and poured himself a glass of water from the bar just inside the doorway of the office. It was warm, but it was water.

"Did you have a nice ride up to the town, Sheriff?" Glorietta asked.

"Just fine, miss. I spotted a campfire on the Wilson ranch, probably have to run off another cattle roamer on the way home, but it was a fine ride," Boone answered.

"I bet you won't."

"What makes you say that, Glorietta?"

"I'd stake a nice dinner on it," she smiled.

"I'll take your bet, but let's not go putting food on the line, miss," he smiled back.

After a short silence, perforated by stolen glances and Miss Glorietta's conflicting desires with Sheriff Boone present, Boss Mason rang the bell for his guest to come in.

Duke walked the steps up to Mason's office on the second floor overlooking the town. As he rounded the corner of the building, Boone saw the paintings of cattle ranchers and Indians fighting on the plains. He saw the pelt of a fox hanging from the wall, the pelt being a new decoration, and a golden frying pan that marked the top of the stairs. Sheriff Boone wasn't sure the golden frying pan had always been there, or what purpose it served. Best he could figure was that it served as what some folks called a "curiosity piece."

When Boone opened the door to Mason's office, the boss man had his chair turned outwards looking at the town below. The noon shadow started to crawl from the back of the city to the ridge looking over the valley below, and the miners embraced the shade's respite. Boss Mason slowly stood and revealed himself to the man at the door.

Mason tried to hide his age with newer clothes and a clean shave every morning, but the brutal life up on the mines did a man no favors, even if his only work with the mines was in the far-forgotten past. Mason's face showed wrinkles and sunspots in crevices that were out of place for a younger man's appearance. Even the sheriff, nearing forty and not much younger than Boss Mason, looked like a spritely young fellow next to the old man at the window.

Ch. 2 | Meeting the Boss

Worry and regret, most likely, had cost the man's hair some color.

But if ever was a man who could be described as having one foot in the grave, Boss Mason had never even met him. The privilege of wealth was often health, and as poor as the old gentleman looked, he acted equally capable to a racehorse, especially in the lively manner with which he always spoke.

Mason surrounded himself with oddities and trinkets from his travels. When the mine nearly dried up several years back, Mason took a trip around the world to visit as many sights as he could. It took him two years to return to Silver Gorge, which was when he reopened the silver mines with much aplomb. Rumors spread that the mines were all dry, but Mason was a shrewd and qualified businessman. If he had men working the mines, it was for a reason, so people's fears about the disappearing silver abated for a while.

He had on one shelf alone a cockleshell from a journey to Spanish coasts, a turquoise figurine with eight arms from the Indian subcontinent, a dried monstrosity that looked like the unfortunate result of a monkey and a fish's unnatural pairing, and an ornately patterned wooden box about a foot long and perhaps half a foot both tall and deep. This box was cut with grooves and fittings that made no sense at first, with triggers and panels that would probably give way if depressed slightly.

From Duke's position at the entrance to Mason's office, he spied one particular trinket that he had trouble placing. Most of the curiosities were clearly ethnic and obviously products of one culture or another. Yet this simple golden frog, a recent pouring from the looks of it, sat in a place of priority on Mason's desk without any clue as to what nation produced it. Perhaps it was just valuable for the gold, Duke thought, rather than any cultural significance.

Sheriff Boone stood inside the door awaiting Mason's

invitation. Standing and waiting on another man's permission to do much of anything bothered the lawman to his core, but when in Mason City, you do what is expected.

"Finally come to talk about our mutual friend, Zeke?"

Duke stood motionless in the door, still stupidly waiting on an invitation he expected may never come.

"Sit, you fool," Mason called out as if berating a mutt for jumping on his lap. "Has the story fallen apart yet?"

"No, the story stands," Duke answered, pulling a leather chair back from in front of Boss Mason's desk.

"You want money to keep silent? Silver's been slow to pour the last few weeks, but I'll see what I can scrape up."

"Don't insult me, Mason. I know you've got most of the money in this valley tied up in your vaults. And it ain't money I'm wanting today."

"Then what is it, man? Spit it out. What was so important you had to come all the way up here for?"

It was a fair question. Sheriff Boone could have sent a letter and requested Boss Mason's presence. He could have just wired a request on the telegraph. What was so vital that the sheriff needed to strap on his boots and hit the dirt to put it to Boss Mason's ear?

"I wanted to talk to you about why Zeke wanted you dead, Mason," Duke recalled. "Why did he hold up three of your men in that saloon, and what made him think that ransoming three meaningless miners would even get your attention?"

Mason seemed caught off guard by the last question, almost as much as Sheriff Boone had been.

"You know full well why he wanted me dead, Boone, and you know better than most. After all, it was your idea," Mason reminded the sheriff.

Ch. 2 | Meeting the Boss

"Don't tell me that my friend died because of a lie, Mason. What really happened? He kept talking about what's in the mine. What's down there?" Duke inquired.

"You sure are a curious fellow, Duke Boone. What's with all the questions?"

"What's with the deflection, Mason? I'm the sheriff. Investigating and asking questions is part of my job. So here I am. Investigating."

Mason leaned back in his chair for a moment, relaxing the threatening pose he had taken up initially, almost regarding this guest as an honest to goodness equal.

The gray gentleman reached down and opened a drawer on his desk, which set off the sheriff's instincts to flashing.

"Relax, friend. I just need a drink," Mason said, stretching his available left hand out towards the nearly drawn officer of peace. "Care for a glass?"

"Unless the drink you're pouring is coffee, I'm fine," Boone answered.

Mason nodded and lazily grabbed a decanter from the drawers beneath his desk and poured what looked to Sheriff Boone like an expensive whiskey into both glasses, despite the officer's protests otherwise.

He picked up his glass and sighed, Boss Mason did, and he looked out the window at his back with a sideways glance that made Sheriff Boone's neck hurt out of sympathy.

Still looking away, Mason downed his drink in a slip of a second and broke up the story for the ridden-in guest.

"Zeke would stumble up this way once every few days just to harass miners in the saloon and taking their break. It was harmless at first, I thought, but it kept persisting and getting worse.

"Now my boys here knew his son, of course, and they weren't looking to cause a fight with a man like Zeke, but they started to complain that he was harassing them, asking them questions about his boy's death and about the silver we shipped off to other parts of the country.

"Like I said, it was harmless at first, but one day he comes in and starts hollering about how my mine is the gateway of Hell on Earth. The plum fool grabs my men by the shirt collar and demands we take him down into the mine, and if not, he's going to start killing. We get him off the property, then the visits stop. My boys get comfortable thinking he's done for good, and then three of them get cornered down in your lovely little town. I never did file the grievance with the city about that like I'd planned. I need to come down one day and get that taken care of," Mason punctuated his story.

"I'll deliver the message for you."

"Look, Sheriff. It's no hard feelings. Zeke was a man who lost his touch with how the world works after his son went belly up. We probably needed to concoct a better story and he might have believed it. As it stands, he knew we were bluffing, but he didn't know how," Mason finished.

The two men sat quietly in the sunlit office atop Mason City, thinking back to what happened with Zeke's son and the resulting chaos. Nobody had expected the simple farmer to become a mercenary when his son died.

"Folks go crazy when life doesn't go their way," Mason thought out loud. "It always amazed me how little it takes for some people to go over the edge."

"Zeke didn't go crazy, Mason. And it wasn't no small thing," Sheriff Boone answered with a hint of warning to his tone. "The man's son died. And he never even had the closure of a burial."

Mason looked up from his empty glass and examined

Ch. 2 | Meeting the Boss

Boone's face.

"Where's the body, Mason?"

"I told you, Sheriff, we don't have one. It's gone," Mason answered, his eyes seemingly darting around the room with a hint of subconscious avoidance. "He stole silver from the mines and ran off out into the desert. We searched and searched for him... I wanted my silver back... but we never found him. For all we know, he ain't even dead."

"You seemed pretty sure when you called me up that night. Where's the body?"

"You are tracking into dangerous territory, Sheriff. You're starting to sound like your crazy friend, the one who fell out over the bar room floor and evaporated into the desert sand. Be careful who you accuse, Duke," Mason hinted.

"When I accuse a man, Mason, I bring a rope. Do you see any rope?"

Neither man dared look down at his drink, each opting to gaze directly into the eyes of his opposite.

Sheriff Boone sat quietly and nodded for a moment, remembering the conversation that had taken place in this office back when the ground was still wet with snow.

"I told you, Sheriff, that a simple mining disaster would've been better," Mason reminded him.

"And I told you then, Mason, that Zeke would dig through a mountain to find his son's body. There had to be a reason we couldn't bury him. I gave you one then, and I'm asking you now where his body is. I'm telling you now, I want to know where his body is, and I want to know what Zeke saw down in the mine. Normal men don't 'spill out' as you put it," Duke raved for a moment before calmly readdressing the captain of industry who sat before him.

"What's going on here, Mason?" Duke watched Boss Mason for a moment, wondering if this earnest appeal would crack the hard-nosed mining boss better than ploys and prying questions. Mason just kept watching Duke for the longest time, playing a game with his eyes that left the Sheriff questioning if he'd even gotten through to the boss.

Mason stood from his desk and slowly came around the edges of the hardwood corners, etched in gold plating that gave the natural dark browns an elegant contrast that belied the hefty nature of this finery. He stood and ignored the sheriff as he headed towards the door. Duke assumed he was being unceremoniously thrown out of the office and out of Mason City, but when Mason reached for the door, he kept walking.

Boone sat and listened to the gentleman's heavy steps until they stopped at the bottom steps of the decorated stairwell, giving Mason time enough to turn back and shout, "Aren't you coming?"

Duke bolted up out of the chair, anticipating answers and closure from a notoriously guarded man. He shut the door behind him and forgot about the untouched show of hospitality on Mason's desk. He hopped down the steps like a boy hearing his father come home from a day in the fields. Mason was already almost through the front doors of the building by the time his ardent follower had spotted daylight from the stairwell.

Mason grabbed his hat on the way out, making him look just a little more like he fit in, even if Mason's hat was the only one for 1,000 miles that was haberdashed in Boston rather than forged by a local trader. The white string that sewed together the various pieces of fabric showed the slightest wear, more often than not protected by the sun-dried leather band that contained the stub of a peacock feather, the blues and greens of which stood out against the drab landscape.

Duke had never taken his hat off.

Ch. 2 | Meeting the Boss

Sheriff Boone jogged a step and caught up to the boss as he approached an abandoned mine car by the maw of Silver Gorge's only working mine. The miners gawked longingly at their boss and his guest, the only men who were not caked in mud and sweat from the morning labor.

"Grab me a light, will you, son?" Mason hollered to the foreman just exiting the mine.

The foreman, initially dumbfounded at who was requesting this favor, cursed himself for the delay all the way to and from the shed where the kerosene lanterns waited to answer the call. He ran back at a hefty pace, spilling more fuel than he could get in the base.

"Thank you kindly," Boss Mason said in his most genuine-sounding voice.

Without another word, Mason hopped on the cart and signaled for a push from the other men standing around enjoying the scene. Sheriff Boone joined him and watched the miners drop their meals and their canteens to rally to their boss's call. Three of them, the three who had seen Zeke that night in town, kept their distance.

As the two partners in transport rolled along their way, deeper and deeper as the mine's downward slope hastened its descent along with them, Mason started opening up.

"I built this mine by hand, you know," he started, his voice somewhat raised to combat the breeze of speed. "I picked the first few swings myself. I lit the fuses on the blasting caps myself. I got the first men myself."

"That's all very noble of you, Boss," Sheriff Boone responded to an unasked question, "but what does that have to do with Zeke?"

"This mine is my life's work, Boone. Every square inch of it. Every speck of dirt that has walked its way out of here on the boots of my miners... that's part of my life, too. This place is full of my own years, toiled away like some kind of wick burning off, you know? Hold up the lantern. What do you see from that burning light?"

Boone did as he was told. He held up the light and caught the cart veer off to the right of a fork with no tracks heading off the other way. Duke looked back to see if there was any way to notice where the other tunnel rejoined this one, but it was fruitless.

"I see… nothing. There's nothing here."

"You're right, friend," Mason laughed. "People have been speculating for years that this mine was going dry, that the silver was all but gone. Well, I'm afraid to say that they're right. We haven't got much in the way of product, you see, but we're still trying. Every once in a while, we'll find a new vein, and the men will follow it. If we were to follow this path all the way down, you'd see it," he said, anticipating a tug from the rope at the back of the cart.

Momentum viciously flung the pair forward into the solid metal side of a once hurtling cart when the rope predictably ran out. Mason had been sitting at the forward side, so he absorbed the brunt of Boone's impact and resulting sudden stop, which of course did wonders for their relationship. Ever the consummate professional, though, Mason straightened himself up as soon as the jarring stop had forced him to break his speech.

"This is a new vein. Zeke didn't see it. That night that he snuck in here, because he did sneak in here, Zeke saw nothing. He knew the silver was depleted, and that's what he went on believing. He assumed that since there was no silver and the men were still busy working, we must be up to no good. He didn't take time to think that we might just be working to find new silver, now did he," Mason suggested with a gleam in his eye.

"So why the… accident at the bar?"

"Which one? The hostage crisis or the spill? Zeke spent

Ch. 2 | Meeting the Boss

too long in the wrong parts of the mine. It happens sometimes. Men come down here and soak up some dangerous gases. That's why we make them bring a caged bird down with them on long shifts. When that bird dies, you know to get out. Zeke probably followed a dead vein into a bad tunnel. My men know better than to follow some trails. Thieves, though, like the grave robbers in the pyramids, don't know which path is real and which one is false. They fall for it every time."

The cart started to gently roll backwards, seemingly by itself as if the mine alone was expelling them, but that was hardly the case. The hill still pulled down, but the rope that trailed the cart pulled tighter and tighter as miners above started to yank backwards.

"One of the perks of being boss. I don't have to haul my own cart back. Or walk," Mason laughed.

It was obvious to Duke that Mason never walked, the fellow's girth belying any notion of beneficial physical activity, though the sheriff was not so bold as to deliver that particular retort aloud.

Sure enough, the cart eased back towards the sunlit surface. Boone had enjoyed the cool air down in the mine, but Mason's story of bad gases made him long for the fresh breezes of being topside. Plus, being a mile deep in Mason's own mine was not what Sheriff Boone would consider neutral ground, and he wasn't fully sold on that story about the silver.

"When I first came out here, Sheriff, there was no town. There were no saloons or trains or law. We watched our own backs, we did. We took care of our own. And we sacrificed to get what we have today, you know. Don't ever forget that," Mason warned. "I know some of you came out on your little expeditions, and they were tough, but riding the trail out west with a wagon train was nothing. I rode the hard lands, and I fought the good fights. I've earned this land, and I won't let anyone jeopardize what we've built here."

33

The cart was moving slower than Sheriff Boone would've liked, and it meant that he would have to listen to Boss Mason romanticize the old days just a little longer than any man with ears to hear could tolerate.

"We dug up this land pile by pile, Sheriff. We pulled mountains of silver from these walls, and I wasn't going to let the lies of one lying fool let people forget that. Tell you the truth, even if I never pulled another scrap of silver in my life, I could keep this mine open for ten more years. Miners are cheap labor, you know. And the only reason most of them are here is because they're too lazy to farm. If only they knew how much easier that life was, am I right?" Mason laughed, slapping Boone's shoulder with surprisingly strong force.

Sunlight came into view, but it took another five minutes for the slow, grinding crawl of the cart to reach the top. Duke could ignore the sound of metal squeezing together when it was drowned out by the rushing wind and the droning of an old man, but now his ears were assaulted by the clanging squeal of their slow rise to the top. Each bump and bounce made it all the worse, as the cart would then push back down on the tracks below.

Cacophonous grinding dulled Boone's senses to the point where he barely noticed what ought to have been an obvious abnormality. The stone floor of Mason's mine glittered at spots where the sunlight touched it, stars blinking at midday with a little help. The striking beauty of this unexpected glitz impressed Boone for a moment, but only a moment before Mason imposed his presence on the scene once more. Just before Mason got up to the freedom of the outside, he looked back at Boone and warned him sternly.

"Boy, you listen to me. Don't tell anyone what I've shown you today. I don't expect anyone to believe it, but let's not test that. Okay? Most of my men know that times are lean, but they still get paid and they still have work. Besides, why do you think we keep them out of town so much?" Mason

Ch. 2 | Meeting the Boss

admitted. "I have something for you when we get to the top. If you'll come back to the office with me, I think you'll like it."

The men popped out of their confined space as soon as the cart came to a stop, mutually ready to be done with each other's company. Still, they had one more dealing to take care of.

Boone's curiosity urged him onward, despite his wariness of what Mason could possibly give him. The men walked on back to the office with the same silence that propelled them to the mines just an hour or so earlier. The clock above the town read half past one, and the shadows grew taller by the minute. Boone would need to leave soon if he were to get into town before dark, but he would have to go back heavy a trinket from the Boss.

"Wait here, Boone," Mason demanded just inside the front door to the office. Glorietta was nowhere to be seen. Perhaps she'd gone home for the day, Sheriff Boone thought.

After a minute, Duke helped himself to the water that had been sitting out on the bar. After five minutes, he helped himself to the jerky that was sitting beside it. He couldn't help but wonder what was taking Mason so long to return. He could hear the footsteps upstairs, and he could hear what sounded like rolling wood over the floorboards, so he knew Mason was opening some secret safe, but for what purpose? What hidden treasure would Mason possibly part with for Sheriff Boone's benefit?

Finally, the sound of boots on wood started coming back down the stairs. When Mason came into view, he was carrying the same wooden box with intricate drawings and details etched on the side that Boone had spotted on his way up the stairs and into the office. Surely this prized possession wasn't the gift promised to the sheriff, was it?

Without explanation, Mason handed the box to Boone. The grooves were rough and uneven, and some pieces appeared to be slit in such a way that they could rotate, but it made no sense to the sheriff. Not one bit.

"Am I supposed to say thank you?" Boone asked.

"No, I don't guess you will. This here is a Japanese trick box, Sheriff. I got it on my travels to Japan, specifically when I was in a place called Hakone, some time ago. This one is quite the little devil. It took me three weeks of tinkering to finally crack, and the man who made it was so impressed that he gave it to me for free. I doubt you'll have the same luck. He boasted that it would take a man his whole life and he'd never find the secret to opening this box. Once I did, I knew it could be relied on to keep one of my dearest possessions safe," Mason explained.

"Your soul?" Boone joked dryly.

"In a manner of speaking, but sadly no, Sheriff. In here, friend, is a memento of my early days here in the Territory. Something… something very precious to me. I've held on to it for… far too long. Take it, please," Mason offered with a reminiscent sadness that puzzled the already hopelessly confused recipient.

"Why would you give me this?"

"This box is a lot like that mine, Sheriff. With enough luck and perseverance, you may just find what you seek. Then again, it may not be what you expect. Enjoy the hunt, Duke. Enjoy the hunt," Mason said as he retreated back upstairs, not once looking back at Boone or the hefty box that supposedly held an invaluable piece of Mason's life.

That man never made much sense, Boone thought. Duke realized then that he liked Boss Mason better when he didn't talk.

-Chapter Three-
The Drifter's Tale

Mason City disappeared behind the Sheriff, who was now riding back a good ten pounds heavier with the Boss's little trick box taking up space in the saddlebags atop Boone's maize-colored horse. Just as it had been the first thing to appear, Mason's golden gleaming clock tower was the last reminder of the town to disappear behind the rocks and the mountainsides that cradled the mining town in its stony bosom.

Boone looked out once more over the green valley he prepared to enter and absorbed the stark contrast of the deep reds behind him. Before him, lush meadows and a sparkling river welcomed the sheriff like a quiet rest under a shade tree. Behind him in Mason City, the parched rocks and the mud-caked walks dared men to tread upon them. Surely, he made the right choice leaving the latter.

The mild meadows just outside the mountain's shadow also served as a nagging reminder of the drifter in Wilson land who would need to be run out on the pass back through.

When Sheriff Duke Boone first immigrated to Nevada Territory, before he had prospects or vague intentions of becoming a sheriff, the sights of terracing rock faces and surprise fields caused the young man to stop and stare, perhaps even watch in wonder for a minute. The farmboy from back east could hardly believe that God would put such beauty on the planet for men to enjoy, but now he had been surrounded by it so long that Duke Boone just forgot what it meant to bask in the Nevada sunset's glow.

Now, looking out over the horizon just reminded Duke of all the work he had not yet done.

As the mountain slope's descent flattened out into level ground, small trees started to appear over a thin blanket of grass. Trickles and rivulets dotted the dirt at spots where the nearby river had splashed over its low banks, drenching the otherwise starved ground. The Wilson claim was one of the most beautiful sights around, as well as one of the most kind on a man who wanted to stay hidden, so it was often preyed upon by unwholesome drifters and solitary free-rangers.

The trees, as sparse as they are at first, provide shelter for those with no roof, as well as cover for those in need of a place to hide. The always-running river, recently refreshed from the melting snows of higher elevations, gave a man all the clean water he could need. If one were so inclined, the roaming herds of Wilson cattle could even keep a man fed for nearly a month if he rationed a single head right.

The pillar of smoke still peaked over the treetops in the distance, making this individual's position a quick find. Still, Boone took the long way around just in case the fire was more of a diversion than a necessity. Silver Gorge was a safer town than many, but paranoia can make for a nice ally when dealing with the kind of people a sheriff has to cross. Some folks called it a lawman's instincts, but Boone knew better. He was just good at checking behind every tree and lifting up every rock.

Duke timidly peeked behind trees and around boulders as he made careful work to stay somehow hidden on a plain where you could be spotted from ten miles out. Clusters of thick trees in mid-spring made for good hiding, along with

Ch. 3 | The Drifter's Tale

piles of rock and soil that had been displaced in this storm or that flood. Sheriff Boone hated these ghost hunts he had to perform time and time again, but that was the nature of his agreement with Mr. Wilson. Boone could come and go as he liked through the property so long as he made sure nobody else did. For all he knew, the fire belonged to Wilson's own boys out minding cattle, but the cautious sheriff was not one to take chances. Besides, what better way for Wilson to know that he was keeping up his end of the bargain than for him to see Duke checking the land?

The sheriff hopped off his horse and tied it up a little north of the smoke, having circled around it for a few minutes. He hadn't noticed any obvious signs of ambush or extra tracks, so he was likely dealing with just one man. With the advancing hour and the dying smoke, Boone figured he might be catching this fellow towards the end of lunch. Good. He'd be too occupied to hear anyone coming.

Boone spotted a tall spruce with manageable limbs, so he started to climb on up in hopes of catching a glimpse of what he was up against. He'd had plenty of practice climbing trees on his family's old farm, but the opportunity to traipse around in the branches hadn't presented itself in quite some time. Most of the branches were thick and could be gripped or stood on with a certain degree of trust. Others looked flimsy and rather more like stretched-out bullwhips than rungs of a ladder. Those were best to be avoided, Boone reminded himself. There was no faster way to lose the element of surprise than to be caught howling while your back caused tree limbs to snap all the way down.

The intrepid tree climber went hand over hand until he got about thirty feet high, high enough to spot the smoldering and occasionally flickering campfire through a gap in the trees. Boone leaned in and out, carefully watching his footing while trying to take stock of the whole campsite. He could see the fire pit lined with stones and what appeared to be rabbit bones freshly planted in the dirt. If nothing else, the sheriff was probably right on his guess about lunchtime. There was a bedroll spread out maybe ten feet from the fire and a sack that probably held sundry odds and ends where a pillow might go. All that was missing was an occupant.

Boone kept his eyes firmly on the fire and the site, assuming somebody might come back any minute now. It hadn't occurred to him, though, that somebody might have spotted his horse tied up to a tree. It hadn't occurred to him that someone might have come back to their campsite by way of the tree he was in at that moment. Sheriff Boone was so intent on watching the vacant camp that he missed the hushed sounds of a lithe body taking up the ground beneath him.

The next sound that Duke heard was nearly the last.

"What are you doing up there, Sheriff?" the voice below shouted up.

Boone fumbled for a branch as he started to slip at the startling announcement, even though he recognized the voice plain as day. The presence of a person he was half-expecting to exist should have never struck him as so surprising, but it sure enough almost ended the sheriff out of fear and a lengthy fall.

"I didn't mean to startle you, sir, but I didn't hardly expect to see a grown man up in a tree so close to me. I nearly shot you from a few yards back, but I knew your horse when I saw it and decided it'd probably be best not to kill a sheriff," the grizzled fellow laughed.

The folks in town called him Greasy on account of how he never seemed to wash, and they said his scraggly mouth was always spitting grease. Boone had never had much trouble with the local drifter and had found him pleasant to be around on occasion, but only on occasion. The rest of the time, he was just bothersome enough that you'd avoid him when you saw him.

"I just finished cutting up a rabbit for m'lunch if you're

hungry. There's probably a little left," Greasy offered as the sheriff climbed back down to grab a hold of his heartbeat. "What were you looking for up there?"

"I was looking for you, apparently, Greasy," Sheriff Boone answered. "I saw the smoke and thought it might be cattle thieves over here after the Wilson herds. What are you doing holing up on Wilson land, Greasy? You ought to know better than to cross them."

"This is Wilson land, Sheriff? Are you sure?" he asked, his few teeth flashing a gleam in the afternoon sun. He'd lost many of them over the years and struggled to keep the remaining ones straight in there with no side support to speak of. After the sheriff finished brushing tree tar off his hat and shirt and got a better look at Greasy's face, Boone remembered why he avoided the man in town. Greasy's hair was shoulder length and stringy, a few discolored strands mixed in with the muted black. His beard looked much the same, except it was maintained to just about an inch below the chin in a triangle shape up to the mutton chops. His clothes were another matter, as the old soldier still preferred to laze around in what was left of his CSA uniform.

The gray wool made for an uncomfortable riding jacket in the western sun, but no drifter stayed warmer at night than Greasy. During the day, he'd just throw the heavy coat over his shoulder so his colors could still show, even if that meant the stench of sweat pooling under his lighter shirt drove away men and women of polite society and weaker sensibilities. Even Sheriff Boone's strong composure struggled to handle the many fragrances and aromas of Greasy.

"I'm positive it's Wilson land, Greasy. Although it hasn't always been, they bought it off of Crooked-eyed Cox a while back so they'd have both sides of the river," Sheriff Boone explained. "I guess I can't fault you for not knowing that, but I'm sure the Wilsons will. You really need to find a new spot to bunk down, friend."

"I can't move, Sheriff. There's not much food left in the valley lately. All there is lives right in here. Plenty of rabbit here because the miners never come through. I guess now I know why," Greasy mused. "If I leave for greener pastures, metaphorically speaking, they won't be real green."

Greasy gave the sheriff a pitiful look that would melt a mother's heart. Too bad for Sheriff Boone that it seemed to work on him, too.

"Couldn't you just talk to them for me, Sheriff? Maybe ask them if I can wait here a little longer until the rains come back through?"

"I make no promises, Greasy, but I'll do what I can," Boone caved.

Old Greasy gave out a hoot and a holler unlike any Duke had ever heard, scaring off every grouse and chicken hawk in the surrounding trees.

"You're good people, Sheriff. Why don't you come sit by the fire and have a rabbit with me? I've already eaten mine, but there's plenty meat left for you," Greasy pleaded in hopes of returning the favor. "I ain't had good company in some time."

Boone knew what that meant. Greasy was fond of sharing his old war stories to anyone who would listen, often to anyone who was just too dumb or too lazy to get up and leave, and company with the Sheriff of all people meant that story time was coming.

The sheriff sat down on an overturned log opposite the subtly deranged vagrant of Silver Gorge and prepared for a story of questionable veracity. A pot of beans sat smoldering at the edge of the fire pit, wafting out dank smoke from the burning metal and grime now likely eternally stuck to it. Greasy's coffee, on the other hand, waited far too distant from the fire to be of any use as it collected ash and dead flies, each one floating on top of the other just beneath the brim.

Ch. 3 | The Drifter's Tale

Pioneer life was difficult for all men, sure, but Greasy seemed to make a tougher go at it than most.

The party's host took up his spot on a barrel of who knows what opposite Boone's position on a charred log while a bevy of roaches scattered from the place where Greasy's feet planted themselves. After a moment, they returned to the familiar plot near his bedraggled leathers, feeling right at home in the shadow of this foul-smelling knave.

"Did I ever tell you I was a sharpshooter back during the War for Southern Independence?" Greasy asked.

"I think you might have mentioned it a time or two," Boone obliged.

"Me and this buddy of mine were sitting on a ridge overlooking this battlefield once. I can't quite remember which one, we sat over top a good many battlefields, but it was one with this big open meadow and a well out in the middle of it. You know the type, they're all over the place back east, surrounded by green grass and not a bare spot for miles," the man started his tale.

"We'd done our fair share of picking off officers and a few infantry men when they'd make themselves visible over a hill, but we were mostly just looking over our own line. There was a small company of gray uniforms beneath us, and I guess we were supposed to protect them in case the fighting escalated over the hill. I don't know, it didn't make much sense to me, but that's what we were doing.

"Well we could see quite a row going on beneath us when these guys kept picking on a shorter fellow and egging him on to do something. He went over to his lieutenants for a minute and asked them a question before gathering up the canteens of the fellows standing around him. I kid you not," Greasy added before taking a breath.

"I never doubted you for a second," Sheriff Boone laughed, as he found himself almost enjoying the story so far.

"Well it was clear to my buddy and me that he was about to try and take that well, even though the meadow below had seen more than a few shellings that day. It was a miracle that the well was even still standing with how many times the yanks had tossed cannons near it.

"Well when we saw him taking off, we knew what we had to do. We started taking shots at him just to give him a bit of a scare. They weren't anywhere all that close to him, just close enough that he might notice a clump of dirt fly up or something. It was a laugh for a minute for us, that's for sure, but then something we didn't expect happened. A group of Unioneers stepped out of the woods to his left and started taking shots at him, too. We didn't even know they were there, but sure enough they started shooting, so we returned their fire."

Greasy stopped for a minute and poured himself a cup of that coffee detritus he'd been brewing all day and he let the story sink in.

Sheriff Boone had found himself engaged in the veteran's old tale, sure enough, and he cursed the coffee cup for draining too slowly.

"What happened to him?"

Greasy kept slugging down the slop he'd heated up as he kept the lawman waiting for resolution of some kind, but eventually there was nothing left to sip and Greasy concluded his story.

"Well, Sheriff. I'll tell you. We were about useless against those shooters on the hill, because they stayed far enough back in the trees that we couldn't get a clear shot on them, but they could keep pouring out shots at our friend in the meadow about as fast as a jack rabbit can get in and out of its hole.

"Well that fool boy even stopped to give water to a dying officer who'd been shelled earlier, for what reason I'll

Ch. 3 | The Drifter's Tale

never know, before he finally got back to his company and out of range of the Yankee rifles. And you know what happened when he got back there, Sheriff?"

"I haven't a clue, Greasy. What happened?" the sheriff responded, finding a bit of humor and suspense in the war story he was hearing. "What did that boy do?"

"He dropped the bucket!"

It was a simple punch line and one without much consequence, but Sheriff Boone and his occasional friend found reason enough to laugh at it. Even though only one of the men had spent time in war, Duke Boone grew up back east during that particular war and had a few memories of it. He remembered what it was like hearing cannons pop in the distance and to see wounded soldiers from both sides visit his father's shed for bandaging.

He had grown up in a part of Virginia where the war constantly traipsed in and out of town over a span of four years, and though Boone never needed to consciously choose a side, he had learned the value of human life from watching these men fight and die over a rich man's game, and he knew that it was all for naught. In Boone's mind, he'd just as soon move out West to avoid the political ramblings of former plantation owners after Virginia's fall. In fact, it was the constant bickering and lynch mobs sprouting up around plantations that caused Boone's father to urge him on towards taking that train ride out to St. Louis where he could join a party of pioneering wagon drivers.

And it was in St. Louis that Sheriff Boone had met Zeke for the first time. As the not-yet sheriff was travelling by himself, just a young man of 15 years when he traveled to St. Louis in 1868 with bushy hair and a sack full of clothes and his father's pistol, Zeke and his family took the boy in and treated him like a second son. The wild-eyed plow boy from Georgia paired well with the greenhorn from south of Virginia's coal territory.

When they all landed in Silver Gorge, the boys would farm together and work together until Zeke took a wife and Duke took to law. They would still spend time together, of course, as the frontier town of Silver Gorge afforded few opportunities to avoid even people you abhorred, much less old friends, but they lost almost all contact a few years back when Zeke's wife left town. The broken man he became let the farm fall into dire disrepair, driving his Josiah into the mines to make any money the pair might hope to have. For several months, Josiah just stopped coming home and stayed put up in Mason City. They weren't all happy memories coming back to the sheriff now, but talk of the war was enough to let him reminisce a fair bit.

Maybe it was the circuitous way that Greasy reminded the lawman of his old friend and the fonder times that made the moment so pleasant. Perhaps Greasy's storytelling had just improved that much. Who knows for sure why Sheriff Boone was so amenable that afternoon? It may have just been because Greasy was better company than Boss Mason, although such a statement said truly little about either one.

Though Boone had originally thought to make quick his visit with Greasy, he would have gladly spent the rest of the dying day right there on that log talking about old battles and glories won and lost had he not noticed the sun hanging low above the westward mountains from which he had just come, and he'd left Mort in charge of the town all day long. Sure, it was good for the kid to learn what it was like to monitor the goings-on of town, but for this long? Besides, he was weak yet. Mort would be getting dressed up to visit his saloon-gal girlfriend soon, and it would do no good to pretend differently.

"Friend, it's been good talking to you. You keep yourself out of trouble, okay, Greasy?"

Sheriff Boone picked his things up off the ground and even contemplated a bite of food before leaving when Greasy

Ch. 3 | The Drifter's Tale

reminded him of his promise.

"And you'll talk to the Wilsons for me, right? You'll tell them I'm here and that I mean no harm? And you'll ask them not to shoot me?" he added, with no small emphasis on that last part.

"I'll do my best for you," Boone answered as he stood and stretched to leave. Duke walked back out of the woods and found his horse waiting right where he'd left her and started to make tracks for the Wilson homestead.

He made quick work of his duties and asked their patriarch not to shoot poor Greasy, and he promised them that he would be no trouble aside from skinning the occasional rabbit or deer, and they begrudgingly agreed to leave Greasy alone as he steered clear of them and their cattle or horses.

Mr. Wilson made plenty of lightly disguised offers at lunch or tea, hoping to snare the sheriff in for one more well-intended meeting with his daughter on their patio overlooking the property, but Duke knew all too well what was at stake. Marrying the Wilson girl, as lovely as she was, would be far too much to manage. People barely trust the law as it is, much less when they think he's working for the wealthy.

Boone gave a courteous nod to the majority of the Wilson family, as a few were still out in the fields attending to the family business, and then made his way back on towards the town. Silver Gorge was a far sight from perfect, but he'd take it without question compared to the frontier or Mason City. The chaos of war and plantation politics was enough to drive Duke out west, but the emptiness of the open range and the harsh climate of the desert rocks were almost enough to force him back to Virginia tobacco.

On the ride back to town, Sheriff Boone found it strange how easily he could think about Zeke now. For the last few weeks, any passing thought of Zeke was cause for distraction and immediate exorcism of the mind, but now it was something lighter and more cherished. For the moment, at least, Zeke found a welcome place in Duke's recollections as opposed to a haunting and malodorous deflection.

It was easier now for the sheriff to remember his friend as a hearty and kind soul who latched on to a scared young man in a bustling train station in the heart of America. He remembered how Zeke had been the one to bear the telegram letting Duke know his father, the man he most admired in the world, had passed away. He also remembered Zeke sitting up with him for the night after Duke heard the news.

Once upon a time, Zeke had been a great friend to Duke. It was a shame, now, what had become of their relationship. It was nothing more than the sad footnote to a life lost in the wake of corruption and suspicious greed. It was a blemish on the mountains and a black spot beneath the saloon in Silver Gorge, which the sheriff could see rising just over the horizon. About time, too, as it was getting more difficult for Duke to push out the cold images of Zeke's final day. It was becoming a trial for Duke to forget what he had seen that day when Zeke came to town.

He tried to seize the pleasantries and the fondness of days gone by, but that reminiscence was gone. All that Duke had now was the harsh truth of what awaited him in Silver Gorge: loneliness.

Either way, seeing the outlines of buildings grow in the oranging silhouettes of sundown brought relief to Duke's ever-quickening chest. With the management of a town to look after, Duke thought, maybe the ghost in his memory will find a way to rest, if only for a time.

-Chapter Four-
The Menace Rides

The drooping sun cast a fierce blaze over Silver Gorge proper, with the sheriff's horse and rider trailing a black shade as long as the street they rode down. Duke never enjoyed sleeping outside of town when it could be helped, so nearing closer to home after a night of no sleep and a day out on the land was about the nearest he'd felt to being ready for sleep in weeks. Yes, the bed was calling.

He had done his best to avoid sleep for a while now, knowing how quickly Zeke would come up to meet him in dreams. Every minute Duke spent with his eyes closed was another minute exposed to an eldritch aberration that was better left alone. Every night, between fits of wakefulness and trembling, a melting figure with no discernible features aside from Zeke's voice stood at attention and asked Sheriff Boone a simple question: *Did they ever even tell you what was down there in that mine, Sheriff?*

The lone lawman of Silver Gorge ventured out to Mason's mine with the regards of sunshine at his side, but daylight and direct dealings had done him little benefit. More and more the sheriff started to believe that he would have to assume Mason was an obstacle more than a victim and that he would have to find ways around the mining boss's attentive glances, although it bothered him just what that would mean.

Aside from potentially offending and further repudiating the most powerful man in Silver Gorge and the surrounding area, Boone feared approaching that mine after dark most of all. Something told him that the mine offered answers, alright, but that those answers would come paired with unsettling truths that would not sit well with his otherwise clean conscience. The town of Silver Gorge would tremble to know what horror had befallen their outcast farmer, despite his recent tendencies for mischief. Nobody should have to see a man falling to pieces and being soaked up into the ground, even if that man is an enemy or a complete stranger; some images just won't go away.

Duke knew all too well how true that was, and he'd as soon die before he let anyone else suffer that same unnerving reality.

Despite their relative proximity to each other, Silver Gorge and Mason City bore no real resemblance other than sharing a general climate. Even that was thrown off by the high winds that occasionally blasted through the town's streets and through the alleys at night. Mason's mountainside retreat shielded him and his men from the worst of the elements at times, although shade could be a bit of a detriment in the winter when the rest of the valley benefited from the sun's warming glow.

There were no gold clock towers to be found in Silver Gorge. There were no fine accouterments of mining littered about the ground or adorning the walls of watchful offices. No, Silver Gorge held a more modest appearance in comparison to its northerly neighbor. The street ran perfectly perpendicular to the horizon, setting a picturesque portrait of the evening dim with the sun's light silhouetting the rising peaks in the distance as the mud-paved road was allowed to run unbent by a mountainside curve. Shops and saloons, largely patronized by farmers and family folk, stood battered

Ch. 4 | The Menace Rides

against the wind and the desert sands. Their walls and walkways showed obvious lapses, the originally imported boards largely missing or rotted away.

Yet the people lived on. There were troubles, sure, but the good people of Silver Gorge had carried on since the town's founding and the mine's initial drying up a few years back before things got going again. As money flowed into Mason City and the first generation of Silver Gorge native-borns started to find a living, whether on the earth or under the earth, things promised to improve. Such was the dilemma that Sheriff Boone faced.

Most of the stores in Silver Gorge had closed up for the day as owners were either headed home to tend to their families or headed to the saloons to tend to their needs. The general store and the stable were both locked up tight for the evening without a patron or a proprietor to be seen. The bankers had left for the day long before the sun kissed the distant peaks and the stage coach office had just one more departure scheduled for the day, and the train station wasn't expecting anything but mine cars through for almost a week.

The one holdout for the night was the town's biggest hotel, and in truth its only hotel with any redeeming qualities, run by the lovely Miss Abilene. The sheriff spotted her at the desk as he rode by. Abilene stood at the front desk wearing the high and tight collar that was the fashion for ladies in town, but her fair hair flowed down to her shoulders and lower. Most of the respectable women in Silver Gorge wore their hair much like the men did, but Abilene had no qualms about letting her beauty impress in this one very public manifestation.

She manned the hotel at all hours of the day and made sure that no guest went without. The lady had even hosted the sheriff a time or two when the domicile and jail were undergoing needed repairs. The two of them were already close acquaintances before that time, but spending a few days under the same roof did much to endear the pair one to another.

Duke strode by on his horse and caught the lady's eye just long enough to tip his hat courteously.

The jailhouse stood at the end of the row from where Sheriff Boone had entered the town, guarding the way to other environs with a steadfast watch. Few structures stood beyond it until you reached the next towns over, and that would require some kind of travel. Boone hopped off of his blonde mare and tied her up to the post outside as he sauntered up to the door carrying his saddlebags. As his boots hit wood, Duke heard a loud crash to the ground as if the jail's doors were thrown open and the roof caved in on them all at once.

Sure enough, when he opened the door, Mort was still sprawled out on the ground with his back nearly pushing through the floorboards.

"Falling asleep on my desk, boy?" the sheriff accused.

Mort, clearly caught, fumbled for a convincing lie long enough to force the sheriff's interest elsewhere.

"You can go, Mort. I know you've got better things to do than sit around here and watch an old man rot away to an early grave," he laughed. "You look nice. That a new suit? Shame you got it all dusty like that."

The young man picked himself off the ground and patted down his clothes. He was off to impress that lady down at the saloon, and he was sure dressed in style. He wore a paisley vest under a bourbon jacket and pants with a barely visible shoulder holster over his right arm carrying a well-cleaned Colt. Mort had never been much of a shot, but he carried the gun with style.

"When you want me back, Sheriff?" Mort sheepishly offered.

Ch. 4 | The Menace Rides

"Sometime before day break would be nice this time, but I don't guess I oughta rush love, should I?"

A devilish grin eased across the dreamer's face as he walked out the door towards his evening paramour.

Having given Mort enough time to wander off without fear that he might slip back, Duke rifled through his saddle bags and pulled out his little treat from Mason. When he shook it around, Boone could hear something rattle inside. Duke wasn't sure why this challenge irked him so much, but knowing that the undermining mine boss would go to bed that night with a grin on his face thinking he'd beaten his adversary? That was probably it.

The box sat on the sheriff's desk where the deputy's feet had just been not five minutes earlier. Its red and yellow hues stared back at him, teasing him to attempt a solution. The raised wooden bars were laid over the red tincture of the box's body. All told, the thing only weighed a couple pounds. It wasn't much of a burden to carry, but it sure was an annoyance to be around.

Duke fiddled with the raised bars on the side and quickly discovered that they were levers, which would be a great find if not for the fact that the four long sides had more than 100 levers in total. The sheer number of combinations he could have tried would have taken the rest of the year, and that would be just the first step. Still, the sheriff plugged away at it with clumsy hands until he stepped away to light a candle as the room went dark.

He could barely see the thing in front of his own face by the time he stood up to bring some light into the room. The sun had completely faded away in the sky and the evening breezes were soon to whip through the crannies and alleys between buildings leaving a whistling wake and some kicked up dust as the only sign of their presence.

The sheriff struck a match and set it to the partially

scorched wick of a half-burned wax candle. He had made the fatal error of not stocking up on candles during the daylight, leaving this as his last one until dawn. Perhaps he would spend another hour or so on the puzzle and get off to sleep this time. It had been a long couple days, and the promise of a dreamless sleep nearly lulled the sheriff into rest with the still lit match nearing his fingers.

The quick and the nail on his thumb both ached with a crescendoing heat as the sheriff's gaze was drawn into the candle-top flame bouncing back and forth, consuming dust and air without prejudice. Crackling wood on the simple match's base urged the flame closer and closer to the sheriff's hand with warnings both visual and tactile that should have made him drop the offender, but it was to no avail. He held on to that match for everything he could, distracted by the light in front of his eyes.

Duke was pulled out of his stupor by a sharp sting of fire on his foremost fingers all at once and dropped the match to the ground with a curse, shaking the offending hand as if that singularly futile action was somehow helping matters. A throbbing red spot melded itself onto his thumb, situated perfectly on top of the knuckle. The sheriff knew enough of burns to know that it would eventually grow into a black scar for a matter of days before disappearing altogether with time. Until then, it would be a fun task convincing people that he hadn't done something stupid to earn the novice's burn.

Back at his seat, the sheriff spent several more minutes trying various combinations on the box, back and forth with different groupings of panels and switches, but it all seemed a circuitous fallacy of skill. For whatever reason Mason had given him that puzzle box, its purpose was anything but as an aid to the investigation. It was a grand distraction that had suckered in the only man who still cared enough about a dead man's dead kid to look into why all of this happened in the first place.

Ch. 4 | The Menace Rides

Confident in the belief that he had done all he could in one extended period of wakefulness, Sheriff Boone finally gave in to the sonorous hallucinations urging him to the bed. Duke took off his star and his hat first, setting one on the desk and the other on a hook near the front door. Next, the one element outside of his usual routine, Boone took the maddening device Mason had presented him and shoved it inside the otherwise vacant safe hidden near his seat.

After putting away the evidence, so the sheriff convinced himself, Duke sauntered to his room beside the main office space and untied his gun belt, grabbing up the candle in his free hand on the way back. Once he was inside and sure the door was secure, he finally removed the weighty guns and set them aside with the minimal care required of such devices.

Sheriff Boone's eyes drooped under the blank moon and the gray glint of night coming in the raised window, and he more quickly than usual gave way to sleep, dropping down to the cotton pad with a deathlike thud. For the first time in a matter of weeks, it seemed, Duke drifted unconsciously without visiting the nascent horror residing in his darkest corners of thought. For once, he slept without dreaming and sought without seeing. For once, he was at rest.

The tranquility of slumber was broken unceremoniously some undisclosed hours later by a shouting Mort carrying on about outlaws and dangers afoot, but the overworked sheriff wanted none of it. His deputy kept begging the sheriff to rouse and work, but the sheriff kept begging Mort to can it and sleep.

Mort clamored on and grabbed the sheriff firmly by the shoulders before giving him a hearty shake rigorous enough to rattle cockroaches out of a watering can. At the deputy's ever so gentle insistence, Duke put his feet on the ground and set his eyes square on the fool boy's face.

"What is it now, Mort? I was a million miles away until

you busted in here screaming up the place," Duke Boone growled with the melancholy of sleep still drowning his frustrations. "This had better be some kind of a real emergency."

"Come quick, Sheriff. Somebody just shot up the hotel. You hear me? A man rode through town and shot up the hotel!" Mort hollered again.

Duke threw on his clothes and his hat as quick as he could, and he grabbed his gun belt on the way out the door. Mort had already relit the last candle, apparently, so there was plenty of light for the sheriff to get ready by. The moon offered some help on that front, as well, as the two men burst out the building and into the streets, those same streets which found themselves a little busier tonight than usual with the uncommon commotion up the way.

The hotel sat near the middle of town so guests would have to come past shops or saloons either way. It also helped that the hotel was near the stage coach and probably one of the closer parts of town to the train station. It was a decent walk for the sheriff and his deputy, but it wasn't so far that they would waste time preparing horses to get there. As they walked side by side, Boone looked over at his man and asked while barely moving his lips, "Was anyone hurt?"

Mort kept walking and acting like he hadn't heard the sheriff's query, so Duke repeated himself and slightly more assertively.

"Was anyone hurt, Deputy?"

"She's fine, Duke. Miss Abilene's alright and nobody else was staying there tonight."

Sheriff Boone had done his best to keep any affections for the lovely innkeeper private, but Mort was an observant enough man and had likely picked up on some of the subtler cues between the two. Not that someone who spent that much time with the sheriff would be hard pressed to discover his

Ch. 4 | The Menace Rides

deepest secret, seeing as how that hotel was by far the most surveilled property in town, but his close relationship to the sheriff gave Mort a few advantages most common men would go without.

Boone's pace dropped off significantly upon hearing the good news, but he hastened his step again when he was close enough to see Miss Abilene standing out in front of her business in a warm nightgown. It was blue and gray with white lace around the collar and the end of the sleeves, and she kept it tied tight in the front so as to not reveal any of her more immodest attributes. Abilene had clearly been sleeping in something more translucent, the sheriff could tell, but the desert winds and the evening chill combined for an inhospitable environment more fitting for long sleeves and a coat than slinky negligées. The lady's hand clutched at her neck with swaths of fabric interwoven with her fingers in order to keep the gown cinched up tight and to keep the wind off her chest, but she let that left hand drop when she saw the sheriff run up to greet her.

"Are you alright, Miss Abilene?" the sheriff tenderly asked, expecting no reply. He simply offered his arms to the shaken woman and took her in. While Mort surveyed the scene and took note of other bystanders out for a midnight stroll, the sheriff did his job as best he could by nestling one of Silver Gorge's most prominent citizens in his secure grasp.

Duke let go only long enough to place his beige coat around the trembling hotelier to reveal his own unprepared attire. Her pale hands crossed over to pull the fur-lined lapels into her chest, her tousled blond hair tucked underneath to protect her neck from the evening air. Sheriff Boone put his exposed arms back over Miss Abilene's shoulders and made no attempt at hiding his affinity for the lady in need.

Though men often carried their guns into town as a show of bravado, it was a rare occurrence that someone would even go so far as to unholster a weapon in the confines of the various buildings and within earshot of the sheriff's office. Even less so was it likely for someone to actually be fool enough to fire one off. Most of the people who worked in town, such as Abilene, lived without any acknowledgement of what such tools could do. Now she had been thrust full on into this new world.

"What happened here, Mort?" the sheriff required of his deputy. "Did these folks see anything?"

"I was just getting ready to ask, boss. Most of them look like they've been roused from their beds, though. They probably heard the gunfire and came running," he answered back, looking at the crowd of clueless eyes and mismatched wardrobes.

One grizzled hand shot up in the crowd, though, to inform everyone that this old-timer had a fair idea of what happened here. Rusty, they called him, lived over the stable and generally made a habit of frequenting the nightspots on a daily basis. He was a few years weary of the frontier life and had come out with some of the first wagon trains to make it as far as Nevada Territory, and it showed in his face and in his eyes.

Rusty stood five feet high with patches of gray hair and no hair under a tattered canvas hat. His uniform of overalls and a stained lime shirt told most people what they needed to know about Rusty, but few would have ever guessed that he was a boxing champion in his younger days. The cracks in his fists and the bent fingers he raised now belied some of his worst injuries, but he still went about his business of pouring back drinks and saddling horses for travelers and locals alike.

"I got a look at him, Sheriff," Rusty started in his even but slow timbre. "The fool sat on the back of a black horse with a gray stripe down the front and he was just shooting at the windows of the hotel and nowhere else. Made no sense, I tell you.

Ch. 4 | The Menace Rides

"Well he wore a bandana on his face and a hat on his head, and you know it was pretty dark, but I could see his eyes alright and his hands. He looked like he had a scar over his left eye and down across his nose from what I could see, and his right hand was missing a little finger. It was tough to tell because he was up on a horse, but I imagine he was about your height, Sheriff. Maybe an inch or two shorter," Rusty surmised, relying on his ability to size up a fight. "He was hunched over and looked a little gangly, if you ask me. He ought not have shot the place up. Instead, he could use a good meal. Put some food on those sickly looking bones."

The two lawmen gave each other glances that said a mouthful, knowing exactly who Rusty had just described. Though they both knew, neither one was ready to put the whole town on edge with news of exactly which unruly gunman had just blown through and interrupted the serenity of Silver Gorge. People had just started to calm down after the last incident. Adding another fiasco to the town's nerves would be ill-advised.

As the sheriff's would-be paramour clung to his chest, he softly pushed her away and lifted her eyes to his. The age that had started to show in his face in the presence of a blistering sun hid under the soft light of a spring moon, rounding off the harsher edges of his chin and cheeks, replacing them with the smooth look of a man half Duke's age as he spoke to the frightened victim.

"Do you want to come stay with me tonight, Miss Abilene?" he asked.

Mustering a laugh and a smile, Miss Abilene answered back, "That'd make you real happy, wouldn't it? No, sir. I've got more than enough rooms of my own to choose from tonight."

Duke smiled at her and gently touched Abilene's shoulders to reassure her that he would do everything in his power to make sure that whoever did this would not come after her again.

"Did you see which way the man went, Rusty?" Boone asked the old gentleman, now at the forefront of the crowd's attention.

"Well. He was shooting across his body with that damaged right hand of his, and it looked like he had just come up from your way, Sheriff, so I guess he went out of town out towards the open plains of the Wilsons' land," Rusty offered in a roundabout sort of way. "We need to round up a posse, Sheriff?"

"Yes, Rusty. Go ready the horses and rouse the men. We'll run off after him as quick as we can," Mort took the liberty of answering.

"Never mind all that tonight, Rusty. If he rode out that way," Boone started, "we'd have as much luck finding a trail by morning as we would of him hearing us coming and laying in ambush. Some men just like to stir up trouble when they can, and we can't go making it a town priority each time they do."

Mort turned on his sheriff with a horrified look, questioning his generally surefire boss's suddenly patient mentality.

"Sir, we've got to go after him," Mort softly disagreed. "You know as well as I do who's out there, and we can't risk him doubling back into town with us being unprepared."

"That's exactly why we can't be going after him, boy," the sheriff responded, now pointing back towards his own office and jailhouse, and more importantly the mountains on the western horizon. "Had he gone that way, his only choice would be to turn around and come back. Then we might have a chance of catching him tonight.

"That ain't what he did, Mort. He went off that way," Boone said, turning his whole body out towards the open plains. "That way is a whole world of possibility. He could be headed east towards Wilson land or Mason City. He could be going north or south to any number of other cities. Nobody's hurt here and nobody needs to be hurt here tonight."

"With all due respect, Sheriff," Mort jumped back, a little less mindful of public decorum this time around, "that man just shot up our town. Look what he did to Miss Abilene, there. Are you going to let that stand? Are you?"

"I will do no such thing!" Boone roared back, enraged by his deputy's lack of respect and restraint. "Of course I intend on making sure everyone in Silver Gorge is safe and protected, and if that means letting one miscreant go unchecked so that we can stay here and guard our walls, then so be it. But I will not sacrifice the well-being of my city in order to quench some bloodlust for a suicide hunt without light and without a trail. If you're volunteering to go alone, be my guest, but you'll get no assistance from me or anyone else tonight. You understand?"

Mort bowed his head respectfully and noticeably shamed before backing away and heading back towards the jailhouse.

"Now, if any of you men want to take up positions on the roofs of those buildings on the end of the street to keep an eye out, that wouldn't be a bad idea. We'll loan you a couple rifles. But I don't want anyone going after our mystery guest tonight. If we're lucky, he just had an itch to scratch and he took care of it with a few shots on a building and not any people. Let's not stroll a bunch of targets out there to give him a few more chances to try," Boone offered before walking his lovely friend back inside.

The crowd started filing away as the excitement had all but died down, so Duke took Abilene by the shoulder and led her back inside and out of the cold. He pulled open the glass front door of the hotel, which boasted one of the few panes not shattered or nicked by a spray of bullets, and took his coat back as they entered the warmer corridor that welcomed guests to the local inn.

The all-wood sitting area held its warmth thanks to a well-fed fire despite the wind whistling through holes in the glass and gusts pouring in through vacant frames. Miss Abilene instinctively started to pour the sheriff a drink from her stocked bar on the wall, but he refused from a leather chair by the corner of the room with the fireplace.

Duke ran his eyes over the room and noticed that a few bullets had worked their way into the back where Miss Abilene stayed, as the visible wall to her place had been perforated by what looked like four separate shots. He'd never personally seen the room himself, but he had seen her walk in and out a few times while he visited. As the sheriff stood and walked over to open the door, passing through the heat of the fireplace, Miss Abilene's eyes started to follow his steps.

With the creak of the door, Duke's gaze fell quickly on the shattered lamp at her bedside table. Even with the muted light of the fireplace and the beams tunneling through bullet holes, flecks of light reflected off the shattered glass on the floor. On Miss Abilene's headboard, the sheriff could see lines where two of the shots had grazed the wood. It was likely one of those that ricocheted off and smashed the lamp.

From the lines of light, Sheriff Boone traced the other two shots into the back wall of her room which bordered the rock wall at the inn's rear. Odds were good that those two had shattered, but the ones slowed by the headboard and the lamp probably still retained most of their shape and could prove useful to confirm or deny his theories as to the shooter's identity.

Miss Abilene's hands shook as she set the decanter back in its spot, glasses clinking against glasses with her uncertain movements. The rattled woman, so normally steady and calm, set her palms against the surface of the bar and let her head drop from exhaustion. Duke wanted nothing more

Ch. 4 | The Menace Rides

than to hold her, but he knew from her posture and veiled expression that this was no moment for romance. This was a moment for letting her be.

As the lady gathered herself up, she turned back towards the sheriff and gently apologized for her manner as if speaking to a customer about poor linens.

"Forgive me, sir, but I'm just not quite myself with all of this excitement tonight," Miss Abilene coyly recited while stepping in the sheriff's general direction. "If there's anything else I can do to make your stay here better, please let me know."

Duke slowly turned and took her hand in his. He had dealt with deaths and shootings, disappearances and robbers, and even one mysterious disappearance into thin air, but watching Miss Abilene break like she had with tonight's violation of safety and calm, nothing had upset the sheriff more.

"You can be honest with me," he whispered, looking into her eyes. "Were you sleeping when this happened?"

The lady in blue slowly lifted her face and looked into his. With a gentle nod, she told Duke Boone all he needed to know about what she had just gone through.

"Just let it come," he said, pulling her close enough to feel her heart beat on his.

And with that reaffirmation, Miss Abilene rested her eyes once more on the sheriff's chest and let loose the tears she had been holding in for far too long.

-Chapter Five-

The Scarecrow's Call

It was but an hour before sunrise by the time Duke made it back to the jailhouse. Miss Abilene had stubbornly refused his requests that she come back to the office where she'd be safer, opting rather for one of her other rooms in the upper floors of the hotel. Since there were no guests at the time of the shooting, and there wouldn't likely be any for another couple weeks, it was that much easier to close the hotel for the time being until Miss Abilene could get the windows fixed and patch the holes in the wall.

Sheriff Boone walked the dirt-paved streets of Silver Gorge in the dark as he had done so many times in the last few weeks, intently watching his feet as he stepped past the Rusty Spittoon. The ritual of aversion came more as a matter of habit this particular morning as Boone's thoughts were still with the lady in blue and less on his own minuscule problems. Abilene was the closest Duke had to a friend in Silver Gorge and he'd be a fool if he let anything happen to her.

A few of the town's men stood on rooftops watching the streets through the iron sights of borrowed rifles. The sheriff grew partially concerned that they would mistake him for a target and take their best shot, but he remembered who all was up there and quickly eased his thoughts.

Ch. 5 | The Scarecrow's Call

On top of the general store stood Joe Miller, a reverend from the Carolinas. His father had fought in the Civil War, but Joe had never picked up a rifle except for the occasional hunt. Duke had been hunting with Joe a couple times, and he'd never witnessed the preacher hit his target.

Above the saloon stood Franz, an immigrant from Europe who got off the boat and hopped on a stage. Franz had spent most of his time working in the printing press, and he was paid well enough to afford food. Again, he wasn't much of a shot.

The only real threat was Erik Harper, the Virginian veteran who had seen his time in service cut short by a shot to the leg. He'd managed to keep that leg through sheer luck, but it still ended his time on the line, probably saving his life. Erik was a keen enough shot, but that was due mostly to his eye. Fortunately for the sheriff, the only man with skill enough to shoot him was the only one with sight well enough to recognize him from on top of the water tower.

Almost as if on cue, Erik shouted down at the sheriff.

"How you doing down there, Duke?" the marksman greeted from on high.

"Doing alright," the sheriff responded. Erik and the sheriff were passing acquaintances at best, but the two men recognized a bit of a kindred spirit one in the other. They had always been men of good terms, swapping tales of farming back east. Although Harper was a few years older than the sheriff, they were the only two Virginians around, and that was a bond that ran deeper than most folks would know.

"We're getting kind of bored up here waiting on a man who ain't coming, Sheriff. What do you say? You got a bottle on you?"

"You're not planning on drinking on the job, are you?" Boone joked.

"No, sir. Just looking for some sport. What do you say?

You got a bottle?"

"Nope. Not on me."

"How 'bout that one over on the rail. To your right," Erik guided. He had a good eye, that's for sure. Duke could barely spot the thing standing five feet away, but Erik had a bead on it from more than 45 feet up. He walked over and picked up the glass bottle. It was clear and empty of anything but air, Duke could tell, and so he gestured to the man on the water tower that it would work.

"Alright. On my count, you toss that bottle up in the air. Let's see if I can still hit it," Erik shouted, grabbing the other two watchmen's attention on himself and his pending trick. "One. Two…" Erik paused, giving Sheriff Boone enough time to properly draw back for the throw. "Now when you let go, Sheriff, you better run. That bottle's coming back down either way, and it might be in a million little razor sharp pieces."

"Quit stalling, Harper. Show us what you've got," Duke smiled, as he could almost make out a grin on his fellow Virginian's face.

"Let me start over. One… two… three!"

With the call of three, Duke tossed the bottle as high as he could and bolted forward. He turned around, though, just in time to see the bottle reach its apex and start to fall. The moment it gave any hint of descent, the rifle in Erik's hand gave off a bang and a puff of smoke. An instant later, Erik's words proved true as the bottle shattered into a brilliant starburst, littering the ground where Duke had previously stood.

"Consider that your warning shot, friend," Erik joked with Duke as he went back to his post.

A few heads poked out their windows expecting a dead body, only to be disappointed by the gleam of a dead liquor bottle buried in the pavement.

Ch. 5 | The Scarecrow's Call

The two statesmen smiled at each other one last time as the confused watchers strode back inside to get out of the street and out of the cold. Sheriff Boone had enjoyed the jest and the game, but there was still plenty of business to tend to. Not surprisingly, Boone noticed that Mort was not one of the many to step outside at the sound of a gunshot. While it would seem strange to some that the only deputy in town would ignore such an event, the sheriff knew him well enough to know that Mort was sitting at the desk awaiting Boone's return, plotting what he would say to the sheriff in defense of his foolhardy actions.

Duke finally reached the step up to the jailhouse and sheriff's office. Boone put an extra emphasis on his next step as a fair warning to the boy inside, per his usual custom, before reaching for the door handle.

As expected, Mort sat waiting on his punishment with a back-up plan in mind, right at the desk where the sheriff would see him upon entering.

Mort had apparently grabbed more matches and candles because the place was quite well lit. It was lit enough, at least, that the sheriff could easily tell that Mort kept his eyes down when Duke walked in the door.

"You and I both know who's just come through town, kid," Duke opened in order to ease the hostilities, "so we can't afford to be going back and forth with each other right now. You hear me?"

"You didn't want to go after him, so why are you lecturing me about him now?" the fool deputy reacted, tossing away the sheriff's laurel offering. "That man will tear through this town like a tornado through a hayfield."

The sheriff looked patiently on his conflicted deputy. As bold as his words were, Mort's gaze stuck to a sole pen in the inkwell. For all his boastfulness, Mort still couldn't look the sheriff in the eyes and go against him.

Sheriff Boone calmly took a seat and burned his stare at the defeated deputy's face and waited for the two to connect one way or another. When the boy finally took on the gumption to look up and meet his boss' face, Sheriff Boone spoke.

"Now, Mort. I told you once why I wouldn't send men after that killer, and you know good and well why we shouldn't. I don't mind you disagreeing with me, after all, I'm just human, but maybe next time hold your gripes to yourself until we're back behind closed doors," Boone chided as Mort's forehead drooped but his eyes stayed locked in with the sheriff's.

"As for the Kansas Scarecrow, we'll wait and see if he comes back. Like I said. For all we know, he was just passing through. There's no reason to disturb the town over a drunk gunman's passing fancy. If he comes back, though, at least now we know who to be looking for."

Mort still wore an inexplicable scowl on his face, though, thoroughly unimpressed with Boone's patience. The young deputy kept looking intently at a fading candle by his propped-up feet, having once again lost the courage to face his boss. It was a short-lived fervor that had allowed Mort's glare to meet Duke squarely, but it had been there for a moment all the same. For now, though, Mort would quietly resume his disapproving indifference to the sheriff's policy.

Sheriff Boone, on the other hand, stood and wondered if it would be worth stepping back to his bed and grabbing another hour or two of sleep. The morning sun was still a good ways off, and if it was true that the Scarecrow was running around Silver Gorge, Duke knew that he may not have many full nights of sleep coming up.

The outlaw known as the Kansas Scarecrow took the name for his unusually gaunt appearance. In their heyday, which had long since passed, the gunmen of the frontier were generally big men with some heft to them, or at least they were average. A man of Duke's height and weight might have done well in that era of gunplay and mindless dispute.

Then again, even a scrawny fellow like the Scarecrow could pull a trigger, as nearly 25 victims had come to know. Sure, some of his conquests had been taken out in a fair fight, but the Scarecrow had come to be known as a ruthless trigger finger with remorseless aim and a blithe, reckless demeanor about death. The Scarecrow had crippled certain towns he frequented with an irreparable fear. His reputation as a heinous, fatal gunslinger had grown so boisterously that he rarely had to even unholster a weapon when he went into a town where people knew who he was. The law had either given up on him or had been bought off by him, and what odds did a normal man or woman stand against the last great shooter?

Knowing full well how comfortable the Scarecrow's life had grown, as he was now so notorious that his name did all the fighting for him, it made no sense to Duke why this character would wander out into the wilderness to face a new challenge and a new town, especially one as disconnected as Silver Gorge. Sheriff Boone and Mort had heard plenty from travelling marshals and the like, but the average person in town had no real concern for a man like the Kansas Scarecrow. He was a ghost. A narrative of no real importance.

Which was exactly why the sheriff knew it was imperative that he go to great lengths to prevent anyone else from hearing about this. The people should know to be protective of themselves and their property, but not enough that they flee in panic or abandon hope. Boone would handle the invader with tact and subtlety if possible. Boone would gladly die before letting the Scarecrow terrify the people of Silver Gorge.

"You've still got a few hours before daybreak, son," Duke said to the still sulking deputy. "You oughta go spend them with your lady friend. We may not have many more free nights coming up with the Scarecrow trying to traipse in on our territory."

Mort's eyes and ears perked up like a dog's when he hears his master unlock the gate. He'd obviously been waiting for an excuse to leave and get away from the sheriff, and this permission was all the notice he needed.

"You sure, Sheriff?" he asked, already halfway out the door.

"Go on. I'm going to go get some sleep, myself. Don't be surprised, though, if I'm gone when you come in. I'm going to go check on Miss Abilene first thing and see if I can help her patch up some things," Duke responded.

Just like that, the boy was gone. After Duke was sure that Mort was nowhere around to see him blow out the candles and grab his hat for departure, the sheriff grabbed his things and headed out to his horse. Duke was surprised to find that Mort's horse had already been untied and ridden out from behind the jailhouse, but there was no time to worry about such things. Before he would be seen, Duke untied his own blonde and saddled her up for an early morning ride out away from the mountains and the western horizon.

The drifting moon would have given Boone plenty of light to see by on a better night, but the cloud cover blanketed the sky and kept prying eyes unaware of his official, unofficial business. All the better, Boone thought. The less people knew about what he was doing, the better off everyone would be.

Boone took a turn once he got out of town and headed towards that mining village in the sky he was so fond of. Although he might catch a glimpse of Mason City at sunrise on that eastern-facing slope, Duke was beyond thankful that his ultimate destination lay far before then. Had he been forced to waste two straight days visiting Boss Mason and taking in that malodorous mine and the equally unsavory people who worked it, that might have been enough to

Ch. 5 | The Scarecrow's Call

convince the sheriff that searching out the Scarecrow was a good idea.

No, Sheriff Boone knew exactly where he was going. He was headed out towards the Wilson farm to give them fair warning as to who may be camped out in their area and who may already be lying in wait for an opportune moment.

Although Boone appreciated the cloud cover, as it gave him the ability to pass through and leave town nearly undetected, it did bring with it one added disadvantage. Had there been better light, Boone may have seen where he joined up a fresh trail outside of Silver Gorge and how he followed it almost all the way in to Wilson property.

Sure enough, Mason City gleamed off the dull rock like a second sun on the wrong horizon just as the original peeked over the eastward plains in that unclaimed territory between the ground and the sky. As the morning glow returned to the world and brushed an orange hue on the already dirty, auburn landscape, Sheriff Boone's eyes squinted with the increased light until he was able to see clearly as he topped the small hill where the Wilson household was.

The Wilson place portrayed an eastern, colonial wealth. It was not unlike the Virginian plantations that Boone had distant dreams of from his youth on the other side of the country, with white columns holding up a white façade dotted in verdant shutters. Immediately behind the impressive two-story palace stood a gallant barn and an immeasurable field with some of the best farmed goods in Nevada. Beyond the produce was vast timber land and grassy plains for cattle and horses to graze when they could, all encompassed by the southern river that divided Wilson's land from everything that Mason claimed as his exclusive right. Though Mason had no legal stake outside of the mountain.

Though it was early, Boone saw the Wilson family rousing from their sleep and opening curtains along the forward-facing windows and coming down for breakfast already dressed in their daily work clothes.

It was rude to interrupt a family breakfast, Duke thought, but it would have to be done. This essential matter would have to outrank the protocols of propriety, even where the wealthy are concerned.

Sheriff Boone strode up to the front door and climbed the landscape staircase that encompassed all of the Wilson front porch in order to announce his arrival. As he did, Wilson's oldest boy, Matthew Jr., flung the door open with his eyes still drooped in a sleepy stupor but a six-gun at his side. Junior was a tall fellow with the type of rugged features that women in town, both young and old, swooned after. His bedraggled brown hair matched the texture of his father's, though it held more of the color that Matthew Sr. had lost to the years.

"It's the sheriff, Pa!" Junior shouted back to his father before inviting the lawman in, a move which his proper paternity chided him for later.

As Matthew Wilson Sr. came to the door, his appearance much like his eldest son's with a couple decades and a lot of hard labor tacked on, the old man fought sleep to bring his assumed friend in from the morning chill.

"Well, I can't say I'm not surprised to see you, Sheriff, but we're always glad to bring a respectable man such as yourself in. Would you care to sit and enjoy a biscuit fresh from the kitchen?" the senior Wilson inquired.

"No, thanks. Not yet, anyway," the business-minded sheriff appealed, looking around and noticing three eager young men and an adorable, bubbly young woman hiding her face behind the door leading into the next rom. With so many ears about, Duke was rather unwilling to speak so openly with the patriarch. "May we retire to somewhere a little more private?"

While Wilson had hoped that the morning's surprise

Ch. 5 | The Scarecrow's Call

meeting involved his daughter, and his initial instinct told him that was even more likely the case as Sheriff Boone requested a more secluded conversation, the lifetime farmer noticed something in his guest's face that told him the discussion would be more dire than a betrothal.

Some people in Silver Gorge saw Wilson and his family as pillars of the town and often spoke highly of him. Others saw the Wilsons as greedy and conniving, and the rumors folks spread were heinous. Whether people spoke ill or spoke well, the Wilson family was never far from conversation.

As with most things, Sheriff Boone saw a little of both in Matt Wilson, Sr. Though he was a farmer and a fine rancher, the venerable man was not beyond shrewd business dealings. Boone remembered well that night he had to talk Grant McCauley down because a land deal with the Wilson patriarch had left him dry and penniless. Wilson knew how to use a contract for his benefit, which was exactly how he managed to snag most of the river's water rights without firing a shot.

It was that last element that most ingratiated the Wilson family to Boone's preservation of peace and order in Silver Gorge. Some men would draw to violence without provocation, but Wilson was not like that. He would respond in kind should someone threaten his home or land, but the gray farmer had lasted so long precisely because he drew a pen first and a gun last.

The two gentlemen, one dressed in riding gear and the other still in his morning robe, made their way across the hall to an oak-laden office with papers and ledgers strewn about. A mounted hare with horns adorned a lampstand in the corner of the office and drew Boone's attention rather singularly. Instead of taking his seat opposite the host as he should've, Boone wandered towards the curiosity and ran his fingers through the gray and brown fur.

It felt real enough. Then the sheriff rubbed the antlers

upon its head, and those seemed real enough. Yet it could not be. The individual elements worked, sure, but together they were an abomination. A monstrosity.

"It's called a jackalope," Wilson offered, smiling before answering a question he didn't need to be asked.

"Don't worry. It ain't real. A friend of mine sent me that after I asked him to mount a jackrabbit I shot a few years back. He's a taxidermist a littler farther west," Wilson went on. "I sent him a perfectly good hare, and he brings me back this little trinket. But, it has advantages, I suppose. People always walk in here and first thing, without fail, they look at my jackalope."

Knowing it was fake, the sheriff could look at the seams between the hare's skull and the antlers and see where the vivisection had occurred, but it was such fine work he never would've noticed the forgery without foreknowledge.

"You show people something they've never seen before and they'll be willing to do anything with you," Matt instructed the sheriff. "That little creature is a lot like what we have here. Our ranch shouldn't exist. We don't kill. We don't harass. We even allow stragglers to take shelter in our woods from time to time, as you well know. In this country, prosperity without bloodshed is a rare thing. You could be a part of that, Sheriff."

"I hate to break up the party, friend, but that bloodshed may have found you," Boone said, finally taking his eyes off the rabbit and putting them on one of the wealthiest men in Nevada.

He had Wilson's attention now as surely as the jackalope had stolen his just a minute before. Boone walked over from the corner of the office to a seat opposite Matthew Wilson and told him what had occurred the night before.

"So as you can see, I came here as quick as I could. There wasn't much concern that our gunman would assault

Ch. 5 | The Scarecrow's Call

the house head on. He's smart enough to know you would have a staff and ranch hands hanging about to gun him down in short time," Boone reassured. "Be that as it may, I wanted to come warn you before you went about your daily work in these woods unprotected. You make sure your sons stay together and watch each other's backs while they're out there."

Wilson nodded his head slightly at first while staring at a book on his desk. Wilson's gaze almost made it seem as if he were more interested in writing up the week's expenses versus protecting his family, but the distraction was just a mental exercise in short-term coping for the family man visiting with the sheriff.

"Nonsense, Boone," Wilson shouted. "My boys won't be watching their backs today. You will be."

The sheriff protested, but it was no use denying Wilson whatever he requested.

"You come here telling me that a gunman got a six-hour head start on me and could be hiding out, watching us talk as we speak," the man said while subtly tossing a look out the window to his left, "and you think I won't be asking you to stay? No, sir. You're staying this morning. First thing after breakfast, we hunt."

Boone gave Wilson a look of dissenting acquiescence, signaling the end of his resistance. So it was settled. Sheriff Boone had tasked himself onto Wilson's posse, and they were about to hunt a scarecrow.

-Chapter Six-

The Scarecrow's Gospel

Sheriff Boone knew two things for certain. First, Matt Wilson owed him big for agreeing to this endeavor. Second, that was the slowest Duke had ever eaten breakfast in his life, for he was in no hurry to take four green cow herders and one senior gentleman farmer out on a manhunt.

All of Wilson's boys were big. They had gotten that size advantage from their father. The oldest, Matthew Jr., was known for wrestling cattle when he was growing up. Junior had won more than a few bar bets by bringing down an unruly steer or bull just by gripping its neck.

The other three were more tame in their own right, likely because Junior threatened to rustle them all the same if they ever showed anything of a wild hair against him. The younger three brothers were equally devoted to their father as they were to their eldest sibling, so it was never much of a worry that they would draw back.

Junior and senior rode at the front of the group with their rifles in one hand and the reins in the other. John and Luke took the middle of the pack seeing as they were the youngest and the least experienced. The twin boys were just about 15 and not much of a shot, so Wilson wanted them buffered on either end. Duke and Mark brought up the rear

Ch. 6 | The Scarecrow's Gospel

guard with an ear on either side and behind with hopes of preventing ambush.

Their numbers alone should have kept the Kansas Scarecrow at bay. He was hardly known for working with a crew as some of the older gunmen had grown accustomed to doing, and he was less likely to jump out of the nearest tree for a spook. Then again, that knowledge didn't prevent Duke and the others from startling at the slightest sound.

Luke and John were especially vulnerable as they'd never encountered such a thing as some notorious myth of a gunman. A deer rustled some bushes off to the group's right and nearly sent the pair of them to the ground in tears.

Mark, seeing their obvious fear from the back, took advantage of the situation. What's worse is he made Sheriff Boone a party to the harassment of his youngest brothers.

"So tell me, Sheriff," Mark asked loudly. "Did the Kansas Scarecrow really take out a whole Wells Fargo caravan in the wide open once?"

"Nah. That was just a myth," Duke answered, and he could see that the twins were visibly relieved. "It was a small crew. Couldn't have been more than six or seven."

The twins glanced at one another and shared a wordless plea for help while the jokers in the back shared a grin. Hearing the commotion behind him, Matt Jr. opted to get in on the fun.

"I heard once that he shot a man for breathing too loud," the oldest brother suggested.

"Why… why would he do something like that?" John questioned, asking nobody in particular.

"Don't know," Matt Jr. responded. "I guess he just has real sensitive hearing. Shoot. He can probably hear a mouse rustle under the grass from 100 yards away. There's no telling how quickly he'd pick up our trail with these horses clomping everywhere."

"These dang horses ain't the problem, boys," Matt Sr. offered. "Now if you four don't shut up and keep your eyes open for our murderous outlaw, I'll make you all split up and search for him on your own. That sound fun? Maybe the Scarecrow will enjoy your jokes."

The brothers never knew their father to be a man of idle threat, so their chattiness subsided real quick. The joking and the laughing had done them one service, though, and that was to prevent the Nevada morning silence from getting too loud. For a few precious minutes, the boys had stopped listening for errant rustling and branches breaking. Now, though, they were back on full alert. The company knew that each crack was more likely the product of some bird landing or the echo of a horse's hoof, but they had to handle the simultaneous fear that it could be their prey tailing them.

Each step was cautious at first, with the riders gently urging their mounts forward. If Luke or John noticed a twig in their horse's path, they did whatever they could to ease his step down on firm ground.

Wilson kept his position at the front, his eyes stretching from side to side and leaping between trees and boulders. He still had the gaze of a farmer looking for a lost sheep, though he hadn't personally ridden for lost property in years. He tossed aside his morning coat for a plain shirt with a collar tight around his neck, much more formally than his sons had dressed.

In all but the collar, though, each of the Wilson boys plainly took after their father. Junior tried the hardest to mirror his father's style, though everyone knew it was Mark who had the deepest resemblance with his father's curls and serious brow. Matt Jr. compensated by constantly furrowing up and tightening his eyes when he was cognizant of the subtle differences.

Ch. 6 | The Scarecrow's Gospel

See, the oldest brother took more after their mother. When he didn't force the stern, blanketed joviality of the landowner's face, Matt's visage betrayed an innate kindness that endeared him to everyone. A harsher man might have looked on his son's appearance as a weakness, but Wilson was wiser. When he saw their mother in those eyes, he saw a man who could deliver more earnestness with brutal friendliness than most. It takes all types to sell and buy cattle, he thought often, and Matt would learn his own approach in time.

Luke and John, well, they were somewhere in the middle. Neither one was old enough to remember their mother well, either, so they lacked the advantage of a model to learn from. Their youthful sensibilities plagued any of that Wilson business sense they would someday likely come by, but for now they were just lost and bleary, playing a game of follow the leader.

It was nearly noon, a good couple of hours after the family posse had started their search, when Wilson hopped off of his horse to follow a small trail up the hill. He spotted what appeared to be tracks in the soft dirt leading up to an overlook, which worried the sheriff more than a little because it put everyone in prime position for an ambush.

"You boys watch my back, you hear?" Wilson whispered loudly as his boots scuffled through the loose brush.

"You want me to come with you, sir?" Matt Jr. asked nervously, knowing what answer he hoped for.

"Stay here and watch your brothers," his father came back before turning his head ever so slightly towards Duke. "And Sheriff. You watch him."

The early heat started to pick up and the five remaining gunmen held out a watch in each direction but down. Luke and John rotated on horseback thinking it would give them better range if they spotted something. Junior moved his eyes every which way, but his rifle always pointed straight ahead. Sheriff Boone was the only one to get off his horse and take a knee as he assumed the rear guard.

The walnut woodgrain of a borrowed rifle felt prickly on his ungloved right hand, but the smooth bore near the barrel felt comfortable. Boone had never liked long guns much, but Wilson's armory of Winchester 1890s came in handy on an outing such as this. The sheriff had loaned out his cupboard of rifles to the men on the roofs, but those guns were antiquated repeaters from not long after the end of the war. These 1890s still had a shine to them. The slide seemed clumsier than a lever-action to Duke, although his opinion on rifles was far from expert.

Wilson's boys started getting nervous when they were yet to hear back from their father. He was stupid to go out by himself, the younger two started to say to each other. He was liable to get himself killed and give away their plan.

"When do we go looking for him, Matt?" Mark asked.

"Quiet, you."

"Matt, we can't let him die up there," Mark retorted.

"He ain't going to die up there, now shut up and listen."

After a minute of restrained patience, "Matt, what's the plan?"

"Have you heard a gunshot?" Matt asked.

"No."

"Have you heard anyone scream?"

"No."

"Have you heard anything to make you think Father needs our help?"

"No," Mark answered sheepishly. "I don't guess I

have."

With the insubordination sorted out, Matt's temper calmed back to normal. "He's going to be fine, Mark. Don't worry. We'll give him a few minutes longer."

While the two older brothers bickered across the line of horses, John and Luke took time to reconvene their earlier conversation despite sitting back to back.

"Do you really think he can turn into a bird, John?"

"I don't know, Luke. I just don't know."

✪   ✪   ✪

Sheriff Boone considered making a fire while he and the Wilson brothers sat and waited for their father to rematerialize out of the wooded trail he slipped down, but he knew a fire would not be conducive to a good manhunt environment. People have a tendency to stare at fires, Duke thought, and the only thing he wanted the Wilson boys staring at was the cluttered horizon. Wilson would return eventually, or so he hoped, and when he did they would likely make their way out of this mess of an endeavor.

If the Scarecrow was ever around, he had likely skipped off unobserved to the other side of the state. They had been looking for much of the day by this point and nobody had noticed him yet. Men like him aren't afraid of a fight, even when outnumbered, so Boone rested easy knowing his assumed adversary was likely long gone.

John and Luke kept the most vigorous watch through the trees as they were the most afraid by a mile. Matt Wilson just occasionally lifted his face away from the gun he was cleaning. Mark kept vigil with the sheriff by a concealing boulder and shared a bit of jerky he traditionally packed for rides on the property.

Duke caught Mark stealing glances at his badge as if it were a woman he wanted to talk to but couldn't work up the gumption. The second brother would purse his lips as his eyes popped on to the glinting medal before just as quickly focusing on the dried beef in his hands or that one tree with a crooked branch. If he felt the sheriff looking his way, his young hands would nervously tear at the jerky or wipe away sweat from his brow. Duke knew what liars looked like, and he knew what it meant when somebody was hiding something. Mark showed all the signs, but there was something rather disarming in his attitude. The way his hopeful longing fixated on the sheriff's badge, Mark's motive was obvious. It was curiosity.

Children were never Boone's strong suit. He'd gotten to be a man of almost 30 before he had to spend any considerable time with kids, and he'd never married or had any of his own, so how to get this young man to explain what exactly he wanted to know bothered the sheriff. Not that Mark Wilson was a child—he was almost 20, after all—but he was acting enough like a child to bring about the comparison in Duke Boone's mind.

"What's it like to be sheriff?" the inquisitive Wilson brother asked, relieving Duke's fears that he'd never get it out of the boy.

"It's a job like any other, I guess," Duke answered, clearly noticing that he hadn't answered the question Mark was really asking.

Unaware of how to rephrase his question, Mark shuffled a bit, clearly at a loss for words.

You don't run cattle when you're sheriff, and you don't grow crops when you're sheriff, so Mark had a hard time understanding how this man knew he had accomplished anything. Mason's miners can see the silver coming out of the ground as they work, so that's a pretty clear indication of work being done. Newspapermen can see the weekly rags

Ch. 6 | The Scarecrow's Gospel

going out and storeowners can see money changing hands and products walking out the door, but a sheriff has nothing to show for his work. Was it worthwhile, Mark wondered?

"I mean... what do you do?" Mark rephrased.

"I keep Silver Gorge safe," Duke responded, rather unhelpfully.

Still searching for the right words to unlock his desired response, Mark started to show visible frustration by the way he raised his voice to the ground while he spoke and how he hit on each word clearly.

"But how do you know that you're keeping Silver Gorge safe?" Mark came back.

The sheriff thought that question over for a second and realized that he'd never really considered it. He knew what it meant for people to be safe, sure, but he never really thought about how he was sure what he was doing was right or how it was working. He wanted to keep the peace in town, that much he knew, but that was about all he could say. So he did.

"I keep the peace, Mark," Sheriff Boone answered, then almost interrupting himself he added to the response to prevent Mark from getting any more heated. "If a day goes by when people don't come calling for me, or if I can stay in my little building there on the street and nobody knows I haven't roamed around, then that's a good day, I guess. If I'm not having to come out here and hunt down outlaws like the Kansas Scarecrow on some endless stretch of land, then it's a good day.

"If people are at peace, then I'm doing my job."

"I guess you bungled it up pretty well back when old Zeke went psycho and tried to kill those three men, didn't you?" Matt quipped from the other side of the makeshift camp.

"Geez, Matt. Go easy on the man, will you?" John

tossed out, uncharacteristically standing up to his older brother. The look Matt shot at John made him wish he hadn't done that.

"No, it's alright, John. Your brother's right. That was a rough day," Duke said, rubbing the back of his neck with his hat in hand. "But here's what you have to understand, Matt. Peace isn't just about keeping bad things from happening. Peace is about keeping bad things from getting worse.

"Bad stuff is always going to happen to you, whether it's someone else's fault or your own. All we can do is respond, you know? All we can do is make sure it doesn't throw everything else off balance. Peace is about keeping the bad from spreading. If Zeke had left the bar that night, if I'd let him walk out of there, the bad would've spread. You probably don't know this, Matt, but Zeke was a friend of mine. I knew him long before anybody else in this town, and it was tough seeing him die… it was tough shooting him," Duke choked.

All four brothers kept their watch on the treeline, but their ears were all attuned keenly on what Sheriff Boone had to say.

"Why'd you have to kill him?" Mark asked in a near whisper.

"Because he was going to kill somebody else, Mark."

"But what if that man deserved it?" Luke thought out loud, making his first sound since they set camp.

"It's not my place to determine who deserves life, Luke. It's my job to keep anyone I can alive."

"But you couldn't keep your friend alive?" Matt came back, softening his tone from the earlier, more accusatory sound.

"There wasn't much choice. He was a good friend, he really was, but he'd been changing. Ever since his son… ever

Ch. 6 | The Scarecrow's Gospel

since then, he'd lost it. He wasn't the same Zeke he was before, and I had to recognize that," Duke explained, falling for his own lies word after word and excuse after excuse.

Turning his eyes from Mark to Matt to Luke to John, hoping that none of them would see the deceit in their sheriff, he kept pouring out filth like the blackness that became Zeke that day.

The truth was, the man Zeke wanted to kill probably did deserve to die. And why couldn't the sheriff be the one to determine that? He was the law in Silver Gorge after all, wasn't he? Wasn't that his whole purpose, to determine who was right and who was wrong?

Not like he could've stopped Zeke's death—that was inevitable—but at least he could've known justice before he died. Interrupting the silence of self-destruction Duke was enduring, Mark finally got around to the root of all this commotion.

"I had thought about being sheriff at one point in time, but I don't know if it's worth it when you put it like that, Sheriff," Mark explained. "I'd hate to be put in a position where I had to kill one of my friends, or one of you guys."

"It's not like you shoot people every day, Mark," Duke retorted while growing tired of this false memory. "Zeke was the first time I'd pulled the trigger on my gun in almost three months that wasn't target practice. People mostly just don't want to get shot, so they stay in line."

The other brothers had stopped paying attention to Duke, though, at Mark's newest revelation. They all just planned on dividing their father's value one day, but Mark had aspirations away from the cattle and away from the lumber. He wanted to be a lawman.

"You want to be like the panty-waist Deputy Mort? No offense, Sheriff," Matt said, covering himself.

"None taken," Duke replied.

"Look, Mark, lawmen don't make much money. You may think you're some tough rider, but we've got it pretty easy compared to most folks in Silver Gorge. You think you could live like this on what he makes? No offense, Sheriff," Matt added.

"None taken," Duke again dutifully replied, this time with an edge to his voice.

"Nobody respects lawmen. Nobody likes lawmen. No offense, Sheriff," Matt said again.

"I kind of take offense to that one," Duke noted.

Ignoring the sheriff, Matt kept right on going.

"You remember that time I tore into Mort at the bar that night? Nobody stopped me. He was standing right there, wearing his badge and his gun and everything, and I cold-cocked him for harassing Miss Billie and Miss Jenny, thinking he was all hot stuff and could grab whatever he wanted," Matt shouted. "He hit the ground like a cow dying of his legs being cut off and nobody said a word. That's not respect, Mark. We have respect with the people in town. They know we work and we can run cattle with any of them. Most sheriffs don't hold that kind of sway, present company excluded, and certainly no deputies."

Seeing that his tirade did nothing to sway Mark's opinion, Matt went to more direct questioning.

"What on earth do you want to be sheriff for?" Matt shouted.

"Why would you want to do that?" John cried, trying to get back in his oldest brother's good graces.

A sheepish Mark, embarrassed that he'd revealed his secret intentions, offered a muted reasoning.

"I don't know," he mewed. "Maybe I... maybe I want to help people."

Ch. 6 | The Scarecrow's Gospel

Seeing that his answer drew nothing but silence, Mark took a different route.

"Maybe I just think I'd get girls with a badge."

And at that, the three other Wilsons just lost it.

Duke Boone had only spent a minute or two with the brothers before that day, but he could already distinctly make out each one's unique laugh. Matt's roaring belly laugh just about shook the boulder Duke was leaning on. He was doubled over on the ground, his gun resting in his lap and pointed straight at nowhere. Luke and John were leaning on each other with near identical laughs, each one a sharp cackle like the giggle an eagle might give upon hearing a particularly funny joke. Then there was the fourth laugh over Duke's shoulder, the one that stood out as featuring long, drawn out exhalations, exaggerated as if trying to draw attention.

They each realized something was wrong at the same time and turned to notice a man towering over them on the hill above. He was a tall, gaunt figure with a scar running the length of his face from brow to chin, and his wide-brimmed black hat covered up his eyes until he wanted to show them off for the burnt brown they were.

"That's the funniest thing you boys have said all day," the stranger howled. "Even funnier than that crack about me turning into a bird and knowing how to fly."

-Chapter Seven-
Meet the Devil

He was good at what he did, make no mistake about it. The Kansas Scarecrow had stalked that party all day and knew when they'd be most susceptible to his move. When they were laughing at Mark's future aspirations, he jumped out of hiding and got the drop on each and every one of them, Silver Gorge's decorated sheriff included.

With the higher ground and a steady rifle aimed at Matt's head, the impressive outlaw ordered Mark to tie each of the four men up using the ropes for their horses. He had a higher voice than any of them had expected, and it rattled with the subtle texture of a coughing spell when he spoke, but his reputation and his imposing stance was enough to keep the men in check. Mark was too scared to refute the orders he was given by the gaunt offender and made quick work of his knot tying.

"If you want to be in law one day, you'll need to get faster at tying these knots," the Scarecrow taunted. "If it'd been me you were tying up, I'd have already slit your throat and run off with your woman."

He leaned around and looked at each wrist Mark tied, examining from a distance for any signs of deceit or lazy workmanship.

Ch. 7 | Meet the Devil

"I give you credit for the knots, though. That's fine work, son. I might not even be able to slip those knots loose," the gunman remarked.

Just our luck, the brothers thought collectively while sharing exasperated glances. *He would pick the one of us who had been a rodeo champ.*

True, the moment looked bleak. Three of the Wilson brothers were being tied up by the fourth, and joining them was the sheriff. They were all at gunpoint and had little chance of getting the jump on a man who just might be the last of the great gunmen.

Sheriff Boone struggled to understand how it had all gone so wrong. He knew it could happen, sure, but he'd never been on such a posse-gone-wrong as this one. To find one man, even one as notable as the great Kansas Scarecrow, the six-man party should have been more than enough.

The wanted outlaw perched atop the boulder that Boone and the boys had imagined would serve them as good protection. His footing was unfortunately and surprisingly steady despite the various cracks and divots under him as he stood in those deep amber boots befitting a plowman more than a gun for hire. Every shooter that Boone had encountered before wore glossy, spit-shined boots and fresh black suits. The hangman standing before them today, however, had more of an everyman feel to him. The Scarecrow's boots matched well with the ankle-length duster he wore which, although a nice shelter from the elements, would have made a thicker man sweat to death.

His spindly fingers reached up and removed the open crown hat he wore. Underneath was a mass of sweat-matted hair, thinner and looser than a dog's coat infected by mange. When the Scarecrow reached up to wipe his partially covered brow, the duster opened wide enough to show off one revolver of what Duke assumed was a pair. This cowboy may not have shown much care for glitzy boots or finer wares, but his pride clearly rested on the freshly polished handguns. Duke carried the same type, a Remington, but the Sheriff's own revolver was clearly an older model. The nickel finish on the Scarecrow's gun was untarnished and as good as new. Almost as if it had never been used. Even though the gun's experience was in question, Duke didn't have the nerve to question its handler. He was clearly experienced enough to make use of such a powerful weapon.

Just as Duke finished examining the Scarecrow's revolver, he met eyes with the man himself. Sheriff Boone jolted backwards ever so slightly upon catching his captor's eye, causing the Scarecrow to tilt his head towards the left enough that his hair shuffled down over the scar that characterized that pale visage of his.

"Why haven't you tied up the sheriff yet, son? He should've been first," the boss said clearly and calmly to his willing servant. "Get on over there now, boy. You can get the others next."

"Yes, sir. Right away," Mark answered.

He had nearly completed Luke's bonds when he skipped over John to get to the sheriff. Duke was the only one looking directly at the Scarecrow, and having seen his face once, he was able to look more confidently now.

"I'm sorry, Sheriff," Mark whispered as he wrapped the cord around Duke's wrist.

Sheriff Boone felt the fibers scratch at his skin and pull the hair out of his arm, and he felt his lungs tighten up a little bit with each pass of the rope. Mark's hands flowed swiftly and effortlessly over one another as his years of experience tying off cattle came to some unfortunate use here.

"I thought if I saved you for last," Mark quietly explained, "it might give you time to make a move. I didn't want to have to tie you up, Duke."

"It's okay, Mark," Boone responded. "If I'd have

Ch. 7 | Meet the Devil

jumped, he would've shot you and me both, and maybe your brothers. Let's see how this plays out, okay?

"And Mark?" Duke added. "No hard feelings."

Although Duke couldn't see the young man standing behind him with a rope in his hands, Mark's face betrayed the shame he felt at binding this living hero of his.

Truth be told, Duke had noticed a moment. When the Scarecrow looked down and lifted his arm to his head, there may have been enough time for a quick action. The sheriff let it pass, though, a choice he started to regret. Now that his hands were tied and soon his feet, there wasn't much he would be able to do.

Then again, he didn't want to force the Scarecrow's hand. Gunmen like him could never be talked out of what they wanted to do, but they could be coerced into doing more than they had originally planned. It was never wise to force a man like that into action.

Mark finished the knots on the sheriff's hands with ease, just as if he were tying up the feet of a colt or a bull that had run astray. The rope was tight, but Mark left it somewhat looser than the others and pinched Duke's arm as he finished in order to indicate as much. It was a subtle sign, but it was enough to get the sheriff's attention.

Mark then took his chances wagering that the Scarecrow wasn't overly knowledgeable when it came to rope and knots. Most men could tie up a horse just fine, but a mess of rope and tangles was often indecipherable to the casual observer. If Mark was right, he thought, he should be able to tie Sheriff Boone's feet up with a running knot which would be pretty easy to escape in a pinch.

The beauty of the running knot, in Mark's mind, was that it would tighten if pulled on from the outside and seem even more secure. But an internal force, like the sheriff quickly pulling his legs apart, would make the knot fall loose and let him run free or at least make a move.

The sheriff-in-waiting ran his hands through the motions around his hero's ankle and attempted to make the knot look as tight as he could. The coarse fibers of the horse's line did their job by rubbing up against each other and sounding tight at the very least, and their captor had taken only nominal interest in the other men's knots, so Mark felt like his plan had merit.

Duke, on the other hand, was concerned. If the Scarecrow took a close look at what was going on, it could be a problem. The gunman stood loosely, his divided attention only somewhat interested in the activity before him. He kept looking around the trees and the rocks, his eyes darting and his head wobbling as if it were just sitting atop his neck and would topple over at the slightest instability.

Sheriff Boone recognized that look on the Scarecrow's face. The jumping eyes and the downward-leaning face — it was all quite familiar to Duke Boone. It was the same look he had caught himself in from time to time ever since Zeke's death. It was the look of a man who no longer trusted the world around him. It was the look of a man for whom sight was no longer enough.

It was the look of paranoia.

Mark finished his running knot and pulled the cord tight on both ends so that it looked secure. He gave the sheriff a knowing glance and held it for just a second, almost a second too long for Boone's comfort, before quickly tying up John, hopping up and getting back over to the boulder where stood the man with the gun.

"They're done," Mark announced, startling the unaware Scarecrow.

"Good, boy. Good job," he sneered, looking over each rope and each prisoner with the interest of a scorpion watching the sky for a hawk.

Ch. 7 | Meet the Devil

His thoughts were elsewhere, Duke could tell, and that fact boded well for the Wilson boys and him.

"Well, folks. Today's your lucky day," the Scarecrow started as he hopped down from the rocks above. "I'm a bit busy and in need of a quick departure, so I'll be on my way leaving you gentlemen to your own devices. Except for you, Mark. I'll need you to come along with me."

The three brothers' moment of ease passed all too quickly when they heard the gunman's plans to kidnap their own. Duke started to his feet before remembering that he wasn't supposed to be able to do that. It came out as more of a shuffle and a crawl from his backside than an attempt at mutiny. The Scarecrow let out his throaty laugh once more.

"It's alright, it's alright. I'll make sure he gets back to you safely, I guess. I just need him for a little bit. I might need somebody watching my back out in the open, you know?" he said, grabbing Mark by the scruff of his neck and yanking him back away from the rest of the unwilling audience.

"Who's after you, Scarecrow?" the sheriff asked, trying to create a moment for Mark to escape.

"Excuse me, Law?"

"Who's after you," Duke repeated confidently, not a hint of a question in his voice.

A grin sliced the Scarecrow's face as he sauntered towards the emboldened officer of the law. Duke could smell the morning whiskey on his counterpart's breath, the man had gotten so close, and he could make out the ruddy, dust-stained chin hairs that the gunman had neglected to shave in his rush to get away. The wiry menace leaned down towards Sheriff Boone's face and held a mutual stare before speaking.

"When you've killed as many men as I have, Sheriff," the Scarecrow spat out with annuciated intention, "you find that the whole world is after you. You know the secret to living with that kind of a chase?"

"What's that?" Boone asked out of sheer spite.

"You keep one hand on the reins and another on your guns."

Duke could see through the veneer of bravado, though. The Scarecrow was running scared from something, and pressing the issue might be his only chance to keep the gunman off-balance.

After his smarmy reply, the Scarecrow got up off of his elbows and turned back towards the boulder he clung to. If Duke had ever planned on making his move, it would have to be soon before the gunman and his indentured companion were gone for good.

"What if you come up against a problem bullets won't fix?" the sheriff tossed out there, clearly intriguing the no longer advancing Scarecrow. "What if you get yourself in a bind you just can't shoot your way out of?"

He'd clearly struck a nerve in the Scarecrow's head with that last comment, but this man was one cool fellow. For the spot of a twitch, just the slightest quiver of his lip and a tightened shrug of the shoulders, the Scarecrow let slip a cocktail of terror and wrath. After a moment's loss of control, the mercenary reversed his calm and answered without ever turning back towards his accuser.

"I ain't found one of those yet, Sheriff, and I don't intend to find one anytime soon," the Scarecrow, rather unconvincingly, retorted.

Perhaps as a threat, however, he added one last corollary.

"Besides. I can throw quite a few bullets at a problem before I run out, Sheriff. You'd do well to remember that."

"Who's holding your chain, lap dog?" Duke Boone shouted, to everyone's surprise including his own.

Whatever outcome he had hoped for the sheriff didn't

Ch. 7 | Meet the Devil

know, but it was probably a far cry from what happened. Without hesitation, a force of fury fell upon Duke Boone's face in the form of a full-metal pistol and repeated blows from the enraged Scarecrow. Blow after blow of focused and directed anger tore at the Sheriff's eyes and mouth and cheeks until his face had grown numb in order to protect itself from the excruciating burns of such a severe beating. Boone tried to shield his face with his tied up hands, forgetting their position behind his back, and the Scarecrow caught on quickly.

The Scarecrow's abuses would have seemed more fitting to the tune of shouts and screams and the heraldry of rage, but the ferocity of his actions came across more vivid to nothing but the crack of bones breaking and the brutal thud of a bare fist upon meager flesh.

He jumped off the defenseless body of a defamed lawman and began abusing Duke's sides with violent stomps of irrefutable severity. The blood from Duke's facial lacerations started to pool while fresh wounds were opening to engorge the flow at his hips. While the sheriff writhed and squirmed, trying whatever he could to quell the volcanic rage he had incited from this unhinged assailant, dirt and grit from the terrain lodged itself inside raw, exposed flesh around his swollen eye sockets and loosened teeth.

The soundless madman let off one final jab at his plaything's ragdoll body with a coarse hobnail boot before he stepped back to admire the brokenness he had inflicted upon a fallen bastion of justice. Sheriff Boone looked back at his tormenter, despite the fact that his eyes offered no light but a bleary screen through tears and blood. Duke was half-conscious of where the Scarecrow stood by how his form blotted out the light, but it could've been any figure standing there. The various features and nuances of the Scarecrow's face, although now burned into the sheriff's mind, were invisible and fell victim to a total loss of detail.

As defiled and broken as he was, Duke Boone tempted

the menace further. He was so far gone that coercing the gunman into murder seemed like a good idea at the time. Duke attempted to slurp out a taunt through useless lips and a shredded tongue.

"What was that, friend?" the Scarecrow inquired, letting loose his first sound since well before the beating began.

"I said… " Duke struggled, trying to manage a couple more words from his blood-soaked mouth, "you're pretty tough for beating up a man in ropes."

Boone could imagine the hate in the Scarecrow's eyes as he saw the shadow loom larger and larger towards his defunct field of vision, but it stopped short of resuming the previous attack. Through what stood for sight now that his eyes were bloodied and ruined, the sheriff could see his attacker look down towards his feet and then turn back towards Mark who was presumably still standing by himself near the boulder.

"Why are this one's knots different from the others, boy?" the Scarecrow asked of Mark.

Sheriff Boone would've been glad to see the darkness move away from him, but knowing where it headed gave Duke new reasons to fear.

"What do you mean?" Mark stuttered. "He's tied up just like you asked."

"Shut it," he commanded. "I'm not blind, you hayseed. What were you planning, huh? Why isn't he tied up like the others? And I mean just like the others."

"I… ran out of rope is all. Yeah. I didn't have enough to tie his feet like theirs, so I had to do something else. That's all," Mark attempted, hoping the lie would be enough to fool his inquisitor.

"Was this your doing, Sheriff Doughface?" the

Ch. 7 | Meet the Devil

Scarecrow asked, turning his attention once more on the defeated corpse huddled in the dirt and the mud. "Did you have some grand escape planned?"

As the Scarecrow moved back into a position over the barely inhabited body of Sheriff Boone, Duke vaguely remembered what he had noticed about the knots around his legs. He remembered something about it, but it was hard to recall with the pounding that slowly returned to his caved-in skull.

While the Scarecrow rambled on with meaningless gibes at the Sheriff's broken state, Duke Boone mustered enough mental acuity to gather his bearings and realize that the Scarecrow was exactly where he wanted him to be. With all the energy he had left in his body, Duke thrust upwards into the gunman's chest with a pair of highly motivated legs, drawing enough force to send his target flying backwards to the ground.

Duke quickly snapped his feet apart and shattered Mark's loosely conceived running knot while the three still-bound brothers marveled at their sheriff's tenacity. The good lawman stumbled off the ground without use of his hands somehow and started towards the shadowy spot he assumed was the Scarecrow before plowing into him at full speed. Duke's plan seemed to be working for a moment as the binds around his arms came loose as a joint result of the beating he had received and the looser knot Mark had so wisely supplied him.

Boone crawled atop the Scarecrow's body and felt around for a gun, finding just pebbles and twigs. Had the sheriff retained his vision, the surprise would have been enough to overpower and subdue the mighty Scarecrow, but as it was, Duke had no means of defeating his mark. After a quick scrum, ending with a sharp elbow from the gunman to the sheriff's left cheek, Duke found himself at the mercy of that Remington pistol he had so admired earlier.

"You done well, Sheriff," the Scarecrow sputtered while catching his breath after the fight. "I've killed bigger men with less of a beating before, I just want you to know that. But you took me down hard, and I can't let that stand. As you so kindly pointed out, I nearly got beat by a man with his hands tied behind his back, and I can't leave a man like that alive to tarnish my good name. Is that clear?"

With all the hate he could muster through a twisted jaw and a pair of sealed-shut eye sockets, Duke Boone's carved lip showed an enhanced snarl that wished hell and damnation on the soul of that vile Scarecrow. Though he accepted the death that was coming, and he welcomed the end of his agony, the proud sheriff detested the giver of death with everything left in him, and he wished to God he could somehow deny that man the pleasure of taking his life.

A seasoned gunman like the Scarecrow was quick and professional, but the sheriff had made this a particularly nasty affair by scuffing the gunman's boots so to speak. The assailant stood tall and proud, lording the Remington and the victory over his man for just a moment longer. Delay was his fatal mistake, though, as that space of time allowed for salvation.

Duke had already closed his eyes in anticipation of the shot to come, but the crack he heard was from much farther away than the revolver in his immediate vicinity. The scuffling of feet and the realization of sustained consciousness told Duke Boone that he was still alive and that the Scarecrow had somehow missed his mark. Somebody had taken a shot at the gunman from a distance, and the Scarecrow wisely ducked out of the scene as quick as he realized that whoever had a bead on him missed ever so slightly.

The four brothers, who had all been struck with silence at the Scarecrow's destruction of Boone's face and body, started shouting and crying for someone to do something or for anybody to answer their call. Mark, as the only one yet

Ch. 7 | Meet the Devil

unbound, gathered himself off the ground and ran over to the fading sheriff.

"Are you alright? Do you hear me, Sheriff?" Mark cried, but Duke barely heard him.

He was slipping away into a needed sleep, no matter how much the boy yelled pleas and prayers into his ears.

"Go… go untie them," Duke ordered, letting loose his last conscious effort.

The next few minutes were fragmented at best for the sheriff as his marginally improving vision helped him to make out Mark untying the brothers and another pair of familiar boots running onto the scene. As brother after brother came free from his ties, the five of them all surrounded the sheriff and tried to lift him onto a vacant horse.

Wilson shouted for somebody's attention and the next thing Duke recalled was resting with his back upon a flat, wood surface. The light had dimmed, but it was just from the canvas cover on a wagon that a ranch hand brought down from the house. Safety bred relaxation for Duke and he let himself drift away though the panic around him was still increasing in fervor.

"Get his gunbelt," one brother ordered.

"Where's the Scarecrow?" another clamored.

With five or more men scuttling off in as many different directions, the last sound Duke heard made little sense, but it was unmistakably a gunshot. The blast was muted as if it travelled a good hundred or more yards through trees to reach Duke's ears, but it was sure enough a gunshot.

Sheriff Boone kept his eyes closed for the rest of that day and for many days after, but in that moment he could make out one last sensation. It was neither sight nor sound that Duke picked up on, but he could swear that a strong odor at some point joined him on that wagon as he picked up on what could only be called an unhappy marriage between stale sweat and unwashed rabbit grease.

-Chapter Eight-
Old Soldiers and Good Stew

Boone healed up well, though he barely woke for the next five days. It was a welcome rest, the sheriff thought to himself, but he could've done without the swelling and the scars. On the first occasion he could grab a mirror and open his eyes, an afternoon maybe three days after the beating when his sight was nearly back to normal, Duke laughed at the mirror in abject fear of who was standing so close to him.

When he realized that the bloated and bruised face was his own, Sheriff Boone was both disgusted and relieved. There was no mangled intruder, true, but Duke hardly looked himself.

Duke found it difficult to eat while his mouth still resembled a deer's side after it's been blasted open with buckshot, but Miss Abilene visited bearing soup a couple times making the days go somewhat smoother. He would've liked to have talked to the lady, especially to see how she was holding up after her own brush with the killer through whom they now shared a common link, but the mealtime conversations were fairly one-sided as Miss Abilene spoke of the hotel and the repairs while the laid-up sheriff dutifully slurped his broth.

It was the fifth morning when Wilson came to visit, and

just in time as the sheriff finally felt awake enough to properly thank the man who saved his life.

"It's good to see you awake for once, Sheriff," Wilson said. "I've been in here a couple times, but you were always sleeping soundly. Dr. Jarvis says you should be fine in no time, minus some minor scars and a little swelling."

"A little swelling?" Boone replied incredulously. "I look like I've been getting rattlesnake kisses for the last month."

Wilson laughed a little, but he tried to maintain respect for the sheriff's condition. It was true, though. The swelling had not yet gone down as much as Duke would like, but it had improved.

"You think you could've taken the shot a little sooner, maybe?" Duke asked. "I know you missed, but hey. Scaring the guy off was nice enough. I just wish you could've done it before he about tore my face in two."

The sheriff's face was still puffy, but his vision was good enough to tell that Wilson's countenance dropped at mention of what happened on the ranch.

"What is it? Is Mark all right? Are your boys good?"

"My boys are fine, Sheriff. We're good," Wilson responded. "But that's the thing. I didn't take the shot, Duke."

There was considerable pain, but Duke sat up to get clearer meaning of what Wilson was saying. He heard a shot and he was pretty sure he saw the Scarecrow run just as Wilson stepped on to the scene, so who else was there to take a shot?

"Look. He saved my life, too. I was out in the woods tracking the Scarecrow when Greasy jumped me from behind. I thought he'd gone crazy. I nearly shot him when I realized he was trying to get me under cover. That accursed Scarecrow of yours had doubled back on me," Wilson narrated. "He's

Ch. 8 | Old Soldiers and Good Stew

good, that one. He's good."

"Greasy was there?" Sheriff Boone asked.

"Yep. Turns out letting him stay on the property was my wisest investment yet. He saved my life and yours. The reason it took so long for us to get that shot off was because he was waiting on me to sneak up behind your villain and leap in case he missed," Wilson explained. "I knew he was a good shot, but he nearly took my ear off. I had gotten turned around and came up on the wrong side of where Greasy told me to get."

"Where was Greasy?"

"He'd climbed up in a tree. The fool said he was taking after you, whatever that means."

Sheriff Boone laughed a little at the nod from his drifter friend.

"Greasy aimed at the Scarecrow and said he would shoot as soon as I was in position, but I guess he couldn't wait any longer. I was proud of the way you mule-kicked that SOB, might I add.

"But anyway, Greasy took a shot at the Scarecrow and scared him off into the woods. I never saw him again, but I ran up on y'all just in time to help Mark untie Junior and Luke and John. They nearly soiled themselves when they heard Greasy's gun go off. They've never seen a man killed before, you know, and they didn't want to start by seeing you die," Wilson surmised.

"So where's Greasy now, Wilson?" Duke asked.

There was an uncomfortable pause from Wilson at the sheriff's question. The gentleman farmer didn't want to answer, but Duke caught on to what his friend was saying.

"Where is he, Wilson?"

"The funeral is this afternoon in about three hours,"

Wilson answered, to which Duke howled in pain enough to bring the doctor running into the room.

"I'm sorry, Sheriff. There was nothing I could do. I thought the Scarecrow was just running away. Turns out he was going off after Greasy and he caught the idiot just coming down out of the tree," Wilson went on. "The doc did all he could, Sheriff, but it was no use. Between the bullet and the fall, he didn't stand a chance."

Dr. Jarvis, a young man who had been apprentice to the town's former doctor and who had worked on the sheriff multiple times before for smaller incidents, tried to give Duke some medicine for the pain, but Boone just shoved him off.

The two men had never seen Sheriff Boone so violent or so passionate before, and they had a hard time believing he could be so physical with the bruised ribs and the immense pain he had to be experiencing. But the sheriff didn't care at all about any of that. Greasy was a good man. One of the few good men left in Silver Gorge, even if he was a half-crazed drifter who reeked of a woodland camp and butchery. Greasy had died for the sheriff, and that was more than the sheriff could handle.

After he calmed down considerably, Sheriff Boone looked up to Wilson and made an earnest decree.

"I'm going to the funeral," he said.

"Now I know you feel guilty about all this, but that's no reason to put yourself back in the grave's clutches, man. You need rest," Wilson urged.

"I need," he paused long enough to swing his legs over the side of the bed, "to honor the man who saved my life. I need to be there. I need to bury him."

The doctor and the rancher begrudged Duke his request, and after much work and considerable pain wrangling him into a wagon up to Cemetery Hill, the trio of men arrived to a small contingent of Silver Gorge's citizenry

Ch. 8 | Old Soldiers and Good Stew

come to bury the local drifter.

The necessary members of society were present, of course, as the undertaker and the gravedigger stood off to the side and partook of the festivities with a bottle of Virginia City brandy. Reverend Hawk and Joe Miller took turns laying Greasy, whose birth name so happened to be Fennimore Grace, to his final rest with recitations of Scripture and formal prayers.

The few who grieved, aside from the sheriff and his escorts, were fellow ne'er-do-wells and vagrants who happened to be in town. Odds are they'd never even met the man that most of Silver Gorge knew as Greasy, but Duke figured it was a part of their nature to mourn their own.

If true, it made them better men than most.

Duke and the two companions stood at the grave, watching as the undertaker's men lowered Greasy's body into a narrow hole. As sheriff, Boone had seen men buried before. He had made several trips to Cemetery Hill, sure, but it was the first time that he had ever felt at all responsible for someone's death.

Of course, Duke remembered the youngest Farrow brother, the one he caught robbing the bank a couple years back. That poor boy was mostly innocent, but his older brothers were ruthless killers. As such, they left their youngest to hang for their own crimes. The sheriff could have spoken against the town hanging him, but a Farrow brother is a Farrow brother, they all thought.

A Hopi man had wandered into town looking for someone to trade with not long after Boone started the job as sheriff. He had warned the fellow that Silver Gorge was not friendly to Indian visitors, but the fool didn't listen. He wound up getting himself shot over a bag of pelts and a particularly coveted bottle of Eastern whiskey.

Most recently, though, had been Zeke and his boy. The

only difference was that neither of those bodies had been buried. Zeke found himself on the rust-red floor of a saloon and Josiah, well. There was never anything found to bury.

Perhaps it was the act of watching the body go down into the ground, then. Hearing the preachers talking of dust and ashes. Duke Boone had always been a hard man. He was kind, but he was also stern. Matters of death made sense to him. Men were born. Many years later, they died.

When he was a boy, Sheriff Boone helped his father slaughter pigs. Death made sense, then. Today, though, death was confusing. Death seemed like it had to be wrong somehow.

The Farrow brother who found himself on a noose in Silver Gorge, even if he was unjustly executed, was nobody to the sheriff. He was a criminal, sure, and his brothers were murderers. It could be explained.

The Hopi trader had fallen victim to an unscrupulous business deal and woke up with 33 knife wounds in his abdomen. It was an awful crime, but it was a crime that Duke understood.

Seeing either of those men buried for actions Duke could follow was fine. Neither one surprised the sheriff to any extent. Thieves and Indians tended to die in the Nevada frontier, so watching them get buried was no problem.

Greasy was an old soldier, though. He'd already survived his war. For Greasy to get gunned down, coming out of a tree helpless and unarmed, was just too wrong. Old soldiers don't die by the gun. Old soldiers deserve peace.

The reverend delivered a pleasant enough eulogy for Greasy, talking about how he was a member of the community and how he had served his country well in a time when it became difficult for men to choose which country they would serve. Greasy may have survived the war in gray, but he loved his country in either shade. It was evident that the

Ch. 8 | Old Soldiers and Good Stew

reverend was not familiar with any of Greasy's stories, though, or if he was, he knew none of them well enough to share with any confidence or authority. Perhaps he, too, avoided Greasy when at all possible.

The time came for the interment of the body and the final return of Greasy's earthly remains to the ground from which he came, or however the preacher had put it. Duke stopped listening and instead chose to think about the box which contained his friend. All that was left to do was to unload the mound of earth back on top into the veteran's occupied grave.

Wilson and the doctor shoveled most of the dirt as Duke could hardly lift his arms to grasp a shovel, but the sheriff made sure to get his hands dirty in honor of the passing friend. He slid the final shovelful of dirt over Greasy's coffin as Reverend Hawk made his final statements and all of the present company headed onwards to the church or the bar one.

Sheriff Boone headed back to the doctor's place on the back of a rickety wagon pulled by two unstable mules. He had managed to stand up for the entire funeral, which was more than Dr. Jarvis had anticipated, but Duke knew he was still a good ways away from being able to walk or ride a horse all on his own. For the time being, he was willing to accept a ride in the back of a two-bit wagon. Sitting there, Duke thought, he would make a point of requesting more funds for the doctor's supplies come the next town meeting.

People in town enjoyed the Tuesday morning air as they went about daily routines. A few of them looked up the sheriff's way and a few others even walked over to his seat of honor behind the doctor and Wilson in order to say they were glad to see him up and out and about.

"It's good to have you back, Sheriff," Mr. Frank Butter said to Duke.

"Welcome back, Sheriff. Hope to see you at the picnic," Ms. Emmajean Mable, the town's resident graying widow, shouted.

"Do be more careful next time," an anonymous voice near the saloon cried. "But we're glad you made it back safely, Sheriff Boone!"

The residents of Silver Gorge appreciated him and gave Duke their commendations and their congratulations on saving the four Wilson boys. They were well-known figures in the town and word had spread quickly when they came home. Mark couldn't keep from telling anybody how the sheriff and Greasy had both dispatched of the Scarecrow. If somebody had a minute where they weren't walking, Mark was up in their ear telling them exactly how Sheriff Boone had goaded the fiend into a blind frenzy, giving Greasy time to take the shot and keep him from killing anybody.

Folks enjoyed the story, but most of them forgot about Greasy's part in the matter just as quickly as they heard Mark tell it. They couldn't go out of their way to give a man like that any credit, could they? After all, he was a drifter and his name was Greasy.

"How was the funeral, Sheriff?" bellowed portly Aaron Oscar, the town's most prominent banker, from across the street.

Duke and company had just pulled up to the doctor's office and were getting ready to unload when the banker opted for yelling instead of politely walking over to see the three men. Wilson and the banker were on fine terms, of course, as the two controlled most of Silver Gorge's money that wasn't tied up in Mason's mines, but Aaron still preferred to conduct his ostensibly public business from afar, not coming any closer than forty feet.

"It was fine, Oscar," the sheriff replied with no obvious enthusiasm to his answer.

Ch. 8 | Old Soldiers and Good Stew

"It was quite the shame about Greasy, wasn't it?" the financier continued. "He deserved better."

Coming from anyone else, the sheriff might've appreciated the sentiments. After all, they were exactly what he had been thinking just an hour before. It was that accursed Aaron Oscar, though, and he was shouting his platitudes for the entire city to hear.

"He surely did, Oscar. You have a good day," Duke yelled back, hoping to end the discourse then and there.

"I tell you, Sheriff, I remember the first time I saw old Greasy. He was covered in booze and ash sauntering into town like all he had left of him was stink," announced the tubby citizen, a compact fellow with little height and enough girth to offset the disappearing hair that had once flourished upon his presently polished scalp.

Aaron Oscar's suit was made from the finest cottons a man could import from Boston, despite the fact that there were sheep farms not a day's ride out of Silver Gorge. His leather shoes were made from New Hampshire cattle and his gold watch, tucked safely inside his vest pocket, ticked at a level where a grown man of no auditory handicap could hear it in any direction.

"Yes, that Greasy was a man of the town, I tell you," Aaron Oscar continued. "He was a fine veteran of the Confederate States, and though his side of the war was lost, we honor him today."

With a visibly crumpled brow and quickening pulse, Sheriff Boone gave the doctor and Wilson a look implying that they needed to get him moved quickly for he could only handle so much more of Oscar's pandering. Anything short of an act of God, though, would have failed to move the sheriff out of earshot in time.

"I do wish he would have lasted until Decoration Day in a few weeks. How grand it might have been to honor

Greasy that day. Perhaps with your blessing, Sheriff, we could host a parade in his honor and memory that day, and in the memory of all of the lost soldiers of Silver Gorge, Nevada," Oscar pontificated.

The insult had gone on long enough, though, as the disingenuous buffoon placated himself to Greasy's memory and to the town's collective penchant for misplaced pity and sorrow. The sheriff would have none of it, though, as he ignored the bruised ribs and the sore lungs in order to hop to his feet and scold the suckled pig of a man where he stood.

Duke was not one for public displays, but Aaron Oscar's vile treatment of the man who saved the sheriff merited a response. The rotund reveler's duplicitousness burned at Duke, producing a seething, loathing rage roiling out in defense of the honored dead.

"That soldier was a far finer man than you'll ever know, Oscar!" Duke shouted as he began his holy tirade against the town's banker. "Greasy cared more about people and about the town of Silver Gorge than anyone I've ever met!

"For someone so interested in honoring Greasy, what did you ever do for him when he was alive? Did you ever buy him lunch? Surely you could afford to buy somebody else a meal," Boone poked as he hobbled forward.

"Wasn't it just last week, Aaron, that I heard you refer to him as 'That befouled mound of muck and feculence?' Did I get that right, Aaron?"

Every vein in the banker's forehead bulged as if preparing to pop, but he controlled himself for the sake of public appearances. After all, he had started speaking with such volume in order to gain the crowd's attention, and so now he was forced to handle himself with the professionalism and decorum demanded of a banker, even if he was at the mercy of Sheriff Boone's verbal abuses.

"You could've paid for him to spend a night or two at

Ch. 8 | Old Soldiers and Good Stew

the inn to shower up, couldn't you have Mr. Oscar? Or better yet, when did you ever invite him in? Were you so concerned with the honor of a Confederate veteran when he was alive, old Greasy may have been something of a sight to see in town. He would've been walking around in your fancy suits and smelling like flowers, wouldn't he have?

"You're the worst kind of man, Aaron Oscar. You shouldn't speak ill of the dead when an innocent man dies, Oscar, but that doesn't mean you should lie and call him your friend. To honor someone's memory means to honor the truth about them," Boone paused.

"And his name wasn't Greasy! His name was Fennimore Grace! So shut your gob and get back to your lunch plate," Duke concluded.

Sheriff Boone had burned with rage to see the way that people ignored Greasy's death like it was of no account to the community, but it was far worse to see someone like Aaron Oscar attempt to increase his own reputation as a caring soul just to drum up business and look like the town saint he portrays himself to be. Aaron Oscar was a lunatic, as far as Sheriff Boone was concerned. Bankers have no place in polite society, according to Duke Boone. Nor in a society as rude as Nevada.

Still visibly stunned, with his bottom lip sewed tight to his nose, Aaron Oscar turned and waddled back to the bank and hid behind the fact that people in town needed him. For Mr. Oscar, that was all the importance that he could handle in one day.

In all of his adrenaline-fueled rage and fury, Duke forgot the indescribable pain tearing at his ribs. As the banker slunk back into his den, however, the surging twinges left as a souvenir by the Kansas Scarecrow started to work their way back into the sheriff's muscles and spine. He would have heroically fallen to the ground if not for the ready hands of Wilson and Dr. Jarvis to prop him up.

111

"Come on, Sheriff. Let's get you back to bed. You've got a few more days of rest before you'll be good to stand, much less storm after wayward denizens of financial impudence," Jarvis mocked.

As beleaguered as Boone was, he hardly minded the quip taken at his expense.

The three men working on four or five legs focused on each step so directly that none of them noticed the gentleman who started to follow them up to the door. The wizened fellow, still sitting atop his cedar horse, followed the three with his eyes and his steps carefully. He bore a keen interest in the middle one, the one who had shouted a name he had searched many weeks to find.

To some it had seemed a fool's errand, but he knew that one day he would indeed find someone who knew of Fennimore Grace. He just never expected the answer to fall so easily in his lap.

★ ★ ★

The frontier doctor had quite a few tools at his disposal that an east coast practitioner might find rudimentary or barbaric, but no physician alive would argue against the liberal application of hearty stew. Duke gobbled up the beef broth while slurping up the cooked carrots and gravy that so ornately filled out the bowl. Jarvis was a middling doctor at best, but his wife's cuisine managed to paradoxically heal the population of Silver Gorge and yet encourage further maladies.

It was the first solid meal that Duke had eaten since he foolishly skipped breakfast with the Wilsons the morning of their manhunt. He'd slept for so long and avoided any such food while he was kept under with a regular prescription of whiskey and ether that this meal took the sheriff just under a

Ch. 8 | Old Soldiers and Good Stew

minute to consume.

"Careful, Sheriff. If my wife comes back in here to find you've already emptied your plate, she might just go so far as to give you my dinner, too," Jarvis warned.

"I might take her up on it, too," Duke answered with a grin, "if you don't offer me anything stronger."

Imogene's stew was just one of her specialties, but it was always Duke's favorite. If she ever managed to get fresh apples, her pies and other baked goods were a worthy treat as well.

Sheriff Boone was preparing to ask for a second helping when an assertive knock came to the door. It was common for the doctor to accept patients into the evening, of course, so the knock itself was no surprise. What was a surprise was when Imogene herself trailed a tall septuagenarian whom nobody had seen before.

"Stop! Sir, I am afraid you cannot go back there! Quit your wandering right now, mister!" Imogene shouted, but the fellow paid her no heed.

His pointed chin had the remnants of a beard long faded away while his shock-white hair maintained much of the vibrancy and body it must have enjoyed in previous years, coloring not withstanding. What drew Duke's attention, though, was the star enclosed in a shield upon his jacket. It seemed that their unknown guest might be of some interest after all.

"Missus. Doctor. Do you mind if the sheriff and I have a moment alone?" the stranger asked with every assumption that his order would be met.

"Now this man is a patient in my care and he will have every respect afforded him that I can offer, and you have no right to…"

"Let it go, Jarvis. We'll be fine," Duke said to the

doctor, more for his benefit than the visiting lawman's. "He's just here to talk business, I'm sure."

The doctor and his wife obediently stepped out of the room, but they did so taking each step backwards as to keep an eye on their guest and their patient for each possible moment.

When they were safely out of ear shot, so Duke assumed, the Silver Gorge local law opened the conversation.

"I assume you're here about the Scarecrow, aren't you? Well, he got away, and I haven't had a chance yet to see where to. He might've gotten the better of me while we were in the open," Duke started.

"Got the better of you might be the kindest way of putting it, Sheriff," the man said without a hint of jest in his voice. "But no, I'm not here about the Scarecrow. He's not mine to contend with. Your friend Fennimore, however, I'd very much like to hear more about."

"Greasy? What do you want him for?"

"That's not important, sir. What is important is where I might find Mr. Grace as quickly as possible," the insistent visitor demanded.

"No reason to hurry, friend," Boone noted. "He's likely to be in the same place now that you'll find him in 20 years. He's up there on Cemetery Hill as of this morning. Then again, the way things are going around here, who knows?"

At the word, Duke's companion showed obvious defeat upon his face. As he turned around and took a seat in the doctor's favorite wooden chair, the lofty fellow's face and eyes dropped with a sigh.

"Well, shoot," was all he said.

"Was he… was he wanted?" Duke asked, hoping he hadn't just vouched for a known felon unknowingly.

Ch. 8 | Old Soldiers and Good Stew

"Fennimore? Heavens, no," the stranger reassured. "That man was a pillar of society if I've ever known one. It's a shame, really, that I couldn't see him one last time before he passed."

"So you two were friends, then? Were you a Johnny Reb, too?"

"We were friends, all right, but I was no secessionaire. I was loyal to the Union through and through. But we did meet in such circumstances, you could say," he said. "Do you know who I am, boy?"

Nobody had called Duke Boone "boy" in quite a while, but a fellow of this man's stature and status could afford the luxury it seemed.

"No, sir. I can't say I recognize you, but I do see your star. Arizona Ranger, right? Captain?"

"You've got good eyes, son. I was a Territorial Ranger, and a Captain, for a short time. The name's John Henry Jackson," the now-identified stranger spoke.

At this revelation, Duke once again forgot his wounds and bolted upright in order to honor the presence of this living legend who sat before him. At least in some circles, Jackson was a legend. For frontier lawmen like Duke Boone, Jackson was a hero.

"You're the Arizona Ranger who shot down Texas Red, right? Captain, I've heard stories of your work for years. It is a right privilege to meet you. Here, have some of Imogene's stew. She's as talented as she is pretty, and you won't regret it," Duke offered, trying to hand the captain Jarvis' dinner.

"That won't be necessary," he declined, too loudly to hear Jarvis protesting the uncalled for hospitality from a few rooms away. "I just came here to meet an old friend. I suppose talking about him now will have to suffice.

"The man you knew as Greasy was an asset in the

115

highest regard to us a few years back. I guess it was almost a decade now, wasn't it? You see, we had a bit of a problem in Arizona with a stray contingent of Confederates during the war, long before I'd ever made the trip out west myself. One of their men was still in our custody, though, and he recommended a few good soldiers to us when we needed help with a little Indian and outlaw problem. They had gotten too rambunctious for us to handle and we needed a good sharpshooter.

"This Confederate suggested I send word for a Fennimore Grace, Georgia, and he would be a valuable man to have on our side. I didn't much like the idea of employing Confederates after all the trouble their kind had put me through in the war, but Governor Tritle convinced me that we needed the help. So I sent word for this Grace and he came out a month later by train. I tell you, I have never been as blessed to be joined by a man as I was that day when he stepped off the train and shook my hand. I didn't know it yet, of course, but I was lucky.

"He was the sharpest eye I'd ever seen. As poor as our rifles were, it was like he knew just how to miss accurately. If a man was within 200 yards, he would either hit the brigand or the fellow standing next to him. At that distance, we didn't much care so long as he helped us clear out the problems," Jackson regaled.

"So you mean to tell me that Greasy, our resident vagrant and wanderer, really was a world-class target shooter?" Duke inquired.

"I don't know much about sport shooting, but he could nail a vagabond in the back of the head in the midst of a sandstorm and a settling fog. Outside of shooting, he turned out to be a good man," Jackson added.

"So that was all it took to get over his past affiliations, the fact that he was a dead-eye shot for you in the present?" Duke went on.

Ch. 8 | Old Soldiers and Good Stew

"Now it wasn't quite that easy, I admit, but it was something he told me once," Jackson admitted. "Fennimore was fond of telling stories, especially war stories, but one in particular he held on to pretty tightly. He wouldn't tell the men this one around the campfires, but he told me once as we shared a cider and a guitar. Are you familiar with the Battle of Chickamauga?"

"Somewhat," Boone replied.

"Well did… what did you know him as… Greasy? Did Greasy ever tell you the story about Chickamauga?"

"He told me so many stories, I can't rightly say. What about it?"

"You'd know this one," Jackson reassured Sheriff Boone. "This one was about a kid and a well."

Duke couldn't believe his luck. Greasy had told the sheriff so many stories over the years that most of them had blurred together like the flies in the coffee that his drifter friend often tried to shill out, but this one was fresh. It being the last story Greasy would ever tell Duke lent it some significance.

"Yes he has, Captain! I remember that story real well," Boone laughed, much to the captain's surprise.

"I don't quite see the humor in it myself, but I guess you're welcome to your mirth if you like," Jackson said with obvious doubt in his eyes.

"Sure it's funny," Duke offered through chuckles and chortles of varying degrees. "It's a great story! He was watching that kid run back up the hill with his water bucket when something happened and he dropped the bucket! That was a great story!"

Jackson sat back in his chair and found a smile himself, though not for the reason Duke expected.

"I guess that is a funny story, but do you know why the

boy dropped his bucket? Did he never tell you that part?"

"No, no he didn't," Duke answered.

As the sheriff leaned forward in his bed, Jackson pulled out an oak pipe and lit the leaves he sprinkled inside.

"I was on the battlefield that day. My men were shooting at that boy as he crossed a field until we noticed that he stopped to give one of my men water. We knew the soldier was dying but we couldn't risk going after him. He was going to die there on that field, and so would each and every one of us if I'd given the order to retrieve his body. In all likelihood, my future friend might've been the one to nail a red badge on me," Captain Jackson sighed as he reminisced about the blood-soaked battle.

"We saw the boy take care of our soldier. This Johnny Reb was giving water to my dying Union cavalryman without a second thought for his own safety. It was a true display of heroism, I tell you. I ordered my men to lower their arms and to give him some space to do his kindness," Captain Jackson went on. "The Confederate lieutenant on Fennimore's side felt differently, though. When he saw that young man in gray offer hospice to an enemy combatant, the lieutenant was outraged. He instantly ordered Fennimore to shoot down the boy. One of his own. A boy he might've called friend had they the chance to meet earlier.

"Well, he refused, naturally. Greasy was a soldier, but he was no murderer. He told his commanding officer that he would do no such thing, but the officer was a forceful man," Jackson illustrated. "He pulled out his revolver and held it on Fennimore's back. The fool warned Fennimore that somebody was going to get shot whether it was the boy or it was the sharpshooter.

"As most men do, Fennimore gave in to his sense of self-preservation and he shot the boy," Jackson concluded.

Duke struggled to reconcile the story he had heard

Ch. 8 | Old Soldiers and Good Stew

some days earlier with this new conclusion. Greasy, a friend, shot down a helpless boy with no means of recourse or defense or even warning. A noble boy, from what it sounded like. Noble or stupid.

"That's horrible! How was that an endearing story?"

"Because of what he told me afterward. You see, Greasy looked at me after telling that story and he said something I don't believe I'll ever forget. He said, 'Captain. I know it's soldiers do the shooting and soldiers do the killing and the dying in war, but it ain't a soldier's game. War is for these groups of men we call governments. War is for those without risk.'

"Then he gave me the most somber stare I've ever seen come from a man and he just said, 'After all, just look at you and me. Here we are sitting in a tent on the frontier sharing a drink and a laugh, when just twenty years ago we might've torn at each other's throats and brandished swords against each other. I might've killed you that day instead of some boy. And here we are at peace. Friends.'"

After an extended pause in which the captain drew on his pipe for a lengthy measure, he stood as if to leave.

"Well, those are old times and old times stay where we left 'em. Since you know the stories about me, you know the Territorial Rangers disbanded not long after. Most of us went on to hunting outlaws and private tracking, but I don't imagine Fennimore ever took to liking that sort of thing without a star or a flag behind him. Strange thing about a man like that," Jackson said before turning to go.

"Wait! You've got to stay," Duke shouted. "I could use a man with your knowledge when I go after the Scarecrow. If you could gun down Texas Red in a fair fight, there's no telling what you and I could do together when we go after the Kansas Scarecrow."

Jackson heard the mystical way Duke said that outlaw's

name and he smiled.

"Boy, there's no way I could hit that kind of a trail again. Why do you think I came looking for Fennimore after all these years? I've given up that life. I wanted to tell him he was right. There wasn't much use in trailing a man just to kill him once you found him. That sort of thing isn't for me anymore," Jackson said over a threadbare gun shoulder on his tan riding jacket. "Besides. I know it don't seem like that long ago to you that I killed Texas Red, but even a few weeks make a big difference on a man my age in this climate. I'm no good to you out there, despite what you might think."

Duke watched his idol walk away with a tip of a hat and the wink of an eye. And with a courteous greeting to his hosts in another room, Captain Jackson was gone. Duke heard the horse's hooves striking the dirt as his rider mounted and bid farewell to the folks of Silver Gorge. A legend like that deserved more pomp, more celebration. He deserved one last good fight.

Instead, he just limped away out past Cemetery Hill to pay his respects to the departed. Duke listened to the hoof beats until he drifted asleep. It was a normal sleep, though, and not the pain-weary sleep Duke had been hypnotized by for what seemed like a lifetime. It was a restful, peaceful sleep at first.

Duke would wake up at one point and imagine what it was like for Greasy to take that shot against his will. He imagined what it must've been like for the soldier in him to do what he had to do, knowing well what the consequences of action versus inaction would be.

As Sheriff Boone pondered Greasy's story and the true ending, he drifted off to dream once again where he saw a dying boy on a field of blood. He saw a broken bucket, splintered by the metal round and matted in mud and death. Then he saw the blood turn to black, and the boy's face melted away like wax under a flame. In the obsidian pool, which

Duke Boone himself stood over, he saw the reflection of Zeke's face as it washed away into the saloon ground. That dream had not left him after all. It was simply waiting for the right time to return.

-Chapter Nine-

Chasing the Black Rider

A veneer of cloud muted the light shadowing off of the ground while the wanted man held his position. After the way things went down between him and the sheriff, the Scarecrow had wanted nothing more than to leave Nevada and make off for the city. Any city. The constantly open air had grown unnerving to the gunman, and he would have bolted if not for a longstanding contract that kept him hanging around.

His breaths were staggered in the chilled air, but it was too dangerous to start a fire. That sheriff took a savage beating and kept on fighting, and there was little doubt in the Scarecrow's mind that the good people of Silver Gorge would come looking for him sooner or later. After all, that was what his employer, Mr. Mason, wanted. He wanted the sheriff out of town, and he wanted him to run into the Scarecrow out in the open plains.

"I oughta just walk up there and shoot the old fool myself," the Scarecrow whispered aloud to no one. "He's got me sleeping in the dirt while he eats steak and bathes in whiskey every night. Not like any of his stinking miners would care, that lousy lot. They might even make me their king… or whatever it is that they do."

The Scarecrow tried to rest with his hat over his eyes

Ch. 9 | Chasing the Black Rider

and his head resting on a mossy stone, but each sound in the night roused his attention. A skittering lizard off to the west nearly forced the gunman to let off a few rounds while a night hare running afoul of a coyote made a scream like that of a green tree popping and whining as it catches flame.

He hadn't rested much since the first night he saw it, the Rider in the Dark. It was a fool's superstition, sure, but the Scarecrow had good eyes. Something had followed him up over the ridge a day or two before he first reached Silver Gorge, and it looked like the thing he'd heard lesser men speak of in hushed tones and drunk manias. All the Scarecrow knew for sure was that he used to enjoy this part of the job. Lying out under the night sky with nothing above you but God's ceiling, that was the perk. That was the only time he found peace in the world, but now that was gone. The Rider had shattered it.

Blackness. That was all the Scarecrow could see when he lifted his hat at each sound. What a pitiable sight this must be, he thought. Here was the most feared gunman for 1,000 miles and he's scared to close his eyes because a ghost might be there. Soldiers and Marshals rode in groups because they hoped to fend off the great Scarecrow, didn't they? Wouldn't they laugh if they looked now and saw the embodiment of their panic huddled up behind a brush pile with a blanket held up as camouflage.

Then it came.

Hoofbeats in the distance stepped at a rhythm under cover of night, and the Kansas Scarecrow froze in hopes that he might look like just another stone on the landscape.

A pistol sat by his hand, but reaching it would mean exposing his flash-white skin to any moonbeams that would perchance escape the clouds.

And the beats kept growing and growing, the sound of the Rider's approach rising with each successively quickening beat of the Scarecrow's heart. Horse's footfalls boomed now like they were an avalanche in the foothills roiling towards the makeshift camp where he would make his final stand.

"Not today. Not like this," the Scarecrow breathed as he tensed his hand to reach for the pistol. "I've faced down Death before. What makes you any better?"

Each tendon in the willing victim's hand tensed as he waited for the perfect moment to reveal his position. The Scarecrow's eyes blazed directly at the back of that hat he used as a blindfold, and the hat would be the first to go.

The Rider ran with a fury over a nearby hill, his mount snorting viciously and his call deafening in the ears of the once fearless Scarecrow. The Rider himself made no sound, but the Scarecrow could hear his own name repeated. A name he hadn't gone by in many years. A name he thought was buried in the sand with the man who made it count.

There would be just a second to strike, so it had to be flawless. His shot would need to be true. Blasting a ghost might not make much of a difference, but the Scarecrow was determined that his last fight would be the best. What could be bolder than an attempt to gun down this rider of Death with a final rage?

Three, the gunman counted silently with his left hand while his right waited to draw the revolver.

The hoofbeats charged closer and closer. The Scarecrow could hear the leather of the reins snap as the Rider pushed his horse towards the finish.

Two.

Dust curled into the sky and fell to the ground, softly rejoining the earth from which it came. Each particle, older than the oldest cities, fell to the will of the Rider that called upon its servitude when drifting once more to the desert floor.

One.

Ch. 9 | Chasing the Black Rider

One last breath the Scarecrow inhaled as he instantly retraced each movement that would have to come in this ultimate ambush.

The gunman flung off his hat as he reached out for the gun to his right and spun up to his feet with a dying, defiant shout accentuated by the wave of his duster and the halo of bullets sent in every direction.

There was nothing there. The Scarecrow had drifted off to sleep, he supposed, and dreamt of his imagined tormenter. No such rider was there, and no such rider probably ever existed.

"Last time I listen to a drunk Mexican in Goldfield," the Scarecrow sneered, rather thankful that nobody had been around to see his failure of constitution.

Then again, the raucous gunfire may not have been for naught after all. A glint of light maybe a mile away revealed what looked to be the mouth of a cave. Somebody was holed up in that cave, and the Scarecrow just had to drop by.

"With all that noise, it won't do much good to stay out here. Let's see what exactly who's out here with us," the Scarecrow planned out loud.

A familiar calm came to the gunman as he refilled the chambers on his revolver and ambled towards the distant cave. The Kansas Scarecrow was good at killing, and knowing that he'd soon be the only living soul on the plains had a way of easing his troubled calm. With a readied gun in his hand and a dusty hat back on his head, the Kansas Scarecrow prepared to do his job.

✪   ✪   ✪

Duke's ribs were still sore, but a few days of rest and a couple more servings of that heavenly stew had done more than enough good to get the sheriff out of Jarvis and Imogene's house and back into the sheriff's quarters. Mort and Miss Abilene walked Sheriff Boone the whole way, acting as supports when he wobbled. The bed-weary lawman was relieved to be up on his feet, but so many days of repose will take the firmness out of a man's legs quicker than anything. With a little bit of help, he was up and moving, and the faster he could get back in riding shape the quicker he could go out after the Scarecrow.

The sheriff held his right arm over Miss Abilene's shoulder while using his free left hand to steady himself on Mort's back. His foot caught a particularly deep rut left by a wagon during a soaking rain the day before, and Duke nearly lost his step as a result.

"Careful, Duke," Miss Abilene pleaded as she bore his weight on her own. "Jarvis says another fall could reinjure your side and keep you out of duty for another month, on top of the week he already says you still owe him."

"I'm not laying in that lumpy bed another minute. I want to get up and move and try out my legs as quick as I can. First thing tomorrow, I'm going out there after the Scarecrow."

The deputy and the innkeeper shared a glance behind Duke's field of view as she urged Mort to speak up and convince his boss to rest. As lovely as Miss Abilene was, she could strike fear in a full-grown man with a cursing eyebrow.

"Uh... boss? Maybe you should let us take care of it," Mort started. "I've had some men out there trying to snag his trail for days now and we can't find him. They've ridden circles around Silver Gorge at least 20 miles out. He just ain't there."

"He's there, Mort. I know it," Duke winced as his foot struck the dirt at an odd angle, causing his side to catch and heave. "He hasn't finished what he came here for. And they

Ch. 9 | Chasing the Black Rider

haven't seen him riding in the daylight, so he'd have to move at night, which he won't do."

"I don't get it," Miss Abilene responded. "You say he has to move at night, but he won't? That doesn't make any sense."

The sheriff smiled and squeezed Miss Abilene's side a little tighter, in part because he wanted to and in part to keep his balance.

"He's scared of something. I don't know what, but he's scared of something out there. He won't ride at night if he can help it, which means he has to be holed up somewhere nearby," Duke explained.

Mort's expression soured at the confidence in Duke Boone's voice. The sheriff believed what he was saying, and Mort knew that meant an expedition was coming. There was no way he could talk the sheriff out of going, so the best he could do was perhaps delay him a bit.

"We need you in town, Sheriff. If he's really still out there, how do we know he won't ride back into town once you leave? If he's watching Silver Gorge, we'll need some protection when you go out on your manhunt," Mort reasoned.

"I'm not fit for a straight fire fight, boy. If I'm going to catch this man, it's going to be with surprise on my side. Besides, you've got help. Just get our rooftop brigade back out. They did a fine job that night the Scarecrow first came through town. You put three or four men up on the roofs with rifles. Even if they aren't good shots, they should do well enough to dissuade the Scarecrow from sticking around too long," Duke retorted.

It was a solid plan, and Mort knew that. The only problem was the limping sheriff. His head still seemed to work all right, but his legs and his ribs were questionable. A hard ride through the wilderness towards a wanted gunman left a hundred options for Duke to reinjure something or, worse, get himself killed.

    For all of Mort's pleading, the sheriff decided to wait at least two more days. That would give him time to heal up a little more and get some supplies together at the very least, though it would also give the Scarecrow time to move if he wanted to. Duke thought he'd pinned down something about that gunman, but he couldn't be sure he'd interpreted the signs correctly.

    Duke saw a familiar fear in the Scarecrow's eyes, for sure, but that gunman was another type of beast altogether. Seemed like the only reaction he knew, true to his word, was to throw bullets at a problem until it was fixed, or at least that's what all the stories used to say. For Sheriff Boone, on the other hand, he had always tried to be a man of patience and understanding. Most problems could be either waited out or worked out, it was just a matter of which one to use when. If the Scarecrow were more like Duke than anyone previously thought, maybe the sheriff would have some luck after all. If the Scarecrow responded just like everyone else thought he probably would when run to ground, Duke knew he might be attending another funeral soon.

    The scalding midday sun gave way to that cooler iridescent glow which foretells the coming night, and Duke was glad to be stepping up into his own office for the first time in more than a week. Mort had been careful not to mess around with too much, apparently, because Duke opened the door to almost the same scene he'd left before going off on his last wild hunt. The cells were still empty, serving as a pleasant reminder of both the sheriff's success at keeping the town safe and a scathing reminder of his inability to bring in the foul gunman. A partially burned candle rested on the platform near Duke's desk, waiting to once more be lit.

    And there on his desk was the puzzle box.

    That foolish puzzle box, which Boss Mason had given

Ch. 9 | Chasing the Black Rider

Duke as a subtle taunt, sat on the Sheriff's oak desk just laughing at him. The few panels he had worked out jutted a half-inch or a quarter-inch from the bulk of the box, giving the wooden figure absurd angles and lines. The shape of the thing was an indictment of nature, just as its as-of-yet revealed secret was an indictment of the sheriff's tenacity.

"Thank you both for your help," Duke offered as he sat down in his chair. "I hate to ask so much of you after you helped carry me here, Mort, but would you mind helping me gather some supplies for my ride?"

Duke's deputy huffed with visible disdain at his boss's request, but it was still his boss's request.

"I know you wanted to see your lady this evening, but I need to restock if I'm going after the Scarecrow. It won't be a one-day ride, for sure. I'd greatly appreciate you helping me out just this once," Duke said while feigning a plea.

"You want me to go get Mark Wilson? He's been begging to come around the office more and help out. I'm sure he'd love to help out," Mort hinted.

"We're not getting Mark or Matt or Junior or any of the Wilsons involved. Now help me get my stuff together and you might just get to see your friend tonight," Duke retorted.

Mort dutifully agreed and walked off to hit up a few shops with Duke's extensive list of needs, and that left the sheriff alone with Miss Abilene.

Ever a lady, Miss Abilene stood by patiently while Duke finished his business with Mort. When the official dealings were finished, however, she eased over to where the sheriff was seated and put her hands on his shoulders for a gentle massage. Even through his leather vest and cotton shirt, Duke could feel the gentle touch of his town's best innkeeper as each finger rolled softly down the length of his arms to his knuckles.

"Miss Abilene, I really don't know if you should…"

Duke protested before the lady clicked her tongue pertly.

"You took care of me, remember? It's just my turn to take care of you," her soft, lingering touch whispered, with her lips brushing upon his ear.

Miss Abilene started by pulling her fingers back to the collar of his shirt, which she quickly removed. The bandages around his side were stained by a week's worth of sweat and blood it seemed, so she gingerly peeled them away to expose his bruised ribs. Duke winced with a subtle, lingering pain as Miss Abilene's hands went to work around his side, but the pain was short-lived with how adeptly she softened his skin and released his tension with her touch.

The lady placed his rags in a pot of water and started a fire in order to boil the pot and heat the room. While she did all that, Miss Abilene directed Duke to move to his bed where he could relax.

Sheriff Boone waited his turn on the bed while Miss Abilene prepared her next surprise. He nearly drifted off with how welcoming the plush surface was to his skin. It had truly been too long since Duke slept in a bed he knew, and Miss Abilene had already lulled him to the point of restfulness.

With her hair down, Miss Abilene was even more strikingly beautiful than what the rest of the town saw of her. In a pioneer town like Silver Gorge once was and still pretended to be, it was to her great benefit to wear her hair up and away. People respected a lady with short hair, she would often say, but Duke admired the woman who entered his doorway through nothing but the light of a fireplace with a candle in her hand. Her draping hair outlined the beautiful frame she would hide with sharp dresses and suits, but that shape was always there just under the surface.

"I thought I told you to lie on your chest," Miss Abilene reminded the sheriff, still lazily reclining on his side.

"You did, you did. But I couldn't pass up this moment,

could I?" Duke teased.

Sheriff Boone was no longer wearing his star and he was no longer wearing his gun. For now, for at least a few minutes, he was just Duke Boone again. And she was no longer the proprietor of a local business; Miss Abilene was just herself.

Muted candlelight flashed orange and black upon Miss Abilene's skin as Duke propped himself up with his elbows and watched this lithe angel circled in a halo of red dust float towards him. Each of the lady's gentle, purposeful steps flowed with obvious intent towards Duke, his body splayed out and tremoring with sweet anxiety. As Miss Abilene approached, she slid her leg across the draped sheets and up to the bed, then knelt down to present her sheriff with a kiss.

The innkeeper's nose sat patiently at the end of her desire, with the slightest space between her and him. With her head low and her eyes looking high, Miss Abilene seduced a man she already had full possession of with a look and a touch. As her left hand slipped up his side, she tried to hide the cringe she felt at his bruises. Duke noticed, but he ignored her momentary shudder. He placed his hand on hers and lifted her chin so that he could better see her full aura in the evening dusk.

Despite the gentle love with which he touched her and welcomed her in, Miss Abilene's mind strayed to the cuts and the wounds upon her love's body.

"I don't want you to go out there," she begged while turning her lips from his.

With a bothered sigh, Duke responded, "You know I have to. He tried to kill you."

"Oh, spare me! More of this inflated sense of duty and protection! I'll be better off if you stay here with me, you know. Stay here. Don't leave me," Miss Abilene urged while pressing her chest against his.

The sheriff kissed his love before softly pressing her to the side so he could stand. Duke nearly stumbled as he bent down to pick up his shirt, but he hid the evidence of pain long enough to get dressed again.

"I can't do this with you right now, you know. My job is to protect this town," Duke boasted. "My job is to protect you, and I can't do that if I'm scared of every threat that might come through. I let this man wait long enough when I didn't go after him the night he came after you, and now Greasy is dead."

"Did you pull the trigger on his gun, Duke?" she questioned. "Did you make that man climb up in a tree and risk his life for you?"

Duke tried to look away in frustration, but the persistent innkeeper pulled his face around and spoke directly to him.

"You listen to me, Duke Boone. Greasy was in those woods because he wanted to help. He made his own choices, not you."

"But he still did it for me, Abb. How am I honoring his decision if I let his killer go free? Besides, that man tried to kill you, too, or have you already forgotten that?" Boone challenged.

"Of course I haven't forgotten about that! I've slept here every night since you've been gone, Duke, just so I wouldn't have to go back to my own hotel. There are still bullet holes in the walls and the lamp by my bed is still in pieces on the ground, but no. I've forgotten that a deranged killer tried to end my life!" she shouted.

Abilene rose to her feet midsentence and stared down her occasional lover, daring him to recant or respond. Wood crackled and spit in the fireplace while the silent pair faced off in a wordless duel. The woman's fiery eyes assaulted Duke while he worked at avoiding her line of sight by staring at the

Ch. 9 | Chasing the Black Rider

walls, the door, and that confounding puzzle box still sitting on a table in the corner of his room.

Still hoping to backtrack from his foolhardy speech, Duke slunk around Abilene and picked up the puzzle box, desperately needing something to engage his fidgeting hands.

He once again shifted pieces and tilted the box hoping for signs of a clue, but moreso as a delay tactic than with any real hope of opening the box.

Abilene glared with crossed arms and a hip popped wide, clearly telegraphing her impatience with the wayward sheriff.

"I'm sorry, Abilene," Duke finally offered after an extended pause. "I don't know what to do. People in this town are on edge. Their sheriff was just beaten up and left helpless on the ground. Sure, he's got a reputation as a bloodthirsty killer, but I let him abuse me. I can't protect the people here if I can't protect myself, can I?"

"You can't protect the people here if you're dead," she coyly pointed out.

Clearly letting go of her anger over Duke's verbal missteps, Abilene walked over to her friend and took the puzzle box out of his hands while softly rubbing his arm and back.

"What is this thing, anyway?"

"A dirty taunt, that's what," Duke responded. "Boss Mason gave it to me about a week or so ago and I haven't had much time to work on it for... well... obvious reasons. If you rattle it, you'll hear there's clearly something in there, but I don't have the slightest idea what it could be."

Abilene rotated the box in her fingers and slid pieces back and forth until she realized just how needlessly complex the blasted thing was.

"It would take more than 1,000 moves, all done in

133

exactly the right order, to get this box open. You say he put something in here?" Abilene asked.

"Yeah, he said it was his greatest treasure, or something like that. I'm not sure I believe him. I know he hides it well, but me and Mason aren't on the best of terms and I'm pretty sure he would never trust me with anything that was his greatest treasure or even his least favorite treasure," Duke mentioned. "Even so, I do wonder what's in there."

"If it's of any importance to Mason," Abilene started, "the best thing to do might be to get rid of it."

"What?"

"I'm just saying, if he wants it, maybe we don't want him to have it. That would really get in his craw, wouldn't it?" Abilene explained while a wry smile took over her face.

"You're out of your mind, woman," Duke laughed while trying to grab the box away from her.

"Ah ah ah," Abilene clucked, yanking the box back. "You can't have it. It's mine now. You gave it to me. Possession is… what's the old saying?"

Duke reached for the box again, but she jumped away. Miss Abilene, still wearing just her nightclothes, bounced around the room and laughed while the sheriff flung himself weakly after her. She climbed over the bed and around the table, leading Duke on a wild chase full of giggling and grunting. He would swat his arms in a wide path, hoping to catch her off guard, but Abilene would just slide out of his way, nearly sending Duke to the ground in a thud. He lunged ahead, but she ducked under his arms to turn around and see Duke hugging the bedpost.

"Come and get me! Come and get me!" Abilene teased with all the glee of a little girl running from her friends. "You'll never catch me, you'll never catch me!"

Ch. 9 | Chasing the Black Rider

Duke knew he would never stop her this way, so he had to be smart. He kept up the charade for a minute longer and lunged with obvious movements that never had any chance of touching her. Finally, though, Duke turned and trapped her in a corner. Abilene realized her position, so she tucked the box behind her back.

The mastermind sheriff slowly and deliberately stepped towards Abilene, leaving his hands in his pockets until the last moment. His vixen slunk further in the corner with the puzzle box right where she wanted it.

As he got within range, Duke leaned in for a kiss and froze Abilene where she stood. He put his hands on her shoulder and smoothed off her lace, slowly running his fingers lower and lower with each touch. The kiss was long. Slow. Perfect. It was a ruse, sure, but Duke loved Abilene and enjoyed his stolen moments with her. As his hands curled around her back for a hug — and to steal the puzzle box — Miss Abilene darted away with a grin.

"Mmm, nice move, Mr. Sheriff. But you'll never catch me, and you'll never get this box back."

In a flash, Abilene playfully shoved Duke back into the wall and tossed the puzzle box into the blazing fire behind her.

It was a move that Duke hardly expected and one he was even less prepared to deal with, so all he could think to do was throw Abilene aside and plunge his hands into the fire. The wooden box had already caught on the edges and started to fade into a bright orange demise, so it was too much for the sheriff to handle.

"Why would you do that!" he kept shouting, hobbling frantically around his compartmentalized room in the jailhouse making quite the pathetic sight. "You're going to burn it! You're going to burn it!"

Although Duke had no idea what it actually was, he

felt that whatever was hidden in Mason's puzzle box was important. Perhaps more importantly, he was worried that Mason might be considerably peeved if it did not return in peak condition.

Miss Abilene looked for a shovel in order to remove the ashes that were once a puzzle box, but none could be found. Duke flung open cabinets and drawers, looking for anything that could retrieve the item that was certainly going to burn up if he didn't hurry. As Duke hurriedly tossed papers and trinkets about, the flames licked at the once ornate wood that contained some kind of a secret, racing against the sheriff and his companion to retrieve the object of so much importance.

Like Shadrach, Meshach and Abednego, the box was summarily tossed into the furnace like refuse for destruction, and the sheriff was resigned to watching in horror while the memories contained in the box followed upward the smoke his fire created.

Almost as quickly as she had left, though, unseen by Duke, Abilene ran back in and hurled a pot of water on the logs in order to quench the flames. A wave of ash and soot washed over Duke's floorboards, but, despite the mess, the water pot had done its deed and done it well.

Gleaming in the dirt was a metal lump, not yet cool enough to be touched by hand. The sheriff took just a moment to spot the slight glint under the veneer of ash, and he used his boot to ease the object out to where it would cool more quickly. Both observers leaned in close and gave the semi-shiny ball a once-over, but neither knew quite what to do next.

Duke tapped the thing cautiously and, having assured himself it was safe to touch, picked up the cool lump of metal and rubbed off most of the soot with minimal effort. He could feel ridges that were supposed to be writing under his fingers as he pushed away the char and the embers, and he finally was able to make out just what the ball of cool silver said.

The full significance of this harbinger was lost on Duke Boone for a moment, but he finally turned and faced Abilene with a queer look and asked a question he'd never even considered.

"Tell me. Does Boss Mason have a brother?"

-Chapter Ten-

His Brother's Keeper

Mason Bros. Mining Company.

It was surely a simple enough message, but the implications of the chiseled claim rushed on the sheriff like the billowing dust clouds that so often plagued Nevada in the late summer. What was it Boss Mason had said about the object inside his puzzle box? That it was one of his dearest possessions?

And the Boss was true to his word. It was a piece of silver, possibly the first one Mason ever pulled out of the mountain if the fancifully engraved "No. 1" on its otherwise smooth surface meant anything. But did he have help digging it out?

Mason and the sheriff were hardly friends, sure, but to think that nobody had ever mentioned a Mason brother surprised Duke. He had lived in Silver Gorge long enough to know most of the folks around with some confidence, but he had never met anybody else who claimed to be a Mason. That was a bloodline of one, he thought, but maybe not. Maybe there was another one somewhere, or maybe even more than one.

"What's that thing there, Duke?"

Ch. 10 | His Brother's Keeper

"I think it might be the first piece of silver Mason ever mined," Duke answered.

"Wow. How much do you think it's worth? And why would he give it to you?" Abilene asked.

"I'm not so concerned about the value of the thing. Look what it says," Duke noted while tossing his elegant companion the piece of etched silver in his hands.

Abilene ran it through her fingers, tenderly smoothing the surface as if it were a fine silk she had planned to hem. She was a lady through and through, but the sight of so much silver and the weight of that much money all in her palms was more than enough to get Abilene thinking some crazy things like how long she could close down the inn for or what kind of wedding could she put together. Could she get away and never come back? Just what could she do with so much silver? The lady knew Nevada was a silver state, and she'd occasionally see miners pass through her inn on their way out of town, but never before had Abilene touched a pure lump coaxed out of the ground.

Her eyes grew wide with the fire of wondrous speculation, nearly causing her to forget why Sheriff Boone handed her the silver in the first place, but her eyes narrowed when they caught a sight of the etching on the flat side.

"Huh," Abilene exhorted instinctively. "Look at that."

Duke held his hand out expecting the silver to return, and it was something of a chore for Abilene to hand it back. Her gaze darted to Duke's face with a flash of sadness, but she dutifully returned the silver to her man. Abilene's hand dropped as if weighted down when she let the silver go, already regretful of the time she held it and the time she felt it leave.

"Yeah. Look at that," Duke echoed.

"So what's the big deal," Abilene requested as her watchful gaze traced the path of Duke's rich right hand. "So the mine was founded by two Masons instead of one. Does that mean something?"

Maybe. Maybe not. It was the purported significance of the thing that made Duke suspicious more than the message. A man like Mason, with all of his trinkets, was rather particular about the objects he chose to keep close, meaning he was also particular about the objects he chose to expel. All that Duke knew was that the mere existence of this silver meant that there was a new piece of the puzzle he was yet to figure out.

"Come, Sheriff," Abilene teased, wrapping Duke's fingers around the cold, metallic puzzle piece that had sucked up his attention rather effectively. "Or did you forget what got us here in the first place?"

Duke weighed the options, of course, but he finally relented to Miss Abilene's touch and placed the silver in his newly discarded right boot. The ever-questioning sheriff hated to spend a minute without it, wondering what it could possibly signify, but the newly excited Abilene kissed his exposed shoulders and let her gentle hands rummage his chest.

"Let me take your mind off that little rock," Abilene said before coming in closer to Duke's ears with a whisper. "Tell me what it'll take to make you forget."

Though that little coo was enough to entice the sheriff for good, Abilene's thoughts all the while were drawn to what sat just a couple feet from her busy hands.

★ ★ ★

Glittering dust and reflections glinted in the Sheriff's reluctant eyes. Had he really slept all through the night? A peaceful rest was more than Duke had hoped for, but Abilene

Ch. 10 | His Brother's Keeper

must have done something right.

"Wake up, beautiful. The sun's up and it's probably about time we consider getting to work," Duke said rolling over.

To his surprise, there was a cool hollow in the bed where a gorgeous woman had been the night before. Smart move, he thought. Abilene had always been adamant that the two keep their private business private in hopes that nobody would suspect favorable treatment from the sheriff, or something like that. Either way, he knew she was probably making the right call and he shrugged off her regrettable absence as just another one of her strategic moves to keep people off their trail.

Duke swung his legs over the bed and reached for whatever clothes he could find. The mornings were still getting warmer, but that left a lingering nip from the night cold still to be burned away by the afternoon sun. Slight chill was no worry for Duke, though, now that he was waking up from the best sleep he'd had in weeks. For a moment, the Sheriff considered spending a little more time with Abilene that night if she was interested. He surely was, and she'd never turned him down before.

He floated around the room whistling, grabbing up his various articles of clothing. Duke threw on a shirt and his undergarments before stepping into his pants and his boots, but he felt like he was barely touching the ground. Nights with Abilene always left the sheriff feeling giddy or relieved, but this one had been especially fine.

Sheriff Boone tossed the door open to find Mort already waiting at the desk with a coffee in his hand and the chair up on two. He was so shocked to see the sheriff that he nearly fell to the ground and took a hot bath.

"I'm so sorry, sir. I didn't know when you planned on coming in, so I didn't think you'd mind if I sat in your chair,"

Mort appealed.

"It's fine, Mort. It's fine," Duke answered with an obvious grin. "Pour me some of that coffee and we'll call it even."

Mort slowly stood and walked to the pot while keeping a sideways watchful eye on the sheriff. He felt around with his hands to grab the pot and a cup, and he poured slowly as not to overfill the cup he clearly had no intention of watching. The young deputy was far too perplexed by Duke's demeanor to focus on his work with the coffee, so he hardly noticed the burning sensation when it started to flow over.

When the boy gave a howl and a curse, Duke just kept smiling and watched out the window towards the inn where Abilene was starting her day, much like he was here, and the sheriff dreamed of what it would be like to just once wake up and enjoy the morning light with her.

"Who is she?" Mort asked, still flinging his hand around to ease the burn and get the remaining liquid off.

"Pardon?" Duke replied as Mort's question hauled him back to the present.

"The woman who was here last night. Who is she?" Mort reiterated.

"What makes you think there was a woman here last night?" Duke inquired.

"Sir. I haven't known you all that long, but I can tell you haven't slept much the last few weeks. After the attack, I figured you'd just be worse off what with the bruising and Greasy's death. But… you're happy. Goodness sakes, Duke, I haven't seen you actually happy since before everything at the saloon," Mort reasoned. "For some men I'd say it was drinking or gold, but seeing as how you've never touched much of either, it has to be a woman. So, again I ask. Who is she?"

Ch. 10 | His Brother's Keeper

"Do I bother you with your dealings at the Cat House? Do I ask you how Charlotte is every day?"

Mort waited to respond, assuming more was coming. After a few moments without sound, he offered a sheepish nod in the negative.

"That's right. I don't," Duke reaffirmed. "Whether or not I have a friend or female companion visiting in the evenings when you're gone, off with your own lovely lady, is of no concern to you. Am I clear?"

The deputy was much quicker in his answer this time around, realizing that Duke had no intention of asking a question with no answer.

"Sir, at least tell me you've given up this fool plan to go out and look for the Scarecrow. Just because you've had a dose of lady and you're feeling all high and mighty the morning after doesn't mean you're not still hurting. Just stay here. Get better," Mort begged.

"I have done no such thing as give up on my plan," Duke quickly and firmly noted while observing the disappointment in Mort's face. "At the same time, something else has come up. Something more interesting. So, I guess I won't be leaving just yet."

Mort started going off about the day's business while displaying obvious relief that his boss would stick around at least a little longer. He listed off cattle thieves and brawls and boundary complaints on the east end of town where the McCalls and the Faulks had their ranches. Duke wasn't hardly listening to a word of it as his mind shifted from the night with Abilene to what they found in Mason's box. Eager Mort had his to-do list planned out for the day and he kept on yammering with something new to add every second, but Duke had better plans. Sure, he might go on a couple of these errands. After all, he was still the sheriff and had work to get done, but he would use his travels as a pretext to dig a little deeper about Mason's family history, starting with the fellow right in front of him.

"Mort," Duke interrupted the ceaseless rambling of his deputy. "You know if Boss Mason ever had a brother?"

The question rolled off of Mort, but the sheriff could tell it shook him a little.

"I'm not sure, sir. You've been in Silver Gorge far longer than I have. I didn't get off the stage but two years ago. If he had a brother, he left or died long before I came here. Especially if you've never seen him. Why you ask?"

"I found something, Mort. Something interesting I might show you sometime," Duke cryptically explained. "Either way, it said something that indicated Boss Mason might have had a brother once upon a time."

"Well if Mason never mentioned him, he couldn't have been all that important," Mort reasoned. "Why would he bother to hide something like that?"

"Could be true," Duke acquiesced.

Duke mulled the thought over and considered it, but he wasn't sold. Mort had asked a fair question, though. Perhaps that was the question that Duke should be asking himself.

The pair sat in weighty silence for a moment, pondering Duke's logical conundrum, when the sheriff finally broke the quiet.

"Aww, heck. Either way, we've got work to do. You take the cattle thieves you seem so high on and I'll head out to the McCall/Faulk boundary to see if we can't settle that. We'll meet back here and go to the bar and try to figure out this brawl business about lunch time. That sound good?" Duke asked, and Mort nodded.

The boy stood to grab his hat and guns to walk out the door, but just before Mort got his hand on the knob he heard Duke cough intentfully.

Ch. 10 | His Brother's Keeper

"Not a word of this to anybody else, you hear? But... don't be afraid to ask anybody if they know anything about Mason's family," Duke suggested. "You made me think of something. Your being new in town might make it less strange asking about a possible relative than if I ask. Now get to it."

The young deputy eased the door shut and walked away, letting Duke hear his footsteps transition from the hard wood just outside to the plodding of dirt pathways through town. It had been nearly two years since the sheriff remembered hearing those same boots crack and creak the weathered walkway leading up to the sheriff's house. A fresh-faced youth from the frozen northeast had decided to leave his life of relative luxury and make his way on the great American frontier.

Duke didn't have the heart then to tell the kid that the frontier was more or less tamed, although it still looked like something out of a Wild Bill show. The gunmen had all but passed on to lives as sideshows in carnivals and the fences of subsistence farmers and local ranchers had divvied up the once open range to an immense degree. What the east coast knew of the western plains was a joke, a laugh shared over chips at a pub while musing over the romance of a life in dust and horse urine. The life was harder than what Boston or New York knew, but it had become, in a word, tame.

That being the case, Duke felt no shame in hiring a greenhorn as a deputy. The young man could get some life experience in a vanilla frontier town before shipping on to the next stop on the railway, the sheriff thought once, but Mort had put in the time and made himself a real fixture in Silver Gorge. People knew him well and most responded to him positively. The miners hated him, but the miners hated Duke, too. All but the three he'd pulled out of the Rusty Spittoon, at least.

In just two years, Mort had thrown off his suit-and-fruit ways for a pleasant life of rugged boredom, and Duke was almost proud of his part in all of it.

Then again, Mort had made it known just how much he longed for the adventure and the sport he expected Wild West sheriffs and deputies took part in. He used to accept assignments with fervor and a loaded gun, but he stopped carrying a weapon after a few months. He would often sit at a table and just spin his Colt artfully around an outstretched finger, itching for an excuse to pull the trigger against something more than an empty bottle.

After a couple months of pained boredom, Sheriff Boone had noticed a change in Mort. The deputy started approaching his job with a sense of duty rather than obligation, and that made all the difference. Mort's sadness turned to focus. For going on a year now, he'd even managed to become a passable and effective deputy in Duke's eyes, and that made the sheriff even more proud.

In the last few weeks, though, something had changed. Where Mort used to gloss over the sheriff when the two were together, tossing passive eyes at Duke if anything at all, he now had a new gleam in his eye when referencing his boss. Ever since the "Grand Shootout at the Rusty Spittoon" between Duke and Zeke, Mort had watched the sheriff with guarded hope and patient resentment. Perhaps it was envy, Duke thought, since Mort could do nothing but stand by and watch while his boss took part in the first shootout Silver Gorge had ever really seen.

Since that day, Duke saw flashes of the old Mort crop up. His duty and effectiveness turned back to adventure-lust and restlessness. Duke couldn't blame the kid, really, since he had been waiting two years to see any semblance of the West he dreamed of. Well, that West had finally arrived, and Mort turned out to be right in the middle of it with Duke Boone, the hero of the Rusty Spittoon.

Duke stood to leave when he felt a sharp point stick in his heel, prompting him to sit right back down and curse these

Ch. 10 | His Brother's Keeper

shoddy boots. He yanked off the hide and pulled his right foot up on to his left knee. Duke rubbed his foot as the sharp stabbing wore off and was replaced by a dull throb. A red splotch provided the evidence that something had happened, but he couldn't see what had caused the bite.

Finally Duke turned up his boot to see a sliver of something fall on the ground with a chink. He might've lost the speck had it not gleamed in the sun as a stark contrast to the muted, matted dusty floor. Sheriff Boone leaned over and picked up the speck and turned it in his hands, recognizing it instantly as a cut of silver.

"Well how'd you get there," Duke asked out loud to an unresponsive bit of valuable metal.

It wasn't until that moment that he remembered something he should have never forgotten. Where was the silver? Where had the chunk of silver from Mason's box gone? He distinctly recalled putting it in his right shoe the night before, but he never removed it to get dressed just moments ago. Had he really been so entranced that he forgot a ball of silver the size of a grown man's fist?

Better question, though. Who could have taken it? Duke jumped out of his chair and ran one-footed into the bedroom, looking under his cabinets and his bed. Perhaps he'd knocked over that boot in his sleep and the silver had rolled under something. Duke crawled along the ground, gathering dust on his hands and knees like a lizard, peering under each object in the room no matter how unlikely the perceived scenario that would end with a silver ball underneath it. But just as the slim light from an early sunrise had provided an obvious gleam from the bit of silver out of Duke's boot, the fuller sun now was unable to bring a more substantial lump to light.

Boxes of ammunition and a rifle cluttered the area under Duke's bed, along with a spare pair of boots. A key that the sheriff had lost a couple years ago sat under the dresser, caked in a half-inch of dust. Duke even went so far as to lift up a chest of trinkets and memorabilia that he kept on the far wall. The chest sat nearly flush with the floor and was opposite anywhere the silver could have gone of its own volition, but Duke had to be thorough. After all, that not-inconsequential silver belonged to one of the most powerful men in Nevada. Going back to Mason without it was tantamount to suicide. And if he couldn't find it, the thought of who must have it was no less disturbing.

Duke resigned himself to failure as he stood to leave. With or without that objet trouve, Sheriff Boone had work to do, and he would have to try and do that work without obsessing over one piece of silver if at all possible.

Before he went to visit the McCalls and the Faulks, Boone thought, he might just stop by the Inn for a short visit. See what Abilene might know about the missing silver.

-Chapter Eleven-
An Honest Name's Worth

Silver Gorge had been nothing but a well-told joke for a while now, even before Mason went on his pilgrimage and left the day-to-day operations of the mine to the sun and the dust. Nobody in town had seen a chunk of silver worth more than lunch in almost five years. Sure, the mine had been back running for going on two or three years now, but the miners certainly never brought silver off the property and very few ever mentioned pulling anything out of the earth but rocks.

Perhaps that was why Abilene had been so foolhardy as to steal Mason's silver, Duke thought. Sure, that ball of metal was probably more than 40 years out of the earth, but it was still silver. And it was still quite valuable.

Boone went back and forth on whether he thought she had actually stolen it. When the silver was first missing, the sheriff pushed it out of his mind that Abilene could have had anything to do with it. He just figured it had been picked up by the wind and rolled away, maybe. But then he got his bearings straight and he was able to think more clearly. Of course she had taken it. Who else could have?

Then again, why would she? What did it benefit Abilene to steal that silver? Aside from a large sum of money, that is.

Sheriff Boone sat outside the hotel on his famous bronze horse, wavering on whether she was a suspect or not. He could have gone in and asked at any moment, but the wondering might have only been half as bad as the worst possible truth. Duke eased his left leg up over the saddle while gripping it with both hands. He finally stepped down, albeit a little clunkily with the front end of his boots catching dirt. Sheriff Boone's mind was preoccupied with the looming conversation, so his usually fluid dismount looked more like a man trying to get on the horse in reverse.

Duke's horse wasn't the only one tied up outside the hotel. There were a couple of grays and a handful of brindles, but one particular horse stood out. She was a beautiful creature, Mark Wilson's horse, standing by the door in a clean black coat. He hadn't taken her out the day of the hunt for the Scarecrow, probably out of fear, but that all-black was certainly Mark's. The Wilson Cross-W brand marked the custom saddle atop this stunning creature rather than the usual shoulder brand as the senior Wilson was adamant that none of his prize horses would have their skin marred. Though it made his horses a frequent target of thieves, the policy to never brand a horse certainly made for beautiful animals.

One of the sheriff's understood privileges is that he can enter just about any public building he wants to without first observing the polite gesture of knocking, but Duke would still make his presence known at this door each time.

"Sheriff Boone," Duke shouted as he knocked at Miss Abilene's door.

That same door swung open quickly to reveal Mark Wilson holding a bag of biscuits out of Miss Abilene's kitchen. The Wilson family would often send somebody into town for food on the days they worked close enough in, and Mark had taken to volunteering more and more lately. Any chance he got to see the sheriff and talk to the sheriff was a day well

Ch. 11 | An Honest Name's Worth

spent.

"Come on in, Sheriff," Mark beamed. Miss Abilene shot the boy a look, though, and he amended his statement.

"Is… is that all right with you if he comes in, ma'am?"

"Come on in, Duke," Miss Abilene smiled.

The sheriff held off his grim demeanor a few minutes, even as disturbed as he was, so he could preserve the topic of conversation for a more private opportunity. That being the case, he just smiled and enjoyed the exchange between Miss Abilene and the Wilson boy.

"What are you and your family working on today, Mark?" Duke asked.

"We're helping the Faulks put up their fence, sir. They bought some beef cattle from us, so me and my brothers are helping Mr. Faulk keep his new purchase reined in," Mark answered.

"You might see me out there in a little bit, then, Mark. I hear Mr. Faulk and Mr. McCall aren't exactly agreeing on where that fence line is," Duke said.

Mark gave his hero a questioning look.

"I don't think I've heard of any dispute. Today's our third day working on this fence and they seem to be cordial," Mark answered. "You want me to get them together to talk about it? I'd be glad to help you out with that."

"No thanks, Mark. Getting men like that to talk about a border can cause a stir where there wasn't one before. Maybe just don't worry about it until I get out there," Duke responded.

Mark said he understood, but his downward eyes and sallow face told another story. He wanted to do something nice for Sheriff Boone. He wanted to help out.

Duke saw the look in his eyes, and so did Miss Abilene.

151

After Mark waved goodbye and stepped on out the door to his impressive mount, she chose to bring that file back up for reference.

"That boy idolizes you, Duke," Miss Abilene explained. "He wants to be just like you."

"Kid's an idiot if he wants to be like me," Duke replied. "He'd be better off being like his dad or his big brother."

"I think you're a fine man, Duke. Not many men in this state could lay claim to the air you breathe," she teased as she walked over and rubbed his shoulders, offering the weary sheriff a kiss.

"Yeah, but his dad's rich," Duke replied, pulling away from Miss Abilene's touch.

His hesitance to hold her scared Abilene. Duke was hardly a soft man, but it was his strong grip that had first impressed Miss Abilene so much. Now the sheriff hardly wanted to put a hand on her, and that baffled the innkeeper, but she had more pressing issues than whether or not Duke felt like being lovey today.

She wanted to stand up for her man and for the kid who adored him.

"Being rich isn't all that great. Plenty of men have the money to go down to the saloon and buy a lady's time, but that doesn't make them loved. I've seen a man buy a cow and three turkeys for a feast, but that didn't give him anyone to share it with. Rich isn't an aspiration worth living for, Duke. But being more like you sure is," Miss Abilene stated firmly. "Why don't you let Mark get close to you? He wants to be a sheriff some day, I think, and it might do him good to see how you do things."

Duke sat down at one of the tables in Miss Abilene's vacant dining room and took a breath. She meant well, but she had no clue.

Ch. 11 | An Honest Name's Worth

"Being around me isn't safe for that kid. Shoot, you saw what happened last time," Duke pointed out.

"That was one time!"

"I'm not done, Abilene," Duke cut her off. "You ever heard the name James Riley?"

"Seems like a pretty common name, but I don't think I know what you're getting at," Miss Abilene admitted.

"James Riley is something of a legend among lawmen, you know. He was this 17-year old kid a few years back who was dying of tuberculosis," Duke paused to pour himself some water from the pitcher and take a sip. "Well, Riley had taken up with the sheriff in town, a fellow named Mike McCluskie. I guess McCluskie thought he was doing right by James by teaching him the life or whatever you want to call it, especially since nobody figured that boy would live real long anyway."

Miss Abilene had been standing on the far side of the room where she was when Duke first walked in and belittled Mark, but she lived for the times Duke would tell a story of the old west. The real Old West where gunmen made their names and lawmen did, too. Miss Abilene slid across the room with the sound of her boots scuffing the wood floor the only noise you could hear until she pulled a chair out from under Duke's table with that common squeal wood makes when rubbed across wood.

"McCluskie was a good man and a good sheriff, you know. I met his brother a few years back. That's where I heard this story," Duke explained. "But you see, he was too good a sheriff. There was a man in the town, a gambler, who had crossed Sheriff McCluskie, and he wanted to cross the sheriff off. Well, McCluskie shoots him first in a fair fight, in self-defense. That's all well and good, but that man had friends. So four of his boys come into town to murder McCluskie in broad daylight."

Miss Abilene leaned forward with her elbows on the table and her head in her hands, just taking it all in.

"Is this where Riley saves the sheriff's life?" she asked, dreams of heroes and cowboys in her eyes.

"No," was all Duke said. "No, I'm afraid not. Those four men shot McCluskie dead without a fight. Not a man in the saloon stood to the defense of their sheriff."

"But what about Riley?" Miss Abilene interrupted.

"I'm getting there," the sheriff answered impatiently. "Riley wasn't quick enough to save McCluskie, but he was smart enough to let the four men who shot his hero dead use up all their rounds before he took a single shot. By the time it was all over, Riley had killed at least two of the gunmen and a couple of innocent bystanders."

"He was trying to save his friend," Miss Abilene insisted.

"He'd snapped," Duke replied. "He got up and walked out into the wilderness and the open plains never to be seen again. He just left."

Miss Abilene gave a curious look to her friend the sheriff, obviously shaken by the story she'd heard. Duke recognized that look quite easily since it was much the same as how he'd looked at the Captain after learning about Greasy, and he wanted to make things better.

"Now, it's okay, Abilene. But do you see why I don't want Mark taking after me?"

She nodded before answering verbally, "I get it, I do, but the kid lived, right? Riley? He didn't die."

"Oh, he's dead. Maybe not that day or maybe not the next, but he died. Riley was about to die on his own bed there, so what chance did he have in the open desert? But it doesn't matter, Abilene. What matters is that he died a changed man. He'd never so much as punched a man before that day, and

Ch. 11 | An Honest Name's Worth

then here he was killing five. Even if Mark did save my life, I don't want him living with that kind of memory. That kind of guilt," Duke trailed off.

"It stays with you."

Abilene took the sheriff's hand in hers and rubbed it softly for a minute. Duke kept looking away at nothing in particular, avoiding Abilene's gaze where he could, but she could see that look on his face all the same. Duke was hurting more than he thought appropriate for a sheriff just doing what he was hired to do.

"Look, Abilene," Sheriff Boone said, pulling his hand back from hers while straightening himself up and delivering a hearty, intentional cough. "We need to talk, and not about old ghost stories. We need to talk about that lump of silver."

"What about it?" she responded, whispering and looking around to see who else might have ears to hear. "I haven't told anybody about it yet, if that's what you're asking. I hadn't really planned to."

The sheriff wouldn't speak. Rather, he just sat there watching her.

"What?" Abilene asked again.

Still no response. Duke's glance sat squarely on her eyes, pressuring the truth out of her. He figured she would hide it, but she could only hide it for so long.

"Duke, quit fooling around. You say we need to talk, so talk. What is so dang important about that ball of silver that you're trying to stare a hole through my head?"

"Where'd you put it?" the sheriff interrogated.

"Excuse me?"

"Where'd you put it, Abilene?"

Now it was her turn to stare back in stupefied silence.

"Don't play with me, Abilene. I wake up this morning and put on my right boot, right where you saw me hide Mason's silver, and now it's gone?" Duke curtailed himself. "Where… where did you put it? What did you do with it?"

"I haven't touched your silver, Duke! How dumb are you? How dumb do you think I am? I didn't do a thing with your silver, and I won't have you talk to me like that in my own lobby!" Abilene shouted before storming out of the room and slamming her still bullet-riddled door.

Duke may be the kind of man to face down gunmen in the streets or miners on a drunken rampage, but even he knew better than to corner a woman like Abilene when she was angry. Women back east could be soft, Duke had heard some of the men say, but the ladies out west fought hard with heart and passion. They weren't the women you wanted to square off against in that sort of situation.

Still, Duke feared what stupid thing Abilene might do with what wasn't hers to start with. If she ran off with Mason's silver, that would mean Duke wouldn't have it to return to him when he inevitably came asking for it. The owner of Silver Gorge's longest lasting mine didn't get to be where he was by letting money go. If he wanted that silver back, he would be coming for it. Even if he did give it away to Duke for the extended headache that was the puzzle box, Mason would come looking for that silver, and it would be very bad if he found it with Abilene.

Duke poured himself a drink from Abilene's private stash under the bar in the corner and he gathered up his things to go. As the sheriff polished off his freebie, he let the glass clink loudly to the bar to signal his departure. It would be rude to leave without saying goodbye, he thought, smiling at how he'd just snuck a sip of Abilene's 50-year brandy for free. Duke smiled again when he reached the door and thought about how she knew exactly what that glass had been filled with just moments before.

Ch. 11 | An Honest Name's Worth

Sunlight caked the floor of Abilene's place when the heavily draped door swung open, but the brim of Duke's hat aided the transition. Otherwise he might not have seen the Wilson boy, Mark, still standing by their two horses with both reins already in hand.

"You said you were headed out to the fence line of the Faulk and McCall place, right?" Mark asked.

"Yeah, that's right."

"Thought we might ride out there together. There wasn't any type of feud when I left, so I'm pretty curious what exactly somebody told you we were doing out there."

The two men rode off out of town, silently for the most part. Mark would try to strike up conversation with Duke, but the sheriff would just rebuff his attempts and keep on moving. Wordlessly. Mark gathered the hint after a bit and stopped forcing the conversation, wondering what he'd done to garner such a cold reception, but that train of thought only occupied the boy's tongue for so long before the urge to speak once again overwhelmed his awkwardness at the pregnant pauses.

"That deputy of yours is a real ass, you know?" Mark offered freely.

"Mind your tongue, son," Duke retorted curtly.

The hurt showed on Mark's face, highlighted by the noon sun directly overhead. The McCall-Faulk border wasn't so far from town that it would take the two long to get there, but it would take longer if the pair kept slowing down to talk, and each minute was grating for Duke.

"Sorry, Duke… Sheriff. It's just that the men my dad hunts with… that's how they talk, and… I just figured you… " Mark stuttered.

"It's okay, Mark. I'm sorry," Duke apologized. "Besides. You're right."

The pair laughed off their momentary discomfort as the

sheriff shifted conversation back to matters of business.

"He does a fine job, though. He's gotten better, at least. Did I ever tell you what Mort did his third day with me?" Duke asked, meeting Mark's look with a grin. "He pulled his gun on Mr. Oscar leaving the bank, shouting at him to put the money on the ground and lay there. I guess it was my fault for not introducing the boy to the town banker, but it was worth it to see the freshly wet mud under where Aaron hit the dirt."

Mark nearly fell off his horse from laughing and Sheriff Boone let loose a meager smile at the memory of Aaron Oscar wetting himself in fear. That was a good day, he thought.

"No, but the kid's getting better. You respect him when you see him, okay Mark?" Duke suggested.

"Yes, sir," Mark replied. "It's just that… I wouldn't mind the job if there's ever an opening."

"No, I figured you wouldn't," Duke said. "Here's the thing, though, Mark. Poor Mort, he'd be all alone if I replaced him. You know he moved out here a couple years ago on some fool whim that he'd be a Wild West sheriff, shooting bad guys and stopping stagecoach robberies. He'd heard too many of the stories old cowboys tell audiences for money. If I let him go, he'd be sunk, Mark. He isn't like you. He doesn't have any family out here that could bail him out."

"He could get a job at the mine," Mark said without thinking. "It's just that I've heard they're hiring now, that's all."

"Stick with your father, Mark. You've got a good life up there. He's teaching you to work real well, and he'll help you out however he can. You mind him and follow his lead, okay?" Duke instructed. "You'll do real well that way."

Wilson's land was lush and green with the river that flowed out of the mountains. The open land headed towards McCall-Faulk territory, on the other hand, was bare and rocky except for patches of purple and yellow wildflowers and beige

Ch. 11 | An Honest Name's Worth

plains of tall grasses. Wilson had settled on the right side of the valley, so to speak, and that left precious little for the other ranchers to graze their herds on. Ranch culture was hard. And ranch culture was changing. That's what brought the Wilson boys out that way, after all. Men were building fences to cut off the land. Free-roaming cattle and horses were a liability. A lost asset. Men needed fences, didn't they?

Sheriff Boone rode in quiet for a little while, opting to let Mark talk about the art of ranching and maintaining such a vast property the rest of the way. He gave a half-hearted effort at listening, but mostly Duke just enjoyed the warm air and the open ride. Each rocky mount jutting out of the ground stood against the bluest sky a Nevada afternoon could provide. The few trees that dared to grow in isolation, offering their bare limbs as a perch for this weary bird or that thirsty lizard, dotted the ground with sinewy shadows that looked like lightning in the night sky.

And then Duke saw the tracks. He had somehow missed the first set, but they were clear now. They looked like disparate steps from several different horses given the gap of their stride, but they were clearly from one horse that must have been leaping between steps somehow. That mysterious first set stopped shy of a second set, though. These tracks were veering off the other way towards what Duke realized was a distant cave nestled in a small, rocky hill. One of those rare trees obscured the entrance, but it was certainly a cave mouth. Duke was sure of it.

How had such a prominent cave gone unnoticed until now? And who was up there? A set of tracks clearly headed off that way, and Duke was hopeful that those same tracks had not yet headed away.

If the scene at the McCall-Faulk border was as calm as Mark had insisted, Duke may just find the time to check out this open cave on the way back to town.

"So do you get what I'm saying about, Sheriff? Snakes

ain't fun, but they're great for keeping other pests away from our horses and our barns, so we just let them go as far as they leave us alone. Make sense?" Mark asked.

"Oh yeah, Mark," the Sheriff lied. "Every word."

-Chapter Twelve-
Open Plains

Mark and the sheriff rode up to the astonishingly quiet scene at the fence line between the McCall and Faulk properties just as the other brothers were finishing up a corner piece.

Not only were the two men okay with the boundary, but Mr. McCall was actually helping the Wilson boys unload lumber from the wagon. Whoever told Mort that there was some kind of dispute going on clearly lied unless there had been an earlier spat, so Duke planned on keeping his visit there short.

"I'm sorry you came out all this way for nothing, Sheriff," Mr. Faulk apologized. "Me and Lucas here haven't had much of a problem at all in the last 35 years, y'know."

"Yeah, we've been getting along just fine," Lucas McCall said in his trademark drawl. "Never had much of a problem, but Lilburn wanted to put this fence up and I helped him find the line."

Even as they talked, Mr. McCall taking twice as long to say half as much, the two men unloaded wood and worked on unwrapping the barbed wire together.

Sheriff Boone offered his greetings and his thanks

without getting off his horse, but not before he thought of something important prior to riding away.

If Lucas McCall and Lilburn Faulk had been working the soil around Silver Gorge for 35 years, they might have known something about Mason's operation when it got started.

"Tell me something, gentlemen," Duke started. "What do you boys remember about Mason's mines when they first got started?"

Lilburn and Lucas stood up straight for a moment and looked at one another as if they had to think through each other's memories before answering. Lilburn would squint and turn his head while looking at Lucas, and Lucas would nod in response to an unasked question.

Finally, it was Lucas who spoke up and told Sheriff Boone what he could remember.

"If I recall," Lucas droned, "Mason started pullin' up silver some time 'round 1862. You remember that, Lilburn?"

"I do, I do," Lilburn responded quickly. "It was about 1862 because we'd just heard about Bull Run… the second one… and I think that was the year I shot your pig, Lucas."

"You shot that pig?" Lucas asked.

"Well, yeah. Don't you remember? I found him rooting around in my fields tearing up my food. I felt bad about it because I didn't know he was yours until I saw your brand on him, so I picked him up and dropped him off on your side of the line with a note tied to his neck," Lilburn answered. "Remember?"

"I ne'er found a note, Lilburn," Lucas said back.

"Well it must've blown away, Lucas."

"Well why dint you say nothin'?"

"You never mentioned it to me, Lucas, so I just sort of

figured you didn't want to talk about it. You know, let sleeping dogs lie. I was plenty happy to let that dog stay down," Lilburn explained.

Lucas McCall gave his friend a stern look and a silent admonition before going back to discussing Mason's early days in Silver Gorge.

"Like I was saying before, Sheriff," Lilburn said. "Mason didn't really come out this way much, but I do remember a little bit about what he was like back then.

"He was skinnier, actually, but so were we," Lilburn laughed while patting Lucas hard on the belly.

Lucas just kept staring at Lilburn with eyes that said death.

"That's great, Lilburn, but do you remember anybody who was working with him?" Duke asked.

"Now that you mention it, Sheriff," Lucas piped up, "I do 'amember this one fella he always rode with. When they first moved to town, Mason and this other guy rode out here couple times looking to buy some cattle to help pull their carts. He said they were getting ready to pull plenty of metal out the ground and would need some way to carry it."

Lucas trailed off, leaving the sheriff and the now-intrigued Wilson boys a little impatient.

"What can you tell us about that other guy, man?" John asked.

"Not much," Lucas said back after a momentary, thoughtful pause. "I just 'amember one time they came out and that man paid for his cattle with some silver 'at said 'Mason Brothers Mining Company.'"

"Goodness, Lucas! That didn't seem like an important detail to tell the sheriff?" Lilburn shouted.

"Nawh. Not really. Especially since the next cattle they

bought from me, that man used several pieces of gold 'at also said Mason Brothers on 'em. I 'amember it because he gave them to me while we got water from your old well, Lilburn," Lucas replied.

"What were you doing using my well, Lucas? Ain't you got water enough of your own to use?" Lilburn inquired. "Why didn't you ask?"

"I guess it dint seem important enough to mention," Lucas retorted.

Now neither man looked real happy, but that was hardly important for what Sheriff Boone needed to know.

"You say he paid in gold? Why would he do that if they were getting so much silver out of the ground? I imagine he had to have had enough silver to pay you a thousand times over," Duke wondered out loud. "But you say it said 'Mason Brothers?' You sure?"

"I'm sure," Lucas nodded. "Mason never told me as much, but I sorta assumed that man was his brother. After a while, that man stopped coming. Shortly after that, when the town started to grow and men started moving to the mines for work, Mason stopped coming. Shame, too. That gold went a long ways."

"I can't believe you didn't tell me that Mason paid you off in gold coins all those years ago," Lilburn protested.

"And I caint believe you shot my pig," Lucas angrily tossed back.

"Well maybe if you'd built this fence 30 years ago when I asked, your pig wouldn't have gotten in my fields to get shot!"

Lucas was a generally quiet man, but the moment Lilburn crossed a line, everybody knew it. That massive farmer's frame exploded with shoulders and muscles all over as he charged at the nearby Lilburn. With a cry of rage and

Ch. 12 | Open Plains

two open paws, Lucas McCall leapt at Lilburn Faulk's throat with intent to do the man harm.

There may not have been a feud earlier that day when Sheriff Boone first heard the reports, but he made sure there was one before he left.

Lilburn was pinned under Lucas' brute strength, writhing and reaching for something to grasp. His twitching fingers finally found a rock the size of a man's foot and smashed it against Lucas' skull. The rock crumbled to pieces, likely since it was more a clod of dirt than a solid rock, but the momentary distraction was enough to get Lucas off of his friend-turned-combatant.

Caught up in the thrill of the fight, the more wiry Lilburn foolishly wrapped his arms around Lucas' waist as he tried to push the big man over. Lucas had a better base at his feet than the lanky Lilburn, so he held his ground and just brushed the dirt out of his hair before bringing a fierce elbow down in the middle of Lilburn's back.

A shrieking howl cut the desert air for miles as Lilburn fell to the ground and rolled over with a hand soothing his beleaguered back, but Lucas was intent to keep the thing going now that it had started.

Before Lucas could reach Lilburn with several crushing kicks to the side, which was clearly his next plan, Sheriff Boone hopped off his horse and tackled Lucas to the dirt. Duke was a formidable man, sure, but even his frame looked meager when Lucas got it in his mind to stretch his chest and fight. The force of the tackle worked, though, as Lucas slowly stood to his feet and Duke quietly winced at the rips and tears in his side and the bruises in his ribs.

As the two figures stood up from the desert floor and Lilburn rose to his feet, Duke accosted both men verbally.

"You two ought to be ashamed," Duke lectured. "Grown men and all just rolling around like a couple of pugs on the floor over nothing? Geez, y'all. Get over it. He shot your pig, he used your well, neither of you knew about the other for a couple of decades, and we were all better off for it. Agreed?"

Lucas and Lilburn reluctantly set their eyes back on each other and extended a friendly hand.

"You never were much help in a fight," Lucas chided his friend with a smirk.

"And you never let anybody else get in a punch," Lilburn grinned.

"What's that old saying about fences and neighbors?" Lucas asked jokingly. "I think we might need thissun more than we thought."

The two old men laughed and got back to work while the Wilson boys just watched with blank confusion covering their eyes.

Duke rolled his eyes and leaned over to grab his hat up off the ground, but he couldn't justify the pain of breathing that came with stumping over like that, so he just stayed there with his hands on his hips while standing at a shallow angle. Noticing how his mentor was hurting, Mark came over and picked up the old hat off the ground before it could blow away and he put it in Duke's hands.

What was that man thinking taking on Lucas like that, Sheriff Boone asked himself. He wasn't sure if he meant Lilburn or himself, though, since neither one had any business getting in a fight with the only man to ever get banned from the Rusty Spittoon and then summarily get himself invited back in by threatening to beat up the bar keeper. Really. Taking on Lucas when he got angry was foolhardy for most any man, but even less so for a man who still ought to be in bed from his last one-sided fight.

Sheriff Boone dusted off his pants and his hat after thanking Mark for his kindness, and then he simply got back

Ch. 12 | Open Plains

up on his horse to leave. In most cases after a fight like that, Duke may have said something or warned the two men to be more careful. With Lucas and Lilburn, though, Sheriff Boone just figured that those two old friends would probably fight again and that they'd probably get together for steaks afterward no matter what.

Or pork chops.

Now that the unexpected and initially nonexistent fight was over with, Duke had time to go check out the cave he had spotted earlier with Mark. He had been careful not to point the place out to Mark, and he was even more cautious when it came time to head back out there. Nobody was following him and nobody seemed to be anywhere around. It was one of those lucky times in the desert surrounding Silver Gorge that Duke could actually be alone.

"Where had that gold come from?" Duke asked himself aloud. When nobody was around, Duke enjoyed taking advantage of the solitude. It was sometimes easier to work things out that way. "He was a silver miner, right? And that's all they had in those mines. After all, nobody's ever found gold here. Or at least that's what Mason… has… told us."

Duke's words trailed off as he realized that evening was quickly approaching and finding that cave might have just gotten more difficult. A red sun started to drip down the sands and the rocks at the farthest western horizon, but it was still bright enough for Duke to ride by. It was not bright enough for Duke to see a distant cave, though.

Was it not wholly possible that Mason had lied about the mine, Duke wondered as he struggled to keep his head on either finding the cave or finding the truth. Perhaps there was gold down there after all, but why would he lie?

"What are you hiding, Mason? What is it you've got down in that mine?" Duke asked himself aloud.

Was it gold that Zeke found? Is that what drove him

to… well, was that all it was? Duke may not have been an expert, but he knew that gold never made a man's body fall to mush on the floor of a saloon.

"No, there has to be more. But the gold. How does that play a part? It has to be involved somehow, right?"

Talking to himself, Duke almost missed the distant sound of a gunshot. He somewhat registered the distinct puff of a gun blast muffled by distance, but he heard pretty cleanly the clink of metal on rock that hit about ten yards to his left. Whoever was shooting out there was shooting at him, and it would be best to keep on moving.

Duke's horse had clearly heard the sound, as well, and it spooked her up a bit. Sheriff Boone managed to hold his reins despite her hard rearing, and the pair went off chaotically to the right of where they had been just a second before. A darkened hill stood at their back and was the likely cover for their current assailant, a mystery figure with a mystery aim. Well, clearly their aim was to lay into Duke Boone, but the reason behind that was the question.

It was a question that the sheriff would worry about some other time if he survived this outing. Duke figured he was getting out of the shooter's range with haste as his beautiful horse put out the speed needed to make their escape happen. A few more cracks shattered the desert silence to Duke's back, but he also spotted the poofs of dust where each bullet fell harmlessly to the ground at either side. The shooter had better range than Duke had expected, but his accuracy was suspect at best, much to Duke's delight. Each shot was more off-center than the last as Duke kept getting farther and farther out, and it seemed he would get away.

Another familiar sound reached Duke's ears, then, when the yips and yells of mounted gunmen chased the sheriff from a distance.

Riflemen up in the hills could lose their target, but guns

Ch. 12 | Open Plains

on horseback tended to make a better chase. As the lone hill fell away at the sheriff's back, the horsemen who came from it gained with ease.

Duke's weakness had always been enduring horses with a strong build rather than the sleek and the quick. In most cases, such a choice would be to his benefit. If he could stay ahead of their guns, it would be today. If not, their burst of speed might be enough to put an end to the sheriff's tenure as a gainfully employed and living lawman.

He had been reluctant to look behind him, relying instead on the sound their hoof beats made to inform the sheriff that it seemed there were three men making chase. Their steady procession of shots told Duke that the men each had a couple of quick-firing revolvers, likely with another already loaded and ready to go should the first set run out. Everything pointed to one conclusion: these men were well funded and probably working on Mason's behalf.

Sending out hired guns was an odd change of strategy for Mason, if they were in fact his. It seemed a bit bold and hurried, almost as if Mason had a deadline he was trying to meet, but that was another question Duke figured he would need to stow away for if he ever got out of this scrape.

Duke's horse huffed and wheezed as the sheriff forced her to run harder than he ever had, but he knew she was strong enough to make that pace last. The two of them had been together long enough to know when they were able to keep going and when they needed to stop, and both the horse and the rider sensed the urgency of making a getaway right now.

Three riders gained on the sheriff, step after step coming closer than the ones before. Duke pressed harder and urged his horse to beat the dirt under hoof, but she could only gain so much. She could hold the pace for a good while, but none of that would matter soon. His guns were heavy and unreliable if not in a straight forward shot, but it was time for

Duke to take some risks. If nothing else, it would keep their eyes off the ground and on his gun.

With a gun over his shoulder, Duke pulled the trigger and let a shot ring in the general direction of his pursuers. Their shots had been inaccurate so far, but they were close enough that he could hear the whizzing of bullets. Now that his gun was out and their focus was divided, the bullets coming towards him were drifting. It was working.

About that time, Duke noticed something coming up in front of him. He saw on the ground the tracks he had planned on following earlier in the day, the ones that directed him towards the cave.

If the cave was occupied by who Duke thought it was, then this might be a stupid plan. Then again, the tracks were old. Perhaps the Scarecrow had dropped in and left. Or maybe he would be there and would object to the men riding towards his hideout with guns drawn. Duke felt like he could make the cave and hold out against three gunmen, but his chances in the open field were looking grim and slim, so the sheriff made the only move he could. He turned off in the direction of a distant cave that might or might not hold some very bad news for him, realizing that potential bad news was better than certain calamity.

Duke veered hard to the right, directing his horse exactly down the path in front of him. As his horse's steps kicked up the dust of a still-visible trail, the men behind him had no idea that there was a plan in place. All they could assume, Duke thought, was that he was running scared.

Off to his right, the sheriff noticed cracked dirt over a wide area. It made no sense for the ground to crack like this here with the rains they had had not long ago, but the gun shots at his back were more pressing to Sheriff Boone than meteorological conundrums. Duke let another bullet loose from his chamber, and a combination of that sound and the dust cloud his horse was leaving distracted the men behind

Ch. 12 | Open Plains

Sheriff Boone enough to miss the obvious pattern that he had spotted.

With a terrifying squeal and the frightful neighing of a broken horse, all echoing as if from a deep tunnel, Duke realized that one of his tails was no longer a problem. The ground beneath the man back and to the right had given way to some kind of sinkhole, and now there were just two.

"There's something wrong with the ground here," one of the fallen man's compatriots shouted to the other. "Watch your step!"

"Of course there's something wrong with the ground, you moron," the man responded. "Jim just got swallowed by the earth! That's not normal!"

"Just keep shooting!" the one right behind Duke yelled right before the other one complied and they got their guns back up.

Duke realized what it was, as he had the advantage of seeing the ground in front of him. The shallower ground must have dried quicker in the sun, he observed. The Scarecrow, or whoever made these tracks, must have also noticed as the trail weaved subtly through the spaces of cracked earth.

It was harder to see the destination with gunshots gaining on him and a precarious trail to follow, but Duke finally looked up and saw that he was closing on the cave he sought after. It was just another few minute's ride ahead if his horse could keep the pace up, and he would have to climb a rocky hill, but it seemed possible.

Just then, the man to his left let out a furious cry that told Duke just one man remained. He risked looking back this once just to make sure, but his ears had heard true. The only man left at his back was the one who rode in the middle, the one who seemed to be in charge.

Duke started taking liberties with the trail as he would weave closer and closer to the cracked earth, and the man followed as expected. Each time he tried this stunt, though, Duke lost some ground as the man's horse regained speed from the turns quicker. But Duke had also noticed that the man stopped shooting. He must have been getting low and was waiting to just run the sheriff down for an easier, more certain kill.

The safe path veered hard to the left through a valley of treacherous dirt, a turn which both horses navigated successfully. Something up ahead filled Duke with both terror and dread, though, after the trail turned back towards the cave. The supposed path of safety, the one he was following now, ended in a blockade of the shallow, fissured ground. There was no exit, no turn. The only escape was to the back, but that path was clearly blocked.

"I hope you can make this count," Duke said to his horse as they reached the end of safety.

With a silent prayer, the sheriff urged his horse to jump over nothing. It must have looked like foolishness to the man behind, because he kept his horse on the ground with disastrous results. Every step of the horse's hoof loosened the baked soil, and where Duke's horse landed did the same. A wide swath of dirt started to give and shift, indicating that a bridge of earth was ready to collapse. Duke could see the end of the line up ahead, and he could still hear the other man's ride trailing him closely. It was simply a matter of reaching that mark first and things should work out just fine.

He was ten steps away, then five, then just one. As Duke's horse cleared the dirt that cascaded downwards, he heard two sounds that gave him a jolt. The first was the unmistakable blast of a rifle as a shot tore the air just over Duke's head. The second was a horse neighing as it fell, absent the cries of a demised rider.

Over his shoulder, the confused and relieved Duke Boone could see that a veritable canyon had claimed the body of his third and final pursuer's horse, but he felt that

Ch. 12 | Open Plains

something else had taken the life of the man upon that horse.

At that moment, a voice called out to Duke Boone and claimed his attention from atop the hill leading to the cliff.

"You want to tell me what you're doing approaching my home, son?" a gray but clean old man shouted, a rifle resting on his shoulder with the barrel pointed straight at the sheriff now caught off-guard.

The figure wore slick, black clothes that Duke had never seen before, but they seemed fine and made the man appear wealthy for a cave dweller. He stood tall upon the rocks, perhaps more than six feet tall, but it was hard to tell as this new figure stood so much higher than the sheriff.

"Speak up, now. I'm not generally patient with my ammunition as your apparent enemy just learned," the mystery gentleman said.

Duke had no idea if it would best suit him to be honest about his profession, as outland people like this one had a reputation for mistrusting and despising the law, but this man seemed different. He wore a fine appearance and spoke with authority, unlike most of the yokels who had shirked any form of society, and he clearly knew how to shoot. Truth it was.

"My name's Duke Boone. I'm the sheriff of Silver Gorge, Nevada, a town not far from here. I was pursuing a fugitive named the Kansas Scarecrow when these three men attacked me. All three have now died, it seems, but they have a sharp-shooter up in the hills a few miles back and I would appreciate it if you let me stay with you a while so that they don't send anyone else after me," Duke pleaded, all before taking a breath.

"Please, sir. Let me in."

Duke's words affected the man, though, as he dropped the barrel of his gun and gave the sheriff a sideways eye, opening his shoulders and letting go of any further suspicion.

"Sheriff?" the man said, as if addressing a lost, familiar friend. "Why didn't you say so? Come on up. I have quite the surprise for you."

-Chapter Thirteen-

Into the Cave

Damp walls and puddled floors of this stranger's cave were noticeably more hospitable than the dusty sands just outside, but Duke Boone held his breath and his pistol tightly as he was still unsure what to think of his host who had apparently lived in the desert for quite some time. Trifles and trinkets were scattered along the floor in varying states of neglect. Some objects looked as if they had always been in one spot whereas others were polished and cleaned with great care.

The sheriff saw toys and pens strewn about with a couple of guns that looked much older than they should given their relatively recent invention. In an opposite pile, Duke saw what looked like a native ornamental piece, but he was a bit hazy on what tribe it belonged to. He had dealt with many of the locals several years ago before the cavalry rode in and dispersed most of them to the mountains beyond Silver Gorge, but none of them had ever worn pieces with such strange blue glass beads and burnt-orange threads. Yet, here it stood, resting upon the chest of some human facsimile carved out of wood.

"Pardon the mess, please, Sheriff," the figure said, looking over his shoulder back towards Duke. "You've, uh…come at a bad time. I haven't had a chance to reorganize yet."

"What is all this stuff? Do you deal with native tribes very often?" the sheriff inquired.

"I used to. Before they were all kicked out, this was one of their favorite posts to stop in and trade. Or at least they would try to trade. I wasn't generally very intent on parting with my things," the man went on.

"You seem to have plenty of things to trade here," Duke added, almost accusatorily.

"How long have you lived in Silver Gorge, Sheriff? About, what, 25 or 30 years?"

Stunned at the man's accuracy, Duke nodded slowly.

"Yeah, that's right. I was with one of the earlier groups out here. The mine had already started up, but there wasn't much else. I started as sheriff about 15 years after," Duke answered.

"And would you say you've acquired some extra stuff in that time? Maybe things you hadn't planned on keeping?"

"Yeah, I guess I would say so," Duke agreed.

"So have I," the man offered as he stopped walking forward and turned to face Duke before dramatically turning back and easing forward. "I've lived in this cave for many years, you know. This place is my home. Always has been, always will be. As you've certainly seen, a man can acquire plenty of things when he stays put long enough," the man mused.

Duke and his counterpart crossed paths with several offshoot tunnels and apparent walkways back into the deeper recesses of the cave system they were in, and the air grew cooler still and more comfortable as they kept going. At times, the sheriff swore he was walking down, and at others he assumed they were walking up. The cave had a way of

Ch. 13 | Into the Cave

twisting Duke's mind, he felt, as the sunlight and the shade both seemed to stay at his back and the occasionally sharp winds often eked out a gentle sigh from deeper still.

"The Ancient Ones called this place Naachama Haaniya-sh'amegani. Loosely translated, it means 'The place eternal,' I think. Something like that," the man explained, looking back towards Duke as if to answer the question he knew was coming.

Each wonder at his feet brought about more questions and each new revelation made Duke more curious than the last as to just what kind of place he had stepped foot into. It was an entirely new world for him, this wondrous cave of hidden beauty, but he was still distracted by the world outside. There was a mission and a man, and Duke realized that this long-time resident of the cave and the desert lands might know a thing or two that could help him clear up some old mysteries.

After all, if the man could spout off mystical native lore with such blessed indifference, maybe he could also offer some insights on more present happenings…

"You say you've lived here for many years, right?" Duke asked.

"That's putting it lightly," the gentleman agreed. Sort of.

"So what do you know about Mason and his men? Do you know about how they got the mine started?" Duke pressed.

"Not much. I know that my native friends weren't real happy with the way that he and his brother came in and made a mess of things…" the man said, losing Duke's attention entirely at the mention of a brother.

"So he did have a brother," Duke mumbled.

"Truth be told, I'm not the one to tell you all you need

177

to know about Mason. I was never a first-hand observer as it is, but I still think I can help you," the man grinned as he and the sheriff stopped in front of a wooden door that read "Private." Duke stood facing the man who held a torch in his left hand and the door handle in his right. The two just stared at each other for a moment, letting the pause drag out a bit longer.

"I thought you'd be taller," the man said to the sheriff with a smile.

"Just open the door, sir," Duke encouraged with a hand at the ready on his gun.

With a nod and a wave, the fellow pulled the door out. It was too dark for Duke to see in at first, but he shortly spotted a surprising sight as soon as the gentleman came around the door with his torch.

"If I'm not mistaken, you two boys have already been introduced," the man pointed out, indicating the missing fugitive bound and gagged in a ratty corner of a dirt-carved hovel. "Sheriff, meet your Scarecrow."

Wails of guttural screams and abominable curses spilled forth from the rag that held the scarecrow's tongue in place at both the sheriff and the stranger who stood over him, one smiling and the other sorely confused.

"How did you pull this one off, Caveman?" Duke shouted with amused relief. "You mean to tell me you've been keeping the Kansas Scarecrow in your closet? For how long?"

"Just a couple days, really. He rolled in here with his guns out thinking he could overtake me pretty handily, but I can hold my own," the fellow responded grinning. "Caveman? Did you just call me Caveman?"

"Sorry about that. It slipped out. I'm not usually a nickname kind of guy," Duke apologized.

"No, it's fine. I like it," Caveman acknowledged,

Ch. 13 | Into the Cave

something like nostalgia peeking through his toothy smile.

So the sheriff and the caveman stood and watched the imprisoned fugitive for a few minutes longer before either one spoke again. After all, there aren't many words to share over a prisoner that could be uttered over a coffee.

"What should we do with him?" Caveman asked.

"Leave him. I'll pick him up before I go," Duke answered.

The scarecrow's eyes widened perceptibly as he started to fear that he might actually be left behind in a rocky cabinet, though he held out a small hope that his time of private incarceration was done now that the sheriff had arrived.

"Alright. Sounds good to me," Caveman said as he closed the door despite his unwilling guest's muffled protests. "Tea?"

"Sure," Duke agreed.

The sheriff's trip out of town had not been a complete waste. Duke had in fact located the gunman and learned that someone certainly wanted him dead. He could surmise that the someone was, in all likelihood, Mason, though he was still unsure as to what turn of events had forced the passive mining boss towards a more aggressive state.

Caveman led the way for Duke once more to a round room carved from the rocks adorned with a tapestry of fanciful reds and yellows and sapphires displaying what the sheriff could only assume were scenes from history, though they were unfamiliar to him. Around the room were shelves, also carved into the rock, each one flowing over with wrapped and bound books. Many of the shelves were full, though a few were haphazardly vacant with a couple volumes here and there. Many of the titles were familiar to Duke, though just as many or more were foreign to him. Some literally so, titled in languages he was unable to read.

As libraries go, Duke had not seen one so well stocked since he was a boy in Virginia. His father had taken him to the University to see their stockpiles of literature and science, but those white columns of Monticello were vastly different from the rutty enclaves that protected these dusty volumes. While most of the books were scattered without preference or apparent organization, a few notable specimens were shelved with care upon prominent displays, one being what appeared to be the collected works of Edgar Allen Poe.

The Caveman warbled on about the number of books he had and how they were from all different cultures and with strange meanings within, but the book of Poe arrested Duke's eyes. While his host was looking off the other way towards a stack of what he said was biographies, Duke wandered over and picked up the volume. It was purple with silver twine laced in the cover to spell out the title and the author's name. The fabric book cover, the texture of small burlap, felt fresh and smooth in Duke's hands. As he opened the book, he could smell the wood fibers in the pages as if he was still standing in the halls of learning on the plains of Virginia. While the mud and the soil surrounding him should have overpowered the smell of a book, the earthy pungence was made secondary whenever Duke opened one, eliciting a noticeable change in the air.

On the inside cover of this particular book read an inscription, addressed to a young woman, presumably the previous owner's daughter: "May your dreams be bright and your fancies dark, my sweet Annabelle Lee, as you travel through this world without me. From your father to my dearest Autu–"

"What are you doing?" Caveman interrupted, snatching the book from Duke's hands before he could finish reading the inscription. "Don't touch anything in this room."

As the obsessive librarian replaced the book of Poe on its stand, he added, "Least of all this book. It's… it's my

Ch. 13 | Into the Cave

favorite."

"I'm sorry, it's just that... I grew up hearing those stories. My own father would read Poe to me at night while I heard cannon fire in the distance. It helped me sleep," Duke said. "It's been many years since I've heard a word of Poe. We don't really have an abundance of reading material in Silver Gorge."

After a moment of watchful concern, Duke decided to prod a little harder.

"Who was she? Was she someone special?"

"You might say that. As a matter of fact, she was special... in a manner of speaking," Caveman sighed, his eyes wandering distantly. "Now come. I promised you tea, didn't I? There's none of that in here. Just books, and those have their own stories to tell. I've read all of them several times over, anyhow. I want to hear your story while I make the tea. You're a good Virginia boy, right, Sheriff? So I assume you'll want sugar in your tea?"

His kitchen was connected by a single door to the library, so the pair of men stepped out of the round reading room and into the more cubical kitchen area. There was a wood stove in the far corner by a barred wooden door, and there was what looked like an icebox on the opposite wall from there. None of what Duke saw in this cave made any sense as such luxuries were uncommon for even the well-to-do residents of Silver Gorge such as the Wilson family, but here was a desert rambler with his own elegant niche of the world quite literally pulled from the rocks that formed a seemingly endless cave.

Duke took a seat and told Caveman all about his life and how he had moved out west from Virginia when the war started. He told the man about what the trip west was like for a young boy without a family and how he had met up with another boy named Zeke. The two became friends and started to build a life on the frontier together until, surely, the other one got married and started a family. Family living had never been much of a goal for Duke, he told Caveman, but that permanently single designation was met with a laugh from the man making tea with water he had poured from a pump.

As annoyed as Boone was at the man's insistence that he would enjoy family life some day, he appreciated being able to move on from the story of his boyhood friend. It was easy to talk about the time that Zeke had convinced Duke to put a dead rattlesnake in the cook's wagon while they were somewhere near the Kansas border just to see how loudly the fat man would scream, and it was fun to bring up the time before he became sheriff that a cloaked Duke and Zeke rode a pair of black horses through town while singing old funeral dirges just to scare the religious folks. Those stories helped, Duke thought. They needed to be told. They were wanting to be told.

It was the newer stories, though, he could not bring up. Duke figured that his host would not be very interested in the way Zeke had burst into the sheriff's office a few years before with his son by the collar for stealing a whiskey barrel, nor would he care much for the time just a few months back when Zeke came tumbling through the door shouting for justice. The man may take an interest in the way that Zeke… died… but that was one story Duke swore never to tell.

"So you've heard my story," Duke said as he sipped on a perfect cup of sweet tea. "What's your deal, Caveman?"

"That about sums it up, to be honest," he answered. "I've lived in this cave for as long as anyone can really remember and that's about it. It's home."

"What do you do? Do you hunt? Do you fish? Do you build things and sell them to passing travelers?" Duke asked before giving way to a lengthy pause that neither man knew how to handle. "I just… I don't get you, you know? All this. How any of it makes sense."

Ch. 13 | Into the Cave

"It's my home, Sheriff. Just like that town of Silver Gorge is yours. I'm sure there are things there that would seem abnormal to a man like me who's been living off by himself for some time. As for loneliness, well, I used to trade with the natives nearby, as you know. They were good men, mostly, but a few violent tribes ran many of them off before those who settled in the middle of nowhere nearby decided the stragglers needed to be dealt with the same way," Caveman concluded.

"That's an awfully sympathetic view you have of the natives," Sheriff said, defending himself from what he presumed to be a subtle jab at the townspeople and folks like them.

Caveman sat back and thought for a minute before answering slowly and deliberately.

"When you've lived as long as I have and you've seen as much as I have, you learn to be sympathetic towards most people. I saw my friends killed, Sheriff," he said evenly without a hint of breaking his tone. "But you know the crazy part? After I saw my friends die, I befriended the men who killed them. Because they were good men, too. And then those men were killed, and I befriended the men who killed them.

"Tell me, Sheriff. When you left Virginia at the brink of war, how much did you hear of the way they ravaged your home? Did you know just how badly your state was being destroyed by the federal government?"

"We heard bits and pieces. By the time I settled out here, the war was already started and people were dying, but there wasn't much in the way of steady information coming out here then. It took weeks, months to hear news. The South had been surrendered for a week before we knew anything of it, and that was the fastest word would travel back then. The wire services help, of course, but there wasn't much we could rely on then," Duke explained to a man who doubtlessly knew all there was to know about that anyway.

"But you know now?"

"Yes, I know now."

"Does that hurt you? Do you burn for the men who died in the war?"

"Of course. Lives lost are lives lost," Duke said. "I never had a leaning towards the cause, you know, but it was home once. To know what they did to it… that hurt me."

"But not anymore?"

"No, not anymore. Virginia is growing and rebuilding. Things are better there now, better than they were," Duke answered.

"It's like that with my friends. Time makes men better, you see. Time makes life better. It would do me no good to shun every man who came behind another. So I move on. I live."

"You make friends with killers," Duke said evenly, though his eyes were downcast in a questioning glance.

"That's funny coming from you," Caveman laughed. "I made friends with the men they were after they were killers, knowing full well what they had done and what made them who they were. Blessed is the man who knows his friends fully. Pitiable is the man who knows his allies for just what they appear to be. Remember that."

Duke stared at the Caveman, unsure of how to take him. He talked of friendships with savages and killers like it was normal. Preferred, even. Still, there was a romance about him, this cave dweller. He had lived by himself, away from society for a lifetime, but he seemed as urbane and suave as the well-to-do back east. Yet he carried himself with an earnestness that was rare, even for common men. Whenever Duke spoke, Caveman was watching him tightly, listening with intent to understand. That was a rare trait for most men the sheriff dealt with.

Ch. 13 | Into the Cave

"And you can call me Connor, by the way."

"That's fine, Caveman," Duke retorted, leaving his host with that same grin he had shown earlier. It was as if Connor was reacting to a silent joke only he understood each time Duke said something. As if Connor remembered an earlier conversation just then.

Though Duke enjoyed annoying Connor with the new nickname he had discovered for him, that earnestness and sincerity with which the man operated in all facets impressed the sheriff to a point where he felt he could trust him. He had already shared much of his life story with the man, so what more could he hold back if pressed? Or even without his asking, Duke thought he could tell this stranger many things, that whatever secrets he shared would remain sealed.

"Listen, Sheriff," Connor said while trying to capture Duke's gaze. "I know you're supposed to take this man back to Silver Gorge, and I know you're not going to listen to me when I tell you this, but don't."

Duke was surprised that the man in the cave would so boldly ask him to forego his responsibility to bring the Scarecrow to justice. After all, taking him into town to a real jail would be a far sight better than leaving him in the closet of a strange cave in the desert.

"Why should I not? That's my job, you know. To take this man to jail. Let him face a trial for all he's done. He's… he's killed good men," Duke responded.

"I know he has, believe me. He should face justice, and he will, but you really shouldn't return to Silver Gorge. Not right now," Connor vaguely hinted.

"What do you know? What aren't you telling me?"

Duke prepared to stand with the thought of curtly explaining the position that Connor had found himself in, but a great crash pulled their attention to the closet in the hall. Somehow, though Duke had no clue as to exactly how, the

Scarecrow had broken loose.

"Got that gun handy?" Duke asked loudly.

"Yep," Connor replied.

"Grab it. Now."

Both men jumped from the table and abandoned their still warm tea for a more pertinent situation.

Duke felt that he was at a disadvantage in the cave since he was new to the surroundings and the Scarecrow had spent at least a couple of days there with Connor, but his fears were relieved when he heard footsteps pattering off deeper into the cave, away from the direction that he figured was the entrance. The Scarecrow was lost and may or may not have still had his hands bound.

Just inside the door, which the Scarecrow had clearly kicked open as evidenced by the broken boards at the bottom and the fact that the top hinge was loose but still attached to the beam, there was a long strand of cloth that had been used to bind his feet. There was not, however, the rag that had bound his hands together.

The deeper Duke strode beyond the closet door, the rarer it was that the sheriff could rely on his eyes more than his ears. He would occasionally hear two sets of steps, though he was unable to tell which was the Scarecrow's and which was Connor's. If he were quiet and he held his breath, Duke felt like he could hear the Scarecrow grunting and writhing as he tried to untie the strips of cloth around his wrists, huddled in some dark corner of the cave hoping neither man would see or hear him. There was the shuffling of a body on the rock floor and then the scraping of rags on a stalactite, a sound like a drunk man's boots shuffling along a gravel road.

Uniquely damp air filled Duke's lungs, the dank and heavy air in this part of the cave betraying just how far they were from the arid desert climate that surrounded them for miles. Sheriff Boone was not the only one who could hear

Ch. 13 | Into the Cave

footsteps, he imagined, as the Scarecrow would alternate his attempts at running and cutting the fabric handcuffs. He could have run to meet the Scarecrow, grab him before he had hands with which to fight back, but Duke preferred a steady, measured approach. His hands were his guide upon the walls as he seemed to find shelves with various objects stacked upon them, veiled by the darkness with the only light remaining near the sheriff's feet as he stepped. When the walls were not plastered with shelves, Duke rubbed the moist granite of the cavern and wiped the grime off on his pants.

A ways ahead of him, Duke heard the clink of a metal door against stone, but it was the sound of a door closing. The Scarecrow had managed to get the unseen door open without alerting the sheriff, and he knew that Connor had heard it as well with both of their steps converging on that spot. Duke's friend, the Caveman, had ducked out of some seemingly hidden space up ahead where the stone walls separated and let in some other pathway, and now the two men were ultimately moving in on their prey together. As the gap between them quickly filled in, Duke placed a soft hand on Connor's back to soundlessly announce his presence.

Calmly and instantly, without a twinge of panic, Connor reached out and opened the bulky, reflective door. Light glinted off the door, betraying its polished silver surface, and the two men managed to lightly step through the portal even more surreptitiously than the Scarecrow had. Duke made sure to place a hand on the door behind him to prevent himself from making that same mistake, but he knew the effort was largely wasted as soon as he stepped into the room.

Every footfall reverberated off the distant, domed walls of their current spot. There were other doors, Duke imagined, but this chamber was so magnificent and vacuous that it was not likely the Scarecrow had found any of them. Drops of moisture, slowly adding length to the stalactites at a rate of an inch every century or so, spelled out just how wide and hopeless this abyssal room really was. Sound went on for days, it seemed, yet it returned to the creator with a richness unlike the usual, natural echoes.

This room was the grand feature of Connor's cave, Duke imagined, though he was entirely unsure of what could be found therein as not a single ray of light advanced beyond that silver door. It could just feature more trinkets like those that lined the walls of the cave outside this glorious, potentially vacant room. For all Duke knew, a great chasm swallowed up everything more than ten feet into this tomb of earth and rock. It was black. Simple as that.

Grunts and shuffles could still be heard from the Scarecrow, though they did little good for Duke in locating this fellow in such a gaping chamber. Each sound he made glanced and reflected off of disparate angles in the rocks, making it nearly impossible to pinpoint which stone was closest to the point of origin. Before long, the Scarecrow might just have his hands and legs free, an unencumbered prisoner obviously being somewhat more problematic.

Though the unwilling, involuntary moans of a labored hand did not give away the Scarecrow's position, the next sound Duke heard did a great deal of good in pinpointing just where this murderer was. From a place slightly below him and to the left, Duke heard a glimmer of tiny metallic fragments scatter across the rocks. Though they could have just fallen on their own will, the twinkling of bouncing coins was unmistakable and was almost guaranteed to be a sign of human interference. The Scarecrow was right there.

The spot was perhaps just 20 feet away, but the darkness between them provided untold horrors for Duke, though Connor seemed to have little trouble navigating the room without use of his eyes. Or at least he stepped more confidently than Duke did.

This time it was Connor who put a hand on Duke's back as he patted the sheriff's right shoulder blade twice before drawing a line on the man's duster, indicating perhaps

Ch. 13 | Into the Cave

that he would go off to the right and come up on the other side of their mutual problem. With an emboldened approach and something of a plan, even if the plan had been formulated without words or signs in a silent, invisible meeting, Duke opted to step forward and address the captive directly.

"Scarecrow," Duke offered. "There's no way out of this for you."

There was no response, but Duke could hear the Scarecrow's gnawing grow more and more furious.

"So you get your hands free. Then what?" Duke shouted.

"I thought I might start by ripping your throat out!" the suddenly maniacal Scarecrow shouted in response. "I'll tear your head from your neck and I'll use it as a canteen!"

Duke was stunned at the show of savagery he'd heard from the usually refined Scarecrow, but it gave him an idea. The room's darkness had bothered Duke in that he was unable to see, but that darkness was likely doing more to the Scarecrow than any of them.

"You know, a torch might help you with those hands. It must be hard to undo when you can't see what's holding you, right?" Duke said.

Scarecrow growled, and Duke kept talking.

"I would've found you by now, Scarecrow, but I can't see a thing in this place. I could be standing right next to you, really. You'd have no idea. I'd have no idea. Wouldn't that be something?" Duke teased.

"Aaaagh! Shut up!" was all the Scarecrow could muster.

"For all you know, we might not be alone in here. There's no telling who all could be stuck in here with us," Duke continued. "Who could be walking up to you at this moment. Who could be watching you, somehow able to see you in this darkness. Who could be upon you right now!"

"No! No! Get off of me! Get away from me!" the Scarecrow screamed.

At that last entreaty, Duke heard the emaciated body of the Kansas Scarecrow drop to the floor and whimper just as a broken glass rattles its pieces about on the ground for a few moments.

Connor had found the Scarecrow, somehow picked him up, and carried him back out the metal door, dragging him headlong into the light with Duke providing support on one side. The Scarecrow writhed occasionally, weakly attempting to shake off his captors, but Duke and Connor had the murderer by the scruff of his neck just about.

"No. No, you can't make me go! I won't go out there! Not in the dark!" the Scarecrow moaned pitiably. "You can't get me out there in that desert! I'm staying here!"

"We'll wait until morning and then we're gone, Scarecrow," Duke informed him. "If we leave at first light, we should have no problem hitting Silver Gorge by the evening at worst."

Duke and Connor shambled along with a spiritually concussed madman slumping between them, his feet generally scraping along the stones more than stepping.

"I really wish you would wait before heading back to Silver Gorge, Sheriff. It's not going to be safe there for you, and it won't be safe for him, either," Connor reiterated. "It may be your job, but who is to protect the city of Silver Gorge with you dead?"

"And who's to protect it if I'm not there in the first place?" Sheriff Boone responded.

"Point taken," Connor acknowledged, sighing defeatedly.

As the two wandered back through the halls of this

Ch. 13 | Into the Cave

indecipherable cave system, dragging their marginally comatose prisoner, the Scarecrow made a clumsy grab at Duke's gun. It was a valiant effort for a man with no discernable cognitive function at the time and hardly any control of his hands, but it was ultimately doomed to failure. Scarecrow let his hands fall a little, and as he stumbled forward while grabbing the men's hips for balance, his right hand drooped low enough to touch the handle on the sheriff's revolver. Duke instantly threw both his arms behind the fool and tossed him to the ground, forcing the Scarecrow to spill out every speck of dust and each item buried in his pockets.

Both men laughed uproariously as the mighty Kansas Scarecrow flopped to the earth-crusted floor face first and splayed his suddenly free hands out on the paved ground as glimmering gold coins shined in the meager light dripping through the tunnel they presently occupied. It had been fruitless and unwise for the still bound Scarecrow to grab at the gold coins Connor had settled away in his expansive catacombs, Duke thought, as there was no way he could have expected to leave with it all intact. Then again, neither man had noticed the veritable treasure walking beside them until this Scarecrow, staggering like a foal at birth, let the coins fall to the ground so carelessly.

Still laughing from the comedy that was the Kansas Scarecrow, now demoted to blithering mess, Duke stooped over and picked up one of these unexpected gold coins. He rubbed it in his hands and felt the fine texture, along with the perfect shine that comes with new things in the desert. It was likely a lovely coin, Duke thought, and it would probably be worth a great bit more if he had more of them.

Sheriff Boone shook his head and banished such temptations without raising much alarm, but the meager light eking into this deep portion of the cave system finally managed to illuminate the words on each coin to a legible degree: Mason Brothers Mining Company.

"I can't believe he was dumb enough to try and reach your gun, Duke," Connor joked. "And he's supposed to be some great outlaw? They must've fallen off a step the last few decades if this man is the cream of the crop."

"He wasn't thinking straight," a distracted Duke replied. "Tell me, Connor. You still got that rifle on you?"

"Yeah, sure," he responded. "What's wrong?"

Almost whipping up a wind around him, the sheriff whirled around and pulled back the hammer on his own revolver in one fluid motion, catching Connor very clearly by surprise.

"Why don't you drop it right there?"

-Chapter Fourteen-
A Toast to Friends, New and Old

Connor instinctively let the rifle hit the ground and threw his hands up in a sign of clear surrender, fearing the trigger-finger of a man who was just moments ago a presumed ally. Duke kept a bead on this age spot right between Connor's eyes if not slightly higher and to the right, refusing to deviate from that small target in the slightest.

"What are you doing, Sheriff? There is a murderer laying at your feet and that's what you want to do? Start waving weapons in my face?" Connor objected.

"Tell me about the coins, Connor," Duke demanded.

Concern and surprise quickly replaced the confusion on Connor's face, or what Duke could see of it in the escaping light. Duke imagined what lies this brigand must be conjuring by reading the change of expression in his eyes. Men caught in a lie are like snakes trapped in the sand. Given enough time they'll find a way around the problem, but the quickest answer usually means attacking the obstacle head on.

"They're relics. Could be 25, 30 years old. I don't know. I know an Apache fellow traded me a sack of coins he said he stole off a wagon train for some food and ammunition a while back. I never had much use for the coins, so they just sat in that bag your friend over there apparently got his hands into,"

Connor said.

"Liar!" Duke shouted. "These coins look brand new, like they just came out of the mint."

"Maybe it's the dry air," Connor protested calmly.

Duke resumed his tightened stance on this man he thought would be a friend, crushed at the immensity of this betrayal.

"You warned me about heading back to Silver Gorge because you know Mason wants to come here and finish us both off, me and him, right? Those men out there were your guards, but they failed. So now it's your turn," Duke explained, filling in the blanks of his audience's story.

"I've never seen those men before and, now that you've killed them, I doubt I'll ever see them again. I don't work for Mason and I'm not lying about the coins," Connor insisted, patiently rebutting each of Duke's points.

"You're a fool if you think I'll swallow that mess of lies, Caveman," Duke answered. "Get your sorry self up, Scarecrow. We're leaving tonight."

"You can't go back tonight, Sheriff. You won't last an hour on the plains in the dark, and who knows how many of Mason's men are out there trying to find you at this very moment," Connor pleaded.

"I know that number will be one less, at least, so that's good," Duke hissed with his revolver at the ready.

Connor leapt for his rifle on the wall, but Duke was quicker than the man assumed. Duke shot once into the stone next to where that rifle stood and sent Connor reeling about a yard back in an instant.

"Do that again and the next bullet will be your dinner," Duke threatened.

"You may not like what you find, Sheriff," Connor

Ch. 14 | A Toast to Friends, New and Old

retorted, the old man displaying a note of severity for the first time in this crucial exchange.

Duke lowered his gun a few inches and gave Connor a cross-eyed look, and that was all the opening the sheriff's host needed to slip away into the everlasting dark. Duke took a step in his direction, but he instantly gave up the search. This place, as detestable and dank as it may be, was obviously Connor's home. He had the upper hand in any scrimmage Duke might attempt, so it would be best to move along with a decidedly stupefied Scarecrow.

The sheriff pushed the shambling prisoner down the narrow cavern that passed for a hall towards the fading evening light that belied the location of the cave's entrance atop that shallow cliff he had first entered a few hours before. At the cabinet that had earlier been the Scarecrow's accommodations, Duke leaned in and found some rope that would serve effectively as the man's new handcuffs for the trip home. It would require them to spend an evening out in the open where Mason's men could overpower the travelers, but Duke hoped that the darkness would be their friend and that the Scarecrow's ropes would be strong enough to last.

A purple haze blanketed the exit. Clouds dotted the little patch of sky that Duke could see through what was momentarily a pin-hole that shortly grew into something that passed for a door. The duo shuffled and stretched towards the hostile open air of a spring Nevada night while they left behind a shelter where their welcome was certainly worn out. Duke figured there was probably a half hour's worth of light left for him to ready the horse and throw the Scarecrow over the back, or drag him behind for that matter. After all, this man had killed his friend and countless other people. What courtesies were he owed?

Just as the slumping Scarecrow and his pursuer were preparing to breach the doorway, a soft voice from a hundred yards deep in the tunnel hollered back at them in Connor's unmistakable tones.

"Don't walk out that door, Sheriff! I'm trying to save your life! It isn't safe in Silver Gorge. It isn't safe!" the man shouted.

Duke walked on.

"Listen to me, you idiot! It's not safe! Stay here at least through the night," Connor pleaded. "There's nothing for you there! Silver Gorge isn't safe!"

Yet Duke walked on.

"Don't you hear me, Duke? Silver Gorge isn't safe! Duke! Duke!"

Sheriff Boone put his feet ahead and left the cave behind him, vowing to forget what that man had done as well as he could. It was a short-lived distraction and nothing more. Now he could get back to his job. Now he could get the Scarecrow back to town.

Duke only had to carry a semi-conscious Scarecrow on the back of his horse for a few minutes as they found what the sheriff presumed to be a horse belonging to one of his would-be assassins wandering aimlessly outside the foul cave. He spotted the horse from a good distance and wondered why it had not yet run back to wherever it belonged, though it became apparent the closer they got. Still attached by his left ankle was the man who had most recently occupied that saddle. Duke seemed to remember him as the man who was on the left, the first one to fall.

His blood, which was profuse from the wound in his head, had mostly dried in a puddle elsewhere, though ovular patches of dusty-red ground outlined the burdened animal's trail for several yards. In brighter light, Duke might could have followed the path of this horse all the way back to before the surprise cavern that protected Connor's entrance. As it were, he needed to work quickly to cut this man's heel loose and to tie the bronze horse, not unlike his own, to his own

Ch. 14 | A Toast to Friends, New and Old

saddle for carrying the Scarecrow efficiently.

Quick strikes with the felled man's own pocket knife made short work of the knot around his ankle and heel, and the Scarecrow had a new mount which he could ride. Still bound and still stupefied, the Scarecrow's gaunt figure seemed more indicative of a feeble body than as an unfair housing for a true killer. Slumped over the reins of a supplicant horse, Scarecrow muttered in his sleep-like state about darkness and a rider. Duke tried to offer him water, fearing that these symptoms might be representative of dehydration, but the Scarecrow just waved his tied up hands as if to signal his lack of interest.

"He comes in the dark," the Scarecrow bleated, his eyes shut and angled at the horse's mane. "The Rider. The Darkness. His is the night. His is the night. Daylight. Daylight. Give me…"

It was a peculiar state the Scarecrow was in, unmistakably terrified of some horror real or imagined. He clearly believed that some terrible rider was pursuing him, and this fear unsettled his more sober traveling companion. Despite his complete awareness and apparent control of the situation, Duke was unnerved by the constant muttering obviously associated with this particular derangement. What had Connor done to him? It was of course within the realm of possibility that Connor had poisoned the Scarecrow in that darkened chamber, and it was also possible that Connor had even poisoned Duke over tea. Whatever effects unsettled the Scarecrow right now could shortly overtake him, Duke thought, making him almost regret his speedy regress from that cave.

Though the incessant muttering continued, the Scarecrow's state of mind seemed to be repairing itself. Such a reality appeased Duke's darker fears, especially those concerning poison, as it was possible that this man would be out of his delirium before they had gone much farther.

"Darkness. He is darkness," the Scarecrow said with the banality of a man recounting his morning's particularly unappealing breakfast.

His eyes were mostly open now and the unwilling speech subsided in favor of groans and a better posture.

"He is… He is… My head. Man, that hurts," the Scarecrow complained, shrugging his shoulders in an attempt to raise his arms to rub his head. "Still got me tied up, huh?"

"As well you will be until we get you into a cell in Silver Gorge," Duke answered.

The Scarecrow's vocal concerns were abating, but his eyes yet darted upon the shadowy horizon where the night's bald half-moon gave an adequate glow.

"What's gotten into you?" Duke asked.

"A great moral shortcoming, most people think. Some say the devil got me at a young age, but I blame society," the Scarecrow laughed nervously.

"What is the Darkness?" Duke asked, this time throwing off the veneer of civility in his tone.

Such pointed questioning clearly bothered the Scarecrow, especially given the topic, but he figured the damage was done and it was time to speak up. After a momentary silence to gather his courage, the Scarecrow gave Duke a glimpse of a world he had never known existed.

"Men in my line of work… gunmen… talk about this fellow called 'The Rider in the Darkness.' He's a foul creature with milk-white skin that curls and falls off his face and hands with greasy black hair that hangs down to his chin or lower," the Scarecrow described. "Or not. You see, most folks think everyone sees the Rider differently. Some people say he's a ghost, others a devil, since he never looks the same to two different people. Again, that's the story."

"And you believe that tripe?" Duke asked.

Ch. 14 | A Toast to Friends, New and Old

"I didn't use to," he replied. "But that was before I'd seen him. That description? That's who I saw. Nobody else gave me those words, and you can swear on the Bible I'm telling the truth."

That face sounded familiar. It sounded like the one Duke had seen a few weeks back before it just fell apart on the floor of that saloon.

"If everybody sees a different face, where does this thing get those faces?"

"I don't know," the Scarecrow responded. "Some folks say he just changes. Others say he pulls the faces of your greatest fears. Others say he stays the same but the way we understand him changes. Who knows which is right? For my money, the cursed thing can keep his faces. I don't care where they come from, I just want to stop seeing them.

"Tell me, Sheriff. Have you ever seen the Darkness: His smoke-black horse and him floating over the sand, leaving a hint of a trail that's just enough to tempt you into following him wherever he wants to take you? Then, if you catch him just right, he'll vanish as if he were never there at all."

Duke leaned back on his horse for a moment in a vain attempt to keep his traveling companion from reading the worry on his brow. Though he had never seen it quite the way the Scarecrow described, with a horse as dark as the smoke from a green tree fire and appearing out of the void, Duke had seen plenty enough things in his day to make a man question what was normal.

"I've never seen your rider, Scarecrow. I'm not a gunman like you," the sheriff said.

"No, but you could've been a fine one. I've seen the way you handle yourself with a pistol," the Scarecrow applauded. "People say I'm the best there is or was and you nearly had me beat in a fair fight out there."

"I guess you consider that a compliment," Duke stated,

letting the tenor in his voice betray the anger behind it. "I'm a long way from a man like you."

"Not so far as you might think, Sheriff. You won't believe me, but I was being groomed up to wear a star myself long time ago. A good man, a sheriff, took me in when I needed someone in a bad way. He tried to teach me to be a good man, too," the Scarecrow reminisced as somber memories overtook his usual jocularity. "I guess it didn't stick."

"Why didn't it stick? What happened to that sheriff friend of yours?" Duke asked, genuinely caring about what the Scarecrow said for once.

"Some fool shot him. Three fools, really," the Scarecrow clarified before trailing off. "I turned around and killed the men who killed my friend and that was it. I left Newton that day and never went back."

Duke was stunned. He heard the story, but he couldn't believe it. None of what the Scarecrow was saying made sense. He could be lying, of course, but it seemed so genuine and real. As if he actually was the man responsible for the Hide Park shootings. As if he actually could be that fellow. Sheriff Boone, stunned by the realizations flooding over him at the moment, stared slack-jawed at the horizon ahead of him. The night sky flickered with countless stars above them, and the long distance to Silver Gorge seemed to blur into an endless road with the ground and the sky showing matching hues of deep purple and black.

Somewhere around a campfire, cowhands and cooks were sitting and listening to an old veteran of the trails tell a ghost story of a boy who stood up for his friend. Somewhere men were admiring the bravery and then bemoaning the unfortunate fate of the man who avenged Sheriff McCluskie before wandering into the desert to die of consumption. Children shuddered at the ghost stories they were told around the amber glow of a waning night fire, and here was Duke

Ch. 14 | A Toast to Friends, New and Old

Boone sitting next to that very ghost himself.

"My word, you're James Riley," Duke said after he could no longer deny the situation.

"That is a name I haven't heard in so many years. The last man to call me that died in the sands north of El Paso. That must've been 15 years, I think," the man who had been living as the Kansas Scarecrow said.

"I don't understand. You should be dead. All the stories I've heard said you were hobbling when you shot those men and you barely managed to walk out of the bar. Wandering into the desert like that should've been a death sentence for you," Duke said.

"Breathing was a death sentence for me, Sheriff. I was dead long before I pulled the trigger on those blowhards in Kansas, I just wanted to make sure I went out doing something that felt right. McCluskie was a scoundrel, sure, but he was more than that. He saved my life… the first time," Riley explained. "I have to agree with you on one thing, though, Sheriff. I should be dead. I can't explain to this day how I walked out of that desert. I went in there prepared to die, honestly, but then something went wrong. Or right. I walked into the desert prepared to die and I walked out of it with no idea how to live. So I took up my guns and made a living that way. Turned out to have a real knack for it."

"But you were a hero! You'd tried to save a sheriff's life. Surely you could've been somebody. Why'd you have to go and ruin all that by living lawlessly?" Duke asked.

"I have two of the most feared names in the country, Sheriff. I think I've become somebody just fine," the Scarecrow laughed. "But I wasn't really all that much of a hero. You know how many of the men I shot that night were actually enemies of McCluskie? Do you? I'll tell you. Just two."

"I've heard the story. I heard you killed five men."

201

"That's close. It was just four. And one of them was McCluskie's best friend. I had an errant bullet drive right through his neck," Riley said. "Two of them were the men who killed my friend, sure, but two of them were just there. You know what I learned that day?"

Duke never answered, but his ears were squarely in the Scarecrow's possession, so the man continued with his story.

"I learned that all men, good and bad, die just as easily with a few well-placed bullets," the Scarecrow said. "So I decided that if I'm going to live rather than die, I might as well be the man who keeps up his end of the bargain and delivers a few souls to the afterlife."

The Scarecrow kept his eyes forward when he spoke, refusing to acknowledge Duke's presence or the fact that his hands were bound as he headed towards the probable application of swift justice. Riding a dead man's horse, the Scarecrow floated ever onwards with the cave behind him and the subdued horror of a phantasmic rider resting like a coil of rope upon his shoulders.

"I always figured I'd be one of those men to die in a hail of gunfire. Or drowning," the Scarecrow smirked, momentarily acting like his old, horrible self. "I never thought my end would come to some vague Darkness that swallows a man's soul whole."

"Your end will come at the end of a rope, Riley," Duke informed the Scarecrow, relishing in the knowledge of this man's name.

"It's all just the same, I guess, if he catches me one day soon or not. I've been living on borrowed time for 20 years and it seems I'll be paying that time back with interest," the Scarecrow said. "But you won't be hanging me in Silver Gorge, Sheriff."

"Why's that?"

For the first time since his recovery from that fear-

Ch. 14 | A Toast to Friends, New and Old

induced coma, the Scarecrow looked to Duke and smiled. It was not a friendly smile, as the Scarecrow was never known for such pleasantry, but it was a wide and crooked smile that revealed most of the Scarecrow's pearl-white teeth.

"What do you know, Riley?"

"Keep using my name and we might just have to see how well I fight without my hands. Maybe I'll bite your nose off?" the Scarecrow laughed, clearly amusing himself.

The fiend just smiled to himself, laughing at a private joke he shared with a party of one. Duke had his head turned over his shoulder watching the Scarecrow's expression with deeply invested interest, but that twisted face revealed little more than it already had. In the little time that Duke had known James Riley, known to the outside world as the Kansas Scarecrow, he had only seen fear of one kind.

The Scarecrow's bulging eyes whenever the Darkness had been mentioned before clearly displayed what the man was feeling. This look, though, was not fear. Even the Darkness failed to terrify the Scarecrow in this moment, and in a bleak, half moonless desert. Scarecrow's eyes, and that wicked grin, showed something else. It was acceptance.

"What do you know, Riley?"

"I really am sorry about killing your friend. Greasy, right? Is that what you called him?" the Scarecrow said, sounding like a genuine apology.

Duke nearly accepted said apology with grace at face value, but he wisely held off for fear of whatever the Scarecrow would say next.

"I never relish killings I'm not paid for. Greasy was free, just a matter of survival," the Scarecrow chuckled. "Closest anyone's come to getting me in a long time, I have to admit. You and him? I respect you gentlemen. It's a shame, then, what's waiting for us in Silver Gorge."

"How would you know anything about what's waiting for us in… shut up. Shut up now!" Duke urged.

With a flash, he leapt down behind his horse and dragged the Scarecrow out of a borrowed saddle. Off to the right, a flurry of hooves scuttled off in the rocks and sand from behind a jagged outcropping. It was difficult to tell in the vacant blackness of that night, but at least three or four riders made out in a hurry towards the blazing lights of Silver Gorge, visible just beneath the next hill. Duke spotted a glinting reflection off what he imagined to be their holstered weapons, two revolvers and a long rifle each, and yet he wondered why they wouldn't take a shot.

"Was any of them your Rider in the Dark?" Duke asked.

"In a manner of speaking. They're here for both of us," his unwilling companion responded in a likewise whisper. "Look, Sheriff. Don't be coy about this. Mason hired me to kill you. That's the only reason I came to town, and he's not going to let me leave while you're still alive. I'm starting to get a feeling that he won't let me leave no matter what happens to you."

Sheriff Boone gave the murderer by his side a thought. If Mason really was behind all this, which of course he had suspected, then carrying the Scarecrow into town as a first-class delivery might not be the smart move. Then again, the gunmen had obviously seen them together at this point, so it would be foolish to break off the path now. They were marked for an appointment with whatever machination Mason had planned in town and that was where they had to go.

Of course, that didn't mean they had to go in unprepared. Duke considered his options at this point, none of which were good, and realized that one might be better than the others.

Apparently, the Scarecrow was thinking the same

Ch. 14 | A Toast to Friends, New and Old

thing.

"Look, Sheriff. I've already been paid a little bit to kill you. Normally I would consider that a binding contract to finish the job, but not when the promise of further payment is likely off the table. So there's no reason to hunt you, really," the Scarecrow offered. "If you let me loose, we might still have a chance."

-Chapter Fifteen-
Reckoning

From the low ridge over the west entrance to Silver Gorge, Duke and the Scarecrow could see torch fires lining the streets with much of the city's population still awake and still around for what was to come next. A grand stage appeared to be standing next to the sheriff's office with a couple of men standing side by side upon it.

The two conspirators had talked through their plan on the ride in, hoping to make sure they knew exactly how to proceed given their uncertain steps ahead. For a law-abiding sheriff, making a deal with this particular devil seemed foolhardy and irredeemable. Yet it also seemed unavoidable.

Perhaps if things went smoothly and they could avoid enacting their violent plan, Duke would be able to lock away the Scarecrow and pretend this conversation never occurred. It would be harder now that the Scarecrow's ropes were tied in such a way that he could release them and grab the revolver hidden under his shirt with just a second's delay, but Duke was counting on that second should he need it.

Sheriff Boone let the Scarecrow lead the way as they topped the ridge and gently let their horses find their way down the main thoroughfare of Silver Gorge. When they got closer, Duke could tell that what he had mistaken for a stage

Ch. 15 | Reckoning

was a gallows. He was no more than 250 yards away now and he could see two ropes hanging from a gallows that had not been there just a day before.

This was the moment. Had he wanted to turn back, now was the time to do it. Sheriff Boone could not yet tell if those present for a promised hanging had spotted either of the two men on horseback riding in well after dark. He recognized several faces in the crowd, from that sniveling banker to Abilene, hiding in plain sight by the door to her hotel, but what surprised him most was seeing Mort up on the gallows.

Deputy Mort was wearing a sheriff's star and standing directly under the leftmost of the two nooses, testing it for undue flexibility or give. He stomped his boot down a couple times on the trap door to make sure it was holding steady for the moment, admiring his accomplishment with gleeful pride. Mort must have pulled in a lot of favors and a lot of helping hands to get this undertaking done in such a short time, and he pulled it off marvelously. It was possible, Duke thought, that Mort was just going along with someone else's plan in order to save his own skin, but such optimism faded instantly upon meeting the apparently promoted deputy's eyes and finding a self-satisfied smile on his face.

One by one, the people of Silver Gorge looked to Mort and then looked to reigning sheriff Duke Boone with his cargo in tow.

"Hey! Sheriff got the Scarecrow! He got him!" came the shout from a portly farmer off to the sheriff's left.

As folks saw for themselves that what this barker said was true, a cheer and applause erupted for Duke. Gentlemen tossed their hats in the air and ladies grabbed their gentlemen to celebrate. The saloon girls kissed the cowboys and some of the roughnecks pulled out their revolvers and sent a volley of pistol shots into the starless night sky.

So. Mort hadn't yet told them why there were two gallows. This could yet work in his favor, Duke thought.

"Congratulations, Sheriff!" Mort shouted, heralding his boss's return and somewhat surprisingly milking the crowd's applause. "You've brought back one of the most dangerous men this country has ever seen! You single-handedly captured the Kansas Scarecrow. You're a hero, Duke!"

Silver Gorge once again let loose their cries of admiration and love for Duke Boone, but Mort was growing impatient as he quickly silenced the crowd with a gesture from his pistol-laden hands.

"Now, since you've brought the Scarecrow back here, we can see that justice is done. Now… it's time for a hanging!" Mort hollered, instantly turning the praise of the crowd and the focus of attention back to himself atop the gallows.

As the citizens cheered and cheered, the Scarecrow broke character for a moment and let slip a worried glance in Duke's direction. He was waiting for a signal to move, and he had promised the sheriff that he would await the signal, but it was clear that nerves were getting to the Scarecrow and that his trigger finger was developing a sudden twitch.

Duke blinked off the Scarecrow, trying to wordlessly indicate the need for patience as he attempted to salvage the slowly but inevitably deteriorating situation.

"We can't have a hanging tonight, Mort, and you know it. That's not how justice is done in this country, and that's certainly not how justice is done in Silver Gorge!"

"He's a murderer, Duke. You know it. You've seen it!" Mort briefed. "He dang well nearly killed you, man."

"Can we talk about this in the office? Send these people home, Mort," Duke begged.

"No. They came to see justice. They came to see Greasy's killer pay for what he's done. What about you?

Ch. 15 | Reckoning

Wasn't Greasy your friend, too?"

Mort was playing the crowd perfectly. The murmurs were small at first, but people started to grow visibly angry with Duke after a bit and he was clearly getting to a point where things were beyond control. Even Abilene, Duke saw, silently voiced her doubts about what the sheriff had planned.

"Of course, Mort. Greasy was a good man. I knew him better than most of you, and that's how I know this is wrong. Greasy had a chance to kill this man, you know. He did," Duke said, turning his horse in a circle as if to address the entire town. "The day Greasy died, he could have killed the Scarecrow without a problem. He didn't. He saved my life without taking another man's, and that is how we ought to honor him today."

"And how did that work out for him, Sheriff? Should we go ask Greasy how mercy played out? Tell you what. How about you run over to Cemetery Hill and see what Greasy thinks about mercy," Mort shouted.

"I'll go if you won't," the Scarecrow said under his breath. "I wouldn't mind a change of scenery."

"What's the problem, Sheriff?" Mort laughed. "You and I both know what this man has done and what he is capable of if we let him stick around this town any longer than we have to. Are you so caught up in an ideal of justice that you won't stand to see the real thing play out?"

Eyes darted to Duke's position, each individual gauging his response before forming their own, but Mort quickly drew their attention back on him.

"Or could it be that you're just afraid of losing your hired gun?" Mort accused.

"That's absurd!" Duke shouted in response, but to no avail.

At Mort's wild insistence, the people of Silver Gorge

mounted an outrage. The bartender from the Rusty Spittoon hurled a stone at Duke's head, but the thankfully drunk man missed by several feet. Mr. Parker from the general store tossed language at the sheriff greatly unbecoming a deacon of his position at the local church.

"I've done nothing wrong!" Duke screamed to nobody and everybody as the crowd's fervor boiled over into a full-on mob. "I haven't done a thing wrong!"

Nobody heard him. The cry of angry men and women muffled out the sound of anything else, and the town of Silver Gorge had turned on their sheriff. This obvious turn of the situation drained what was left of the Scarecrow's patience as time for a drastic action had come and probably passed. So, disregarding the plan and the promise of a sign, the Scarecrow acted on his own.

"Come on, Sheriff! You're twenty minutes past late. Time to g-" the Scarecrow proclaimed, but he was interrupted.

With just one hand unbound and the other clutching the concealed gun and a swollen rope constricting his motion, the Scarecrow fell quiet at the crash of a fired bullet buried deep within his chest. Though he had felt the sting of the hot metal break his sternum and embed itself in the clutches of bone and sinew and lean muscle, it was the sound that had alerted the Scarecrow as to just what had gone wrong. The crack of the gun preceded the crack of his bones by just a moment, but it was enough. The Scarecrow had been shot.

Duke Boone hopped off his horse and bolted for the spot where his companion of convenience lay in the dust, thick black ichor coming out of the wound and rejoining the Scarecrow to his earthen roots. Nobody moved at all except for the Scarecrow and Duke, and most of that movement belonged to Duke's hurried attempt at closing the wound on the cleaved fellow's chest with a hand and a spare scarf. It looked to be right near the heart, and as much blood came gushing out of it, that was probably the case.

Ch. 15 | Reckoning

Such impromptu attempts at medicine did a fine job of plugging the leak for a moment, but the rag was quickly sated and in need of replacement. As the scarf filled up with blood, so too were Duke's hands covered over by the same.

"Quickly. Quickly. Somebody give me a rag or a towel or something," Duke rattled in a hushed but urgent whisper.

Nobody moved. Nobody came to the sheriff's aid.

As he looked around into the faces of his townspeople, Duke was angered by their inaction.

"Won't somebody help me? Won't anybody get this man a rag!" Duke shouted in protestation of their cowardice.

Sheriff Boone scanned the eyes of the people he had known and considered family for so long, and he was overcome with rage and disappointment. Through the flickering light of wrathful torches, Duke could see the likes of Will Hampton, a farmer he had once saved from a rattlesnake bite. There stood Miranda Sanchez, a widow who had frequently relied on Duke to scatter the bandits who came to harass her late husband's few head of cattle and modest crop of corn and wheat. Phillip Jones was standing beside her, a young man who would be dead now if not for the time Duke dove into a flash flood to pull him out as a boy.

Even Abilene stood by, watching without motion, as her latest betrayal still stung fresh on Duke's mind.

Silver Gorge had turned against Duke Boone over a matter of hours and they would not come to his aid now.

"Don't you see? A man is dying, people! This man was shot down in cold blood because he knows something that false deputy wants to keep hidden from you," Duke urged. "Please! Do not be complicit in this man's death!"

"He drew on me, Duke. You saw it. They saw it. He's no innocent man," Mort retorted from his podium above the crowd, pointing and waving wildly.

The sheriff held his hand firm on the fallen gunman's chest, yet it was for naught. Within minutes, or seconds, the Scarecrow would be no more.

"It's... it's okay, Sheriff. You knew this was the result, one way or another," the Scarecrow said. "Besides. I always knew it would come to this. I'd rather this than... than..."

The Scarecrow's eyes grew wider, whether for death or fear Duke was unsure. After spending the last few weeks trying to outrun the Rider, here he was splayed out in the dirt for anyone to see. The greatest gunman in recent memory sat here, the first victim of an anxious but generally gutless deputy with no previously displayed semblance of a trigger finger. Yet claiming the life of the Kansas Scarecrow would now be the feather in Mort's recently made cap.

"You've got a trial coming up, Riley. You're not getting out of it like this," Duke begged.

"Don't... don't tell me... you've gone soft," the Scarecrow said, releasing one last grin. "All men... all men die easy, Sheriff. Make Mason next."

As the Scarecrow closed his eyes, Duke eased his hand off the blood-soaked cloth that covered the Scarecrow's trademark black duster and charcoal-gray shirt. The Scarecrow's throat gurgled out droplets of blood onto the dirt that was his final rest as his head violently shook and rattled with death throes. Yet, with one last effort, the Scarecrow chose to amend his final words.

"Now that... now that I think about it... " he stammered through fits of hemorrhaging coughs, "maybe make that fool deputy of yours next."

Duke laughed a little as the Scarecrow's faint final words were in fact final this time; Duke could see the Scarecrow's throat and mouth fill up with blood, though his lips still flapped in an attempt to hold on to the world just a moment more.

Ch. 15 | Reckoning

Shortly after, he had truly passed. Presumably out of reach for the Rider he feared so much.

"Get up, Sheriff," Mort bellowed with a command he had never before hinted at.

"You murderer!" Duke snarled in defiance. "This man was in my custody. He was going to stand trial!"

"He went to pull a gun on me because you let him," Mort replied. "Do you people see what your beloved sheriff has done? He betrayed you by consorting with a murderer. With a violent man who would just as soon end you as he would walk out on paying for his drinks. This Scarecrow came here, likely on the Sheriff's orders, to scare you good people. Is that what you want?"

The crowd's initial reaction was a hushed fervor, giving Duke the slightest hope that things could still go his way. But it was partially true. He had enacted plans with the Scarecrow, with James Riley, in order to counteract Mort and Mason's scheme. How could he explain that to the people?

But that was the answer! Duke knew it was his final chance. He had to explain to everyone how Mason had…

"And this," Mort announced, producing a small object from his empty holster.

Duke couldn't quite make it out from that distance initially, but the quick glint of silver off of someone's torch drove a pit into the once-trusted sheriff's stomach. It was Mort, in fact, who had snagged the chunk of silver that night rather than Abilene. Worse than that, Duke realized he'd been played.

"What I hold in my hand is a fairly large piece of silver pulled out of Mason's mine, bearing Mason's insignia. Where did I find it?" Mort asked, turning and facing each man and woman in the street. "I pulled this from Duke's own pocket the other night while he slept with a married woman in that very office."

213

For a moonless, breezy night on the plains of barren Nevada, Duke noted a sudden surge in the heat around him. A subdued rage contorted the sheriff's face as Mort pushed the lie deeper and deeper, scandalizing a once proud man.

"I won't do any of you the indignity of revealing your family's infidelity, let that be your own business, but I will not let stand Duke Boone's failures to protect this town and its people from danger and moral degradation!" Mort cheered.

Silver Gorge, nearly in entirety, let rage the mob that had formed at Duke's presumed dishonor. Boone's place in town was gone, that was certain, and it seemed that the second noose's intended occupant was becoming clearer and clearer by the minute. Mort had succeeded in creating the moral indignation against Duke Boone that would require action from a lynch mob. Death had not yet departed Silver Gorge and there would doubtlessly be a second body joining the Scarecrow shortly.

Through their deafening jeers and audible hatred, Duke slumped helplessly in the dirt. A once imposing man, a figure who could stand tall and turn back the less determined villain, the sheriff now fell into a lump at the epicenter of a fearful gaggle. Perhaps his death would bring some measure of calm to Silver Gorge. Perhaps even peace. Though if that was the case, Duke knew he had failed. The absence of law is preferable to the presence of law misplaced.

Every familiar voice shouting death upon Duke Boone condemned him further, though it was the silence of one voice that held him through. Even after he had scorned her for a traitor and a thief, and even after she had stood by and watched while the Scarecrow slipped away, Abilene watched the Sheriff with pity and silent tears. She could not, she would not rally against the man she loved. She would not abandon him now, even if all that meant was her silence in the face of those who terrorized.

Duke gave her a longing glimpse, cherishing one last

Ch. 15 | Reckoning

time the smile of a woman who loved him as much as she did. He gathered the little feeling he had left to leave her with a smile, and she offered the same with tears streaming down her face. He feared for her life and thought to turn away, but Mort must have known it was her if he stole away the silver. He must have known and chose to leave her alone. The risk was great, but the risk was worth it for their one last private rendezvous.

"I'm going to put my gun down now, Sheriff," Mort said. "But don't get any ideas. Lest you forget, we've still got our watchmen on duty. Look over your shoulder, Duke. See them on the roofs? You remember them. You appointed them, after all. Say hi, gentlemen."

The three riflemen stood, looking down on the sheriff who had been their friend. To his right was Joe Miller, the preacher. To Duke's left was Franz. At his back, most unfortunately, was Erik Harper. Each man reluctantly waved at the sheriff and returned their hand to the trigger guard on the rifle stock. Duke could tell, and he knew it well, that it was easy for the mob to scream death. It was much more difficult for the lone man to distribute it.

Mort tossed his gun down on the gallows and walked over to the other man on the raised wooden platform, a man Duke now recognized to be Aaron Oscar, and started making inaudible orders. The rotund, still finely dressed banker stepped off the grand stage and into the bar for a moment as Mort once again started to address the crowd and the sheriff specifically.

"Given your years of service to the town and the people of Silver Gorge, we are going to give you a choice," the faulty deputy proclaimed. "Duke Boone, former sheriff of Silver Gorge, you may either walk up to the gallows yourself and let us bring you to justice for your role in the death of Greasy and for conspiracy against this town or you can take your best shot at escape."

That option seemed fine for a moment until Oscar came back to the gallows with his prescribed items. In Oscar's left hand was a bottle of the Rusty Spittoon's clearest, strongest liquor. In his right hand was a rag.

Oscar handed the dangerous combination to Mort, and the deputy turned sheriff turned executioner made quick work of his now obvious task. Mort doused the rag with a slight quantity of the liquor and stuffed it back through the neck of the bottle. With a torch borrowed from someone at the front of the eager crowd, Mort lit the rag and held aloft his backup plan.

"Say you choose to run. Say Harper misses. Say you take refuge in one of these buildings for a moment," Mort listed. "We could let the people tear you apart for your transgressions, but I have a better idea. Whatever building you choose to cower in, we burn it to the ground. Your death will once more remind the people of Silver Gorge just how selfish and careless you were as their lawless sheriff. Sound good?"

Duke took a step forward. Slowly he lifted himself off the ground and put his right foot out in front. He lifted the left foot and put it down in front of the right one, slowly advancing to his final moment. Greasy's death was on Duke's hands, true, but the people of Silver Gorge would never understand why. Perhaps this sentence was what Duke deserved after all. Mort may have won, and Mason may have won, but Boone would not let them tarnish his death with more wanton destruction. This would be the end of it, one way or another.

"I really am sorry about all this, Sheriff," Harper shouted, breaking up the interminable silence while still staring down the barrel of a rifle. "Too bad it can't be like last time we spoke."

The last time. Yes. Too bad. That had been a good night, Duke supposed, when Harper showed off a little. It was

Ch. 15 | Reckoning

still stunning how he had decimated a glass bottle with a long rifle in the dark of the night from that distance. Duke was a good shot, but Harper was better. He knew it. He knew it was hopeless to run. Duke might could get off one shot before Harper would have him, but that wouldn't be right. How could Duke force his friend to take that step?

As Duke agonized over each step, and Mort patiently waited for the deposed lawman to finish his last walk, Harper's words echoed. Last time. That was the key. That glimmer of hope that had died with the Scarecrow and with the sheen of silver's reflection in Mort's hand came surging back. There was a way out, wasn't there?

"I'm sorry it had to be like this, Duke. You were a good friend. That's what makes this hurt so much, the way that you betrayed us. The way you betrayed Greasy," Mort said.

Duke had mostly closed the distance between himself and the deputy now, and that was close enough. It was manageable now.

"I'm sorry I failed you, Mort," Duke said as he stopped walking, still holding his eyes to the ground. "I'm sorry I didn't teach you better how to be a good sheriff."

Mort lowered the flaming bottle and looked on Duke with surprise. He had never expected the proud sheriff to go along with a lie so easily, yet here he was. He was admitting it. All of it. But why?

"You… it wasn't your fault, Duke. These things just happen, and when they do we just have to go with them," Mort replied.

"Get on with it, man. Your time is up," Aaron Oscar urged, preaching further without a hint of irony. "Let this be a lesson, people! We will not be persuaded. We will not be moved by the wealthy and the powerful here in Silver Gorge! All men are subject to the law."

"Quiet, Oscar," Mort rebuked. "Let the man die with

dignity. He's earned it."

Oscar sneered obediently in Mort's direction and held his place. Given what was coming next, Duke almost regretted that the banker retreated.

"No, I'm serious. I failed you, Mort. I never really did make sure you learned the most important lesson I could've taught you," Duke said, raising his voice to the level where everyone could hear it.

"What lesson is that, Duke? What was so important that you have to teach me at this moment right now?" Mort asked with a blend of ridicule and genuine curiosity in his voice.

"You never really learned, Mort. What did I always tell you? When you draw on a star…"

"You'd better be prepared to finish it," Mort concluded.

His moment of realization came a split second too late. Mort's eyes widened and his arm tensed as he once again raised the glass above his head. From this distance, however, Duke needed just a moment to make his shot work.

While Boone felt each action pass by individually, as if he were crossing each one off a list as it happened, reality was quite different. The irrevocable action passed in a flash. As soon as he had spoken his warning to Mort, Duke took a long breath and pulled his revolver out of the holster. As soon as the gun was at height, and Duke was sure his aim was steady, he pulled the trigger.

First came the crack of the pistol. In the same moment, hidden by the first shot, was a bullet from Harper's rifle. Boone's bullet found itself buried in Mort's chest. Then came the crack of the glass. Everything after that was confused by a blinding flash and the shrill agony of a man screaming for mercy. Flames engulfed Mort's body as the liquid fire rolled down his sleeves and onto his chest, burning at the flesh underneath. Smaller droplets of flame converged into rolling

Ch. 15 | Reckoning

tongues that caught his hair and his face, and the mob stood stunned in utter terror of the sight they were witnessing.

Moving more quickly than he ever had before, Aaron Oscar leapt from the stage to the mob below as the entire gallows burned and seethed. The roiling flames had seized upon the bitterly dry planks in a matter of moments, engulfing the entire gallows in burning light before anyone could react. All anyone could do was watch as two infernal ropes dangled in the night, devoured by the flames like a snake biting its way through the body of another. Mort's screams persisted at a horrendous pitch, piercing the peace that had been the tranquil mob a moment earlier. Even still, the people heard nothing through the roar of the expanding flames. As the great wooden altar collapsed, the banker turned towards Mort's followers and shocked them out of their stupor with cries of justice and panic.

The crowd heard Oscar's entreaty after a moment, but Duke realized the dire need of the situation first. As the crowd slowly grasped that their purpose had not yet been fulfilled, Duke Boone ran back to his horse and leapt in the saddle with the urgency of a coyote caught in a brushfire. A few clever men in the mob gave chase, but the snipers on the roof held them at bay with their presumably wayward shooting. It was curious to some how the watchmen had withheld their shooting until then, but it was a subject of minor importance given the nature of the evening.

Before any of the mob was able to break away from town, Duke had escaped the confines of the city street and made his roundabout escape for the woods surrounding Wilson land. If the mob was going to follow, he would make sure that they had to work for it.

-Chapter Sixteen-

Sanctuary

Calls from morning birds started to infiltrate the night silence as the once-named Sheriff Boone urged his mount to reach the woods before daybreak. He might could manage to hide out for a short time if he reached the woods ahead of the mob he had left behind him in Silver Gorge, but he could hear their rabble and shouts quickly gaining on him. Duke Boone was quickly losing ground and options.

Golden hair and a thick brown mane rushed through the open of the desert, aided by the cool of night, but Duke's famous horse had given all she could. After a few minutes at this speed, that horse would cease to be useful. Duke loved his horse and he had no intention of harming her, but neither did he intend to feel the burn of a lynch mob's rope around his neck. He would have to keep going just a little longer. Perhaps once he reached the woods, Duke thought, he could find refuge. Few people knew the Wilson land like he did, except for perhaps the Wilsons and Greasy.

Another minute now. The cover of trees promised Duke rest, since he had not slept in nearly a day, and the barely healed bruises from his more violent encounter with the Scarecrow started to pull and strain. Like most men, Duke hoped he could last long enough to die of old age. He just

Ch. 16 | Sanctuary

hoped that it would not be today when the effects of old age would get the better of him.

Plopping hooves and beleaguered breathing taught Duke the rhythm of his getaway, but the trees grew larger in the ever-decreasing distance. It would not be long now before he would finally have something that resembled cover.

Whether it was the stories that he had heard from the gunman known as the Scarecrow or some vague awareness of a second rhythm of hoof beats back and to the left, Duke suddenly had to fight off the urge to check his periphery for a veiled rider. As Duke charged ahead towards the forest, he felt the chill shrinking the night air around him, suffocating his vision as an unnamed menace pressed onward in his direction.

Just a quick look and he would know what it was that Riley had seen. Just a peek and Duke might glimpse this figure that haunted the man who for two decades was the undisputed terror of Nevada and the wide swath of the territories. Muscles in his neck spasmed, twisting the sinew in directions they perhaps shouldn't go. His gaze held straight forward as the sharp burn in his neck made riding nigh unbearable, yet Duke pressed on. Looking back would do him no service now, whether an otherworldly horror gave pursuit or not. He must face forward and meet the forest with a ready gaze.

Sheriff Boone's figure contorted as half his body rebelled and attempted to twist towards the anonymous phantasm he imagined was back there, but the greater measure of control kept Duke's eyes ahead as long as could be maintained. His resistance was successful, or so it was for the time being, as the specter of being followed gave way as soon as Duke reached the edge of the woods. Traversing such a landscape was horrid for the newcomer at night, so, even if the pursuing herd could stay together, he would have the advantage. As it were, the trees in the thicket were too tight in most places and the rocky soil was too loose to allow for any measure of close riding. For a moment's rest, Duke Boone had evaded the self-formed posse and the apparition that haunted James Riley, if the latter was ever there at all.

Daybreak would come over the eastern sky in a matter of an hour or so, Duke thought, as the songs of the earliest birds were joined by the late risers, evermore replacing the chirps of bats out of their distant caverns. Light was a long way off, but the symptoms and signs of better times started to appear with enough authority to calm Duke's fears.

He no longer pressed his horse with the urgency that had driven him into the woods, and he even allowed the animal to rest for a while as he heard the pack of riders stop shy of the treeline. They knew as well as he did that it was a pointless effort to ride into the woods in the dark, so they would wait until he had to leave. Several of the riders peeled off and headed around the woods to surround him, but that left plenty of acreage along the boundary upon which he could try to escape when the time came.

Even with the separation of some of the swifter riders, the primary body of the current mob still stood at more than 50 men and horses, and Duke knew that they would eventually come after him. It was just a matter of time and opportunity now, so he had to make sure that he took less time to claim an opportunity.

Sunlight's warm glow teased Duke with hints of orange streaking across the southernmost border of the sky, though he barely spotted a glimpse of this display through the trees and the brush. What Duke could see, however, was the rose-red hue that the night sky all at once began fading into as morning recaptured her position. Each songbird made its own presence known with the pleasant whistling that Duke had heard before now growing into a unanimous chorus from all around, yet the previous day was not yet done.

For all of morning's stupid optimism and naïve hope,

Ch. 16 | Sanctuary

the day before had still happened. Riley was dead. Mort was dead. Duke was alone. No number of dawning suns could clear the actions of the one before. If anything, rather than welcome the sun's coming, Duke knew he ought to be outrunning it. Nothing good would come of this sunrise or any that followed. And the sheriff was desperately in need of rest, his eyes confirming this fact by how readily they sought to escape the privilege of morning's first light. Tight lids squeezed around his tired eyes as the suggestion of sunlight gave way to the great light's first step over the horizon. Former-sheriff Boone turned his horse away from the sun and ran deeper into the woods, hoping soon to find a cool, dark place to sleep that would provide him some shelter from the mob.

Perhaps it was the brilliance of stupor or inspiration bred out of necessity that gave Duke Boone his saving idea. Had Greasy not camped out in these same woods for an indiscernible amount of time? As savvy an outdoorsman as he was, Greasy would no doubt have had a well-planned hiding place to rest at his camp. Duke never noticed such a spot in the short time that he visited the camp, but surely something would be there that he could make use of. The only way Duke found the cleverly hidden camp at all was because Greasy lit an ill-advised fire to cook lunch. Without the aid of a smoke trail, Duke probably would have wandered within feet of the camp and not noticed it was there at all.

Duke turned and started slowly trotting in the direction that he thought the camp was in, that task being made considerably easier now by the illuminating sunlight that flooded the forest floor. With an angry mob trailing him, Duke knew he needed to find concealment as quickly as he could. Sunlight benefited Duke in simpler transportation, but it benefited the mob in every way that mattered. His tracks would be easier to spot. His horse stood out rather easily against the greenery of the forest, though boulders and dusty hills on occasion helped her camouflage. Duke recalled once spotting a bandit taking refuge behind a tree because of the glint of sunlight off his pistol's barrel, so there was no shortage of inconsequential items that could betray the presence of a man who wanted to stay hidden.

A menagerie of rocks and unruly shrubs dotted the landscape between trees both meager and towering, and the ever-present shroud of dust that caked each leaf and filled the air parted for Duke as he and his horse kept stepping through the landscape in search of a hiding place. Initially, Duke was confident that he could find his way back to the camp, but such pleasant notions fell away as the various sights all merged and twisted together like two snakes fighting over a mouse. It was difficult to tell what was memory and what was wishful, creative recognition. Oh, that rock? He had passed it that morning on his way by the hidden campsite, certainly. This bush? It looked like the one where he saw a rabbit run just before looking up and seeing the smoke that indicated where Greasy was hiding out.

Were Duke honest with himself, he'd acknowledge that he was in no condition to traverse these trees and locate this supposed sanctuary. He would still be lost tomorrow, probably, if not captured or dead. In his frustration and his feeble attempts at using the sun as a compass towards unknown destinations, Duke looked up in a tree and by wild chance spotted Greasy's rifle perched upon two branches. Fate smiled down, so Duke imagined, as he was gifted with something that might prove ever useful in the coming days or hours. Whoever was entrusted with delivering Greasy's body, which had to have been found nearby this tree, must have missed the rifle that the man had haphazardly hidden in the woods. Near this spot, Duke thought, a good man lost his life.

Such somber reminiscence brought a quick end to Duke's moment of triumph, though, as he quickly measured out the fact that Greasy's perch on the day he was killed sat nearly two miles from the camp, and these two spots were separated almost unavoidably by the Wilson home. It would

Ch. 16 | Sanctuary

be possible to sneak around the main house and the barn, but it would add precious time to the journey. Duke knew not whether the mob was resting or still pursuing, so assuming they were preparing an incursion of the woods seemed the prudent attitude to take. As such was the case, Duke wearily resumed his course, albeit in a more accurate direction.

After a few missteps on weakly stacked rocks and fighting his horse's hesitancy to move on towards the planned destination, Duke finally managed to earn a little progress. It was not so long before he found the Wilson home and prepared to breach the clearing that surrounded it when he heard the unmistakable din of a chattering mob and the plopping of slowly shuffled horse's feet en masse.

Just moments before Duke was to step out into the wide open clearing, Mort's legacy mob did the same from the direction of the main road. Of course, at the head was that bloated banker who had stood right by Mort the night before. Behind the banker trailed something like 50 men with torches and rifles aloft. They had done better than the sheriff at keeping up their energy, likely with the promise of more shooting or a hanging keeping their spirits alive.

As Oscar dropped from his finest imported horse and sauntered to the front door of the Wilson home, Duke heard a couple of cow hands he recognized as frequent patrons of the Rusty Spittoon about 15 yards away from the edge of the woods rehashing coarse jokes regarding Wilson's daughter and how they would enjoy a few moments alone with her willing flesh. Duke noted that he would shoot them first if it came down to it.

Through the din of hearty conversation and the vacuum of distance, Duke barely heard the rapping of Oscar's knuckles on the great oak door at the head of the Wilson threshold. Moments later, Wilson was heard opening the door and greeting Oscar impatiently without immediately noticing the mass of people at his back.

"This is a fine way to greet your customers, Oscar. What in the name of…" Wilson stopped. "Oscar? What's with the extra company?"

"Why weren't you in town with us last night, Mr. Wilson?" Oscar asked. "You and your boys were noticeably absent at a time when we could have used your support."

"We were busy," Wilson gritted out.

"Do you happen to know what our enterprise in town was last night that you were obviously too occupied to attend? As a pillar of this community, you have a duty to uphold justice in Silver Gorge when you see the chance to do so," Oscar lectured.

"I can't say I did know, but I trust the sheriff in how he handles these matters," Wilson retorted. "When he interrupts breakfast, at least it's for good reason. So far all you've done is asked me about my schedule and present conflicts with the community calendar. You care to explain yourself, Aaron?"

"Perhaps invoking the sheriff's name wasn't the most prudent move at this time, Wilson, since it's actually his misdeeds that have brought us here," the shifty banker explained.

As Aaron Oscar laid out the list of charges levied upon Duke's shoulders, Boone called on each measure of restraint he could in order not to break out in fitful shouting with each lie that was said against him. These were monstrous accusations, the most of them, with a couple of accurate, if not misinterpreted, actions relayed to the landowner and one present ally the sheriff had left. Oscar spoke of sedition and conspiracy with the gunman known as the Kansas Scarecrow, a charge that Wilson flatly knew to be a lie given his own involvement with the events of that month. Oscar accused Duke of furtive contracts signed, agreed to in private meetings with Boss Mason, and he even charged Boone with aiding the Scarecrow's efforts to murder Deputy Mort.

Ch. 16 | Sanctuary

That last one was actually true in a manner of speaking, Duke thought, a self-admission that may not do much to further his cause.

"Yes, Sheriff Duncan L. Boone has crossed the thin line separating lawman from outlaw, and it is our sworn duty as the upright, honorable, armed citizens of Silver Gorge to bring that man to justice," Oscar said, addressing the crowd more than Wilson at this point.

Aside from the fact that the town's imbecilic banker had just called Duke by the wrong name, since Duke wasn't short for anything and it certainly wasn't short for Duncan, Boone felt like the banker's pitiful plea would surely fall on deaf ears. Wilson had always been a reasonable man, and when that failed he hated getting involved too heavily in the political or legislative affairs of Silver Gorge. It would be just minutes before he would send the raiders on their way and Duke would be able to move about undetected.

"You really expect me to believe that Sheriff Boone shot and killed his own deputy and that he was actually trying to help that Scarecrow all along? Did none of you even see what our sheriff looked like when the Scarecrow was finally done pounding on him?" Wilson asked. "And you're telling me he signed up for it? Or that maybe it was even his own idea?"

A few of Aaron Oscar's supporters shuffled upon presentation of logic, but they were hardly given the chance to really consider what any of it meant.

"We all saw it, Mr. Wilson. The sheriff, your friend, pulled the trigger and murdered Mort in cold blood, in a way most foul that I doubt any of us will ever be able to forget those horrendous screams. What a horrible noise he made!" Oscar exaggerated.

Wilson returned the banker's pleas with a weary look, almost begging the man to leave his porch so as to end this pointless conversation.

"Get out of here, Oscar. Neither me nor any of my family are going to join you on your hunt. If Boone broke the law, I see why you feel you must go after him. But I will not be partaking," Wilson concluded as he slammed the door shut right in Oscar's face.

Either empowered by or shamed by the collective gazes of the mob at his back, Oscar refused to let that insult go unpunished. He shouted curses and slanderous names up at Wilson's ivory tower, hoping that they would stick like turpentine to a child's hands.

"Sheriff Boone is a murderer and a traitor to this town, Wilson! And anyone who stands in our way stands on his side, you hear me? Is that where you want to be when the true men of law and justice come down hard on Sheriff Boone with the swift sword of righteousness? There will be a holy fire, Wilson, and you'd better decide now if you want to be holding the torch or lighted up underneath it!" Oscar proclaimed.

Wilson's front door slammed open with a mighty thwack upon the walls of the home as it swung to the limit and Aaron Oscar jumped back in surprise. He no longer stood on the pedestal stairs that led to the front door, leaving just Wilson's second son perched up above everyone else.

"You hear me, sir," Mark scolded. "Sheriff Boone is a fine man and a fair sheriff. He was suspicious of Mort and whatever that deputy had going on. He asked me what I knew about him just a couple days ago. If Sheriff Boone killed Mort, it was because he knew it was the right thing to do."

"Now, son. You ought not say these things. It's unwise to speak ill of the dead," Oscar chided.

"I'll speak ill of any man who earns it," Mark returned. "And by all accounts, Mort earned it. If Sheriff Boone shot him down, it was only because Mort betrayed him first. You mark my words, Aaron Oscar. Sheriff Duke Boone will have his

Ch. 16 | Sanctuary

day. You think your mob can scare him? What's a mob but a bunch of men too scared to do something brave on their own? And how scared you all must be if you need 50 men just to ride out against one."

It made Boone proud to hear this young man stand up for him, and it made him smile to see the mob that Oscar had gathered step back a bit at what Mark said. These things had never occurred to them, apparently, and the suddenness of their corporate strength devolving into individual fear exposed their internal weakness and brought to the surface their reluctance towards heroism.

"I wouldn't be surprised if Sheriff Boone is up in those trees around us right now," Mark shouted, forcing the riders in the mob to turn about with worried eyes piercing the surroundings. "He's probably up there somewhere right now with a bead on one of your heads at this very moment."

Oscar had lost the mob, in truth, as a few of the men on the outside edge of the pack turned tail and ran immediately. A few others had the look of desperation wash over them as they considered leaving, but the majority were off in their own circles and fretting over what to do. The banker tried to shout them down and bolster their courage, but the jig was up. Their resolve had been broken by a teenager with a pedestal and Oscar was boiling red with fury.

"Just in case he ain't out there, though, I figure I'd do my part at coming prepared," Mark explained vaguely as he reached back in the door and pulled out his father's shotgun. "Now if you men don't leave my family's land right now, at least three of you will be leaving with holes in you."

Mark's insistence on pulling a gun forced Oscar to pull a gun, likely expecting his men to follow suit. They did not, however, and the crowd quickly fell into a frenzy.

"He's just a boy," one man shouted.

"Let's leave before the sheriff gets here," another

advised.

None of the men there wanted to see Oscar shoot a kid, and none of them were devoted enough to the cause to help him do it.

"What are you doing, Mark? Get back in here!" came a voice from inside the house. The rustle of other Wilsons behind the door caught Oscar's attention. As the doorknob started to turn, the banker aimed his gun ever so slightly away from the boy in front of him.

"Anyone else walks through that door, them and the boy gets to taste a fresh one," Oscar vainly taunted. His attempts at intimidation came across as shaky and fraudulent, just as they ought to from a banker playing at gunman. Even so, his threats effectively barred the other Wilsons firmly inside.

At the sight of his truest friend being held at gunpoint, Duke did just what Mark suggested he do moments earlier. The sheriff swiftly but noiselessly clambered off his horse and up into a tree near the clearing while pulling Greasy's gun in tow. Mark and Oscar were polite enough to let their standoff hold while Duke got in place, which was no easy task given how long it had been since he climbed a tree with a gun, and the sheriff made up the third man in this particular trio.

His bleary eyes made seeing properly rather difficult, but Duke checked the sights on the weathered rifle and unsteadily aimed at the back of Oscar's head. He could gently squeeze the trigger and likely end the threat, but it was difficult to get a clear shot. Though it was a light breeze that morning, the branches on every tree around Duke sought to expand their reach into the nearby landscape. The stacking of the branches on Duke's tree made it difficult to steady the rifle. Oscar kept swaying out of fear, a sign of a man who had never really been standing at gunpoint for any duration of time.

Ch. 16 | Sanctuary

Should his shot miss, Duke could easily ignite a furor that would be impossible to quench, but a true shot would fell the banker and send the rest of his compatriots running. Then again, it could be good for Mark to talk the banker down with a gun in his face. Yet neither the banker nor the boy spoke, and Duke held his spot as long as he could with inaction.

The crowd of onlookers calmed their nervous apprehension after a few minutes of no shooting and they watched as the boy and their apparent boss held opposing arms in the other's direction. Mark was steady and sure, Oscar weary and shaking. The moment would come now, any minute, and the banker would turn and run and put an end to this silly threat.

Duke's eyes began to droop, forcing the gun out of his spot, but he caught it in time to prevent a total loss of control. Oscar held tight in the distance and his resolve appeared to grow the longer the situation went. He was quickly warming up to the idea that he could end Mark's life, apparently, without much in the way of consequences. Mark recognized Oscar's new boldness and reacted accordingly, reaffirming his position as the man with the integrity, experience, and high ground to win the day.

Although Duke tried to keep his gaze clear and his head aloft, torpor and exhaustion got the better of him and, in a tragic moment, pulled his weary head down to sleep with a startling wake-up.

In a moment of panic, there were two gunshots.

Two bullets escaped their chambers and hurtled towards a target at irrevocable speeds, yet just one connected.

As Duke saw what had been done, James Riley's prescient words echoed.

The bullet that connected, the one shot that found a place to land, did not end up where it had been meant to go.

-Chapter Seventeen-
Fallen

True to Duke's expectations, the surprise gunshot from the left peaks sent Aaron Oscar's mob into a panicked evacuation. In their haste to leave, none of the men saw how Duke Boone ran from his perch in the tree to the front step of Wilson's home.

"Mark! Mark, are you hurt?" Duke shouted over the boy. "Get up, Mark. We've got to get you inside."

"I can't move, Sheriff," Mark groaned before letting out a howl.

The bullet had lodged itself deep in the muscle tissue of Mark's right side about halfway between his hip and his heart, and each movement helped the bullet tear the flesh from the inside out as the young man winced and cried and shouted with the rage of unbearable pain.

"I've got to get you on a flatter surface. You can't stay out here on the stairs, Mark. Can you give me your arm?" Duke asked fruitlessly as Mark's eyes started to lose focus. "Mark? Mark! Come on, Mark!"

There had finally been enough commotion to stir the rest of the Wilson family and bring them to the front porch. Matthew Jr. poured through the door first and had the

Ch. 17 | Fallen

presence of mind to get under his brother's legs and help the sheriff take him to the first bed they could reach, a guest room just inside the door and to the left.

Red covered the planks and boards that made up the front porch, Mark's blood staining the green paint and dripping down the stairs to the dust below. Droplets dotted the path from the front door to the guest room and a worrisome flow started soaking the sheets as soon as Mark's limp body was laid down.

Though Silver Gorge was generally known as a peaceful town, Duke had seen his share of gunshot wounds and knew how to handle them. While it took a moment for most of the siblings to come around from their initial shock of seeing Mark bloody and wounded, Duke was able to bark out the right orders to get them moving. John was running for the cistern to get some water to clean the wound while Luke ran off to find some clean linens. Matthew Jr. made sure to hold a cloth tight on his little brother's wound while Rosemary, their lone sister, held Mark's hand at the side of his bed. Rosemary and Mark were about the same age and so the two always held a closer bond than the other brothers had. Matt Jr. had always tried to act too much like a father to Rosemary while Luke and John were young enough that she often felt like she was raising them. But Mark was different. Those two had been a team, really, and Duke could tell in her eyes that she was hurting to see her friend, her brother in such a dire situation.

"Sheriff? Sheriff, you still here?" Mark coughed with a ragged voice.

"I'm here, Mark. Rest now. Stay quiet," Duke ordered gently.

"Sheriff. Thank you for coming back for me," the boy said. "I guess that was kind of dumb facing down Oscar myself."

"It was right brave of you, son, now save your strength," Duke complimented the boy while tearing sheets of clean linen to make a bandage.

"Listen. Listen to me, Sheriff," Mark struggled to say. "You take care… you take care of Rosemary for me."

The young woman whimpered at her brother's seeming admission of his fate, but Duke would not have it.

"You've got plenty of time to take care of her yourself, boy," Duke reprimanded.

"You're a good man, Sheriff, but a terrible… terrible liar," the boy said, trying to laugh between fits of coughing and screaming as the pull in his sides shifted the bullet with disastrous results.

The siblings all did their jobs admirably while Duke coordinated the efforts and Mark slipped from consciousness. Sheriff Boone recognized the lolling face in front of him and knew that time was short to do anything he might need to do, so he made a choice.

"Mark, I need to tell you something," Duke said, catching Matt's questioning gaze.

"I know," the boy said before grinning. "I would've been a terrible deputy."

"Be serious for a minute, boy."

"I am being serious. I got shot by a banker. Who does that?"

The three attendants let out a small laugh through their tears, not even noticing that Matthew Sr. had been standing in the room for a moment.

"Can you two leave me alone with the sheriff for a moment?" Matthew Sr. asked.

"But Pa, we're working on…"

Ch. 17 | Fallen

"I said now!" their elder roared.

Duke offered Junior a nod and traded places with him, putting his hands on the blood-soaked rag that, for the moment, was keeping Mark alive.

"I've sent John and Luke into town to get Dr. Jarvis. Matthew will escort you off my land and you will never see or touch Rosemary again. Do you understand?" Wilson asked.

"Are you crazy? Your son is dying and you're sitting there talking about getting me out of… "

"My son is dying because of you!" Wilson charged, turning on Duke and bearing a pointed finger on the sheriff's chest with a clenched hand suddenly gripping the sheriff's collar. "You have brought death to my family for the last time, Sheriff Boone. Those men were here looking for you because they knew this is where you would come. I'd hoped to be wrong, but you sure enough showed up here with no mind of what anybody else needed. And now my son… you let that fool Aaron Oscar shoot my boy!"

"I tried to stop him. I swear to you, I tried to stop him," Duke pleaded.

"But you failed. That bullet in my son's chest belongs to you, Sheriff," Wilson said, emphasizing that last word with bite, and scaring Duke with what he might know. "I don't care if you didn't pull the trigger yourself, this is still on you. If my boy dies, it's on you."

Wilson's growl finally stopped, but the fire in his cheeks and his eyes stood in stark contrast to the colorless white of his hair. The threat in Wilson's words did not pass over Duke unnoticed, and it was a very real threat that Wilson could easily enforce. He had the manpower to rival Oscar's posse and he had the funds to own Oscar's posse. Wilson had always had these things, but now he had something more: the will to act.

"As I was saying, Matthew will escort you off my land.

If you come back, I will kill you," the elder Matt Wilson said, towering over the sheriff in a way only he could.

Duke glanced back at Mark, who was by this time fully asleep, and walked out of the room. His hands were crimson and carried that paradoxical combination of slipperiness and stickiness that blood leaves behind, but Duke knew he would not be welcome to stoop and rinse Mark's blood off his hands. Perhaps it was best that he keep that one reminder, after all.

Matthew and the sheriff took a silent ride away from the home, confused about how to properly end their amicable acquaintance, as this would surely be the last time they could ever speak.

"I'm not going to kill you, Duke," Junior said.

"That's good to know," the sheriff responded.

"Father wants me to shoot you. He told me to cut you down at the slightest reason, his words, but I won't do it. Even though I know the truth," Matt continued.

"I really do appreciate… "

"It's not for you," Matt added without hesitation. "Don't get me wrong, you've always been a good man to me and I know you mean well, but it's not for you. Mark really loved… loves you. He wants to be just like you, and I hope he gets there. Assuming my brother pulls through from this thing, it would be a shame if he woke up to find that his big brother had killed his hero.

"I used to be jealous of you, Duke. I was. I hated that my brother looked up to you so much and wanted so badly to be you that he just overlooked me," Matt went on. "The thing is, though, I was always the one to get him into trouble. I'd get into some bar fight that he would try to get me out of. I'd try to fix him up with this rancher's daughter and he would end up having to outrun a bull that the man had turned loose after him. I was always the one getting him into danger and I figured you would be safer for him. I guess the joke's on me,

Ch. 17 | Fallen

really."

Duke rode in silence, just letting the soft sounds of a Nevada morning try to hide the stiff, still quiet between the brother of a dying boy and the man who accidentally shot him. Thinking on that topic, the sheriff wasn't sure if that was the truth that Matt hinted he knew or not, but Duke was in no hurry to find out. The quiet air and the breeze of an early sun would be enough to pad the ride without any further uncomfortable topics.

The pair dutifully rode towards the dusty border of Wilson's land, heeding the commands of a grieving father to the letter. Matt made no effort to let Duke go and Duke made no effort to leave. They would stick together as far as the line and the sheriff would not offer a protest to the contrary.

At a spot some ways off from the main house, and yet a good couple miles from the river that made up Wilson's boundary on that end, Matt wordlessly hopped off of his horse and tied her up to a tree. The area was new to Duke, though he had ridden through Wilson land countless times before, but it clearly held meaning to Matthew.

"Give me that rifle," the oldest Wilson brother demanded gently.

Duke obliged, though he feared that Matt's earlier promise now proved false. Matt tenderly held the rifle in his hands and stroked the wood grain that made up the stock. He raised the rifle to his shoulder, momentarily jolting Duke, but then he aimed the rifle towards no particular tree in the opposite direction.

"He taught me to shoot out here sometimes," Matt said. Duke assumed the man Matt referred to was his father, Matthew, Sr. "He would always say, 'Look down the barrel, not down the sights.' That's what he would say. But I never listened. I never could break the habit of looking down the sights of this dang rifle. He'd say, 'The barrel makes a longer line than the sight does. Longer line makes for a better shot. Which line you want to use, boy?'"

Duke was still confused, of course, but he let his fear slip away as Matt's behavior leaned more towards the reminiscent than the angry.

"In order to teach me better, he bent the sight on this rifle to the right. I finally had to break my habit," Matt explained. "That's why Greasy thought he could stay on our land. Because I told him he could. He would bring me out here and teach me how to shoot by getting me to aim at that branch over there. He had a tin can he would set up there and I would have to hit it."

Duke looked at the branch Matt indicated and, sure enough, it was dotted with holes from wayward rifle rounds and occasional buckshot. More importantly, Duke realized what Matt was trying to say.

"You weren't trying to shoot my brother, Duke. That much is obvious," Matt said. "We both loved that boy, and I know you'd never want to hurt him."

"I was aiming for Oscar. I don't... I don't know how I shot so far off. It makes sense now, I guess, but... I'm so sorry, Matt," Duke said evenly. "I thought maybe I was too tired or my eyes were too crossed. I haven't slept in a day, Matt. I could've aimed better."

"You aimed fine. You had no way of knowing that Greasy bent the sights on this gun just like Pa had no way of knowing that Greasy was teaching me to shoot," Matt offered. "It's the secrets we keep that hurt the people we love. If I hadn't begged Greasy to teach me how to shoot like he could... none of this would've happened. He wouldn't be dead and you wouldn't have used his rifle to shoot my brother."

Matt turned around and hugged Duke after dropping the rifle. Matt Wilson eclipsed Duke in size and width, and his

Ch. 17 | Fallen

arms wrapped around the sheriff like clouds around a mountain peak, squeezing him tighter as the minutes passed. Nothing would be said of this moment, but it was one they both needed.

After they parted, Matt picked up Greasy's rifle and balanced it against a tree as a memorial. Duke and the young man stared at the gun for a moment while Matt said a prayer of hope for his brother.

"Amen," Duke echoed.

"Look, Sheriff. I've gotta get back. My brother needs me. Can you find your way out without me?" Matt asked.

"No problem. Pull him through, Matt. Pull him through," Duke said.

Never before had Duke been so ineffective. As sheriff, Duke commanded respect and authority. He had a measure of control over his life and the town of Silver Gorge. As Matt Wilson, Jr. mounted his horse and headed back towards the mortally wounded Mark, Duke considered how little control he really had. Every effort that Duke had put toward altering the course of events had resulted in death. People who stood on his side kept winding up dead. Duke Boone had created a path of destruction like the flash floods that were known to spring up overnight and sweep up every building and soul in their way.

For the first time since Zeke's horrifying end, Duke was truly directionless. There was no path, no goal that stood before him. Every option had been eradicated. And while Duke still had a few friends he could rely on, just a few vestiges of safe harbor, he dared not put them in the path of destruction that had claimed so many innocent men already.

And yet, the objective had never been clearer. Leaving now simply meant abandoning the people Duke cared about to ruin. Though running was the safest course to follow, Duke knew that he had already caused too many people to pay too high a price. If he were to bring justice to Greasy. To Zeke. To Josiah. To Riley. To Silver Gorge. To Mark. If Duke were to bring those forfeited souls peace, the only direction he could travel in now was forward.

Burning light dripped through the brush and between the green leaves that were starting to show up all over Wilson land once again. Duke closed his eyes for a moment and basked in the weaving of shadow and sun that was the great oasis around him. Though his heart broke for Mark and for Rosemary and for all those who had given more than they should to help the sheriff now cast down, an impossible calm came over Duke sitting atop his famous mount with reins in hand. Though Duke would never be able to fix what was behind, the next steps ahead would start to make things right. Justice would only come in one way, and that was the way that Duke had to go.

-Chapter Eighteen-
Valley of Ghosts

Weary, Sheriff Boone mindlessly hopped off his horse and tied the golden beast to a post outside the office as he had done countless times before. The monotony of routine saved him the hassle of thinking too much while in the dullness of exhaustion, allowing the world-worn sheriff to open his door and walk right in the jailhouse without raising an eye or even letting his gaze come up from the floor.

He was so worn, in fact, that he missed the obvious sign of footprints in the dust that seemed to line the path ahead before Duke took his steps. Thirst and torpor conquered Duke's thoughts, not observant acuity, so even blatant hints of misdeed or surprise passed by him unchecked.

As Duke's hands turned the handle and his boots made no small announcement of his presence, the door creaked open to announce the entrance of an additional party to the room. Off in the corner of said room, the only room that Duke generally felt comfortable entering without scanning, stood a shadow-veiled figure, his eyes hidden under the brim of a weathered black hat, while the sun poured through the window and distracted the balance in Duke's eyes. The figure stood silent, waiting for someone to arrive and break the coarse silence that was his impatience.

Even still, the sheriff did not see the figure at the corner of the room until he was already fully in the doorway and had nearly closed the door behind him. Neither was the figure as keenly aware of a new presence in the room as he should have been given his current occupation of the jailhouse, which gave Duke a moment to collect the gravity of the situation and draw his weapon on the man who stood there before him.

"Whoa, whoa!" the figure hollered as Duke hesitantly released the pressure on a half-squeezed trigger.

If Zeke had been born any less smart or lucky, Duke often said, he would've died out years ago. His brains and his fortune balanced out this time, it seemed, as the man opted not to wait outside when he could come in and scare the sheriff within an inch of someone else's life.

"Zeke, what in the world are you doing in here?" Duke asked, feeling the pulse in his neck slowly coming down from the peak of a recent shock.

"I'm sorry, Duke, er, Sheriff. I just wanted to come by and see you for a bit and I didn't think you would mind if I came on in," the farmer answered.

Zeke was a tall man, standing even above the sheriff when he stood straight, but his dark features often hid the handsomeness that had once been his meal ticket. The sunken eyes complemented a perpetually clean-shaven chin, but his distinguishing hair was the real treat. Zeke had been known around Silver Gorge's female population as the lover with the locks, a name he encouraged for obvious reasons, in his younger days. Now a man of more than 40 years with a son of his own, Zeke's scorch-black hair still fell long upon his shoulders and was the one thing that would still impress a woman interested in his company.

"I don't so much mind, I guess, but you nearly made me shoot you," Duke chided. "Don't do that."

Once the initial warning had been shared, Duke

Ch. 18 | Valley of Ghosts

warmed up and greeted his old friend as a companion and a guest, pouring some undesirably cool coffee into a mug and passing it over. Zeke being a polite fellow accepted the coffee and cordially guzzled it down in light of the fact that he owed the sheriff a little for that rude fright earlier.

"What brings you into town today? Did I forget an appointment?" Duke wondered.

"No, we're not due to go hunting for a week. But I do have a small favor to ask you," Zeke asserted. "See, it's Josiah. I'm afraid something's wrong."

"Is he okay? I thought he was working up at Mason City?"

"He is, and I think he's fine, but something doesn't sit right with me," Zeke explained. "See, I know Mason ain't paying his men all that much, and most of it is in that worthless crib he calls Mason Money, but my boy keeps showing up at the farm with fancy clothes and extra money for me to run the place with and pay everything off. It don't make much sense."

"What's that old saying about gift horses and teeth, Zeke?" Duke joked.

"Yeah, yeah, I know. I shouldn't worry about it, but it doesn't make any sense. I'm afraid he's stealing money from Mason and that he's going to get himself into trouble. Boss Mason ain't exactly a reasonable man in the best of times, so I know he won't deal too kindly with Josiah if it turns out that's what's going on," Zeke said.

"Have you tried talking to him?"

"Well. No, I guess not," Zeke responded while Duke laughed derisively. "But listen, it's not like he's home very much as it is. He stays up there on that mountain and in the mine and it seems like he only comes home when he's got more money to stash somewhere. He always comes home in his mining outfit, and he leaves in his mining outfit, but I always see him wearing these fancy clothes he shouldn't be able to afford while he's around with me. And he has all these saddlebags full of... well, I don't know. Stuff. He won't ever let me see it, but he has some kind of stuff in there. I'm telling you, Duke, my boy is going to get himself killed if he's stealing from Boss Mason.

"Besides. I never see him anymore and I don't want to start a fight with him," Zeke concluded.

"Well what do you want me to do about it? Follow him?" Duke foolishly suggested, assuming his old friend would see the idiocy in such a notion.

"Yeah, that's a great idea! You can follow him up to Mason City and then follow him back to see what he's got hiding in those saddlebags," Zeke rejoined.

Angry with himself for tempting a desperate father, Duke begrudgingly agreed to take on this added mission.

"I'll do what I can, but I make no promises. If I catch him stealing, you know I have to arrest him," Duke explained.

"Yeah, sure. That's fine. It'd be a far sight better if he ended up in your jail than if he ended up buried in some corner of Mason's mine up there," Zeke noted, subconsciously rubbing a spot on his chin where a thick, dark blood-like substance started to seep.

"You cut yourself shaving this morning, Zeke?"

"Yeah, I must've. Huh. That wasn't there a moment ago."

In a flash of visions, Duke saw himself trailing the boy Josiah through the desert at night and he saw himself watching Josiah unload a saddlebag full of indeterminate trinkets at the mouth of Mason's mine. Josiah carried a pole twice as long as he was tall with a net dangling from one end, the fabric and the wood tar-stained for three feet on that end. Duke crouched on the edge of the butte and watched Josiah

Ch. 18 | Valley of Ghosts

wander into the mine and back out some hour or so later with the same saddlebag, and it seemed to have gained no mass but considerable weight. Josiah grabbed another and headed back down, but this time there would be no ascension.

Duke heard shouting and a blast that sounded like powder, and with the influx of men crowding the mine, the sheriff left his perch without once seeing what became of Josiah or the first bag he had pulled from the mine.

In another flash, Duke stood between Mason and Zeke on the steps in front of the mining boss's office atop the mountain. The chill of this cloudless December night made it easy for Duke to see the wrath in his friend's eyes and the worry in Mason's bloodless cheeks.

Zeke kept screaming for his friend to do something, begging him to arrest Mason or shoot Mason, his violent pleas bringing tears to the face of the hardest man Duke had ever known. Unswayed he stood, though, and Duke did all he could in the eyes of the law when he stepped between his friend and the target. Betrayal washed over Zeke's face as he lowered his gun and backed away in defeat, but he never saw the miners with rifles and pistols camped out in doorways and windows of surrounding buildings. Mason walked up behind Duke in view of Zeke and put a thankful hand upon the sheriff's shoulder, but Duke impudently shrugged it off. That was perhaps an unwise move, as it was never wise to cross Mason, but Duke loathed his own oath at that moment and wished he would have let Zeke have revenge, even if it meant death.

As Zeke turned to mount his horse, a patch of black, bilious mucus overtook the lower quarters of his face and contorted his wrathful grimace into a wretched, twisted maw that bellowed forth a silent scream. Duke could not reel in horror, for that was not how he saw Zeke that night, but there was an undeniable veracity in the transformation upon his former friend's face.

Time flashed once more in the eyes of Duke Boone as his next vision came from the saloon on that day not so long ago when Zeke cornered three presumably innocent men in an attempt to lure Mason away from his stronghold on top of the mountain. Duke reasoned with his friend and pleaded for the lives of those three miners, but it was useless. Zeke held a curved knife at their backs and threatened action if Mason were not summoned at once. The putrescence crept out of the corners of Zeke's mouth at first, slowly and deliberately to start, but it eventually wrapped around his entire visage and swathed the rancher's features in an oily sheen that gave way to a roiling, bubbling stew of indescribable darkness and unknowable stench. Zeke's entire person converted to this hateful liquid which billowed like smoke temporarily trapped in a human form, yet he stood firm.

Forcing his way around the three captors, what was once Zeke barreled down upon Duke and shouted hateful curses upon him.

"Do you even know what is in that mine, Sheriff?" the hideous thing mocked. "Do you know what is in that mine?"

His body shook and trembled, and it was perhaps the physical scraping of skin and hair against rock that aroused Duke from his disastrous rest. This horrid amalgam of recognition and dreams had affected him unnaturally, and the terror took hold of him just as awfully in waking as it had in sleep.

Duke was conscious of a terrified yelping, full of uttered prayers and proclaimed blessings, though he was initially unaware that it was his own primal reaction to the fevered and greatly intensified return of his previous dreams. Before, his dreams of Zeke had just been the worst memories from that day in the saloon revisited with detestable repetition. Now, it seemed, Duke's mind played deeper and more sinister games with the memories that had put him in this position.

Ch. 18 | Valley of Ghosts

As the sheriff sat up and gathered his thoughts, he blindly reached out and felt the gritty rocks that made up his bed and his cover. He had found shelter in a place just outside the Wilson territory and taken a rest, though the term turned out to be less restful than he would have hoped. Duke was shaded from the worst of the elements in this hollow, but even there he could tell that evening was coming upon him in a hurry. He did not hear the cries of a posse's ill-advised bloodlust, so Duke pleasantly assumed that he had not been tracked to this point as a way of recovering from the earlier unpleasantness.

Such an assumption was proven untrue, however, when Duke slipped his head out from under the rocks and caught sight of a silhouette's leg in the low sun. The single limb he spotted wore beige canvas pants and had a Remington pistol with a custom embossed pearl handle at the hip, and Duke feared that this was one of the paid assassins that Mason had ordered to end whatever threat the deposed sheriff still measured up to.

Rather, it was a sight much more welcome as Duke realized when he saw her hair fall down out of her hat and onto her shoulders. Even when outshined by the sun, Miss Abilene's golden waves were obvious and enticing.

"I'm glad you finally came out of there on your own. All that racket you threw up and I was afraid I'd have to crawl in after you," Abilene remarked.

The tangible fear of an interloper had worked to shake Duke out of the intrinsic dread he felt at Zeke's unreal transformation, and the comforting realization that his guest meant him no harm helped ease the final transition. Sheriff Boone crawled out of the hole he had burrowed into earlier and took his feet back in order to face Abilene at nearly eye level.

"How'd you find me, Abs? I was buried under that rock pretty far," Duke asked.

"Yeah, but your horse was right here. Not exactly tough work to spot that one, plus you were screaming like an angry toddler just now," Abilene responded.

The shock of his horrid dreams had woken Duke only so much or else he might have noticed the obvious truth that his horse was sitting in plain sight. Such a foolish mistake could have been costly, but his error wrought no permanent damage. Just a tired horse and a visit from someone who actually wanted to keep him alive.

"We've got to get you out of the sun, Duke. You've been laying here all day. Is there anywhere we can go?" she asked, hoping he had a plan.

If he'd had a plan, Duke thought, he might not have curled up under a rock.

"There's nowhere to go but to leave, Miss Abilene. I can't go back to Silver Gorge or else I'll be hanged. I can't stay here or else Mason will come and take me himself. What are my options, then?" Duke laid out.

In his heart, Duke had resolved to ride until the sky and the sun were one and there was nowhere left to ride. Leaving was not enough, Duke thought, but making his final ride would be. As long as he was around, Duke was a danger to everyone who chose to follow him.

"What possible choice is there?" Boone shouted.

As he spoke, the sheriff gathered up his things and started to prepare his horse's saddle for a long ride out, but Miss Abilene ran over and yanked the reins out of his hand.

"You will do no such thing, Sheriff Boone," she scolded. "You are going to end this."

"End what? End Mason? Because he's got me. He won. My deputy is dead, which is of no consequence since he was the one who wanted me dead in the first place. I killed Mark Wilson. The only people who were still behind me have every

Ch. 18 | Valley of Ghosts

reason to hate me, and most of the town turned out to watch me hang, including a woman I thought I loved," Duke taunted.

"I had to be out there, Duke Boone! You know what they would have done if I hadn't stood there and watched them hang you?"

She paused as if to let Duke answer, but his guilt at insinuating her implicit passivity had started to bubble up. Duke knew he had made a mistake and he was ready to accept the punishment.

"They would have strung me up right next to you. Mason's men would have had their mob drag me out of the hotel by my hair and added a third rope for me right there between you and that killer," she concluded.

"And we can't have them ruining your beautiful hair," Duke teased, stepping closer to the fair lady in farm clothes and a flat-brim straw hat before she rebuked him with a firm hand to the chest.

"Don't you try any of that now, you hear? You are still far from being in the clear. First of all, you accuse me of wanting to hang you. What gives you the right to say such a thing? And what do you mean you killed Mark Wilson?"

Duke turned and stared at his feet intently for a minute, finally answering with a soft whisper.

"I shot him."

"What'd you say?"

"I shot him," Duke yelled. "I shot him. I was trying to hit Oscar, who was pointing his gun at Mark, but I missed. I killed Wilson's kid. Or at least I guess he's dead. I stayed with him as long as I could, he was alive when I left, but I've never seen anybody survive something that bad."

Abilene eased up behind Duke, wrapping her left arm around his and resting her head on his shoulder. The sheriff caressed her right hand, which had been inserted under his arm and placed on his chest, and he just let the lady hold him tight. In the dying heat of a Nevada evening, Duke turned and pulled her body close to his, taking to her lips like a hummingbird to a flower.

As sweet as the moment was, Duke knew that Abilene's first thought was right. They could not stay out in the open all night, not if they hoped to survive, and it occurred to the sheriff that he had two options. The first, which was certainly out of the question, was the cave. That man had gold that belonged to Mason and he could not be trusted. His second option was safer in the short run, but it presented certain other problems.

Duke pulled away from Abilene's embrace and rubbed her shoulders with both of his hands, all the while avoiding her gaze. Concern blanketed the woman's face, which Duke tried to deflect with a tender smile. He was unsuccessful.

"I have an idea of where we can go. That is, if you're still up for sticking with me through this," Duke said.

"Sure. You know I'll go anywhere with you, Duke, but why do I get the feeling that you're not happy about this?" she wisely surmised.

"Just… just trust me," Duke said. "And forgive me."

Abilene, fraught with curious distress, mounted up and followed Duke on the star-lit path towards Mason City. Night had covered the desert before long, especially in the moon shadow of Mason's private butte, but Duke traveled as if he needed no semblance of light or direction to discern his path. Even a treacherous river crossing that took them uncomfortably near to Mason City passed over Duke without so much as a bother, though he was certain to turn back to aid Abilene in her journey. Duke had clearly wandered this path many times, more than once at night.

After a while, the two travelers came upon a small,

Ch. 18 | Valley of Ghosts

wood-thatch house with smoke pouring from the chimney. The cozy abode was nestled up against a lower crest of the butte that provided Mason with his fortress, though it was not in direct view of the mining facility as it lay to the western side of the feature and towards the back. Barking could be heard coming from inside, likely warning the occupant that someone approached, and Duke noticed several lamps light up at once. Duke could smell the aroma of an evening stew with rabbit, potatoes and beef broth gently spiced as it broke the monotony of dust and sweat.

Just as he expected they would, Duke and Abilene were interrupting their unexpecting host just moments after dinner and before bed. Abilene kept tossing furtive looks at Duke, but he shooed them away with his disarming smile and a nervous face. This blend of emotions confused Abilene at first, though its explanation was all too obvious upon her later remembrances of the scene. She and the sheriff passed through the fence and sent the guard dog into a momentary fervor before the sounds died out altogether. It knew who was coming and it felt comfortable.

Duke and Abilene were close enough to walk the rest of the way as they dismounted and stepped towards the door after roping their horses up to the post. Between the stars of a clear sky and the lantern light squeezing under the shutters, Duke could see just well enough to make out the front door. Though he didn't need to see the front door, as the path was exactly how he remembered it.

A sharp knock rattled the door, signaling the severity of this visit, and Duke heard rustling of fabric and rope behind the wall. From the sound of things, it was silk. This would not be good at all, he imagined.

After a moment's pause, likely due to her insistence on glancing out the crack in the door to see who approached, the door flew open to show off most all of Miss Glorietta as she stood backlit by the fire in the chimney and the lamps on her table.

"Finally come to pay up on that bet you made?" Miss Glorietta teased, her tender hands rubbing the doorposts where a prayer might be, unveiling the silhouette of a woman ready for bed.

The woman's tender hands, no longer hidden by black gloves, delicately touched the wood that framed her entrance, though Duke was quick to clear his throat and step out of the way to where Miss Glorietta could see their other companion. Upon the realization that a third party stood witness to their exchange, the lady wrapped her garment more tightly around herself and stepped away back into the house.

"We need your help, Glorietta," Duke pleaded. "We need a place to stay and someone to help us put an end to Boss Mason."

-Chapter Nineteen-
Deeper Still

Glorietta reluctantly stepped out of the door frame to let her unexpected guests make their way inside. The sun had been fully down for nearly an hour now, so the pair had either been staked out waiting for dark or their needs were as serious as advertised. A woman living alone so near the mining camp would be wise to keep a rifle near the door, which she did, but the miners were smarter than to leave Mason City at night. They were smarter, still, than to attempt a pass at Glorietta.

"Why is it you want to put me out of business," the lady asked, subtly letting her chiffon gown slink over her shoulder in a teasing ploy. "Mason's been good to me. Almost as good to me as you once were, Sheriff."

Duke attempted to shake off her blatant gestures and ill-timed innuendos. The scene had almost reached Boone's limit for excruciating discomfort, though he was hardly surprised by Glorietta's behavior in Miss Abilene's presence. Even so, he had to stay focused.

"I've lost count of how many times Mason has tried to have me killed in the last two days, Glorietta," Duke explained, drawing a curious look from his former paramour. "Should I list it for you? He sent assassins after me in the desert. He somehow convinced my own deputy to build a gallows in town, not lacking a noose with my name on it. He sent an armed brigade of more than 50 citizens after me."

Glorietta tested Duke's accusations, measuring out their effectiveness on her will. Mason had openly spoken against Duke in private conversations, of course, but would he have gone so far as to attack the sheriff of Silver Gorge? True, it would probably suit his interests to replace Duke Boone with someone more favorable to the mine, but murder for hire was a new step for Mason. It seemed unlikely.

"Not to mention whatever it is he's got penned up in that mine down there," Duke said.

That caught her attention. Glorietta turned on Duke with a flash and nearly pushed Abilene out of the way to approach him.

"What do you know about that?" she charged.

"I'll know more when you tell me," Duke retorted.

She bit her lip and darted her eyes fiercely around the room as if to check for prying ears, and Glorietta leaned in close to Duke before letting fly what she knew.

"The mine isn't empty, Duke," she teased. "We all thought it was back when he left a few years ago, but it wasn't. We just had to look a little deeper."

"What'd you find?" Abilene shouted, losing herself in the mystery.

The audience of two watched Glorietta and waited for her response, but the woman was a master at her craft. Glorietta's look slowly drifted from one face to the other while she stretched out the tension in the room as far as it could bend. With a determined grin, Glorietta exposed her boss's secret.

"We found gold," she smirked.

Ch. 19 | Deeper Still

"Gold? You found gold?" Duke bellowed. "You're a fool if you expect me to believe that for a moment, Glorietta."

"It's the truth, Duke! There's gold in that mine, and plenty of it by the numbers I've heard Mason talking about. We've got more gold than men, I think," Glorietta mused.

"There is no gold in that mine, woman. There's never been gold found in all of Nevada, but you expect me to believe that Mason found a million-dollar vein overnight?" Duke responded.

"You know good and well they found gold in Carlin a few years back," she reiterated.

"A trickle! Nothing like what you're trumping up, Glorietta. What's really going on?" Duke urged.

Glorietta sat the crew down and explained her side of the issue in an attempt to quell the swelling emotions. She, like everyone else, thought the mine had gone empty a few years back when Mason up and left Nevada for foreign lands. With Mason's departure, the small band of miners who were in the area left for gold mines near the California wilderness. A straggling few were loyal to Mason and had stuck around out of respect for the man, but his absence meant they were eventually free from any such burden.

When Mason came back, he hired an all new crew to work on the lowest vent where silver had been found. At least most of the crew had done so.

"I'm not really supposed to know any of this, I don't think," Glorietta warned, as if forbidden knowledge made a difference to a man running for his life. "Most of the men work in the silver mine, never really finding much but a rock here or there. There's a smaller group, though, that works on a side shaft. They take heavy carts of equipment down there every evening when the rest of the miners are already asleep or off doing God knows what and they stay throughout the night. I've usually gone by the time the B Crew goes in, but

255

I've seen them by chance a time or two. It's a very secretive group, the B Crew. Your three friends from the saloon were promoted to it just last week, but it's not easy to get that detail. I first spotted B Crew just a couple weeks after Zeke's kid went missing, come to think of it."

"I don't buy it, Glorietta. Gold don't explain what I've seen. Men don't change like that because of gold," Duke rebuked.

"Then you've not seen enough gold. For as much gold as I think Mason's found, men will do quite a lot that you've never seen," Glorietta added. "Production really ramped up after Zeke's kid went missing, I think. They never get all they could out of there, probably because the other miners would notice it and get suspicious, but they get a good bit. But if I'm being honest with you, come to think of it, Zeke's kid ain't the only one to go missing recently."

The way that Glorietta said that the boy had gone missing rather than died worried Duke, as if the facts were far worse than misrepresented earlier and that she knew something more. It also reinforced one of the most pernicious ideas that would pervade a parent's mind, and that's the notion that no body means no death. For the longing of a wounded parent, the lack of a corpse can only mean that the child is still alive. Perhaps not in great circumstances, but alive nonetheless.

Duke had never had any children himself, but it made sense. Burying your child must be an unimaginable hell, and the ambition of blind hope, no matter how torturous not knowing can be, preserves some semblance of sanity for a while. In Zeke's case, that hope drove him to do an awful thing.

Glorietta told Duke of miners going down with the B Crew and never being seen again. They'll usually get a few weeks with the crew before they go missing, but men have been known to disappear as quickly as their second day with

Ch. 19 | Deeper Still

B Crew. Rumors in the camp would be worse if not for how effectively Mason keeps his B Crew men sequestered. Promotion to B Crew is dubious and notorious for the men in Mason City as they never really know what to expect. After moving to the separate housing, Glorietta explained, B Crew men get a bump in pay. It's still in Mason's own currency, but it is an enviable raise from their previous wages.

A man might grow to enjoy his time with B Crew, even if it means he can rarely ever speak with the men in his old crews, and he might even get comfortable on B Crew. Then after a few weeks, there he goes. Nobody ever hears from him again, B Crew can't acknowledge that he used to be with them, and work goes on like always. Nothing new in their minds.

"Listen, Glorietta," Duke pleaded. "We have got to find out what's in that mine."

"How? What makes you think I can help you with that? Or that I would help you?"

"I know you never met Zeke, the man who took Mason's miners hostage in town, but he was a close friend of mine. When his boy went missing, it tore him up," Duke explained. "And there wasn't a thing I could do. I couldn't get in there to look for a body. I couldn't charge Mason with anything. All I could do was watch. All I could do was stand back and let Mason get away with ruining my friend. All because of that… that cursed star.

"But that's gone now. I can make a move. I can do something. Right before Zeke… right before he died, he was talking about the mine," Duke concluded. "His last words to me were about whatever Mason has hiding down in that mine. I have to know what it is, Glorietta. And I have to stop Mason."

"Last words don't have to mean anything," Glorietta challenged, deflecting Duke's accusation. "I was a little girl when my grandfather died, but I still remember the last thing he said. You know what he said, Duke?"

The man shook his head.

Effecting her best gravelly, senior voice, Glorietta said, "'Fetch me a mule saddle. I'm hungry.' That's what my grandpa said just seconds before he died. You know what a mule saddle is? Nothing. It doesn't exist and you sure can't eat it. And there was a miner a year back who broke his neck when he was horsing around on the water tower. Know what he said? 'The stars. I feel the stars on my skin.' It was lunchtime. There were no stars."

Glorietta had shamed Duke with her stories and had nearly convinced him to give up the significance of those words, but she went a step too far.

"Besides. All the men who have died like that were too far gone at the end to really be trusted," Glorietta eked out, realizing her mistake the moment it was said.

As Boss Mason's secretary stopped and hesitantly turned her grimacing face back towards Duke, the sheriff had already charged, immediately pinning her up against the wall before the shouting commenced.

"What do you mean? You knew! And there were more of them! What's going on up there, Glorietta!? You better tell us and tell us now, or so help me I'll make sure you never speak again," Duke bellowed as Glorietta pleaded.

Though his show of force probably went a long way towards convincing the largely silent and merely observant Abilene that no semblance of a spark was left between the two people who were currently caught up in a different kind of embrace, watching Duke react so feverishly shocked her into action. Using a gentle tug, Abilene reached across Duke's chest and tried to pull him away from the gagging, convulsing woman pinned to the wall. As he backed away and she fell, Glorietta let out a howl that rattled the horses outside.

Ch. 19 | Deeper Still

Gathering her breath, Glorietta shot a burning stare through Duke's bowed chest as if tearing at his insides with a trowel. Duke's show of force had betrayed Glorietta's trust in inviting him in, and the passion with which he attacked her now was the most vigor she had seen from the former sheriff in a couple years. To feel his hands again, yet in as violent a manner as this, was a betrayal that Glorietta would hardly let go of.

"Yes, there were more," Glorietta spit. "I saw two of them, two men who one day complained that they couldn't feel their noses in the cold air. On Monday, they're telling me that they can't feel part of their face. By Wednesday morning, their hands are dripping black and oozing all over my office. That night, they both just... well, you know. They just spilled out everywhere. It was horrible, Duke! It was horrible! And I needed you. Tell me something, Sheriff. Do you have the nightmares? Because I do. Every night, I lay in that bed wishing for death because I can't sleep without seeing the hollow, horrified eyes of a man just before his body turns to sludge and seeps back into the ground. You have that experience, Duke?"

While Glorietta sat on the ground huffing and wheezing in fury, her balled fists supporting her weight and turning white with gripped rage, Abilene walked over to place a blanket over her apparent competitor's shoulder. In her right mind, Glorietta might have protested being touched by a woman in Abilene's position, yet her gaze fixed on Duke with unwavering hatred.

For the once-sheriff, his realization was complete. Not just that Mason really was doing something horrible, but that it had happened before. Zeke was not alone in that wretched death, even if Glorietta had been alone in dealing with it. Just like he had been, Duke thought. As much as he struggled to barricade those memories away, it was a losing fight. Duke had seen men die before, but watching a man's body collapse like that was a soul-crushing reality. At least twice, Glorietta had seen the same thing. She knew the sound of juicy flesh giving way to inky black bile and plopping onto parched earth. She knew the smell of previously decayed meat advancing further into deeper and more mature stages of rot. She knew the horror of what Duke had seen and she had handled it alone.

"I'm sorry," was all the sheriff could say.

Abilene helped Glorietta stand, the latter worn and weary from her fit of terror and hatred. The two women walked towards Glorietta's door when the homeowner slowly faced her male guest.

"I forgive you. You know I can't stay mad at you, Duke Boone," she started. "I'll help you. I'll help you both however I can."

Duke and Abilene shared a look before thanking Glorietta for her sacrifice and her kindness.

"You can stay here the night, of course, but I've just got the one bed. One of you can join me, and Abilene, you can sleep on the furniture in here," she went on, tapping Abilene on the back as the female guest carried her host to bed.

"I'm not sleeping with you tonight," Duke offered simply.

"Can't blame me for trying," Glorietta said, her slinky night things seductively slipping off her several surfaces. "Come on, honey. Looks like you and me this time."

Nearly an hour passed and Duke still sat up firmly in one of Glorietta's fine chairs, sipping on his second bowl of stew from the pot. She had always been a fine cook, Duke reminisced, and she had plenty of other handy talents, too.

It was then that a creaking door caught his attention and his host softly escaped her room with unusual surreptitiousness for someone in her own home. Duke looked at her with annoyance, but he was actually quite glad to see

Ch. 19 | Deeper Still

her face. There was much to discuss about tomorrow's endeavors and Duke had no knack for planning such a thing on his own. Plus, it could be nice to talk about the old days for a moment, even though he had not yet fully admitted to himself or to Abilene that the old days had happened between him and Glorietta.

Rather than her colorful gown, Glorietta now bore a plush robe of some exotic design, likely given to her by Mason upon his return from those exotic locales. The cotton garment was wrapped conservatively around her shoulders and chest, sealing out chilling breezes and prying eyes. Her dark hair still stood stark against the waning candles as it flowed across her shoulders and down her back for a ways. Even when she tried to put it away, Glorietta's beauty was unmistakable.

"I won't sleep with you tonight," an exasperated but conflicted Duke offered without request.

"Would you shut up about that," Glorietta laughed. "I'm not here to jump you, Duke. I just want to talk."

Talking was good between them when it was done right. That's all they had done for a while, really. Duke would ride out to Mason City and visit Glorietta for a dinner afterwards. One night a storm came up that kept him from riding home, and the undeniable, encompassing presence of Glorietta was all it took to convince Duke that this woman's company was worth keeping.

After that night, they talked much less frequently.

"She's a good woman, Duke," Glorietta examined without invite. "Be good to her. Be better to her."

"I'm sorry about my actions earlier. That was wrong," Duke apologized.

"It was," she sighed, trying to forget his earlier brutality, coupled with his selfishness in ignoring her needs. "You didn't know that I'd seen what you saw, so you had no way of knowing what I was going through."

"But I did know, Glorietta. For God's sake, I'm the only man on the planet who really knows what you're going through. We could've talked about this. We could've been there for each other."

She backed away laughing, aware of where that talk might lead.

"You are a charmer, Duke, and your chest is still as sexy as ever," she giggled, as Duke had long taken his shirt off after Glorietta and Abilene's initial departure, "but we're done. That's not what I want to talk about. I want to talk about how you're going to supposedly destroy Mason. What is it going to do to know what he's got going on down there? My guess, he'll just kill you to keep it a secret, much like he's already wanting to do to you. So what's your big plan?"

Duke grinned and looked at Glorietta for a second, admiring her sharp demeanor for a moment before revealing the one aspect of a plan he really had.

"We're going to blow the mine," Duke admitted.

"Great, so you've closed up the entrance. Now what? It's a mine. Those men are made to haul rocks," she answered reasonably.

"I'll think of something. There are ways to keep miners from working," Duke hinted.

"Yeah. It's called killing the man who signs the checks. When you talk about blowing the mine, you don't just mean the structure. You want Mason dead," she intimated.

"Or in jail. I'm not too particular," Duke softly barked.

"Listen to me, Duke. This is not the road you want to go down. If you kill him, his people will come after you. There's no telling how many of them he really has or what he is fully capable of, especially if he can manage to subdue the Kansas Scarecrow. Mason is a dangerous man dead or alive. I hope you know what you're doing," she warned.

Ch. 19 | Deeper Still

"The only thing I can do, Glorietta. Something," Duke said.

Their talking done, the former lovers sat quiet in an ever darkening room as the candles melted down their wax and built white drip castles next to the low flame while the third slept in a stranger's bed. Duke had forgotten the feeling of home that he knew when he was with Glorietta. He and Abilene both lived at work, so to speak, so the notion of getting away and being in Glorietta's home was rejuvenating for the sheriff.

Outside the window, Duke's and Abilene's horses stood tied to a post, listening to the glimmer of stars and tiny bugs skittering across the dirt. Wolves ran the night in their hunting packs, tracking down something savory to eat. A warm moon signaled the end of cooler evenings as the heat of the sun lingered longer and longer with each passing day.

And with all of this going on, up on a ridge sat two riders who sped off towards the north in the direction of Mason City.

-Chapter Twenty-

Secrets Within

      Before the sun had come up, Glorietta gathered a small breakfast for her two guests and pondered what the events of her day would be like. There would be the usual ride up the butte to Mason City, conjoined with the usual whistles from wayward miners who had not yet been taught better. After a short while spent preparing Boss Mason's morning particulars, a glass of whiskey and toast served up beside the pertinent telegrams, Glorietta would retreat to her own office space to pore over inventory sheets and productivity numbers. She would, as usual, pretend to ignore the discrepancies that Boss Mason paid her to ignore while mentally plotting out where her discussion of the numbers would go. As always, she would creatively skirt the topics of missing men and inventory while wholesale ignoring the inflated output numbers. After lunch, she would slip away and pull a crate of dynamite from inventory for Duke's plot to end Mason once and for all. So that was new.

      Ham and eggs sat on the chipped-blue stoneware plates that Glorietta placed on the table. She had hardly slept at all that night, what with her late conversations with Duke and the presence of another flailing woman in her bed made for one. It was different when a man joined her. After all, lying close beside a man is warm and romantic. Lying beside a

Ch. 20 | Secrets Within

woman is hot, uncomfortable, and dangerous. And Abilene snored.

Abilene's company was welcome, though. It had been a couple years since anyone had joined Glorietta in her bed, and certainly not since the nightmares began. Another body beside her gave Glorietta the confidence to close her eyes and rest. By herself, Glorietta instinctively feared that those visions and hellscapes would still be there when she awoke. Having Duke sleep just a few yards away while Abilene pulled up close to her back made Glorietta rest better. Then again, it might have just been that Abilene's snoring prevented Glorietta from sleeping deeply enough to dream. Either way, the nightmares stayed at bay for one night, and that was a blessing worthy of the exhaustion she would suffer through the day.

Mason's aide had already put on her usual attire, a loose-fitting dress of black cotton and purple stitching. It was nowhere near as ornate as the saloon girls wore, but then her job required more than being pretty and laughing. Glorietta managed a mine while Mason watched from his office window, likely napping through most of the day in his leather throne.

Glorietta spotted a glint of sunlight through her back window, meaning that it would come time to leave very soon. Gathering the last of her things, she gobbled down a quick bite of the feast she had prepared for her former love and his new woman. What a messed up scene this was, Glorietta thought, with Abilene in her bed and Duke resting half-dressed in a chair right by the table, gleaming in the morning haze. She took a moment to admire his physique and his mere presence, though the moment was shattered once more by the sound of Abilene's throaty roar reverberating beyond the shut door. Duke responded in kind, letting his own ululation echo twice as sharply as Abilene's had.

"You two are perfect for each other," Glorietta quipped to the occasionally silent room as she leaned down and kissed her guest on the forehead. "Rest well and I'll see you tonight."

"You sleep well?" Duke groaned, slightly startling Glorietta who was back to operating in the confines of her routine without real awareness of anyone's presence.

"Yeah, I slept well," she smiled.

"Nightmares?"

"Nope. No nightmares."

"Good."

Glorietta grabbed up her pouch and headed to the door, turning back once more to look at Duke and pray for success.

"God, I hope this works," she sighed.

As Glorietta walked out the door and led her horse out of the stalls in the back, Duke and Abilene started up their nocturnal duet with raucous vigor and a clear timbre.

Several hours later, Duke shook himself from sleep with a violent tremor and a shout. Abilene nearly jumped out of her shoes as she stood at the window with her back turned away from the rest of the room. This startling event was not the result of a nightmare, or at least not one of the usual variety, but simply Duke yielding to the strange familiarity of his surroundings. It had been too many days since he slept in his own bed, between the night in the cave and the days on the run, yet here before him was the woman who had been there with him that last night. Seeing Abilene in one of Glorietta's aprons was odd and equally startling, but Duke came to himself quickly and smiled at the backlit beauty who grinned back at him.

Abilene woke up shortly after Glorietta's departure that morning and ate the provided breakfast. She ended up eating both breakfasts when it took Duke so long to get up, and then she dressed in some of Glorietta's clothes due to her own apparel's fatigued and dusty state.

Ch. 20 | Secrets Within

Duke waited on a moment of clarity to let the fog of sleep and sudden waking drift from his mind before he relayed to Abilene the plan that he and Glorietta fabricated the night before. They had decided that the only way to seal the mine would be to blast it with dynamite. To that end, Glorietta would pilfer a couple crates from the supply and place them behind a few aberrant boulders at the mouth of the cave. Glorietta would leave Mason City at the end of the day and would come back home to grab Duke and Abilene. Together, the three of them would go back up to the mine and cause a ruckus for B Crew, prompting Mason himself to step down into the second shaft of the mine.

At that point, things got difficult. Duke would have to occupy Mason and B Crew long enough to let Abilene slip away and go light the fuses on the dynamite. It was crucial that Abilene make it out of the second shaft quickly so she could race to the top of the mine and light the fuses. Duke would stay behind and make certain nobody would escape or trail Abilene. If he were able to do so, he could follow behind Abilene and make an escape. Should he not be able to do so, he would accept that reality.

Abilene was kept in the dark on this part of the plan, but Glorietta knew her instructions well. It was her responsibility to get Abilene to safety if nothing else. There was no guarantee that Duke could return to his former life, even if he did dispatch of Mason and prove to Silver Gorge that he was a good man. Without proof, Duke might have to resort to the life of an outlaw, and that was not what he wanted for himself or Abilene. She was still clean and could get out of this mess unscathed and unsullied.

To guard Abilene from knowing the full extent of the plan, Duke told her a simple lie. To her knowledge, the plan was that they would run out and blast the mine together. She expressed doubts on the timeline of certain things, no matter how many iterations of the plan they ran through waiting for Glorietta's return, but Duke was convinced that Abilene knew her part and that she would be able to achieve it without fail.

They ran through the plan several times, detailing each step of the way from their hidden ascent of the mountain to their contingency meet-up plans should a wrinkle appear at each point along the way. It was crucial for each one to know where they must go if an irreversible error prompted a cancellation, and that generally involved meeting at the bottom of the mountain and heading off in the direction of somewhere else for good. If things failed, Duke and Abilene knew there would be no returning to Silver Gorge or anywhere near Nevada.

Lunch came and went with conversation over the plan, then a few hours more passed as the duo worked through each step so far as each one was aware. When they were confident that the plan had been sized up with sufficiency and efficiency and extraneous proficiency, they agreed to rest for a short while before Glorietta returned.

Duke and Abilene braved the covers of Glorietta's bed, knowing how perturbed she would be to come home and see them there. Duke wrapped his arm around the woman laying with him now, reminding himself of Glorietta's conditions. Be good to her, she had said. Be better to her.

"When we get out of there tonight, you promise me one thing," Abilene urged Duke while they both drifted away. "We don't look back. This is the end of it. No more mine, no more secrets, no more vendettas. No more nightmares. You understand me, Duke Boone?"

He smiled, caressing her soft hands between his rope-calloused fingers. It was useless to deny her pleading eyes when they begged as they did now.

"Of course. No more nightmares," Duke agreed.

Duke held up his bargain that afternoon as he slept peacefully until well after dark. Groggy eyes slipped open to see Abilene still resting while the moon pulled itself up over the horizon and the last orange in the clouds retreated back to wherever color waited. Though he realized what this departure from the plan likely meant, Duke stumbled softly out of the bed while untangling himself from Abilene's embrace just to be sure.

"Glorietta," he whispered, wandering from the bedroom to the rest of the house. "Glorietta."

No answer. She wasn't home at all.

"Get up, Abs. Get up," Duke urged. "Something's not right."

"What… what's happening? What do you mean? How late is it?"

"It's late. And she's not back. We have to move now," Duke calmly insisted, nearly shaking Abilene in order to rouse her weary body.

Abilene shook off the bonds of fatigue quickly in order to dress herself in dark riding clothes and a borrowed duster while Duke gathered his guns and put his hat atop his head. Glorietta was a strong woman, it was true, but her absence gave Duke plenty reason to be nervous. There were no good options as to what was keeping her away, and in fact the best option was that she or her horse had been bitten by a rattlesnake on the way home. If not a snake, then a devil had done her in.

Duke and Abilene were ready to go in a moment as they rushed out the door and to their horses still tied up and waiting. Their plan was simple enough that it mostly required their presence at the top of the butte, so there were relatively few supplies needed that could slow the pair down. Duke had his guns, of course, and Abilene had some matches. Otherwise, they needed just the will to put everything in motion.

Loose stones and dark paths made up their journey to Mason City as Duke and Abilene rode quietly up the steady incline to their chosen destination. At the end of this road, the path they had decided to follow, was a town and a mine and something evil. At the end of this road, Duke would know what had happened to his friend.

The moon had been bright for several recent nights, but cloud cover blanketed the desert with a bleak, indifferent gray that prevented too much detail from showing through. A keen ear could hear the steps of Duke and Abilene's horses, but no eye was likely to spot them quite yet on the gentle slope up to Mason City.

Such cloud cover worked as both a boon and a bust for the surreptitious pair. Though they were less likely to be seen, it was also much harder to see. Twice Duke nearly led his horse off the edge of the path. Abilene had been tempted to pull out her matches and provide them with some kind of light, but it was too dangerous to give away their position. People rarely ever traversed this path without sunlight, and for obvious reasons. The miners almost always came and went in the daylight if they had to, though most of them preferred to just stay topside. The few regulars who lived offsite, such as Glorietta, would always be sure to come in at sunrise and out before sunset. Boss Mason never bothered to concern himself with the safety of those who traveled at night.

Duke had come this way once when he tracked Zeke's son to the mines at night, and that had been a similarly difficult path, but that night he was just avoiding the gaze of a kid. It had been fairly simple to make the path work then, especially with limited light to aid his efforts. Duke now had to avoid the entirety of Mason's company, a decidedly more difficult task.

They reached the top of the trail and proceeded with caution. Duke's favorite features of Mason City, the gleaming copper fixtures, sat matte in the dark as they barely reflected the flat moonlight that managed to slink through the perforated clouds. After a quick glance over the horizon,

Ch. 20 | Secrets Within

making sure that nobody wandered the floor at this late hour, Duke and Abilene crested the trail and tied their horses to a hitching post that was out of the way behind the town's company-approved saloon.

"We need to find Glorietta," Duke said.

Abilene gave him a questioning look and nearly protested, especially since she had assumed that Glorietta's state of being was not in question, but a subtler understanding of what Duke meant urged her to continue. It was not the person or the partner they were seeking at this point. Duke wanted to find the body.

After he surveyed their surroundings and realized that not a single candle was lit in any of the official quarters, Duke suggested that they head towards the main office. If Mason had done any foul business, he reasoned, it would have been done there.

The swinging doors of the main building creaked noisily in the otherwise silent town, and Duke winced when the wooden slats shuttered together at their midpoint. It was certainly a loud entrance, but Duke hoped that he had calculated correctly. If Glorietta was right, Mason was down in the secondary mine with his B Crew, leaving the office entirely unguarded. Even if Mason had figured out that Glorietta was up to something, wouldn't he have held to his schedule? Duke ascended the stairs, this time without invitation, and rubbed his fingers over many of Mason's trinkets of travels to unknown corners of the world. Asian dolls and African charms adorned the wall up to Mason's office, that temple to his opulence, and the two of them steadily eased their way up the stairs in order to minimize any further creaking.

Mason's door was cracked open at the top of the stairs, prompting Duke to open it with extreme caution, but nobody could be found. It was truly empty. Duke and Abilene wandered the room, paying caution to avoid the window, yet there was no sign of Glorietta nor any other human. Mason's prized chair was cool to the touch, so he had been out of it for several hours now. Sitting atop Mason's desk, still placed next to the paper and the inkwell, rested the golden frog that had drawn so much of Duke's admiration upon his last visit to the space. Yet it seemed cleaner than the rest of the table, even with a spot of dust missing around the base of the frog.

Duke sat down and proceeded to write a short note out with Mason's pen and ink, something that the boss would have hated if he could see it. Abilene was too busy checking behind cabinets and near the bar for a body or sign of illicit affairs, perhaps, to notice that Duke was not searching the room at all. By the time she noticed, the letter was done.

"Listen to me, Abs," Duke said, drawing her attention. "I've written a letter to the sheriff in Carlin. He's an old friend and he'll come up here to help you."

"With what?" Abilene asked.

"With all… this. This. I hope I can take care of the future here now, tonight, but if I can't, you have to go to Carlin with this message and explain what all has happened here," Duke responded.

Abilene was aware that something could go wrong, and she was aware that something probably already had for Glorietta, but she refused to believe that Duke was to be in any danger or that things could go wrong for him. Her resistance upset Duke, but she eventually took the letter and stuffed it away in one of her pockets.

"Now help me get this desk back together the way it was before we head off into the mine," Duke urged.

"Why? What's it matter? If we succeed, Mason won't be using his office any more. If we fail, he's going to know we were here anyway. It's a waste of time," Abilene said.

"And what is your arguing doing to help? Come on, help me out," Duke pleaded.

Ch. 20 | Secrets Within

"No. In fact, I'm taking this," Abilene said, reaching down and stealing the ink bottle placed on Mason's desk. "And this. And this."

Duke's features were fuming with anger, but he couldn't help but laugh at Abilene's antics. In the last few seconds, she had managed to stuff Mason's ink, a few dollars in coins and a gold pin for his tie.

"Oooh. This looks fancy. I think I'll take it, too," Abilene said, indicating the golden frog that Mason loved so much.

As Abilene went to pick it up from the desk, she found that the frog would not budge. The thing was solidly attached in such a way that it would not move. Duke laughed for a moment, then he realized that her struggle was genuine and not an act of embellishment.

"Get over here and help me," Abilene commanded.

"Just leave it. We don't have time," Duke responded.

"No, I've almost got it. It wiggles a little bit, so maybe it'll screw out."

As Abilene rotated the frog on Mason's desk, the bar along the right side wall slid to the side, revealing a reasonably large hole. Duke and Abilene stared at the door first, fearing that the loud noise would elicit some kind of attention. Satisfied that no wayward guards were coming, the inept cat burglars went to the hole and peeked inside. It was dark, sure, so Duke pulled a candle in to see better.

It was at that moment that the reflection off of countless gold coins and artifacts bedazzled the sheriff and nearly caused him to drop the candle.

"What? What do you see?" Abilene asked.

"Look for yourself," Duke said, stepping out of the way and handing her the candle.

For a brief moment, Duke and Abilene felt wealthy. Obscene amounts of gold rested in this secure vault that nobody could have guessed existed. After all, so few people are welcome into Mason's office that his secret could have been kept safe for decades if not for Duke and Abilene's blind luck.

They picked up the coins and let them jingle in their hands, contemplating the idea of ransacking Mason's store and taking the bounty as their own. It was a combination of Duke's virtue and Abilene's keen eyes that prevented such theft from occurring, though, when the lady looked to the back of the vault and spotted something particularly peculiar.

"Look, Duke. You see this? Am I imagining that?" she asked, handing Duke the candle.

As the light grew on the distant figure's front surface, Duke realized what he was looking at.

"My stars, that's a statue of Josiah. Zeke's kid," Duke clarified.

"Yeah, I remember who Josiah was, but why is there a statue of him here? And why is it gold?" Abilene smartly asked.

It was clearly Josiah, Duke thought, but why? Abilene's question had been his own, and now the sheriff was even more puzzled than before. Men had died in Mason's mines before. That was a fairly common occurrence, according to Glorietta. Yet nobody else had a gold statue cut out for them. Josiah was the only one, and it was done with such marvelous detail, though the thing was placed oddly with its feet pressing into the floor as if the thing were trying to leap. It was possible that Mason was trying to alleviate some of the bad blood between he and Zeke. It was entirely possible that Mason was working on a statue such as this to appease Zeke, yet he never got the chance to reveal it.

"It looks just like Josiah. There's no telling how much it

cost Mason to make this thing. Look at the detail here on his cheek where he was starting to grow a beard. Or up here on his ear, that spot where he cut himself fishing one day as a kid," Duke pointed out. "Too bad Zeke never found this thing while he was snooping around Mason's camp. It might have helped smooth things over."

"Or it might have pushed him over the edge sooner," Abilene glumly offered, drawing a sharp look from Duke.

The duo turned and left the hovel where Josiah's statue stood, along with a relatively expansive fortune in gold coins and art, and they headed back towards the door. As strange as Josiah's image meeting them in the office was, Duke and Abilene had more important tasks ahead than admiring a memorial to a fallen miner.

Each creaky step forced Duke to pause, even though they had already established that nobody was around to hear whatever noises they were making. In boots, it was difficult for Duke to slowly ease his heel down on the next step without putting too much weight down too quickly. Abilene, who already had the advantage of weighing 70 pounds less than Duke, managed the stairwell more efficiently.

After easing down the stairs, Duke and Abilene met with their most difficult challenge yet. They would need to traverse the open courtyard between Mason's office and the entrance to the mine. Cloud cover still benefited the pair with a darker shade of blue, but the task ahead of them would not be met without considerably more effective stealth than Duke and Abilene had already shown an aptitude for.

Gently they pushed open the swinging doors of Mason's office, and gently they helped the doors close. Duke estimated the walk to be about 100 yards of open air with several windows and elevated perches on the mountain side and nothing but an empty drop-off on the other. If Boss Mason knew they were coming, the long walk from the office to the mine would be the best place for an ambush. Duke took it upon himself to test out this new theory by taking the first step.

One foot. Another foot. His legs felt like bent twigs ready to snap with anxious pressure building up in his calves and at his ankles.

The third step. The fourth step. Each time Duke got a little farther out, the more he realized how mentally taxing this process would be. It was true that he was getting closer and closer to the mine with each step he took, but Duke was also aware that each step meant he had been exposed a little bit longer and that someone could easily be drawing their bead. His thoughts bounced from optimistic fervor to dread with each clicking insect or wind-blown pebble shuffling along the dirt.

After Duke had gone about 15 steps, he waved for Abilene with a silent hand gesture. Her steps were more limber and less precise than his as she stepped confidently out into the open. After she caught and overtook Duke, their movements together improved. Abilene was a step ahead of Duke, minding only the entrance and potential dangers therein. Duke's thoughts rested on each window that seemed to glint or gleam even without the aid of a reflecting moon.

A couple minutes later, after Duke had finished walking a tightrope 30 feet wide, they reached the opening of Mason's mine. Duke pumped out a great sigh upon reaching the shelter of the mine, gladly removing himself from line of sight. Then again, had he known what waited further down in the mine, Duke may have chosen the bullet.

What Duke had remembered as gray rock seemed now more like onyx on all sides. They could only see it, though, because Glorietta had done her job after all. Multiple crates of dynamite adorned a hidden corner at the mouth of the mine, and a few flame-ready torches sat there as well. Duke quietly questioned the wisdom of placing such volatile torches right next to the dynamite, but an early explosion would hardly be

Ch. 20 | Secrets Within

the worst thing that happened to this mission.

Deeper into the mine, Duke started to notice flecks of gold scattered across the ground. Some seemed to be bits and pieces of processed nuggets while others appeared to be grown into the floor of the mine. It was astounding to the former sheriff how none of the other miners questioned this foreign element or how he himself had overlooked this significant detail the first time around. It was unmistakable, though, what Mason had hiding in his second tunnel. There was gold in the mountain and Mason wanted to keep each bit of it for himself.

It was greed that had cost Josiah his life, both Mason's and his own. The boy had gone into the mine and started stealing from Mason's guarded gold vein. Or, perhaps less likely, Josiah had actually discovered the vein and was simply using his own time to smuggle out enough gold to fund a new life in the city for three generations. No matter what Josiah's involvement amounted to, Mason's involvement had produced murder. It had started as just one dead child, then a dead father. After such a slate of other unnecessary deaths had been charged to the mine boss' account, now it seemed to Duke that the only option was complete annihilation of Mason and those loyal to him.

Torch light gleamed off the trail of gold that led deeper into the earth as Duke realized that the torch light was precisely why he had no trouble seeing the glinting, glittering gold droplets now. Daylight died quickly upon a mine's doorstep, but enough receding light painted the floor of the mine that it would blanket the glimmering of gold and mute its presence. With such a black night, however, the gold stood out rather plainly. Abilene occasionally bent over and inspected one of the loose nuggets. Miraculously, those nuggets never made a sound dropping back to the ground.

"Why don't we hear anybody?" Abilene asked in hushed tones.

"They must be too deep in the mine for us to hear them. Let's keep going," Duke said. "And stay quiet."

It took an excessively long time to walk the path without the miracle of mine carts, but Duke and Abilene eventually found the place where the path splits off on Mason's secret fork. The cart tracks appeared to end there with the only intact line heading deeper into the traditional mine, but Duke spotted a clever little trick he had missed on the first pass. Mason had installed a camouflaged switch that would allow the B Crew miners to move their product in and out at night and then return the line to its normal destination.

Abilene urged Duke for a momentary rest to massage her feet. Mine floors were not meant to be walked on for long, of course, since the uneven terrain mixed with pebbles and divots made for an unfriendly jaunt after the first mile or so. Duke would scarce admit it, but he welcomed the rest, too.

As they approached the switch and went off in that new direction, Duke thought more about Abilene's earlier question. After all, mine work was loud. It was usually a symphony of picks and hammers, all mixed over the backdrop of grinding metal upon the rails. Mason's mine tonight, however, sounded more like a hollow tomb in the still, quiet hours. Duke's plan had been to trap Mason in the mine. If he wasn't there, Duke realized, they were walking themselves into either a trap or a wasted opportunity. Clearly one option was better than the other.

Just as Duke's optimism had reached a bit of a low, Abilene gripped his arm tightly to silently communicate some great revelation. Duke furrowed his brow and tossed her a look, to which Abilene responded by widening her eyes and nodding in a generally downward direction. If Duke were too dense to catch the silent cues, she added a few high grunts to accentuate the direction her head bobbing aimed. After a moment of this confused exchange, Duke finally took her hints seriously and squinted off in the generally black area

Ch. 20 | Secrets Within

that Abilene indicated. The picture was bleak at first, but when Abilene took Duke's torch away and tossed it further behind them, Duke finally made out what had excited Abilene. A further hundred yards up, Duke's eyes just realized a hint of lamplight peaking around the corner of some door.

They had at last arrived and the plan was still, for the moment, viable. Duke was aware that the path was still silent, meaning that the miners were likely not in, but that was okay. If the lamps were still lit, that meant they were likely to return soon and then Duke could corner Mason and force a confession out of him. At the very least, he would get to look in Mason's eyes when it occurred to him that the mine would be forever sealed shut with him inside.

Briskly the two hurried upon this secondary mine with rock and timbers encapsulating the tunnel further into the belly of the butte. For Duke, the pursuit of justice at all costs had finally come to fruition. For Abilene, the chance at seeing that much gold presented a wonderful possibility. For both of them, the end was close.

And yet, when they rounded the corner of the carved doorway and the timbers that held it up, there was precious little gold. Instead, the lamps shone on a bleak room not unlike the rest of the mine. There was no great vein of gold, nor were there any bars or ingots of any kind. Even the dripped path of gold had ceased before the door, and there was hardly a nugget to be found. It seemed to Duke that they had been played and his hand quickly slipped down to the pistol at his belt. If a trick had been played, Mason might yet enter the mine and present a decisive opportunity for action.

Once again, it was Abilene's keen eyesight that noticed first the oddity at the back of the cavern. It was a spacious area, perhaps bordering on 130 feet in any direction, but none of it appeared carved except for the door. Even that only appeared to have been widened rather than cut out. Similarly, much of the path into this cavern had been rougher and more natural in appearance.

With her torch held high, Abilene spotted a greasy reflection coming from the farthest corners of the cavern. As they approached it, Duke managed to hear a bubbling and gasping as if a kettle of soup were on somewhere in front of him. When it finally became clear, the sight their torches revealed was far from appetizing. The hideously grotesque nature of the thing was shocking, and both Abilene and Duke instinctively reached for each other's familiar bodies when presented with its horror.

The roiling, bilious fluid bubbled with such malicious viscosity that Duke Boone swore it was alive. A slick sheen covered the top of this wretched pool, reflecting and almost glowing in the presence of their torches. Whether it was a trick of the light or not Duke never knew, but it seemed to pull towards him and Abilene as they walked closer to the shores of this abyssal lake. The thing could have been a mile deep or just an inch. The simple fact was that no light escaped this pool to give any inclination of depth, and the surface of it was awful enough. What made the thing so wretched to Duke was that he had seen and smelled such unnatural obscenities before. It was this very same fluid that poured out of what was once Zeke's body those weeks ago in the saloon.

She would later say it was the response of some innate bewitching that caused her to do this, but Abilene inexplicably bent down and tried to place her hand atop the writhing liquid. As her hand was just an inch away, Duke pulled down and yanked it back. Abilene fell backwards to the ground and kicked up a great cloud of dust, but it was that dust which snapped the both of them out of the pool's vexation, for it was all gold.

Any dust or dirt or stone or pebble that rested near enough the pool to be touched by it was gold. A thin line of demarcation stretched out perhaps five or six inches from the

Ch. 20 | Secrets Within

edge of the boiling blackness with tinier flecks dotting the surface of the sand slightly further out. At this observation, Duke stepped back and picked up a stone he had spotted near the entrance. It was smooth and thin and fit comfortably in his palm, making it the perfect stone for this little test.

Duke presumed the posture of a boy at play, positioning his outer foot near the pool and his other foot perpendicular to it. As he bent his knees, Duke handed Abilene his torch and reared back a powerful right arm. With a quick flick of the wrist, Duke sent his favored stone skipping all the way to the back of the cave wall where it was met with a solid clink. It was not the scraping of rock against rock that Duke and Abilene heard, though, and it was not the ruddy orange of dusty rock that they had seen bounce and sink into the pit. Though it was beyond all reason, Duke and Abilene were both in agreement that the stone had somehow transformed into a solid chunk of gold after the slightest touch on the obsidian waves of this bubbling bile.

"What is this place, Duke? Is this magic?" Abilene asked.

"I don't know, Abs, but I'd wager it's something else entirely. Something older. Something darker," Duke answered, the necessary word escaping him for awe at the things he had seen.

"Either way, I'm glad you pulled my hand back. Do you think it would have turned me into gold?" Abilene asked again.

"I imagine it would have done something far, far worse," Duke answered yet again.

A third, familiar voice rang out in the cave back near the entrance, informing Duke and Abilene that they had let themselves fall under the pit's spell for a minute too long.

"You're a smart man, former Sheriff Boone," Mason bellowed. "Too bad your friend Zeke or my brother hadn't been quite as smart."

-Chapter Twenty-One-

Out of the Black

Mason had of course not come alone. Three hired gunmen flanked him on all sides, barring any attempt at escape. On one side, Duke and Abilene faced an unknowable blackness that consumed the life and being of anything unfortunate enough to meet it. On the other, there was a black pit that turned stuff gold.

More surprising than Mason's presence was what he held in his hand. Duke would have expected a gun from most men, true, but Mason already had them outnumbered in that department. No, it was something else that Duke had never expected to see again. In Mason's right hand there was a fist-sized chunk of silver. Though he could not read it from this distance, Duke was certain what was etched on the bottom: Mason Bros. Mining Company.

"So. There was a Mason brother," Duke smiled, as if this new knowledge were an achievement or a help in their present circumstance.

"Yes, Duke, I had a brother. Good man. He would've hated you," Mason laughed. "You see, we came out here together as young men among some of the first pioneers. No, we weren't the great trailblazers that carved out this territory and made it something, but we found the land around Silver

Gorge before any of you railroad riders to come after us. And me and him, we took up shelter on this rock.

"Me and Michael were so excited when we found the silver here in this cave. We knew we'd struck it rich. The only problem was that we barely had enough equipment or money to start a mining operation, and we couldn't tell anybody about it for fear that they might try to run us off and do it themselves. But I guess you can figure out what comes next in the story, can't you, Sheriff?"

Duke thought about taking a go at the gunmen, but they looked to be true professionals. He'd never clear leather before they had shot him and Abilene both, so it was wise to play along with Mason's games.

"Yes, I can figure what happened. You explored further into the cave, didn't you, and that's when you found this messy black pool," Duke surmised.

"That's right. See, boys? I told you he wasn't half as dumb as he acted," Mason teased, though not even the men he had paid to be there laughed.

"That's great, now can we just shoot him and get paid?" grunted the one to Mason's left. "We've done everything you asked."

"You'll get your money, just shut up for a minute and let me enjoy this," Mason ordered. "It's my money, it'll be my process."

The three fellows all shared annoyed glances with each other and begrudgingly let the moneyman do as he wished.

"When did your brother mess it all up?" Duke asked. "I mean, he clearly touched the stuff."

"Not immediately, actually," Mason started to explain. "You see, it all went smoothly for a while. We found rocks and things that turned into gold. We could take a little bit of the fluid out of there in a glass and pour it out on a wooden wagon wheel or whatever else we had laying around and, sure enough, it would turn the thing gold. We tried it once or twice with little lizards, but nothing happened to them. They just skittered away and the stuff fell into the ground.

"We actually had a life out here for several years. Before the town of Silver Gorge really got going, Mason City was already at its peak. Michael, well, he managed to get married. Had a baby. Named it after our father. Things were great at first. Me and him would come down here to make gold coins, and we'd use the gold to pay workers to mine the silver. It was a great system, but Michael wanted more," Mason said gravely. "You see, it all happened one night when we came down here to turn some broken rope into a gold cord. We didn't realize that a frog had snuck down here in the sack we kept the rope in, but it did. And sure enough, that frog hopped itself down into the pool and took a little swim. A minute later, we see the gold frog sitting hunched up on the shore. Oh. And take his guns. We don't want a repeat of what happened in town."

The shortest of the three men stepped toward Duke at his boss's insistence, which of course came at Mason's insistence. This shorter fellow had a foot-long beard and eyebrows that needed to be burned off, and Duke was sure that he wouldn't be much of a challenge in a fight, but the other two fellows had their guns trained right on Duke's head. The bearded, grizzled gunman handed Mason the revolver that had been Duke's and took his place up on Mason's right.

"Once my brother knew that it was possible to turn living things into gold, we never stopped trying new things. Some of our experiments worked, some didn't. We had to keep buying new nets to dip things in the pool because the old ones would turn gold and be just useless, but it wasn't so hard to afford all the nets we needed," Mason narrated. "We'd dip frogs, lizards, chickens, pigs. Whatever we could get, and we did so with mixed success.

"Finally, Michael couldn't take it. He stuck his hand down in there and just had to see what would happen. And nothing did for a while," Mason admitted.

Talking about his brother pushed Mason into a new territory mentally, Duke thought. He had never seen Mason spend much time talking about the past. Even when he had suddenly returned from years abroad to reopen the mine, Mason just talked about looking ahead and moving ahead. Except for a few anecdotes of his time spent absorbing exotic locales or foreign cultures, Mason never really talked about what had been. The distraction of recalling his brother's fate was a likely culprit for why he avoided the topic.

"It was after that when we started noticing that the animals we couldn't turn the first time around were acting strange. The pigs would groan and languish away ever so slowly. The chickens lost most of their feathers, but the few they kept all turned black and rigid. It was a nightmare, Duke. We thought there was a disease in the camp, but there wasn't. You know, of course, what was going on," Mason acknowledged. "And once the animals started oozing black juices out of their once healthy bodies, we had a pretty good guess.

"It was then that Michael sent his wife and son off to live with her family back east. He wanted Mortimer to grow up in a safer environment, not the mines and deserts of Nevada Territory," Mason said.

The name had nearly slipped past Duke, but the full realization came on in time. When it did, a new fervor and rage built up that caused the sheriff to act rather irrationally by charging Mason, baring his teeth and threatening with his fists. The bearded fellow stepped up and leveled Duke with a well-aimed punch to the chest, and a wounded, weakened Duke hobbled back towards Abilene. He fell face-first into the shoreline of the black pool, his hands coming to rest just inches short of the deadly liquid.

Ch. 21 | Out of the Black

"Did I forget to mention that? I guess I did. Yes, little Mort was my nephew. I wasn't very happy with what you did to him, but I guess I can't blame you. He could be a fool-hardy young boy," Mason said.

"That's how you made everything happen. You knew you had a man in my corner, and you even had him retrieve the silver for you," Duke reasoned.

"It was the last thing I had of my brother. Aside from Mort, I guess. But I couldn't let you keep it. Or sell it. Especially since it was crucial that it look like I'd paid you to betray the town. I went through all this trouble teaching Mort how to open that puzzle box, since I was certain you wouldn't. Then I trusted him to get it back for me if you somehow ever had opened the box, and imagine my surprise when he brought me back this piece of silver no longer in the box. How did you open it, anyway? I'm genuinely curious how an uncultured buffoon like you could have…"

"I burned the box and took out the silver," Duke answered, interrupting Mason's speech.

"Makes sense. It's clever, but not exactly sporting of you," Mason acknowledged. "Either way, my brother was dying. We both knew it, yet there was nothing we could do. He just… well… he leaked out one day. It wasn't like I could hold a funeral for him, so I just fired all the miners and started over after that. From then on, we ignored the pool and all my men just believed it was a dangerous section of the mine. That is… until Josiah."

Duke burned at hearing Mason reference the boy with such flippancy, as if he had been mildly inconvenienced by Josiah's presence. Mason's grievous insults would not be tolerated, but Duke was frozen. Turns out you can insult just about anyone when you have all the guns.

"I don't know what compelled Josiah to sneak down here, or how long he had been doing it before we caught him, but some of my men started noticing droplets of gold on the ground. I didn't believe them, but then I saw it for myself. Had Josiah been more careful than to let golden pebbles fall from his converted wares, he might still be stealing from me and I might still be wringing my hands over an empty silver mine," Mason admitted. "But he failed to conceal his actions properly, and I had my men ambush him in the mine."

"So you shot him," Duke guessed.

Mason's sly grin turned into a hearty chuckle as he leaned back and crossed his arms before finishing this part of the story.

"We tried to, sure. But we missed. You see, he dove into the pool to escape, probably without thinking. That or he knew half of what I knew about living flesh. But then the strangest thing happened," Mason said. "After Josiah hadn't come up for about 20 minutes, we knew he was dead. So we took a rope and tried to lasso him out of there, but he felt about 300 pounds heavier than he should have."

Duke connected the dots before Mason could explicitly come out and say it, and the former sheriff reeled in horror, nearly stepping his own heel into the abyssal fluid. Mason only ever said that there was no body to show off. No body he could give Zeke. And yet, there was a body. It was just gold and stashed away in Mason's office.

Mason could see that Duke had the ending figured out by the twisted horror on his face, and thus returned a more voluminous, bellowing laugh from the boss. Yet Mason had not fully revealed his list of horrors, and the greatest was to come.

"So you've seen it? I couldn't give Zeke a golden statue of his son. That would've been heartless," Mason said without a hint of irony. "I kept the statue, thinking we would figure out what to do with it, but in time we got plenty of opportunities to research how exactly the process worked on

Ch. 21 | Out of the Black

people. After a few trials, we learned that people and any other living things have to be completely submerged. Some kind of strange quirk, I guess. So unlike your friend Zeke and my brother, people could be reliably turned into gold. We had a way of making it work. Now all we needed were volunteers."

Once again, Duke's perceptive mind had worked out the details. Mason's B Crew helped him finance the mine by turning things into gold and retrieving them, but some people were not very careful. If a miner were hit by the black fluid, Mason would immediately have them cast into the lagoon and submerged. Ultimately wasting time mining or working with a plentiful supply of potential converts, Mason wanted to one day take the entire fleet of mine workers and have them tossed in.

"Josiah was not a suitable volunteer for obvious reasons. He actually had family here. Someone to notice he was gone," Mason said. "When Zeke came around asking questions and getting belligerent, we had a real problem. I don't know when he slipped into the mine and found this place, but he did. Most people don't last more than two weeks after they touch the pool, so it was probably about then.

"So Zeke was gone, and that just left you, Sheriff. See, I had thought about bringing you in on the plan, but I never imagined you'd really be okay with it. And you're not dumb, so I'm sure you would've caught on eventually. Even if they were just vagrants and undesirables, you would have noticed the numbers dwindling. That's why I had the Scarecrow track you down, but he was supposed to kill you. He wasn't supposed to lead you right to my door and kill my nephew," Mason explained. "Which reminds me. Now that you know, I obviously have to kill you. You know that. But because you killed my nephew, I'm going to have to make sure that your death is fitting."

Without his guns, Duke was unable to shoot a way out

of this particular corner. It was likely that Mason intended for Duke to wither away like Zeke did in order to pay for his transgressions, but that intent would not be suffered. All Duke needed was a way out.

"Please. You can kill me however you want, but let Abilene go. She's done nothing wrong, Mason. She's here because of me," Duke pleaded, though Abilene protested.

"Well… she can't leave, but I suppose I could use a new secretary," Mason chuckled. "I had to let go of my last one, but that was a real shame. She was top-notch, Miss Glorietta. Worth her weight in gold, you might say."

Mason was pleased with himself, but Duke took the opportunity to embrace his love rather than mock the mine boss's horrid jokes. The lovers grabbed onto each other tightly with Duke's wandering hands checking each crevice of Abilene's fittings as if searching for a particular spot. Duke spun Abilene around and planted a wonderful kiss on her lips while he kept rubbing her back and feeling her thighs, most surprising the lady when he slipped his hand into her pocket and surreptitiously pulled something out. Abilene broke their bond for a moment to silently express her confusion, but Duke just reinitiated the embrace and ignored her concern.

After a moment or two, Mason's patience with the death-row romance had ceased. He stepped towards the lovers and violently separated them, shoving Abilene back towards the gunmen while keeping Duke in his grasp at the edge of the pool. As Mason gripped Duke's collar, staring straight into his eyes, a raging fire bellowed up behind the mining boss's glare. What Duke saw in Mason's eyes now was not unlike what he had seen in the Scarecrow's face that day in the woods, if not more primal. Though Duke's considerable height advantage on Mason might have made the scene laughable in another circumstance, the diminutive madman held tight like forged steel and burned with anticipation.

"You have been in my way for too long, Sheriff. Mort

Ch. 21 | Out of the Black

couldn't finish you off, but I imagine I'll have no such problem here," Mason teased.

"It's good to have a healthy imagination," Duke responded, rather unwisely.

An outburst of furious anger and malicious rage tore through Mason, pulsing from his chest and out his mouth in a guttural shout, as Duke suddenly found himself buried in the gold-flecked sand so near the edge of the pool. Mason repeatedly abused Duke's face with his potent fists, letting the cold metal of his various rings tear through the flesh and bruise the bone. Duke attempted to fight back, but he was just one-handed at the moment. After grabbing a pebble in his left hand, Duke was completely unable to fight back without sacrificing his one move.

Mason spritely flew from his knees to his feet and continued the barrage of abuses both physical and verbal. Curses and kicks pummeled Duke as his already bruised ribs throbbed in great pain and blood poured from the fresh cut in his side. Yet Mason had little concern with Duke's health problems as a hefty work boot found a spot on Boone's side that seemed perfect for the kicking. Again and again, Mason tore into Duke, punishing him for the death of a brother and nephew Duke had never been aware of. After a particularly prurient bout of savagery, Mason stepped back and walked over to the gunmen to borrow Duke's own pistol, giving Duke a moment to act.

Though he was in great agony, Duke rolled over to his chest and pushed himself up off the ground. With his hands just shy of the pool, Duke knew now was the time it would have to be done if it were to happen. As he heard the footsteps of Mason coming back towards the pool, Duke tossed the pebble in with one hand and swiped at the top of the liquid's surface with his right. In one fluid motion, Duke uncapped a hidden ink well in order to smear the black liquid all over his hand while he dropped the glass bottle straightaway into the murky pool.

Mason stood behind Duke, jeering loudly at the fallen man's apparent fate, while Abilene protested and cried. Duke, on the other hand, stayed on his knees and waited for Mason to be fully distracted. With imperfect speed and precision, Duke rounded on Mason and smeared a great swath of the black stuff upon his captor's face.

Horrified, Mason threw his hands to his face and reeled from his own body at the sight of black upon them, hardly believing that this could be his fate. His laughter turned to moaning and wailing as streaks of viscous, coal-black liquid flowed down his retching face, and Mason fell to the ground trying to rub the remnant off.

"Get it off me! Get it off me! Won't somebody do something?" Mason shouted to Duke and the stunned gunmen, who had not been paid to deal with otherworldly fluids.

Mason pulled handfuls of dust out of the ground and rubbed his skin raw trying to remove any trace of the black, but all he could do was smear the liquid over the entirety of his face. Bits of gold dust and clay blended under his eyes and around his mouth, giving the normally sharp man a wild and ravaged look. His expression twisted between mortified and pleading, with eyes that went tender whenever they momentarily locked with another's.

As Mason accepted his fate, he turned and looked towards the only option he had for a quick and resolute end. He bounded to his feet and, shoving Duke out of the way, dove into the black pool intent on going out now rather than later. Mason bathed in the fluid and rolled around like a pig trying to stay cool in the summer sun, but the pool defiantly pulled away from him. Mason could rub the stuff all he wanted, but the pool would not allow him the mercy of immersion.

Ch. 21 | Out of the Black

Frantically flailing, Boss Mason splashed the fluid about, disrupting the usually thick and cohesive surface tension as if he were drowning. Yet the opposite was true. He couldn't get enough of the stuff on him, and panic eventually overtook his better judgment.

After a pitiable display of writhing, Boss Mason bobbed in the pool and bargained for death, looking straight ahead with a wordless request. Each of Mason's hired guns looked at each other as if passing off the job, yet none could do it.

"Please," Mason begged.

Reluctantly, the bearded man tossed Mason Duke's pistol, yet the mine boss's hands were covered in filth and sweat and unable to grip the cool metal, so the gun fell flat into the pool. Mason had expended his available energy with the earlier flopping about, so there was no frantic search for the fallen firearm. Rather, Mason just looked out at the five souls before him with one final plea.

"Please. Someone. Save me," Mason asked. "Please."

He went to speak again, but the words came out like vomit from an ill child as a trickle of black rolled from the man's tongue and down his cheek. All at once, Mason's head rolled back and his arms fell limp as each orifice expelled the self-same fluid that had earlier been so eager to escape his reach. In a moment of horror, it was over. All that was left of Mason was a slowly receding mound of goop at the center of the bilious pool, along with now-gilded clothes that presumably rested somewhere underneath the surface.

-Chapter Twenty-Two-

Into the Dawn

Once the sense of dread that overtook each of the horrified witnesses passed, they slowly came to the realization of what their current situation entailed. Present company included three gunmen, two condemned prisoners, and a back room full of gold that had just come open in all the fuss.

"You men still want to kill me?" Duke asked.

"What's it matter? There ain't nobody to pay us for it, and you're a dead man anyway as far as I can figure," the tall one said.

"And her?"

"Mason wanted her to live, so we'll let her live," the tall one again confirmed. "Seeing as you killed our contractor, however, we will be taking this gold as something of a recompense. That seem fair?"

The man's outstretched and cocked gun put an exclamation on the question and assured Duke what his answer would be.

"No objections here," Duke affirmed, to some silent protestation by Abilene.

Duke and Abilene waited while the three gunmen

Ch. 22 | Into the Dawn

grabbed their full share of the gold that was waiting around for nobody in particular, and the three men had their fill of a cart after nearly twenty minutes of slow work. It was a tense twenty minutes, too, as Duke and Abilene knew well that at any moment the gunmen could change their minds about the whole thing and just shoot them to death on the spot. The bearded one gave his companions some looks that were cause for concern, but the affair went off without incident.

As they started to leave, the tall one turned back around and addressed Duke with a stern tone.

"You wait for us to get up there, you hear me? Give us a five-minute head start before you leave. We don't want you sneaking up behind us on the way out of here and stealing our gold," the tall man warned.

"No problem. Five minutes," Duke echoed calmly.

"I mean it," he reiterated, pointing a shaky gun in Duke's direction. "We'll be looking."

Duke grinned as the men went off in the other direction and left Duke and Abilene behind, safe and sound for the first time in a while.

Abilene let out a sigh of relief now that there were no more guns trained on her, and she took Duke's hand in hers for a brief second before realizing what could have been her fatal error. When she felt the moisture of his hand and looked down at the splotches on his skin, she remembered what had happened just moments before and started running around the room in an absolute tizzy, waving her own hands about and trying to wipe the stain off.

Duke ran to her and threw a bear hug around her waist, trying to calm her nerves however he could.

"It's okay, it's okay. You're going to be fine, Abs, you're going to be fine," he repeated to little avail.

"But you're gonna die, Duke. And now I'm gonna die,

too!" she shouted.

Duke's response at first seemed callous, but his laughter at least drew her attention long enough for him to explain what he had done.

"Check your pockets," he ordered.

Confused, she obeyed and found the regular cache of items she had snatched from Mason's desk. Except for one.

As she looked up from her own ink-stained hands, Abilene noticed Duke palming the glass inkbottle, cradling their salvation between his smudged fingers. The idea flashed on her mind and she had full knowledge of what he had done to reverse their fortune and end their captivity. It was a moment of brilliance on his part, and of appreciation on her part, when Abilene threw down her small treasures and pulled Duke close for the best kiss she had ever given him.

"What do you say we blow this place?" Duke asked as soon as she would let him.

Abilene smiled and quickly bent over to pick up her things. Duke turned to give one last look at the impossible pool that rested contentedly behind him, and he was about to leave when he noticed one last thing. It was his own gun, but it was different, for the pool had taken effect. Duke's gun had somehow washed back up, yet now it was fully gold. He was at first hesitant to pick it up, but Duke eventually leaned over and reholstered his newly plated weapon.

The two of them grabbed some of the oil lanterns that Mason had prepared earlier, and with that the pair and the light left the black cave for good.

Their walk back out of the mine had been much easier than the walk down had been, what with the threat of death largely beyond them, so Duke and Abilene took the time to talk considerably about something they had largely ignored for so long: their future.

Ch. 22 | Into the Dawn

Abilene proposed that they run away and forget Silver Gorge, though Duke's plan to give it one last try won out. They thought about getting married in June, which was after all just a couple months away, and perhaps building a house. Duke refused to live in the hotel and Abilene refused to live in the jail house, so building a house just seemed right.

Abilene suggested moving into Glorietta's place, since it would be open now, but that house's distance from town and corresponding nearness to the darkness of the doomed mine forbade that suggestion almost instantly.

There was a future at the end of this long walk for them, and Abilene once again carried Duke's hand in hers: this time without panic and without fear.

They could see moonlight once again pouring into the cave, catching the flecks of gold in such a way that the path before them looked like stars with tiny constellations as their walkway. Up ahead, the stars led to a perfect moonlit night that quickly neared dawn, but something else stood at the exit to the mine. It appeared to be three figures stacking boxes, and Duke knew what was going on the moment he saw them. Duke and Abilene doused their lanterns, but they had already alerted the gunmen to their presence.

"Hey there, Sheriff!" the bearded one shouted down as the other two turned to look.

"Just in time. I wasn't sure we'd get to say goodbye," the tall one chimed in. "You see, we've been talking. We figured that since all this gold was Mason's, he really did pay us to kill you in a way. And since we can't have you running around after we got paid to do a job, seeing as how that would be real bad for business, we're going to have to leave you down there."

At that, the tall man took one of the torches and walked out of the mine's entrance. The boxes of dynamite were deeper in the mine than they had been when Duke and

Abilene went in, which might be good and bad. They would need to cover less ground, of course, but it also meant that the blast would be more strongly contained inside the mine. Moments after the tall man disappeared from view, Duke and Abilene heard the unmistakable hiss of a lit fuse, and that was their signal to run. The gunmen may well be waiting at the exit to shoot on sight, but the duo figured they stood a better chance with three gunmen than a cave-in.

  Duke and Abilene ran as fast as they could for the exit, their weary limbs rebelling in the face of chaos. Each step brought them closer to the exit where the fuse burned sharply and quickly. They were a hundred yards away. Then seventy-five. Fifty yards. Twenty-five yards. Duke could see the light of the fuse and estimated that they would pass it up just ten seconds before detonation. In preparation for the imminent faceoff, Duke pulled his gun. His nervous hands dropped the revolver as it clanged on the ground, costing him precious seconds to pick it up.

  "What are you doing, Duke? Come on!" Abilene urged.

  "Go! Go! I'm right behind you!" he shouted back.

  Abilene had a ten-step lead on Duke and she cleared the dynamite boxes first. Duke nearly dropped in anguish when he heard shouting and the crack of gunfire just as she left his sight, but Duke knew that his escape was the only chance she would have. Abilene's likely peril pushed Duke on, each bound more urgent than the last as he came to the barricade of crates and saw only a rattlesnake's length of fuse still burning a frantic path toward the dynamite. He would have no more than five seconds before the blast, Duke thought to himself, so he had to run no matter what stood at the end of the line.

  He had leapt as soon as the flash of light and the deafening boom surged all around him, and Duke could feel the push of the blast behind him as fissures opened up in the ground below. Severed stone that once made up the entrance

Ch. 22 | Into the Dawn

to the mine fell away in chunks as dust and stones rushed to fill the crevice they left behind. The sheriff had never been an athletic man, but the threat of demise provided ample force to shove his body through the air. Duke barely maintained consciousness as his flight came to an end just shy of solid ground. He could hear Abilene crying for him to hold on, though the ringing in his ears muffled the sound dramatically. The rock was wet and slippery, and his grip was quickly failing, but a strong hand thrust itself forward and took Duke by the wrist just before he could fall.

Duke used his other hand to grab onto the mystery wrist, fearing that the gunmen were just seeking an opportunity to finish their humiliation of him, but the hand did not belong to any hostile body. That was confirmed to Duke, now, though he had once doubted the fellow's intentions.

"You should really wear gloves," Connor laughed.

"And you should tell me how you did that," Duke wheezed, still struggling to gain his breath.

Despite the unceremonious way they had parted before, Duke graciously hugged Connor and thanked him for the save.

"You know this man?" Abilene asked.

"You could say we're old friends," Connor smiled. "I see you held on to that gun. Good job. May I see it?"

Duke handed the revolver over to Connor, who was obviously a good shot himself with how thoroughly he had dispatched of Mason's last hired guns, their bodies slumped to the side a few yards away.

"It looks good like this," Connor noted. "Never seen anybody else with a golden gun."

As was his way, apparently, Connor laughed at a joke that neither Duke nor Abilene got.

"How did you know to be here?" Duke wondered.

"Would you believe that I heard these gunmen talking as they rode past my cave earlier?" Connor asked, to which Duke shook his head. "Eh, it's just as well. I was never a good liar. Maybe I'll tell you that story some day."

"And that's one of many stories I'd love to hear," Duke replied.

Truth be told, Duke barely cared why or how Connor had showed up in their hour of need. What mattered was that he and Abilene were safe and that they could move on from this wreck of a mining town.

Sunlight peaked behind Mason City, though Duke and Abilene were unaware of it. The valley beneath them would quickly fill up with vibrant blues and oranges as the nightlife of the desert crept back into holes and burrows under rocks. Up on top of Mason City, miners would quickly rush to the mine and see that the mouth had been blasted away. They would search for their missing boss, but the men knew about B Crew and they knew that Mason had made a habit of digging at night, so they would likely assume he had gone down with the blast.

In time, Mason City would fall to dust as the miners raided what closets and storerooms they could find before heading off to the next camp or the next job. Life atop the butte would all but cease to exist, except for the occasional straggler and drifter who misguidedly sought shelter among the crackling structures that had been left to rot.

Silver Gorge would slowly lose the last vestiges of their mining town reputation as the generally calm state of things would return and people would just whisper about legends and half-truths that took place at the local saloon one day in early spring. Assuming they welcomed him back, Duke thought, the people of Silver Gorge would likely forget about the time they watched their deputy try to hang the sheriff, and

Ch. 22 | Into the Dawn

they would likely never know how Mason had orchestrated it all.

He and Abilene would hold each other to promises made in the quiet of their walk back up the mine and they would change their lives for the better. Duke knew all of these things to be true, and peace about the days ahead in Silver Gorge washed over him as the trio untied their horses and eased down the slowly illumined path to level ground. Every so often, Duke looked up from the road ahead to Abilene.

In the dying night, he could see her eyes gleam with apprehension and promise, and he knew that they would never again speak of what had happened to Zeke. And to Mason. It was a lifetime gone, they would agree, and all that mattered was the life that waited down the mountain in Silver Gorge. Nothing behind them would matter, and the secret of the mine would one day be buried with them and the few souls who escaped B Crew unharmed.

"Anyone ever tell you that's a beautiful horse you got there?" Connor asked.

"Quite a bit, actually," Duke said.

"She have a name?"

"No, but I've been thinking about giving her one lately."

"And?"

"Sunrise. I think I like Sunrise."

Connor smiled at Duke and leaned over to pat Sunrise's mane, making a mock coronation part of their descent. The name seemed right, Duke said, in that it perfectly accounted for how he felt at that moment. The sunrise was coming, and a new life was coming with it.

Duke looked over his shoulder to see Abilene riding a short length behind him as the sunrise nearly caught up with the contours of Mason's mountain. What little light had curled around the butte beamed through Abilene's hair, giving her the appearance of an angel to Duke. He would tell her that one day, that this moment was the most beautiful she had ever been.

    What Duke would not tell her, though, was the shape he saw in the shadow behind her. How he had kept his face from betraying the grizzly sight was a mystery even to him, but it was undeniable what Duke spotted several yards back on a ledge nearest to Mason City. Though a thick fog curled around it, dripping liquid like the pool hidden away underneath miles of rock, there stood a black horse. Perched on top of the horse, slumped and bent in an inhuman angle, was a rider equally black and foul, and underneath the grimy, matted hair was a face that Duke had seen too often in his dreams and that would ever haunt his most unpleasant memories.

Acknowledgments

This book could not have happened without the incredible efforts of my editor, Mark Bilbrey. Mark was far more instrumental in making sure I looked like I knew what I was doing than even I was, and this book would not be what it is without him.

All of my initial readers were so good about providing insight and comments that helped me refine little things and big things. So many friends and family members took these pages to their heart and gave me back something better, but I especially want to thank Rylan Wade and Chad Mozley for their thoughts and endless encouragement.

Speaking of my editor, it was my parents who actually gave me the money to pay my editor. I made a deal with them that I would cut their grass for a while to earn the check, and I'm pretty sure I got the best hourly rate ever for simply cutting grass. Thank you for helping me get here. In this way, and in so many others.

Thanks to everyone who bought my first collection, <u>Call of the Mountains</u>. I will never forget sitting at lunch with Franklin Scott and telling him about my first book, only for him to immediately order three copies while I sat with him and ate. Everyone should have a Franklin Scott in their life.

And to my wife. Without her, this book would still just be a quaint little 1,200-word short story about a shootout that never happened. When she asked me one pivotal question, this book was born: "Well, what *was* in that mine?"

Also from Author Adam Wynn

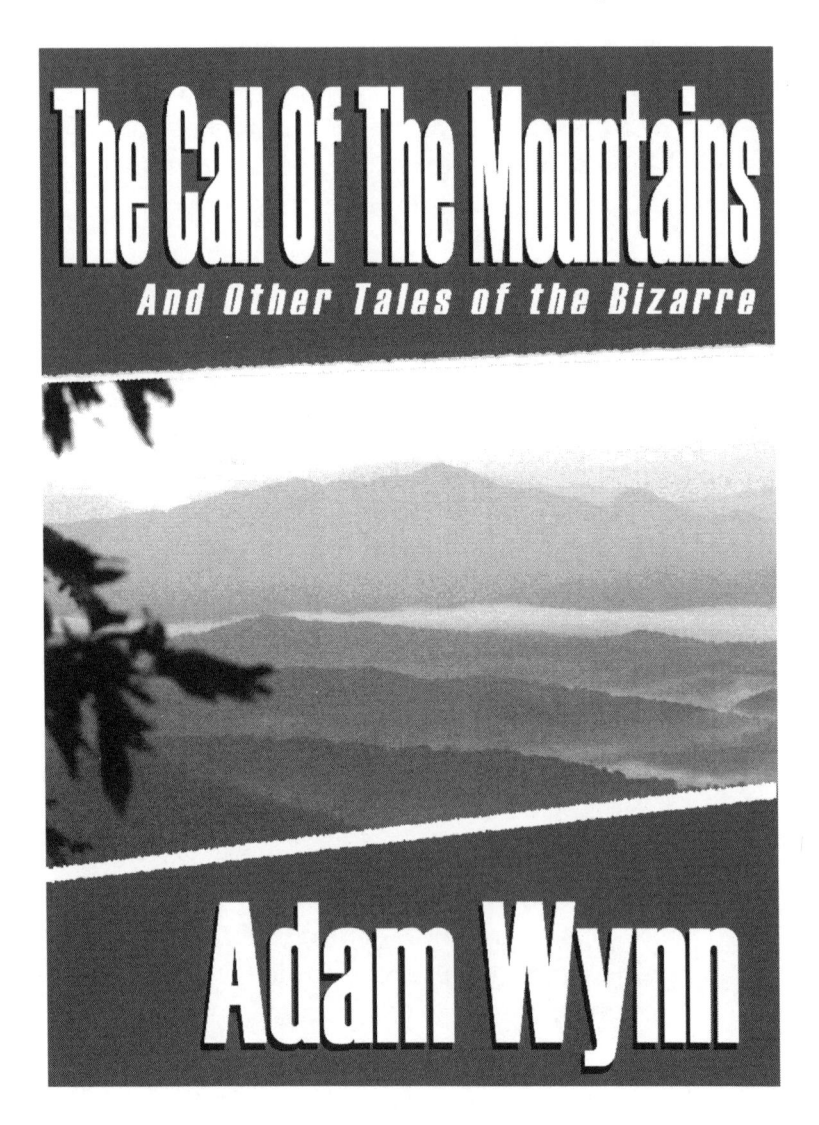

The Call Of The Mountains
And Other Tales of the Bizarre

Adam Wynn

A young couple faces uncertain horrors in the ancient mountains of Tennessee. A conspiracy theorist tells two wary listeners about an earth-shattering secret. An unorthodox interrogation takes a strange turn. This compilation features 11 tales of horror and hopelessness and the bizarre partly inspired by famed horror writer H.P. Lovecraft.

Made in the USA
Columbia, SC
02 March 2022